BY TENEKA WOODS

Hot August Nights

Wednesday at Noon

TENEKA WOODS

Wednesday at Noon

a novel

AMENITYpress

Copyright © 2020 by Teneka Woods
ISBN 978-1-7336787-2-8 (paperback)
ISBN 978-1-7336787-3-5 (ebook)

Cover design: Stefanie Fontecha
Formatting: Polgarus Studio

ONE

Nate drummed his fingers on the steering wheel in frustration. He was caught on the 610 West Loop South just before The Galleria, traffic inching forward at a snail's pace, which only reminded him why he avoided this side of Houston at all costs. No matter what day of the week or what time of day there was always a traffic jam. It was Wednesday afternoon. Their lunch date was scheduled for two o'clock and he was already a half-hour late. To her, that half-hour translated to two hours. She was no doubt sitting at the table fuming by now, swallowing down her iced tea as she contemplated calling him a third time to find out his location. He's been on her bad side for several months and he hoped they could enjoy a peaceful lunch together for once without talk about the money.

But she said she had something to tell him. A surprise. And he had no idea what that could have meant.

The address she'd given led him to a small sandwich shop on Westheimer Road with limited parking. Nate knew something was up because a sandwich shop was definitely not her usual style, even if it was located just a few minutes away from her sprawling River Oaks home. He found street parking a couple blocks over and walked back to the restaurant.

Her back was to him as he entered but the mirrored wall facing her table announced his arrival.

"Is this a joke?" he said as he approached.

"Your sister chose this place."

He leaned down to kiss her forehead. "Hey, Mama."

"Hello my son." Her cup of tea was almost empty.

Nate removed his keys and smartphone from his pockets, threw them on the table before sitting down across from her. "Is that why we're here? Is this the surprise? Because you've never been one to partake in an establishment in the business of cold cuts."

She rolled her eyes at his sarcasm. "Of course not, but I let Sunny convince me to try something new today. She said their soups are really good."

Nate scanned the small eatery with its exposed brick walls, kooky art décor, and mix of high and low table seating that gave it a jumbled appearance. With the exception of one cashier, they were the only brown patrons in sight, surrounded by the college student-type crowd. "Where is she anyway?"

"She's in the ladies' room. She'd just left the table right before you walked in."

Nate bobbed his head. "Did y'all order already? I'm starving." He grabbed a menu from the holder at the center of the table.

The corners of his mother's mouth curved. "Now why would we do that? Unlike other folks I know, we have manners and are considerate of other people. We wouldn't dare have lunch without our guest. Even if they show up *extremely* late. To *everything. All the time.* Oh no. We wouldn't do that."

Nate could only laugh as he'd set himself up for that one. "Mama, you know how it is with my clients. I'm there for them. If they need me a few extra minutes beyond their session for some more pep talk and encouragement then I have to stay. It's my gift to them for their support."

She huffed. "Sure, son. It's always the *client's* fault."

It never failed. She stressed the word client because, in her mind, the clients he worked with were not real clients. They were not the type of clients she—Mrs. Victoria Helena Walker—raised him to work with. To her, they were just people lacking common sense and self-control, paying him a few dollars per hour to show them how to eat healthy and exercise. She wanted her son to follow in the family's footsteps and have a successful career in law or science. She wanted her son to have the career she and his father paid for him to have.

And he'd followed their dream and attended law school, passed the bar with flying colors, and worked as an attorney for a couple years. But his heart was never in it. His heart was in fitness and nutrition. Instead of mulling over criminal case files, he would rather demonstrate the different ways to perform a sit-up.

This is what Victoria had a problem with. Sending him to law school was a waste of their money and she would not let him forget. "It's the truth, Mama. It's a valid excuse. I have no reason to lie about anything like this."

"What are you lying about not lying about now?"

It was his sister Sunny. A big, rotund belly suddenly appeared in his peripheral view as she made her way back to the table. She was only six months pregnant but looked as if she should have delivered his niece a month ago. "What's up, baby sis? How are you doing?"

She blew out a breath as she sat down. "How do I look like I'm doing? Fat. Exhausted. Fat." She laughed weakly.

He laughed with her. "I think you look good. Skin glowing. I like your hair." It looked freshly done. The golden ringlets bounced easily with the slightest movement. It reminded him of the curly fries with mustard they loved to share when they were kids.

"Thank you, but now that you're here we can finally eat. Baby Sunny is not happy at all. Mama and I know what we want, and since you were late *again* the bill is on you."

They told him what they wanted from the menu and sent him to the counter to place the order and to refill their drinks at the soda machine. "Alright," he said, once back at the table, "what is this surprise you had for me, Mama?"

"I'll let your sister tell you."

Nate looked from his mother to his sister.

Sunny's mouth spread into a wide grin. "Well… brother, I'm a little disappointed that you didn't notice. I'd expect my best friend, my twin, to know right away the reason my skin is all aglow as you observed." She moved her hand from beneath the table and thrust it towards him. "We're getting married!"

She said it too loud because suddenly it was quiet in the restaurant and everyone was looking their way. And then, slowly, they started clapping. Sunny grinned some more and Victoria nodded, mouthing a quiet 'Thank you' all around the room.

Nate could not share in his sister's excitement. He narrowed his eyes at the two of them, sitting back in his seat. "This is the surprise?"

"Yes," Sunny continued to beam, her hand outstretched in front of her as she stared at the ring. "We're finally doing it."

Victoria said, "Aren't you happy for your sister, son? As you can see she is over the moon about it."

They knew his sister's boyfriend was his least favorite person in the world. A man he believed was not worthy at all of his beautiful and smart sister. He wanted to be happy because being married to the love of her life was a dream come true for his sister, but he wished she was marrying someone else. Someone who truly respected her and his family. "Well, I've never bitten my tongue about anything when it comes to that dude, and I'm not about to bite it now. What made him finally decide to pop the question? This is baby number three. He was making promises to marry you after baby number one." He didn't give her a chance to respond. "Oh, I know. It's to seal the deal now that you've made partner. He can continue to sit on his ass while you bust yours every day."

Sunny's face twisted.

"Nate, looking after children is a full-time job in itself," Victoria said. "If it works for them what do you have to say about it?"

"Mama, I get that, but how many times do we have to hear it from her own mouth about how Levi really is at home? How he does the bare minimum for my niece and nephew? Doesn't even get them dressed for the day, doesn't cook, doesn't clean or take them out to the park for fresh air and play? And he still expects Sunny to cook him a hot meal when she gets home after a long day in the office? Huh? Or about how she can't even make it in the door good and hang up the car keys before he takes off to *go to the gym*?" Sunny dropped her eyes and he knew he hurt her feelings.

"I thought you would be happy for me, Nate," she said.

Nate shook his head. "You can do so much better, baby sis. So much better than that bum dude."

"He told me he's thinking about getting back in school to finally finish his degree. He's been looking into online programs. Maybe law school, too."

Nate grunted. "And I guess you'll be paying for that too."

Victoria asked, "Nate, if the roles were reversed would you be saying the same thing? Would it be a problem if Sunny was the stay-at-home mom and her husband financed her schooling? And you are one to talk about someone paying for another's education. At least Levi's making plans to do better. *He's* considering law school. You know… something promising? Something sustainable?"

"Oh, so now what I do isn't promising or sustainable?" He shook his head and was glad when the waiter came over with their orders. This was not the type of conversation he wanted to have over lunch. He pushed back from the table. "I'm going to wash my hands." In the restroom he scrubbed his hands clean all the while thinking about this surprise. His sister was everything to him and he wanted her to be happy, but for her to be such a smart woman she made the dumbest choice of a father to her children and a soon-to-be husband. And now he would have to attend a wedding he didn't care to witness.

"We're throwing the engagement party at a ballroom downtown," Victoria said when he returned to the table. "It'll be formal."

Nate rolled his eyes. His mother lived for extravagance. Since they were kids there was always an affair she and his dad had to attend or host in their home. She would dress him and his older brothers in suits, Sunny in a little girl's gown, and introduce them to their colleagues and bask in the compliments about how neatly dressed and well-behaved her children were. If one of the neighbors came over to talk about the weather, it was reason enough for Victoria to pull out her most expensive tea set or dinnerware.

He picked up the pepper shaker to sprinkle some over his salad.

"And this is the bonus surprise," Sunny said, smiling at him, "I invited Kaneesa. She's going to be in the wedding. And she's walking with you."

Nate stared at his sister as he continued to spice up his bowl of mixed greens. Kaneesa was his one-night mistake, although he'd known her for ten years. She was just an intern at the medical center where his mother worked when Victoria invited her to one of their dinner parties and first introduced them. Nate recognized her attraction for him right away and soon after she was showing up to all of their family events. For ten years he ignored her as he was in and out of relationships of his own and, by then, she had become like another sister to him. But one night after one too many drinks at the Christmas party he retreated to a room upstairs to recuperate and when he finally emerged Kaneesa was right there to push him back in. For nearly an hour she did things to him in that room he wasn't aware the nerdy and uptight Kaneesa was capable of.

The next morning he woke up to find her preparing breakfast for him in his apartment. He didn't have the heart to ask her to leave.

That was several months ago. Kaneesa is still looking for a chance to spend another night with him.

"Aren't you supposed to ask people if they want to be in your wedding? You already know I do not approve of the groom, so... you may have to get somebody else to walk with Kaneesa."

Sunny threw down her fork. "Nate, are you serious? You're not coming to my wedding?"

Nate shook his head. "I hate to break it to you, baby sis, but no. Or the engagement party. I don't want to see you make the biggest mistake of your life."

"Son, don't be ridiculous," Victoria said. "It's been five years already and they're on their third child. Why wouldn't they marry?"

His mother's question fell on deaf ears because his attention was stolen by the woman that walked through the doors of the sandwich shop. A tall, statuesque beauty with legs that appeared to go on forever. His eyes followed her as she strutted over to the counter, completely oblivious to the heads turning with curiosity in her path. She removed the oversized sunglasses from her eyes, resting them atop her head as she perused the menu hanging on the wall. The tattoo spanning the length of her torso piqued his interest.

"Now he doesn't have anything to say."

"Obviously because something's got his mind elsewhere."

Nate could not remember the last time he was so taken by a woman at first sight. "Speaking of marriage... I think I see my wife."

"What?" his mother and sister said at the same time. They turned to see for themselves who he was talking about.

Sunny sucked her teeth and turned back around. "Oh God, no."

"You can't be serious, son," Victoria said.

"She is beautiful."

"She is trashy," Sunny replied. "What the hell does she have on? Kaneesa wouldn't be caught dead wearing something like that."

His mother agreed with a nod. "But of course Kaneesa is not the young lady he wants. She's too classy."

The woman wore a pair of short denim shorts, a white shredded T-shirt just long enough to cover her breasts, and shoes that looked like combat boots with a stiletto heel. He knew the long sheer floral jacket she topped the outfit with was called a kimono. His mother wore them often.

The woman smiled at the cashier as she accepted her order number flag, and walked over to the wall next to the soda machine to wait. Nate did not know what he was going to say, but he knew he had to say something to her. "Y'all don't understand," he said as he grabbed his cup, getting up from the table, "that's confidence. There's nothing trashy about it."

He pulled the top off his cup of water and walked to the soda machine. She was looking at her smartphone. He poured out the water and pressed the button to refill it. "Hello," he said.

She looked up from her phone. "Hello."

"I like your tattoo." It was a tribal print of elongated curves and sharp points. Now that he was close up he could see it was shiny, red and puffy around the edges. She'd just gotten it done.

"Thanks," she said, her attention quickly returning to her phone.

Nate studied her profile: short forehead, concave nose and chin. A trio of miniscule moles dotted her right cheekbone. She was perfect.

He grabbed a straw and tapped it against the counter. "How long did that take?"

She looked at him with a slight smile and he wasn't sure if it was a genuine smile or a smile that she was annoyed. "Three, four hours. I don't remember to be honest."

He nodded. "I was thinking about getting a sleeve myself. Those look pretty cool."

Her eyes roved over him. "I can see that. It would look good on you."

He smiled and extended his hand. "I'm Nate Walker. What's your name?"

"Tora," she said as she shook his hand.

"I like that. You come here a lot?"

"No. This is my first time. I just left the tattoo parlor down the street and decided to try it."

Nate took a sip from his cup before setting it on the counter. "It's my first time here, too. Nice vibe."

She nodded, glancing around the room. "Yeah. I love the artwork."

"Tora, do you mind if I give you a call sometime? Maybe we can meet up for lunch one day?"

She dropped the phone in her purse when her order number was called. Smiling, she said, "Thanks, but no. I don't want to waste your time. It was nice talking to you."

He watched her walk away and towards the counter to pick up her meal.

"Did she spit in your face and tell you to get lost?" Sunny laughed when he returned to the table.

"Naw, she said she didn't wanna waste my time."

"Waste your time?" Victoria said. "So, in other words, you're beneath her?"

Nate picked up his fork. "I'm sure she has a man. That's all."

Victoria said, "That's not it. If she had one, she would have said so."

Nate noticed Tora still standing at the counter chatting with the cashier. He couldn't take his eyes off her honey brown complexion, flat stomach, and long legs. She pulled something out of her purse and handed it to the clerk before walking out the door as sexily as she'd walked in.

His mother was probably right. *There goes my wife.*

TWO

"I can't believe I let you talk me into this." Tora sat next to her coworker at a table in the mall food court. Candace was on her phone, completing a dating profile with Tora's information.

"This is how it is now. People are so busy these days, so online dating is the way to go if you really want to meet someone."

"How does that make sense? If they're so busy, how would they have time for dating?"

"It just makes the process easier," Candace said. "Between traveling to work and home, and other obligations, people don't have the chance to get out like they used to."

Tora rolled her eyes. "It's just giving people an excuse to be lazy. That's the problem… people don't talk anymore. Everyone wants to hide behind a screen."

Candace sighed and popped her gum. "Well… at least this way you have the control over the man you choose. Since you're always complaining about the type of men that approach you. Look, see—" Candace held the phone up so Tora could see the screen "—they have a field where you can enter your height requirements. It will automatically rule out the short guys."

Tora sucked her teeth. "I'm sure a lot of guys exaggerate their height on there."

Candace laughed. "I don't think so. This is a dating site you have to pay for, so I believe the people on here are more serious than those free sites. And a driver license is required, so maybe the site checks the information against the ID."

Tora shrugged. "All of it just seems so desperate to me. What happened to the days when men and women weren't afraid to talk to each other?"

"It hasn't changed. People just talk online and by text now." Candace handed the phone to Tora. "Here, now upload a couple of pictures."

"I'd rather not. Just leave it blank."

"Tora, you have to upload a picture! This will increase the chances your profile gets views."

"How about I upload a picture of Mink? At least they'd know up front that I'm a cat lover, and only cat lovers need apply."

Candace's eyes narrowed and she pursed her lips. "Seriously?"

Tora laughed. "Alright. But only one." Tora scrolled through her phone to find a black and white photo she'd recently taken.

"This is perfect," Candace said when Tora gave the phone back to her. "Now you will be able to meet your own Ruki."

"Is this the site where you met him? Soul Meet?" Ruki was Candace's fiancé, a sexy Nigerian orthodontist. They had been dating for a year when he asked her to marry him. Her family loved him, but his family despised his choosing an American for a wife.

She grinned. "Yep."

"Well, I guess I'll give it a chance if they have more guys on here that look like him."

Candace laughed, shaking her head. "I don't know if there's anybody else out there as handsome as he is, so don't get your hopes up."

"Oh, please!" Tora rolled her eyes and gathered her trash from the table. "We need to get back so we can finish setting up for the sale."

Tora pulled a pair of gray slacks onto a mannequin. She loved her job as Visual Merchandiser at Driskell & Co.—a chain of clothing stores dedicated to the stylish and sophisticated young adult. The workload kept her busy and required travel to a different location around the city every other week, so she felt like she was not stuck in the same place every day. Candace was the floor manager of the Willowbrook Mall store—the location where Tora spent most of her time.

Tora said, "So, tell me exactly how this online dating thing works."

"I can't believe you've never tried online dating. Where have you been?"

"Existing in the real world."

Candace laughed as she started to work on the four-way display in front of her, sizing the shirts from smallest to largest. "Online dating *is* the real world. It's just another avenue to meet somebody."

"I imagine it's full of loony people hiding behind a screen to play out their sick fantasies."

"Tora, you can't go in with a negative attitude already. It's true there are a bunch of crazy people out there, but I feel more comfortable with the paid sites. I don't think any sane person would spend their money just to harass folks."

"Those are the ones that have the money to burn. Because they have nothing else going on in their lives, they spend their extra funds on sick and twisted pastimes."

Candace rolled her eyes heavenward. "Do you really think I would recommend something I'm not sure of? Ruki is the best thing that's happened to me and I'm pretty confident you will find someone who's good for you, too, but you have to have an open mind and put yourself out there. What do you have to lose?"

Tora sighed and buttoned the black and white checkered shirt on the mannequin. "I'll try it," she answered, "but it better be worth my money. I can't believe I'm even *spending money* just to meet a guy! It's crazy to me!"

"All you have to do is find a profile you like and send him a message. Exchange numbers to get to know each other over the phone, see if y'all click, and then schedule a date."

"No way," Tora shook her head. "I'm not giving out my phone number. I prefer we meet up first… that way, I'm not wasting my time on a bad candidate."

Candace shrugged. "That could work, too. However you want to do it. But I preferred to spend a few weeks talking to gauge how we vibe together before I determined he was worth moving to the next step in the process."

"Well, I disagree. If I don't like him, I don't want him calling me."

Laughing, Candace said, "You are a trip."

"I'm just being honest about it. It doesn't make sense to give out my number to someone I'm not interested in."

Tora relaxed in bed later that night, stroking Silk's fine coat as he lay at her side. Silk was one of her Blue Point Siamese cats; Mink was the other—a female. Whereas Silk was calm and laidback, and preferred to be coddled, Mink was her adventurous and talkative one. She liked to roam the apartment out of Tora's sight most of the time. And she slept in the den in her cat bed.

It was nearing midnight on the east coast, but Tora picked up her phone to call her mother before she called her father as she did every night before bed. Her parents—Sharon and Myles—lived in her hometown of Pittsburgh, Pennsylvania, and both were night owls with mid-day and third-shift jobs. When she announced to them seven years ago she was moving down south for a change of atmosphere and warmer weather year-round, they were in complete disbelief. Her father cried for two days and her mother didn't talk to her for a week. They did not understand why their child—their only child—would want to be so far away from them, breaking up the family. But Tora's mind was made up. She'd already applied for a job, secured an apartment, and had the movers scheduled. On that day, as she hugged her parents tightly and her tears mixed with theirs, she promised to come back home around the holidays and to call them every day.

And since then she's upheld the promise.

"Hi, Mommy," Tora said when her mother answered. "What are you doing?"

"The same thing I'm always doing when you call me around this hour, sweetheart."

Tora knew she had just made it home from her job at the call center and was probably getting ready to eat dinner. "How was your day?"

"Busy as usual. We had two people call in sick, so I had to step in and answer some calls myself."

"Mom, as long as you've been at that job, you should be the last person to have to work the phones. You've put in more than your share of customer service."

She laughed softly. "That's what I'm paid to do, sweetheart. I have to be willing to step down and assist wherever there's a need."

And it was that type of attitude that made Sharon a favorite in the workplace and, although it took nearly fifteen years for her work ethic to be fully recognized and rewarded, she became Call Center Manager at the 24-hour security answering service.

"You won't believe what I did today," Tora said.

Sharon remained silent, waiting for her to continue.

"I let my coworker convince me to sign up for a dating service."

"So now you're turning into your Aunt Kit."

Tora laughed. Aunt Kit was her dad's sister, a serial dater who lived for all types of matchmaking services and speed dating. She had a new "gentleman friend" every few months. Her motto was 'Keep trying until you get Mr. Right'.

"I'm not going to go that far," Tora said. "I'm only doing it because it's the site where she met her fiancé. And he's a handsome guy. And tall."

Sharon chuckled. "Your poor father cursed you with all that beautiful height, didn't he?"

It was true she inherited her stature from her father: tall and naturally lean, with long feet. Tora wished she'd gotten at least some of her mother's curviness. However, her height is what she believed contributed to her lack of success in the dating arena, not her lack of curves. Even as a teen she was always taller than most of her classmates and teachers. And the few tall guys in her school were already taken. It was the same in her adult life.

A ping sounded in Tora's ear and she pulled the phone away to check the message. It was an email notification from the dating site alerting her of a new private message. "It's a blessing and a curse at the same time. I just want to finally meet someone *I* can look up to," she said.

"And you *will* meet him," Sharon assured her. "It takes time to meet somebody special. But are you sure you're making yourself available? Not being too picky? We discussed this before if I remember correctly."

Tora talked to her mother about everything. Almost everything. She informed her all about the woes of dating and her desire to be in a serious relationship. "We did. But I still say having standards is not being picky."

"It sounds pretty picky to me if your main concern is whether or not he's tall enough for *you* to look up at *him*."

"It's not the main thing, just an important thing. What woman wants to look down at her man?"

"Well... I'm not going to say I understand your frustration because clearly I don't. I just think you need to come down off your high horse and give somebody a chance. Pun intended."

They laughed together.

"I'm going to give this dating service a try and see what happens," Tora said.

"You may get lucky like Aunt Kit... you never know."

"Can we really consider Aunt Kit lucky if she's still looking?"

Sharon's easy laugh made Tora smile.

"I guess it depends on what you're looking for. In her case, anytime she has a new boyfriend she's struck gold."

Silk nudged Tora's arm and she made room for him to settle across her lap. "I just thought I'd be in a long-term, committed relationship by now... on my way to marriage. I haven't even had a date for two years now." She sighed.

"Sweetheart, you're still young. You've got plenty of time. Just forget about it, have fun, and let the universe send him to you."

"Thirty-two is not so young. Plus, you and daddy were already married and had me by the time you were my age."

"Yeah, but you see it didn't last long at all. And I want you to tell that knucklehead when you call him tonight to return my weed eater he borrowed and promised to bring right back. It's been a whole month."

Tora shook her head at the craziness of her parents. They divorced when she was five years old, both went on to marry other people, divorced again, but somehow the two remained close friends. And they bickered and fought as if they were still married. She teased them all the time that they should just put the other out of their misery and get back together. But Sharon claimed Myles was stuck in his ways, and Myles claimed Sharon was stuck in the past.

"Why don't you just call him yourself, Mom?"

"I'm not calling him. He'll have me on the phone for hours."

Tora understood. Her father was definitely a talker—another trait she inherited from him, although hers was not as extreme. "That's because he's still in love with you." Sharon made a sound and Tora imagined she was sitting at the dining table rolling her eyes.

"He is a mess. Always has been," her mother chuckled.

"I'm going to let you go now so you can eat your dinner and relax. Talk to you tomorrow. I love you."

"I love you," Sharon said.

There were eleven private messages when Tora signed onto the dating site. Of the eleven, only two interested her enough to view their profiles. One was a very good-looking man who, according to his profile, was tired of racing through life alone and was ready to meet his sidekick. A scroll through his photos revealed he was part of a motorcycle club. She'd been on the back of a motorcycle only once in her life and she remembered it being both a hair-raising and exciting experience. She left a reply.

The other was a music recording artist and producer. He was not as striking as the first, but his photos caught her attention. Although dark and brooding, they showed the artist hard at work in the studio. His message to her said: *Every day I'm always looking for inspiration for a new song. Sometimes it comes, but many times it don't. Inspiration came to me today.*

She replied back, signed off, and then pressed the button on the phone to call her dad.

"WMYL… this is your voice of the night, coming to you live from

P.A.," Myles answered in his baritone voice. "Anything you need, I got it, just hit me up on the phone lines and I'll make it happen for you."

Tora laughed out loud. Her father never picked up the phone with a simple 'hello.' He always had something outlandish to say. "Hey, Daddy. I need three—"

"Uh-oh… there's static in the line. I think we're losing the call. Please hang up and try us again in a few minutes."

Tora wished she was there with him to give him a playful smack. "How are you doing? Are you on your way to work?"

"Just making it in. What's going on, baby girl?"

"Nothing. Mommy said you better bring back her weed eater."

"What? That old raggedy thing?"

"Hey, I'm just the messenger." Tora scratched Silk's chin and he tilted his head back, closing his eyes in satisfaction as her fingertips worked their magic.

"I ended up having to buy one, so I went ahead and replaced hers too. I just haven't had the time to take it to her."

And there was that, too. Myles still looked out for Sharon, doing nice things for her here and there.

"But I have to go now, baby girl. I tell the guys no personal calls on the shop floor, so it's only right that I do the same. I'll call you back when I go on break."

"No worries. I'll just talk to you tomorrow. Love you, Daddy."

"Alright. I love you, too."

She noticed the musician had replied to her message when she logged back onto Soul Meet. He wanted to have a live chat.

    xoTakeTwo: Hello.

    music_man85: how are you this evening?

    xoTakeTwo: I'm fine. How about you?

    music_man85: i'm well… just got back from the studio

xoTakeTwo: Recording my song?

music_man85: lol

music_man85: yeah

xoTakeTwo: What's the name of it?

music_man85: Rapture

xoTakeTwo: Interesting title.

music_man85: thx… it's the first thing that came to mind as soon as i saw your pic

xoTakeTwo: OK

music_man85: so tell me about yourself…

xoTakeTwo: Where would you like to meet?

music_man85: h

music_man85: you move fast? lol…

xoTakeTwo: I have no time to waste.

music_man85: interesting…

music_man85: what part of town are you on?

xoTakeTwo: It doesn't matter. I can meet you anywhere.

music_man85: wow

xoTakeTwo: Do you drink tea? We can meet at True Tea on Memorial.

music_man85: when?

xoTakeTwo: Is Saturday OK? At 12?

music_man85: yeah. that's cool.

xoTakeTwo: OK. I will see you Saturday at noon.

music_man85: what's your phone number so i can call you?

xoTakeTwo: I prefer not to exchange numbers just yet.

music_man85: then how will i know who you are?

xoTakeTwo: I will be wearing a turquoise shirt.

music_man85: ok

xoTakeTwo: See you Saturday at noon.

music_man85: you're signing off now?

music_man85: you really don't waste any time.

xoTakeTwo: Yes. Off to bed.

music_man85: OK. Can I get your name at least?

xoTakeTwo: Tora

music_man85: so you're a tiger?

xoTakeTwo: I'm impressed. Not too many people know that.

music_man85: i lived in Japan for a while.

xoTakeTwo: Oh wow. I can't wait to hear about that on Saturday.

music_man85: i look forward to meeting you.

music_man85: good night

THREE

Nate had a half-hour before his next client was scheduled to arrive. He took a seat at his desk and pulled his smartphone out of the drawer to make a quick call.

She giggled as soon as she answered.

"You must be guilty of something," he smiled. "Send me a picture right now. No excuses."

"How do you know?" she laughed again. "*How do you just know?*"

"Because I know you. We've been working at this for almost three months now, so… I know your habits. You take your lunch every day at twelve-thirty."

"Alright, but I promise it's not as bad as you think."

Nate shook his head. "Not as bad as I think? It shouldn't be bad at all."

She laughed again. "It's just cheesecake. And only a small slice—not even three bites—I promise. But I'm eating a spinach wrap. I got my water."

Nate chuckled. Jordyn was a client who'd come to him seeking help to lose twenty-five pounds in preparation for a tropical vacation with her girlfriends late in the summer. Nate made it a point to support his clients throughout their journey to a fit and healthy lifestyle, and one of the things he enjoyed most was the spontaneous calls to monitor their progress throughout the week. The phone calls were not part of the training package, but he believed a two or three-minute call could make a difference and show how much he cared about their success beyond the gym's walls.

He said, "I want you to answer this for me: what's more important to you right now? That cheesecake that's going to derail your efforts or wearing the swimsuit that's hanging on your bedroom wall?"

Jordyn groaned. "I swear it's just a small slice, Nate. It's been so long since I've had a piece of cheesecake and I've been craving—"

"I understand," he said, "but you said it yourself how hard it is for you to get right back on track if you allow yourself a treat. Am I right?"

"I know, I know," she whined. "But I feel I can handle it today. I'm just going to have this small slice and then get right back to eating what I'm supposed to be eating. I swear. Besides… I can't just throw it away now. That would be a waste." She sounded desperate.

"You don't have to throw it away. Give it away."

She was silent a few seconds then let out a sigh. "I guess so, Nate."

"Either that, or you will have to do fifty extra squat-thrusts during our next session." She hated squat-thrusts with a passion.

"Alright, alright! I said I'm going to get rid of it."

He smiled. "Trust me, you will be glad you did."

She grunted and offered a dry 'Goodbye' before ending the call.

Nate hung up and scrolled through his contacts list for another client to hassle.

* * *

Her photos were stunning. Nate sat at his computer desk, his hand perched on top of the mouse as he examined every picture. He was supposed to be editing the podcast video he'd recorded last night to upload later, but got distracted as soon as he logged on to her website.

Take Two… photography by Tora. Candid shots were her niche he noticed as he studied her portfolio, but she also had a knack for bringing out the best in her clients' still shots. She knew just the right angles and lighting to capture their perfect moment.

He turned over the black business card with turquoise script in his hand. Her phone number was listed and he wished to call her, but what would he say? *Hello, I am the guy you met a couple days ago at Southlake Sandwich Shop. If you're concerned about wasting my time then I've got time to waste.*

He quickly decided his own website could use some updating, starting with recent photographs of himself, so he sent her a message via her site to request a quote.

Friday nights were usually low-key and uneventful since he had a private training session on Saturday mornings at 8 a.m. On occasion he would meet up for drinks with friends after they've hounded him for never having time to hang with the guys but, for the most part, it was just him on the couch with the television tuned to ESPN as he ate a healthy dinner until he retreated to his room for bed.

His smartphone rang as soon as he settled on the couch with the plate of food in his lap. He groaned as he looked at the phone's screen sitting on the arm of the sofa and reluctantly pressed the button to answer the call on speaker. It was Kaneesa. "What's up?"

"Hey, Nate," she said, drawing out the words as she always did when she called him or saw him. He used to think her childlike voice was cute and innocent, but lately it's become a bit of an annoyance. "What're you up to?"

"Not much. Just relaxing. Watching TV."

"Oh, so you're at home?"

Now he wished he wasn't. And he knew she probably already had the answer to her question and was just testing him. He took a bite of his steamed chicken breast. "Yeah, why?" he said.

"I was calling to see if maybe you wanted to hang out. I'm in the area and don't want to go home just yet. You wanna go to Top Golf?"

It was always the same explanation—that she just happened to be in the area. He lived in the Energy Corridor; she lived way out in Fresno. "Naw. I'm in for the night and don't feel like doing anything. I have to get up early tomorrow."

"Well… how about I come over there? You want me to grab some takeout?"

Nate shook his head. "I'm good. I'm eating right now, Kaneesa, and I'll be going to bed after this."

She whined, "You suck, Nate. Who goes to bed this early on a Friday night?"

"The people that have to be to work early like I do."

"If you say so," she retorted.

"I'll talk to you later," he told her and hung up after she said goodbye.

Ten minutes later there was a knock on his door. He got up from the sofa to peer through the peephole and a new wave of irritation washed over him at the sight of her on the other side. He snatched the door open. "Kaneesa, I told you you can't keep showing up to my place like this! What's up with you?"

She smiled, trying to move past him. "I'm sorry, but traffic is at a standstill on I-Ten and I have to use the bathroom."

"You passed up plenty of restrooms just to get here." He glared at her. Trying to convince the apartment complex to change the gate access code would be useless because then she would just sit and wait for another resident to enter and follow in behind them.

"I know, but I didn't want to go in any of these filthy restaurants. Are you seriously not going to let me use the bathroom?" She looked up at him blocking the door, her eyes pleading with him.

Nate shook his head again. He had no doubt it was all an act. She was always trying his patience. "This is not cool, man. You know it's not." He stepped to the side and she bolted towards his bathroom.

He grabbed his phone to pull up the Maps app to confirm her lie.

She was not lying. A bright red line signifying severe traffic stretched from Fry Road all the way to Wilcrest. Nate returned to his dinner on the couch before it went cold.

"There was no way I would have been able to hold it until I made it home," she said when she returned and went to his kitchen to get a paper towel from the holder on the counter. "Oooh… you cooked, Nate? What is this?"

He shook his head as he heard her lifting the pot tops.

"Chicken, rice, broccoli. It smells good, too."

Nate stood and walked to the door, waiting for her. He needed her gone.

"I'll just eat some of this," she said, her back to him as she opened the cabinet for a plate.

He dropped his hand from the doorknob and headed for the kitchen. "Kaneesa. You have to go. What are you doing?"

She flashed him that innocent, dimpled smile. "I told you I was hungry, Nate. What? You're not sharing tonight?"

He took the plate from her hand and began to fill a Tupperware bowl instead. "You have to take it to go." From the drawer he gave her a real fork. "Here you go," he said, touching her shoulder to steer her towards the front door.

Kaneesa let go an exasperated breath. "Are you serious, Nate? I can't eat this here until the traffic dies down? The freeway is a parking lot. I had to take a back street just to make it here and even that was a mess because everybody else had the same idea."

Desperation showed on her lovely face. Kaneesa was a beautiful woman. Standing at five feet, two inches she was petite, but curvy.

Nate loved her hair the most. It was thick and bouncy just like Sunny's, falling just past her shoulders in black and red curls. The deep dimples in her cheeks were his second favorite. But for her to be as pretty as she was it was just something about her that didn't move him.

He sighed. Perhaps he was being a little insensitive. "I'm just tired that's all," he told her and left for the living room. "You can stay a few minutes."

She made a noise that sounded like a rubber duck being squeezed and rushed past him to the couch. "What're you watching?" she asked, plopping down in the exact spot where he had been sitting.

He took the opposite end. *What does it look like?* he wanted to say, but instead asked, "Is there something you wanna watch?"

"Put it on Investigation Discovery. I love that channel."

He handed her the remote instead and reached for his smartphone.

"See, I told you." She said, "Look at that."

It was a breaking news story. A big rig driver lost his load and some sort of chemical spilled, so the freeway was shut down completely as they waited for HAZMAT crew to clear the scene. The helicopter panned out to show the sea of red brake lights all the way to Grand Parkway now.

Nate grunted, nodding his head.

"There's no telling how long that's going to take. I feel sorry for the people stuck in that. Can you imagine? What if someone was on their way to the airport or something?"

He really did not feel like talking and just wanted to be alone. "Yeah," was all he could offer in response.

"This is the juiciest chicken breast I've ever had, Nate. It is so good." She finished off her plate and set it on the coffee table. "Where are your manners, Nate? You didn't even ask me if I wanted something to drink."

If you say my name one more time.... He looked over at her. "Would you like some water, Kaneesa?"

"That's all you have? No juice or anything?"

"You know I don't," he said and got up to take her plate to the kitchen.

"A tall glass of water it is then." She settled back in the couch, pulling her skinny legs up to her chest. If his mother were here she would ask Kaneesa where *her* manners are because she should know one does not sit with their feet in the sofa.

"Oh… I've got so much to do," she started when he returned with her water. "Do you have a straw?" She accepted the glass from him.

"Nope. I don't." He watched her take the tiniest sip from the glass and set it down. Either she wasn't as thirsty as she wanted him to believe or she lost interest since she didn't have a straw.

"I've got so much to do," she said again and he knew she was waiting for him to engage her.

He picked up his smartphone.

"Nate! What is wrong with you? Are you going to ignore me all night?"

"What are you talking about? I'm just looking at something on my phone. I hear you."

She smiled, crossed her legs Indian-style, and pulled the throw pillow into her lap. "We have to find a caterer and live band. Victoria said she wants to have valet to park the cars, too."

Nate shook his head. If they were doing all of this just for the engagement party, he could only imagine what the actual wedding would be like.

"So we have to start looking this weekend for the caterer at least. When are you free?"

He looked up from his phone. Surely Sunny had told her he was not attending any of the festivities. "Y'all go ahead without me. I'm not in it."

"What do you mean you're not in it? I've already told Victoria we're gonna start our part of the planning this weekend."

"I'm not sure why you lied to my mama like that. She was there when I told Sunny I wasn't going to the party or the wedding."

Kaneesa's mouth dropped open. "What do you mean you're not going to the wedding?"

It was clear now neither Sunny nor his mother told her the news. "Kaneesa, you know I don't like Levi. I don't support it, so I'm not going."

"Well that's selfish of you, Nate," she scolded. "This has nothing to do with you. This is for your sister. You *have to* be there, Nate. This is an exciting time for her."

"No I don't. And I'm not going just because people say it's the right thing to do. To be there would be fake. It's not gonna happen." He reached for the remote since she never did put the television on *Investigation Discovery*.

"I know you're joking, right? Sunny would have said something about this if it were true."

He shook his head again. "I'm serious. You can call and ask her yourself."

Kaneesa was not taking his word for it and grabbed her phone from her purse.

Sunny didn't answer.

She laughed then. "I think you're just pulling my leg, Nate. We're walking together in the wedding. How can you not be there?"

He looked her right in the eye to let her know he was serious.

A frown knitted her eyebrows. "I'm calling Victoria."

Nate shrugged and got up from the sofa to connect his phone to the charger in his bedroom and to use the bathroom. When he returned Kaneesa's arms were folded across her chest and her lips were poked out like a child that had been denied candy.

"I really can't believe you would do this to her," she said. "Even if you don't like him you still—"

Nate waved his hand. "Kaneesa, this is not up for discussion. I'm not going and that's just it." He sat down at the computer to start the podcast video edit. He no longer felt like doing it, but he couldn't be on the couch next to Kaneesa either.

"Can I have a blanket?" she asked. "I'm cold."

Without a word he got up to retrieve one from the hall closet.

She didn't even say thank you when he handed it to her.

He returned to the desk and covered his ears with his headphones. He worked for an hour before he finally looked back to see Kaneesa had fallen asleep. His bed was calling him, too.

"Hey," he gently touched her shoulder. It took a second gentle shake before she looked up at him. "Let me walk you out."

"I'm tired, Nate. Just let me sleep here tonight." She pulled the blanket up to her chin and closed her eyes again.

"Kaneesa, I work early tomorrow morning. You have to go."

She ignored him and turned over on her side, her face buried into the back of the sofa.

Nate shook his head. He didn't have the energy and it wasn't even worth arguing about. He turned off the lights and television, put the pots in the refrigerator, and went to his room.

* * *

"I'm offended that you found it necessary to lock your door."

She startled him when he stepped into the living room the next morning. He'd forgotten she was there. And he'd just wondered when he left his bedroom why the door was closed and locked.

Kaneesa was sitting at his computer desk. "The sofa got really uncomfortable after a while last night," she said. "I expected you to be enough of a gentleman to let me sleep in the bed."

"Kaneesa…" He didn't have a response. He went to the kitchen to make one of his usual breakfasts: over-easy eggs, sautéed spinach and mushrooms. He added some chicken leftover from last night. "I'm leaving in fifteen minutes to meet my client," he said.

She got up from her seat and met him in the kitchen where he stood eating at the counter. "Why do you keep trying to pretend what happened between us didn't happen, Nate?" A soft hand touched his back.

He stiffened under her touch. He should've had on a shirt. Sighing, he said, "I'm not pretending anything. But I think we both know it's best we keep the line drawn between us."

She wrapped her arms around his waist. "I don't think so. We're perfect for each other, so I don't understand why you're trying to fight it."

Nate grabbed her hands and tried to step to the side. She pressed her body against his, pinning him to the counter. "Kaneesa…" He didn't want to have to shove her tiny ass aside. He turned his body to face her. "Kaneesa," he said again, staring down at her. "Me and you will never be together. I love you like a sister. That's how I see you."

She flashed those chocolate dimples. "Are you afraid to fall in love with me? Good friendships make the best relationships."

"And I don't want to ruin our friendship," he told her.

Before Sunny met Levi and before the kids came, they were three peas in a pod and often hung out together.

Kaneesa stepped closer. "Nate, all these years I've been waiting for a chance to be with you. I see the way you look at me. Even Victoria and Sunny notice the way you look at me. There's definitely energy between us."

He had no idea what she was talking about. If he was looking at her it was probably because she'd just walked into a room or was speaking. It was a natural reaction.

"You wanna do something before you go?" She squeezed his penis.

He jerked back from her grasp. "You need to go, Kaneesa."

She giggled and reached for him again.

He grabbed her by the elbow and walked her to the living room. His patience was on empty. "Let's go, man."

"That's not what you were saying to me the night of the Christmas party." He released her arm and she sat on the couch, taking her time to put on her shoes. "Or the morning after."

Nate stood with the door propped open, waiting for her to exit.

She finally stood and grabbed her purse from the coffee table. Looking up at him on her way out, she said, "But you refuse to acknowledge that part, am I right?"

FOUR

"Tora? It's been a while since I've seen you!" The small woman's eyes glistened as she smiled, extending her arms. "I must've been in the back when you walked in."

Tora stood from the table to accept the hug. "I think so. And it has been a while, Ms. Trooty, how are you?"

Trooty's hands remained fastened on Tora's arms as she leaned back, staring up at her. She shook her head as she took in the hair and makeup and outfit. "Absolutely stunning, dear. You're all dressed up for tea?"

Tora laughed softly. "Just thought I'd try to be a little cute today since I'm meeting someone here."

"Oh, you're so modest. You're beautiful all the time." Trooty patted her arm and motioned for her to return to her seat as she took the one across from her. "What's been going on with you?"

"Not too much, just working hard. The usual. How is Myrna?"

Trooty's slim shoulders shook as she laughed and threw a hand to her heart. Myrna was her 1959 Cadillac Eldorado—the one Tora side-swiped trying to dodge a Pomeranian that ran out in the road ahead of her as she drove down Memorial Drive about six months ago. It had already been a stressful day, so when she got out of her vehicle to assess the damage she'd caused to that shiny mauve convertible spaceship with the milk-white seats and tires, and at the puppy that lay bleeding and twitching in the street, she was hysterical.

With her easy smile and soothing voice Trooty had calmed her and told her that automobile was the least of her worries and she was glad the two of them were all right. From her car she offered Tora the cup of tea that did not topple over and spill across the floor during the impact. It was the one she was taking home to her husband.

"Did William tell you about the new lemon bars? I think you'll love them. They're perfect for your favorite tea."

Tora nodded. "He did, but I'm going to wait until the guy I'm meeting gets here."

Trooty lifted her bushy black brows. Tora loved the contrast against her wavy gray hair. "Is this a special guy?"

"This is my first time meeting him, actually," Tora said. "I met him online."

"Oh really?"

"Yeah. So I don't know."

"So it's more of a blind date, am I right?"

"That's how I view online dating, anyway. Because you really don't know what you're going to get until they show up. I saw his photo, but who's to say it's really him?" She shook her head at the possibility. "I'm only trying this because my coworker suggested it."

Trooty reached across the table and touched her hand. "You give me a signal if you need an escape, okay darling?"

Laughing, Tora said, "Right! I hope I won't, but that's a good idea. If you see me tugging at the back of my hair like this, I need an out."

Lines appeared at the corners of Trooty's eyes as she chuckled. "I'll let William know, too," she said.

When he walked in Tora's first thought was the picture was old. Years old. She knew it was him because he looked as out of place as she did amongst the half-dozen silver-haired customers sipping tea and eating pastries. He was the right height, but the rest of him was all wrong. She had the mind to pull her hair right away but didn't want to be rude and decided to let him enjoy one of Trooty's savory beverages at least.

He stuck out his hand when he approached the table. "How're you doing today? You're even more beautiful in person."

"Thank you," Tora smiled.

He glanced around as he sat down. "What made you choose this place?"

"Besides it being the best tea I've ever had in my life and worth the drive all the way over here? I know the owner."

He nodded. "Oh okay."

"Are you going to tell me your name?" she asked.

"I'm sorry, sweetheart," he stuck out his hand again. "I'm Jason."

Trooty walked over. She looked at Tora and gave her a thumbs-up. Tora responded with a slight nod. "Here are the menus. Just let me know when you're ready to order," she said before turning away again.

They looked over the small, single-sided menus in silence before Jason finally said, "Now you have to tell me everything about you."

"I don't know about *everything*, but…"

He laughed. "What made you join Soul Meet? I would think a woman like you to be spoken for already."

"It's not something I normally do, but I decided to give it a try. Like everyone else I'm just hoping to meet a nice person and see where it leads."

"Well, I can say with confidence right now you can stop looking."

Tora looked at him a couple seconds before the laugh burst out of her mouth. A few of the diners' heads turned their way and their eyes gave a look as if to say *Of course they would be the loud ones.* She couldn't care less.

"Let's not get ahead of ourselves. This is only our first meeting," she told him.

"I just know that I'm a good man and I got the reputation to prove it."

"Oh really? Do you know what you want to order?" She was going to need her tea for this one.

"Yeah, the corn beef sandwich sounds good. And I wanna try that tea you say is so great."

Tora waved Trooty over and relayed their orders. When she left, Tora propped her elbows on the table, resting her chin on her hands. "Tell me about your reputation."

Jason cleared his throat. "Well, all the women I've been with—"

"How many have you been with?" she interrupted.

A sly grin curved his lips and Tora had to admit he had a sexy smile. But, height notwithstanding, it was the only other thing he had going for him physically.

"Isn't there a saying that it's not polite to ask a guy—or girl—how many partners they had?" He laughed.

Tora pursed her lips.

"Seriously… everybody will tell you I'm all about working hard to make sure I become a success so my family can be a success. I'm talking generational wealth. Leaving something so my kids and my kids' kids don't have to work so hard."

Tora nodded. "That's understandable. A great outlook."

"Every day I'm grinding," he continued. "I'm always in the studio writing or recording or with my partners putting tracks together. Music is my life. It's in my blood. I eat, sleep, breathe it."

"Okay."

"So if you know it's what's going to get us to the top why would it be a problem?"

"I agree."

He smiled again. "Women say that all the time though. Do you really see what I'm saying?"

"Yeah, if music is your passion you should definitely pursue it."

"Exactly," he nodded, "so if we have this understanding beforehand why would it all of a sudden be an issue five or six months into our relationship?"

Tora's forehead crinkled. He touched her arm.

"Let me ask you this: what type of work do you do?"

"I'm a visual merchandiser."

"What's that?"

"I make the store look good to attract customers."

"You love what you do? Is that your dream job?"

"I enjoy it, but I also do photography on the side. It's what I really love."

"Alright, so photography is what you really wanna do, right?"

Tora nodded again. "Well, it's one of many. I have several hobbies."

"Okay, so let's say above all else it's what you want to do. Now, if I was your man and you came to me and said, 'Baby, I really wanna pursue this photography thing. It's my heart, it's my passion… it's what I wanna do and I believe it will get us the financial freedom we're striving for.' As your man I'm going to see to it that you do that."

"I like the sound of that," Tora said.

"Exactly. But let me take it a step further. If I knew that you needed a lot of free time to really pursue your dream and do what you have to do, and if I were in a position to support you financially in the meantime, I would do that too."

Tora raised a brow at him. She should have known there was a catch.

Trooty set their plates and pot of tea with matching cups in front of them.

"Thanks, Ms. Trooty," Tora said.

"Can I get y'all any extra condiments or anything?" she asked.

Tora shook her head no while Jason requested Tabasco sauce. He didn't wait for Trooty to return and dove right into his sandwich as soon as she walked away.

"I can tell by the look on your face you're already seeing the negative," he said.

"I get what you're saying, but chasing your dream is one thing. Wanting somebody to take care of you while you do it is another."

"That's not what you just said. Just a minute ago you said you like the way it sounds for your man to help you reach your goal."

That sly grin appeared again. This time it wasn't as sexy with the glob of mayonnaise stuck on the corner of his mouth. And he kept chewing and talking as if he didn't feel it. She had to look down at her own plate to keep from regurgitating the forkful of pot pie she'd just swallowed.

"So now let me ask you this: how much work do you put in working on your dream?"

Tora shrugged. "I don't know. I mean… I take my camera with me everywhere I go. Every chance I get I'm always promoting my services."

Trooty set the hot sauce in front of him. He twisted the cap off and set the bottle down next to his plate. "But you're not able to devote to it full time though, right? Because of your other job?"

"Well, no, but—"

"And that's exactly what I'm talking about. How can you expect for your photography business to get off the ground if you're only able to work at it for one or two hours a day?"

It was true she could not take on as many jobs as she liked because the biggest money makers and opportunities for exposure were events that took place on weekends, and Driskell & Co. required her to work most weekends. But she always saw the situation as a glass half full and believed all she needed was one awesome shot to bring her steady business. So she approached every shoot with that mindset. "Are you telling me that you only date rich women?"

He laughed and strings of mayo and red cabbage slaw stretched from the roof of his mouth to his tongue. Tora pushed her chicken pot pie aside. She was done.

"No, not necessarily. But I believe in making sacrifices."

"Jason, what exactly are you saying?"

"I'm saying if we're in a relationship and committed to growing together, building something, and you know my music is what's gonna get us there, then we can do without certain things so I can commit to it full time."

"So in other words you're looking for a woman to take care of you, to make sacrifices for you? A woman you're not married to?"

He took a sip of tea before setting the cup down delicately on its saucer. "I'm looking for a woman that's supportive of my dream. Isn't that what relationships are about?"

"How long have you been doing music?"

"All my life. Well… since I was thirteen, fourteen."

"And how old are you now?"

"I'm thirty-four."

"And you haven't had any success with it yet?"

"I got two albums, co-wrote and produced one of my partner's albums, and did some music for a stage play. I got a notebook full of songs."

"But you haven't gotten signed or anything?"

"We did, but then the label kept putting off the album, saying they were going through some changes. I got tired of waiting and told them if they weren't gonna put it out that year, I was taking my music elsewhere."

"Did they?"

He shook his head. "They dropped us."

"How long ago did that happen?"

"About twelve years."

"So for twelve years you've been in relationships with women who have taken care of you while you work on music full time? Were you married to any of these women?"

"No. I was engaged once. Like I say… they were all down with me in the beginning. Then their attitude changed."

"But can you blame them? You're asking them to finance your dream, basically, and have nothing to show for it or offer in return for all the years they've invested in you. Be serious now."

He nodded. "It's a testament of their belief in me. My dream won't die. I have to keep working at it to see it through."

Tora rolled her eyes. "Jason, you can't be serious. At some point you have to realize you got to try something else if it's not working. You can't just live off people."

He looked at her as if he were seeing an alien with three heads. "That's the craziest thing I've ever heard. I would never tell someone to give up on their dream if it's not working. How would you feel if I told you to give up photography? And I see you have temporary amnesia because just a minute ago you had no problem with the idea of your man taking care of you while you strived for the top, but now that I'm presenting you the situation in reverse it's a problem." He chuckled. "Come on now. *You* be serious."

She folded her arms on the table to combat the urge to slap him. "I'm not saying to give up on your dream, Jason. Many of us are chasing our dreams and would love to be able to commit to them full time, but bills have to be paid. You have to do what you can until you get there is all I'm saying. And I'm not sure what type of women you're used to dealing with, but my parents raised me to not depend on anyone financially. Especially someone I'm not married to. I will never not have a job that brings me income—even if it's just part time."

He grunted, shaking his head. "And it's that type of attitude that keeps us from advancing together as a people, as a community. We're never supportive of each other in relationships. We're always looking out for ourselves. As your man you *should be* able to depend on me financially… and vice versa."

"Long gone are the days where families can survive on one income."

"It doesn't take much to run a household," he countered. "All you need is food, water, and electricity. Everything else is just extracurricular."

She picked up her fork to take a bite of the pie. He had finished his sandwich and her stomach was growling. But what she really should have done was call Trooty over to ask for a to-go plate. It was clear now, Jason was a bum and she had no reason to waste any more time on this meeting.

"I was about to ask you if your food wasn't good since you weren't eating it," he said.

No, it's because I had to wait until the horse sitting next to me closed his mouth long enough so I can enjoy my lunch without gagging. "I was just letting it cool down a bit. The last time I got it it burned my tongue," she lied.

He let her take several more bites before he spoke again. "So… Tora the Tiger. I still don't know much about—"

"That's right," she cut him off, "you were supposed to tell me about your time in Japan. How did you end up there? You said you lived there for a while, right?"

He waved his hand and poured more tea into his cup. "This tea is very good by the way. I see what you mean."

"I told you," Tora agreed.

"Everything is always about the music," he said. "One of my partners is from there. He was here for a while in school, but decided he could be more successful in Japan for the type of music he was producing, so he went back. He told me I should come with him so we could work on some things together. And me and my girl had just broken up, I was down about it and figured why not. It was the opportunity for a fresh start. Plus, he convinced me of how big the music scene is out there—especially hip hop."

"Is that the type of music you're into?"

"I'm more R&B. Soul. But I can do hip hop tracks. I can do it all, really."

"Did you like it there? Why did you end up coming back to the states?"

"Aww, man. Japan is cool. I was surprised to see more of us out there. I wasn't expecting that. But I got more connections here, so it just made sense for me to be home. I was there for three years though. We worked on the album I was telling you about that I co-wrote. It got some play, but didn't really take off like we hoped."

Tora nodded.

"But I definitely need to get back soon. It's been a minute since I've seen my little Hoshi."

Tora gave a quizzical look.

"My daughter," he clarified.

She couldn't recall whether or not his Soul Meet profile mentioned any children he might have had. "She lives in Japan?"

"With her mother, yes."

"Is this the woman you were engaged to?"

"No. Not her."

"When's the last time you saw her? Your daughter I mean?"

"Not since I left. About five years."

"How old is she?"

"She's eight now."

"What's stopping you?"

He sighed and laughed a little. "Those flight tickets are pretty steep."

Tora was in disbelief. It was getting worse by the second. "So let me get this straight," she said, "your friend asks you to move to Japan and, because you broke up with your girlfriend, you decide to go. You meet another woman there and get her pregnant and, because the music scene wasn't right for you, you decide to leave your family and return to the U.S.? And because you don't believe in working a job outside of music to support yourself, you can't come up with the money to go and visit your daughter? And you don't see a problem in that?"

His grin showed her that he didn't see the problem.

He said, "That's why I'm working hard to make sure I win. She will be well-taken care of when her daddy gets Hoshi Music out here on the scene."

Tora rolled her eyes again. "Well… I'm sure she will be glad to see that you cared enough to use her name in your work." She was disgusted.

His lip curved into a smile and she decided he looked like a lizard.

She raised her arm, waving Trooty over. "We're ready for the check. It will be separate."

FIVE

"Uncle Nate! Uncle Nate!"

The patter of little feet came rushing down the hall as Nate stepped into the foyer. The security system's three beeps sounded whenever the front door opened and, as always, his eldest niece, Bryanna, wanted to see who the latest visitor was for Sunday dinner at her grandmother's house. And because she was the eldest of the bunch his other niece and nephews followed right behind her. Tiny limbs and hands encircled his waist and thighs and knees as the five of them hugged him at the same time.

"Hey little munchkins. What's up?" he said, looking back into the little brown faces that stared up at him bright-eyed and grinning. He rubbed their heads and patted their backs before Bryanna grabbed his hand, leading him towards the dining room.

"Nana's waiting for you so we can eat," she said in a stern tone Nate was sure she'd picked up from either her mother or her grandmother.

"Nana's waiting for you so we can eat!" his youngest niece repeated before skipping ahead of them.

The adults were seated and in conversation around the table: his father Gerald III at the head, Victoria at his right; Sunny, Levi, his eldest brother Bryan and his wife, his other brother Gerald IV—

whom they called Geo—and his wife. The kids took their places between their parents.

"Hey everybody," Nate said as he took his usual seat at the end of the table opposite his father.

"Only ten minutes late this time, brother?" Sunny said. "I'm impressed."

"Which is perfect because the rolls should be ready," Victoria added as she stood. "I'll go and get them now and we can get started."

"How's everything with you, son?" Nate's father asked him. It was customary for the family to discuss any good news or issues they experienced throughout the week over Sunday dinner. "I was just telling them about my newest big project. A merger."

Nate nodded. "My week was good. Picked up another private client yesterday through the lady I train on Saturday mornings. It's her son, but she paid me up-front for three months' worth of sessions for him."

"That's good. I'm not sure how much money it brings you, but my guess is a lot. I imagine you can charge a high price for your private sessions."

"Well, I try to keep it as affordable for the clients as I can." Nate never disclosed the specifics of his salary with his family because, unlike most of them, it was not something he felt the need to boast about. Besides, he knew they all knew his income could not compete with theirs and it didn't make sense to even make it an issue.

Victoria grunted as she returned to the table carrying a basket of the fresh dinner rolls. "Gerald, I doubt that," she said, addressing his father. "Which is why he basically has to work two jobs. Every day I question his logic in that venture."

Bryan and Levi laughed while Sunny shook her head.

He'd only been there a good five minutes and his mother was already starting in on him. But what pissed him off more than anything was Levi having the audacity to laugh about the situation. "At least I have a job," he said, eyeing Levi. "That's more than what you can say though, right?"

"I work," Levi countered. "I work with my kids at home. Schooling them. Taking care of them. Something you know nothing about."

"That's a lie and you know it."

"Alright, you guys," Victoria looked at Nate. "That's enough and we are not going to have this discussion in front of the kids, okay?"

Nate glared at Levi before moving his eyes over to Sunny. She looked away from him.

Victoria grabbed the dish sitting in front of her and began to fill his father's plate. "Let's eat," she said.

Dishes were passed around the table and Nate helped himself to everything. Only on Sundays did he relax his clean eating routine and indulge in the soul-filling goodness that was his mother's cooking.

"What's the latest on the engagement party plans?" Evelyn asked Sunny. Evelyn was Geo's wife.

Sunny beamed as if she had been waiting all day for someone to broach the subject.

"We got the building as you already know. Ma is handling the guest list and invitations, and the parking and entry attendants. Kaneesa said she'll find the caterer and band." She glanced at Nate, but his attention was fixated on the plate in front of him.

"I'm just so happy you guys are finally getting married," Evelyn said.

"Me too," Sharday, Bryan's wife, added. "But what about a photographer? You're gonna have someone take photos, right?"

Sunny said, "Ma's getting the photographer, too."

"No I'm not," Victoria shook her head. "That's on the list of what you're supposed to do."

"Is it?" Sunny laughed. "I thought all I had to do was show up with my love looking cute?" She grabbed Levi's hand and gave it a squeeze.

"You know you're in charge of getting your own photographer and decorator."

Nate's ears perked up when he heard photographer. He'd hoped to receive a call back from Tora, but here it was Sunday and still nothing.

Gerald said, "I just want to remind you all while you're making these elaborate plans just to tell folks you're getting hitched that I'm only responsible for the actual wedding ceremony. My money will not be going towards this engagement party."

Victoria rolled her eyes at her husband. "Oh be quiet, Gerald. No one's asked you to pay for anything. Sunny and I got this covered." She winked at Sunny and the two of them, along with the daughters-in-law, laughed.

"So you know what that means, Dad," Bryan said.

"Yeah. They think they're slick." Gerald gave a skeptical look at his wife.

She blew a kiss his way and he folded.

"Oooh," sang Bryanna, and the other little ones followed suit, mimicking her.

"Oh stop," Victoria smiled at her grandchildren.

Sharday asked Sunny, "What made you want a band instead of a deejay? Remember it was my cousin who worked me and Bryan's wedding? I can check if she's available for that day."

"Well, the live band was Ma's idea. She thought it would be more appropriate for a formal event."

"But it's your party. You should have whatever you want."

"I don't mind. I like the idea of a live band. We're keeping it classy since there will be a lot of my attorney friends there."

Victoria added, "And because we remember how a few of your family members got a little out of hand when a certain song was played."

Nate couldn't help himself and he laughed with the rest of them at the memory of the night of his brother's wedding. He couldn't recall the name of the song, but he remembered vividly the guests from the bride's side of the family that held everyone captive, their mouths wide open as they stared at them as butts shook and hips gyrated and pelvises pumped and humped the floor.

Victoria was livid and had pulled her son to the side away from the wedding party to ask if he was certain he was marrying into the right family because she couldn't imagine her son associated with such an uncouth group of people. Bryan told Nate he had to call Sharday over and she assured her new mother-in-law she was nothing like 'those people from her daddy's side of the family—the roguish side'.

Sunny agreed with Victoria. "We definitely don't need any of that at my party."

"I just want to say marriage is the most beautiful thing and I'm glad y'all are finally doing it," Evelyn said. "But you haven't told us what made you go ahead and propose for real this time, Levi."

Nate's attention immediately went to Levi, eager to hear what story he would tell.

Sunny laced her fingers with Levi's as she stared at him like he was the best thing this side of heaven.

"It was just the right time. I didn't wanna keep her waiting anymore because she deserves it. I'm not going nowhere. She's not going nowhere." He turned to her. "And because I love her."

"Aww, babe," Sunny cooed. "I love you, too."

Nate grunted and took another bite of his food.

Sharday said, "It's nothing like being married. I don't care how much people like to claim living together is the same as being married, it is not. There's nothing like the comfort of knowing that he is really serious about being with you and is committed to you for a lifetime."

Victoria raised her glass. "I second that."

"We're all happy for you," Bryan said, looking at Sunny. "Bryanna's already made up her mind that she's going to be the flower girl."

"Yeah!" Bryanna chimed in. "I'm the flower girl."

Sunny laughed. "Well, I guess two flower girls are better than one because I had only thought about your cousin Anaya as the flower girl."

"I wanna be the flower girl, too," Anaya whined.

Sunny looked over at her daughter. "Anaya, you *are* going to be mommy's flower girl, okay?"

"It is an exciting time indeed," Gerald said. "I'm glad to know my daughter is making her family official."

"What about you, Nate?" Levi said. "You're the only quiet one. You happy I'm finally gonna marry your sister?"

Silence fell over the room and all eyes were on Nate. Even the children were uncharacteristically quiet as if they knew it was an off-hand question.

Nate looked squarely at Levi, his loosely-closed fist thumping lightly against the marble tabletop. "You want a pretty lie or the ugly truth?"

Levi gave him a look as if to say if he could crack his plate over Nate's head he would do it without thinking.

Nate's gaze didn't waver.

"Kids," Victoria started, "are you guys ready for dessert now? How about we all have dessert?" She got up from the table. She looked at Sunny and her daughters-in-law. "Clear the table and get the kids some ice cream. Let them eat it outside on the patio." Then she turned to Nate. "Come see me in my office."

Nate stood looking at the books and family photos on his mother's shelf. They were books and family photos he'd seen many times before, but he needed to stand after waiting for nearly a half-hour for his mother to come and talk to him as she'd said she would. He was tired of waiting, but it beat having to sit and listen to his family gush about the impending nuptials between his twin sister and her tool of a boyfriend. He couldn't stand to be in the same room with Levi. Just looking at the guy got under his skin.

His mother finally walked in. She'd changed clothes and her hair was pulled back into a sophisticated bun at the nape of her neck. It was how she wore her hair when she was going to work. She sat in the oversized brown leather chair behind her desk and pointed to the one in front of it.

It was the same feeling since he was a kid. Like going to the principal's office when he was in trouble.

"What's going on with you, Nate?" she asked as he sat down.

"What're you talking about?"

"Why are you always picking on Levi?"

"Picking on Levi? You make it sound like we're ten years old or something."

"Well that's what you two act like sometimes."

"He's always saying something to me. You know that. It's not the other way around."

"Nate, all he asked was if you were happy for them. What's wrong with that?"

Nate shook his head. "He knows how I feel, so he just said that to get at me."

"And you could have been the bigger person and just said 'yes' and let it go."

"Say yes for what?"

Victoria sighed and reached to turn on her desktop computer. "Nate, he's going to be your sister's husband. He's your nieces and nephew's father, which means he will be a part of this family for the rest of his life. You two *have to* put whatever grievances you have with each other aside."

Nate blew out a breath and sat back in the chair. "It wouldn't bother me one bit if I never said anything else to that dude for the rest of my life."

"You know I won't tolerate this type of strife in my household—especially at my dinner table."

He looked at his mother. "Why don't you ever say anything to him?"

"Because *you* are my son. And you know how I raised you all to conduct yourselves. We uphold a standard of civility in the Walker family. Got it?"

He sucked his teeth and reluctantly nodded his head.

She pulled a folder from the drawer and a stapled document out of it. "Now, to discuss your behavior towards your brother-in-law is not the only reason why I called you in here." She pushed the document towards him.

Nate looked at it but didn't touch it.

"Do you have any idea how much we spent on you to attend UT?"

His eyes went back down to the paper.

"Take a serious look at it," Victoria said.

He picked up the document. She'd typed up a report of every dollar she spent towards his tuition and fees and supplies for his entire college life. He flipped the pages.

"I have the same record for your brothers and sister."

"Okay." He frowned, realizing where the conversation was going.

"Nate, when your father and I got married and decided to have children, I had a vision of what I wanted for my family. I wanted you all to be the best kids, the smartest kids. And I wanted you to be a success. Gerald and I agreed that we would work hard to be the example and ensure you understood the types of careers that would afford you a certain lifestyle—the type of lifestyle we wanted for ourselves. When you graduated from college we didn't want you all to be inundated with a bunch of debt like so many college graduates are and that's why we paid for your education." She sat back in her seat. "Nate, with your sister and brothers we can see the return on our investment. They have nice homes. Bryan and Geo's kids are in good private schools. They're doing well."

Nate shook his head wearily.

"But you?" she continued. "It really upsets me how nonchalant you are about throwing our money away."

"Mama, I didn't throw your money away. I went to law school. I *was* a lawyer, remember?"

"But you're not a lawyer now—"

"I love what I do."

She shook her head at him this time. "I've come up with a plan for you to start repaying us."

"Mama, are you serious?"

She clicked on the computer screen and the printer started to whir. "I'm very serious, Nate. I've told you this plenty of times before." She grabbed the sheet of paper from the printer and gave it to him. "I figured half of what we paid for your education is fair enough. I'll give you a month to prepare, but beginning the first week of August I want seventy-five dollars per week."

Nate was furious. "Seventy-five dollars per week? I can't afford to give you seventy-five dollars a week."

Victoria shrugged. "You do what you have to do, son. Cut back on your expenses, take on extra clients, record more podcasts. I don't care, but I want my money."

Nate grabbed the documents from her desk and walked out.

SIX

Nate Walker? Why does that name sound familiar?

Tora halted her steps and aimed her camera as Mink sniffed around the buds of a floral bush. Just as her tiny paw reached up to touch the pink flower Tora captured the shot. They were taking a stroll through the apartment complex. Tora liked to bring the cats out for fresh air at least a couple times a week, but Silk wanted no parts of the outdoors today, so she left him inside the apartment. The outdoors made him nervous and the times when he didn't put up a fuss and let her bring him out she had to carry him the majority of the time. Mink, on the other hand, waltzed ahead on her leash as if she owned the universe and dared a mutt to come running up to her barking like he was crazy.

Mink stopped every few feet to pounce on a fallen leaf or dig at the bark chips beneath the bushes. *Maybe she thinks she's a dog,* Tora thought, and continued to snap photos as Mink romped through the grass and pranced the edges of the sidewalk.

Nate Walker wanted to know her pricing for a photo shoot, which caused Tora to purse her lips as she read the short message earlier. He offered no other information except that he admired her work from the pictures she had posted on her website and was interested in having his professional photos taken by her. The contact form clearly stated to be as specific as possible when requesting a quote. She'd replied to his message with several questions to answer for more details on his needs.

"Are you ready to go inside?" Tora said to Mink.

Her mobile phone rang and she knew it would be Candace finally returning her call to hear about the fiasco that was her first experience with the dating site candidate.

It was a number that was not saved in her phone as a contact.

"Hello, this is Tora," she answered.

"Hi, Tora, this is Nate Walker. I contacted you requesting a quote for photos."

"Yes," she said. She tried to come up with the image of his face in her head that would go along with the name and voice. Nothing came.

"I hope you don't mind that I'm giving you a call back, but I thought it would be easier to talk to you instead of going back and forth through email."

"No, it's not a problem at all." She scooped up Mink and walked to a table in the courtyard and sat down. "I don't have anything to write with on me right now, so I'm going to place you on speaker and type some notes in my phone. Is that okay?"

"Sure," he said. "No problem."

Tora wrapped Mink's leash around the table leg and tied it tightly so she wouldn't try to get away. "Will this be a personal shoot or for a bigger party or—"

"A personal shoot. I want to get some recent photos of myself for my website."

She didn't want to assume anything, but she needed to know. "What type of website is it?"

"It's my personal site. I'm a fitness trainer."

"Oh, okay," she nodded. She'd been hired to take photos for

graduations, family portraits, a wedding, a quinceañera, an arboretum, but never a personal trainer. She imagined he would need full body shots, possibly topless, and possibly wearing skimpy biker shorts or—even worse—the dreaded Speedo. "What do you have in mind for the setting? Will this be an indoor shoot at a gym or do you want a studio background with props?"

"Uhh… I'm thinking outdoors, but if you suggest something better that will be cool, too."

"If we do outdoors you have to consider the weather. Will there be any wardrobe changes or anything?" He laughed and she wondered what was funny about the question.

"I didn't think about that. But I guess I can bring a change of clothes. For a different effect in some of the shots."

"Do you have a particular place in mind for this outdoor shoot?"

"Hmm…." After several seconds of thought he said, "There's a park not too far from where I live called Bear Creek Park, but I'm not sure what part of town you're on."

Bear Creek Park? That's five minutes away from me! That's it, she thought. Maybe she'd seen him somewhere around here. "It's okay. I normally charge a mileage fee if it's far out, but I will waive it as a courtesy to you." After explaining her hourly rate, she asked, "Do you have a particular day in mind? How soon do you need them done?"

"How soon is your next available appointment? Are there any openings on Wednesday?"

Another coincidence? Wednesday was her off day. "Yes, that would be perfect. Is twelve o'clock a good time for you?"

"That's cool. Are you familiar with Bear Creek Park? I will be in the picnic area."

"I've heard of it," she said, "but I've never been. First, I need your email address to send you a deposit invoice." He called out the address and she typed it into the Notes app on her phone. "I'll find the park and call you when I get there."

"Thanks, Tora. See you Wednesday."

* * *

"I'm canceling my membership."

"What?" Candace followed Tora to the storage area in the back of the store. Tora needed a display sign post and Candace needed to get a roll of quarters for the sales clerk. "Canceling why?" She sat down behind the desk to get the cash box. "Oh! Was he that good?"

Tora rolled her eyes. "He was bad. Very bad."

Candace laughed. "Really? What happened?"

"First of all the picture he has posted on his profile must be a decade old—"

"Noo… he didn't pull that one did he?" Candace shook her head. "And guys try to say women are the ones who do things like that."

"Exactly. Second, he wasn't too clean-cut… ill-fitted clothing, bad body. Wasn't attractive at all."

"Oh my god."

"But wait… it gets worse."

Candace closed the cash box and returned it to the drawer. She folded her arms in front of her on the desk, anticipating the best parts of the story.

"The guy must not have been raised with any kind of table manners because he talked and chewed with his mouth open, mayonnaise and saliva everywhere."

Candace twisted her lips in disgust. "Okay, eww."

"It was sick!" Tora almost gagged again at the memory. "And more than anything… he was just a lazy loser who mooches off women." She sat down in the chair. "Do you know that fool believes women should take care of him while he works on his music?"

Candace raised a perfectly arched brow.

"Yeah," Tora nodded, "he said that's our biggest problem in relationships because we don't support each other. He should be able to pursue his dream full-time and not have to work. Meanwhile his girlfriends—mind you… he's never been married—are going to work every day to support his ass with only a promise that he will marry them *after* he becomes a success. But he's been trying to get his music off the ground for damn-near twenty years!"

"*What?* You have got to be lying," Candace laughed.

"I wish I was, but no. And that's still not the worst of it—"

"You mean there's more?" She popped her gum.

"He has a daughter on the other side of the world in Japan that he makes no effort to take care of or see because the plane tickets are expensive—"

"Huh?" Candace frowned. "How did that happen?"

Tora waved her hand. "He moved there with one of his friends—somebody that's into music like him. But can you believe that? Because the plane tickets are too expensive? I mean… I would think a man would do what he has to do to make money: deliver pizzas, wash cars, cut grass. Hell, work at Burger King… I don't know."

Candace shook her head in disgust too.

"The nail in the coffin for me, though, was when he told me the girl would be well-taken care of *after* his music makes it big."

"I hate to laugh," Candace said as she covered her mouth with her hand and her body shook, "but this sounds like a prank date."

Tora sighed. "Which is why I'm signing on to request a refund. I don't need a full thirty days to know this is not for me." She pulled her phone out of her jacket pocket.

"Aww, Tora. You can't give up after just one date. It was a whole year of misses before I met Ruki."

"Nope," Tora shook her head. "I'm not wasting my money just

to meet a bunch of losers."

Candace laughed again. "That's why I told you you should talk to them on the phone and get to know them before you meet in person. Y'all would've never moved past the phone conversation by the sound of it."

"That's a negative as well. I need to *see them.* Suppose we vibe over the phone, but then finally meet and he turns out to be a porcupine in the face?"

A laugh burst out of Candace that Tora was certain the customers on the other side of the wall could hear.

"Shhh," Tora hissed. "You're gonna have people thinking we're back here goofing around."

Candace covered her mouth and slid down in the seat as the laugh overtook her.

"I'm canceling right now. I'm serious."

Candace righted herself in her chair and reached across the desk for Tora's phone. "Don't! Give it some time, girl."

Tora twisted away from her. "See," she said, holding the phone in the air, "this is exactly what I was talking about. Five messages from Jason."

"Who's Jason?"

"That's his name. Mr. Yuck Mouth also known as The Mooch. If he had my phone number these messages would have been missed calls and or voicemails."

"What did he say?"

"I don't know and I don't care. I'm not reading them," she said and pressed the button to delete each message.

Candace sucked her teeth. "You could've at least seen what he had to say, Tora. Maybe he became an over-night success."

Tora had to laugh at that one. "Nope. Not wasting time. Oh… but here's one from the other guy—the cute one." There were fifteen more messages from other members, but her eyes settled on his. "This is the one looking for his sidekick."

"Oh, he is handsome." Candace snatched the phone away from Tora. "Damn," she said as she looked closely at the screen.

Tora nodded. "Yep. That's the same thing I said."

"I *know* you're going to meet him, right?"

"I don't know. I get a feeling I'll only be disappointed. His picture is probably old, too."

Candace batted her hand. "Don't think like that. Just because the first date was a disaster, don't let it get you down. It's all a part of the process. Like I said, it took about a year before I met my prince. And look…." She wiggled the hand with the stunning diamond ring in front of her face.

Tora rolled her eyes. "Shut up."

Candace laughed.

"Candace?" One of the sales associates appeared at the door of the small office. "Brittney needs some quarters."

SEVEN

He was tall and oval-shaped with sloped shoulders, breasts, soft belly, and heavy legs. He wore a red snug-fitting University of Houston hoodie over a pair of black gym shorts. His mother had told Nate he was fourteen. He didn't have any friends, spent most of his time at home locked in his room, spoke rarely, and she worried he suffered from depression. She'd wanted her son to see a therapist, but he refused, so she was turning to Nate in hopes that he could help him get active and lose weight to build his self-esteem.

Nate hugged Leticia before holding his hand out to her son who stood with his hands shoved into the kangaroo pocket of the hoodie. It was ninety degrees outside.

Ms. Leticia nudged her son with her elbow. "Take your hands out of your pocket, Vaughn."

Annoyance crossed the kid's face and he reluctantly pulled a hand from his pocket and offered Nate a limp handshake.

"What's up, man? You doing all right today?" Nate asked him.

Vaughn didn't answer, but looked somewhere over Nate's head.

"He didn't wanna come," Leticia said, "but I told him he has no choice."

Nate nodded. "Alright, well, hopefully that'll change in a few minutes." He smiled at Vaughn. "We're gonna have some fun today, alright man? I'm gonna tell you a little bit about what you can expect from me, I'll get your measurements, and then we'll take a tour of the gym to get you familiar with the equipment and everything. Then we'll talk a bit about nutrition and what you can do when you're at home to make sure you don't jeopardize all the hard work you put in here so you see some results. And then we'll get us a workout in, alright?"

A crease appeared above Vaughn's brow, but he said nothing.

Leticia laid a hand on her son's arm. "Son, this man is here to help you. Don't give him a hard time, okay?" She looked at Nate with a mix of desperation and sympathy in her eyes. "It's a start I guess. How long do you think you'll need?"

"About an hour should be good today. Just to go over some things."

"Alright," Leticia said. "You have my number. I'm gonna go down to that coffee shop right there on the corner and wait for him. Just call me when he's ready, okay?"

"Yes, ma'am. I will do that."

"See you in a while, Vaughn," she said before turning to go out the door.

Nate looked up at Vaughn, "Alright, you ready, man? Let's get started. Step over here with me to my desk." The kid sucked his teeth quietly and followed behind Nate. Nate stopped at the small refrigerator to grab a bottle of water for him. "You ever worked out in a gym before?" he asked as he sat down behind the desk. Vaughn plopped down in the chair in front of it.

He didn't answer and Nate realized this was going to be his most challenging client. He was used to the ones that were eager to get the weight off and get fit. They walked through the doors with a purpose. Even the ones like Jordyn, whom he had to coax a lot of times through the workouts when she was feeling unmotivated. She hated every minute of them, but she still showed up. More than anything, he was able to laugh and talk through the workout sessions with his clients.

Vaughn wouldn't even answer his most basic questions.

But Nate wasn't giving up. Leticia was depending on him. "Tell me a little bit about you. What school do you go to?" He decided to take a personal approach.

Still nothing.

Nate sighed. "Alright. I'll just start it off and tell you a little bit about me…"

Vaughn pulled a hand out of the hoodie pocket, examined his barely-there fingernails before raising them to his mouth to bite one.

"I went to Lamar High School. When I was a kid and all throughout school I played sports… all kinds: basketball, football, kickboxing, baseball. Loved it. I was always into active sports. I even used to go rollerblading with my sister."

Vaughn frowned and Nate appreciated that he was at least listening to him.

"I went to college to be a lawyer, but then I realized I really wanted to work in a field where I could help people. And since I loved exercise, I figured why not help people exercise and get healthy? So here I am. And that's why I'm here. To help you, too."

Nate continued, "Your mom told me I'll be working with you three days a week. We'll be doing a combination of cardio and weight training. I promise you won't be bored, man. Once we start working out you'll feel better and see how exercise really helps your body and builds your confidence. I mean… you'll look better, have more energy. Even in school you'll see the difference because exercise and eating healthy fuels your brain and gets rid of all the toxins, the bad stuff." He opened a drawer for his measurement tools and client worksheet. "Let's step over here to this room so I can get your stats."

With his clipboard in tow Nate walked over to the room adjacent to the trainers' area. "Step up here real quick so I can get your weight. Let's see where we're starting at."

Vaughn stepped on the scale.

"Step off," Nate said and waited for the screen to reset. "Now step on again." He recorded the results. "Alright, now for your measurements. You gotta take your hoodie off though."

Vaughn looked away.

"You don't have on a shirt underneath?" he asked him. Vaughn shook his head, but Nate could clearly see the edge of a black T-shirt at the boy's neck. He knew trying to use the fat caliper would be useless then too, so he laid it on the floor. "It's cool," he said. "Just raise your arms for me."

Vaughn lifted his arms and Nate wrapped the tape measure around his chest. He did the same for each arm, his waist, hips, thighs, and then calves. He wrote the results on the client worksheet in between. "Alright, we'll take the tour now so you can get familiar with the facility and see what kind of equipment we'll be using." Nate returned the clipboard to his desk. "This way," he said and Vaughn followed him.

It was like walking around talking to himself because Vaughn did not utter a word as Nate pointed out the cardio area, weight machines, free weights, fitness and spin class studios, the sauna, and swimming pool room. He thought there was an inkling of excitement in the boy's face when he showed him the basketball court and Vaughn paused for a minute to watch the pick-up game going on.

"You like basketball?" Nate had asked him, but he just gave a half shake of his head and turned away from the glass.

They walked back to the cardio area and Nate led him to a treadmill. "I'm gonna start you with a warm-up just to get the blood flowing, man. We'll do this for fifteen minutes. You ever been on a treadmill before?"

The televisions hanging from the ceiling above had Vaughn's attention. He pulled a pair of ear buds and mobile phone from the pocket of his hoodie, plugged his ears, and pressed the Start button on the treadmill.

Nate hopped on the one beside him and started his machine. When the fifteen minutes was up and Nate wanted to increase the pace a bit, Vaughn refused. He also refused moving on to another area. Nate didn't have to call Leticia because Vaughn did it himself before the last couple minutes on the treadmill timer had run out. He didn't know whether he should feel disappointment that he couldn't encourage the kid to open up to him or glad their session was over for the day.

"How was it?" Leticia asked when she came to pick up her son.

Vaughn shrugged his shoulders and Leticia looked at Nate.

"I think he just has to get used to me," he told her. "We took it easy today and just did some walking on the treadmill. Next time we'll do some other things. I'll see you in a couple days, man." Nate patted Vaughn on the back.

"Thank you," Leticia smiled.

Nate watched them walk out the door and to their car in the parking lot. Vaughn walked slowly, his head down. The kid was a giant next to his mom. Nate wondered what was going on with him. What type of trouble did he have at fourteen years old that caused the sadness in his eyes, the weight on his shoulders, the silence?

EIGHT

After one look at the ebony locks twisted into a single braid hanging just past his shoulders, and skin the color of aged copper, Tora recognized him. He was sitting on top of a picnic table, his feet on the bench.

She sat in her jeep watching him for several minutes pondering the coincidence. *How in the heck did he find me?* She looked around at the few people in the area, thinking maybe he was there with someone else and that he was not *the* Nate Walker she was scheduled to meet.

But the name sounded too familiar. She was certain it was what he told her that day in Southlake Sandwich Shop.

He reached into his pocket when she called his phone. "I just wanted to make sure I'm on the right side," she said when he answered.

He looked up and then towards the parking lot. "Hey. I'm in the picnic area."

"I see you. I'm in the red Jeep Wrangler."

He smiled and stood.

She grabbed her bag from the backseat floor and got out.

"How you doing," he said, his hand extended as he moved towards her, meeting her halfway.

"Good. Have we met before?" she asked, second-guessing herself even though she knew it was him. How could she forget that gorgeous face and made-for-caressing body? Her eyes fell on his chest the same way they did that day near the soda machine. It was the type of pectoral muscles that would make a woman forget all her troubles as she lay on his chest at night.

He smiled. "Yeah. Actually, we did."

Tora nodded. "I thought so. But if I remember correctly we didn't exchange phone numbers, so how did you find me?"

"Oh… uh… I got your card from the girl behind the counter."

"You did?"

"She threw it in the trash and I asked her if I could have it when I found out you do photography."

Tora looked doubtful.

"No lie," he said. "I hope you're okay with that."

She adjusted her bag on her shoulder. "Where do you want to have the pictures done?" She didn't know how to take his claim and wondered if she should find it creepy or flattering that he would seek her business card out of a trash can.

Looking behind him he said, "Right here in this open field is what I had in mind."

Tora pulled her camera from the bag and set the bag on the bench where he had a few personal items. "I just want to do a couple test shots first," she said and aimed the camera at him, clicking twice.

"Oh! Just like that, huh? No time to warm up and get my pose right or nothing?" He laughed.

"Don't worry. These don't count and will be deleted." She checked the photos on the LCD screen. The weather was perfect: clear-blue cloudless sky, high sun.

Nate walked further into the center of the field. "I'm just going to do some basic poses, alright? Nothing too over-the-top," he said.

He turned around to face her and stood with his legs slightly apart, his fists at his hips.

Tora raised the camera and his face went into serious mode: set brow, no-nonsense eyes, tight jaw.

She clicked.

He turned slightly, moving his arms behind him, clasping his hands.

Those arms. Tora clicked away as he moved from one pose to the next. He was beautiful. The sun beaming down on him, the perspiration that was beginning to form on his forehead and across his shoulders was making it difficult to concentrate and the shoot had only just begun.

"Maybe we should've waited until later in the day when the sun is not so high up," he said, and turned his back to her.

"You think?" Tora said. "I don't know. I kinda like the way they're coming out. Maybe you should take off—"

He was removing his tank top before she could finish her sentence.

Tora swallowed the *Damn!* that threatened to escape her mouth. *This is a client. Remain professional at all times,* she told herself. "This looks good," she said to him instead as her eyes took in his symmetry: wide back, tapered waist, tight ass. The camouflage pants he wore were sexy on him. "You should undo your locks."

"Oh okay. That's cool." He reached up to remove the tie and Tora watched as the muscles flexed beneath his skin.

Another click.

"Don't you have gloves on the table? You should get those and put them on."

He jogged over to the table and Tora dropped a hand from the camera, rubbing it down the front of her shorts, and then the other hand. Her palms were sweaty.

"Got 'em," he said when he returned and slipped his hands into the fingerless gloves.

"I like this look." Tora aimed and clicked. "Shake your head a bit to loosen the locks some more." Another click. She squat down in front of him. "Look down at me." His hair fell, framing his face. "Perfect."

He smiled and Tora squint her eye to remain on the task at hand: keeping her mind on getting a great shot and not on the rivulets of sweat traveling down his abs. "Now, run your hand through your hair like this," she said, demonstrating.

He chuckled. "Umm… this is for my fitness website. I don't think that will be a good look. It won't fly with the male clientele."

"Fine," she laughed. He went through five more poses, including a handstand and a crouching position—which Tora thought was the sexiest pose of them all—before she stepped next to him to let him review the shots. Heat radiated off his body, his breathing labored from trying to get that handstand just right.

"Let's go back under the shade," he said. "I have some water in my truck if you need some." He picked up his shirt from the grass.

"Yes, I'll take one." She sat at the picnic table while he went to his vehicle. It was the hottest shoot she'd ever done, and she wasn't referring to the weather. She clicked through the photos reliving those poses. The man was gorgeous and knew how to look into the camera to make her feel his intense stare.

"I'm sorry, they're not as cold now." He set a bottle down on the table and took a seat next to her on the bench.

Her arm flinched slightly because she wasn't expecting it.

"Oh, I'm sorry," he said, moving a few inches away from her. "I don't mean to crowd your space. I just thought we were going to look at them together."

Tora laughed nervously. *Why am I nervous? I never get nervous.*

"It's okay. I just… I just…." She fumbled with the camera. "My hands are a little sweaty," she said and set the camera down gently in front of him.

He picked it up and she tried to keep her eyes on the table as long as she could, but they had a mind of their own and slowly traveled the length of his arm up to his elbow. Traveled up and over the rock-hard bicep, the curve of his shoulder. His neck. The Adam's apple that bobbed in slow motion. They settled on his mouth.

He caught her staring. "Huh?"

"I said they look good. I like 'em."

"Oh. Okay." She took back the camera. "Is there another place you want to have some taken?"

He chewed his bottom lip. "Let's go to the fitness area. There's some bars over there I think will make some pretty cool shots."

They walked from the picnic lot down to the fitness area. For the next half-hour she had the pleasure of watching that body flex as he performed pull-ups, flags, push-ups, and more handstands. He was drenched in sweat by then and Tora kept clicking. He used a nearby restroom to towel off and change into a pair of shorts and matching sleeveless hoodie. She suggested he take a few photos in front of some trees.

"Well, that was cool," he said when she snapped the final photo. "Can't wait to see how they turn out."

"I will start working on these tonight and get the link over to you no later than tomorrow evening. You can choose however many you want, but only five edited shots are included in the price of this session." She turned off the camera and placed it in her bag. Holding her hand out to him she said, "It was nice meeting with you, Nate. I will email you soon"

"Wait… you're leaving already?"

"Is there something else you want me to do?"

He smiled. "Well, I was about to get me a bite to eat and wanna know if you would like to join me."

She returned the smile, but in her mind she was wondering why it was the same scenario each time. She was looking down on him when she wanted to look up. "Thanks for the offer, but no. I don't wanna—"

"Waste my time?" he said. "It's not a waste of my time. What does that mean anyway? Are you involved with someone?"

A lot of times—more often than not—when she was asked the question she would say yes, that she was involved with someone even if she wasn't. It was a way to spare the gentleman's feelings, to say she was taken versus 'you're not my type.' This one, however, had everything right in the looks department, but still, there was that one thing.

"It's just lunch," he said. "Nothing major."

She looked at him. "When is it ever *just lunch*?"

His brow furrowed.

"No man asks a woman out without a motive behind it," she said.

He chuckled. "Well, it's my way of trying to get to know you better. Why do you think I had that cashier dig your business card out of the trash?"

Tora's eyes went to his arms again. It was difficult not to stare. "I don't believe you."

"Huh?"

"You said it's nothing major."

Confusion crossed his face.

"If we go to lunch then you will expect another lunch and so on and so on."

He nodded. "Well, yeah, if we have a good time, I can't lie, I will ask you out again."

"Exactly. Which is why I said I don't want to waste your time."

"So you are involved with somebody."

Why is it always like this, too? Why can't they take no for an answer and move on? "Nate," she said, "I just know I wouldn't be a good fit for you." It was easier to make the situation about her. She adjusted the bag on her shoulder and stuck her hand out again. "I'm going home to get to work on your photos."

He took her hand. "Alright. Talk to you later, Tora."

She got into her jeep and threw her head back on the headrest. She wanted to scream. He had to be the finest man to approach her in years. The finest man to approach her, period. There had been many: handsome ones, tall ones, skinny ones, a few overweight ones, but even the tall and handsome men of her past couldn't compete with what she witnessed behind her camera lens today. She could still see the slow stream of sweat traveling down his smooth stomach and settling in his navel. The way his muscles pulsed with each pull-up.

"It was torture, Mom," Tora said to Sharon later that night.

"I'm sure it was," she laughed, "but you could've at least taken him up on the lunch offer. He was being nice."

Tora sighed. "I don't even want to get his hopes up."

"Your daddy wasn't my type either, but he still found a way to make me fall in love with him."

"Mom, are you serious? You never told me that." Tora settled underneath the covers.

"Oh yeah. I didn't like him in the beginning. He talked too much and was too loud. I didn't have time for all of that. My girlfriend Jan thought he was so handsome and charming. She liked him, not me, but he didn't want her. Go figure."

"Isn't that the craziest thing? That's what I don't understand. The people we don't want are the ones to hound us the most."

Her mother laughed again. "It is."

"But how did your friend feel after you and Dad got together?"

"I think she was a little upset about it at first, but she quickly got over it. It wasn't as if I'd stolen her husband or something."

Tora pulled her laptop over to her and logged onto Soul Meet's website. The biker had left her another message earlier and she'd replied back with the same information she told Jason—that she preferred they meet in person versus messaging back and forth and talking over the phone. He said he was free anytime during the upcoming weekend. "Well, I'm going to go now so I can call Dad. I work the opening shift tomorrow and should've been asleep a long time ago."

They exchanged I love yous, and then she hung up and called Myles.

Before she logged off the computer for the night she agreed to meet the biker at a sports bar Friday night.

It has to be much better than that fiasco with Jason, she thought, and rolled over on her side and closed her eyes.

NINE

He flipped through each page. He couldn't bring himself to look at the report again until now, after he'd gotten over being angry. His mother was the most meticulous woman he knew and it didn't surprise him how detailed she was in recording his college expenses. She'd even included the postage for the care package she sent, which included several boxes of condoms after he and his girlfriend at the time had a pregnancy scare. Nate shook his head. Why was she doing this to him? He appreciated everything his parents did for him and he'd taken his career as a criminal attorney seriously, so for Victoria to say he blew their money was not fair. There was no way he could add an extra job to his already busy schedule and still maintain his client list.

Grabbing the remote from the coffee table, he blew out a breath. He wished he had somewhere to go, someone to spend time with that would take his mind off things. It was late and Tora still hadn't sent him the email she promised. He took a chance and called her anyway. It was Thursday night and he was bored.

"Hey, Tora. This is Nate. I hope I didn't catch you at a bad time."

"Nate? What's going on?"

"I was just calling to check on that email you were supposed to send me. I haven't received it yet."

"You didn't? I sent it a few hours ago."

"I didn't get it." He went to his computer to check his email again. "Did I catch you at a bad time? I was just anxious to see how they turned out." What he really wanted to tell her was that he was anxious to talk to her again. She'd said she wouldn't be a good fit for him, which had been stirring in his mind ever since, and he was curious about what she meant.

"It's okay," she said. "It's not a bother and I want to make sure you get it. I will send the link to you again."

"Thanks. And I'll hang on in the meantime." He couldn't let her get off the phone.

"Alright, just give me a minute to get my laptop going."

He cleared his throat. "So how was your day?" he asked as he waited.

"It was good. Thanks for asking. How was yours?"

"Cool. But I couldn't stop thinking about what you said. What did you mean when you told me you wouldn't be a good fit for me?"

She made a sound that was half laugh half snort. "Oh god."

"What? It's a fair question, right? Since you didn't tell me?"

"Mr. Walker, are you sure you didn't receive the email? I show it delivered at five-thirty. Have you checked your junk folder?"

"Mr. Walker?" He chuckled. "I guess that means I'm strictly in the client zone and can't ask any personal questions, huh?"

"Yes, I prefer to keep it that way."

The message was in his junk folder, but he wasn't ready to give up just yet. He said, "Well, it's been bothering me. From the day you walked in that sandwich shop I knew I had to get to know you. Why do you think I went through the garbage? I was serious." Her laughter made him smile.

"Sounds kinda creepy don't you think?"

"Not to me. That cashier you gave your card to had no use for you, but I did. One person's trash is another one's treasure."

She sucked her teeth. "Mr. Walker…"

"Tora, I'm serious," he said. "How do you know you're not right for me if you don't even know me? What is it? You don't like guys with locks?"

"I just sent the link again. Did you get it this time?"

He refreshed his inbox. Now he had two of the same message. "Yes, it's here now. But—"

"Just select the five you want and I'll get those touched up for you as soon as you reply back. The email has more detailed instructions."

Her avoidance of his questions only made his curiosity that much greater. "Just answer this one question for me and I'll drop the issue. How do you know you're not a good fit for me if you won't even meet me for lunch to have a conversation?"

There was a long silence.

"Tora?"

"Look… I just know, okay? Can we leave it at that?"

"Unacceptable. You can't even give me a legitimate reason."

She laughed, then quickly said, "Mr. Walker, I will be waiting for your email. Good night."

He hung up the phone smiling and shaking his head at the same time. There was no way he was letting her go that easily. Why wouldn't she just come out and tell him why she could not have lunch with him? He decided he was going to have to come up with another excuse to see her again.

* * *

"Give me one more. Come on." Nate stood at the head of the weight bench, his hands hovering beneath the bar as Jordyn struggled through her final chest press. Her arms trembled, she grit her teeth and he knew she had nothing left, so he gripped the bar lightly and helped guide it to its resting place. She let out a scream and he laughed.

"I'm so tired of this!" she said, sitting up.

"It's been three months. You should be used to it by now, Jordyn."

"I will never get used to exercise. I hate it! Hate it. Hate it."

"Why? Look at the results so far. I'm seeing a difference in your shoulders. Look at your legs."

Jordyn stood up and walked over to the mirror, turning sideways to check out her legs. "Yeah, but my weight isn't budging all that much."

"That's because you're building muscle. It may seem like you're not losing weight, but it's just that muscle is heavier, more dense, so I wouldn't focus too much on the scale."

Jordyn sighed. "I just want to be my college weight again. It was the last time I wore a two-piece bikini."

Nate grabbed her bottle of water from the floor and led her to a pulley machine. "You'll get there, but you gotta stay committed. And leave the snack cakes alone."

He coached her through three more exercises to work her chest and back before they moved to the floor for core training.

"I won't be here Monday, Nate," Jordyn said as they completed their final stretch, ending the workout session. "My family reunion's this weekend, which is why I came in early today."

"Oh, that's cool. Where is the reunion?"

"In Beaumont. It's an all-weekend event, which means lots of good food and beer!"

Nate chuckled. "Had I known that I would've made you do a little extra today."

"I'm telling you right now I'm having a slice of my Aunt Randy's German chocolate cake. Without question."

"Alright, since it's a special occasion I won't give you a hard time, but just promise me you'll still get some exercise in."

She rolled her eyes. "I don't even know if this hotel has a gym, Nate. The one we're staying in really isn't top tier. More like a Best Western-type."

"You don't necessarily need a gym. Just go for a walk or do some of the exercises we do here. You can do jumping jacks, some high knees, mountain climbers right in your room."

Jordyn let out an exasperated sigh. "I just want to relax this weekend. I need a few days off."

Laughing, Nate told her, "Jordyn, I only see you three times a week. You already have four days off. Come on... you have to remember your why. Why are you doing this? To get into your swimsuit for your Virgin Islands vacation and to get down to your college weight, remember?"

"I know."

He held up his hand to give her a high-five. "I'll call you this weekend to check up on you, alright? You did a good job today."

"I don't think I get good phone signal out there in Beaumont, Nate," Jordyn laughed.

"You're a piece of work," he shook his head. "See you Tuesday, Jordyn."

She turned the corner and headed towards the women's locker room.

He sat at his desk waiting for Vaughn. Leticia had sent him a text message letting him know they were stuck in traffic and would be a few minutes late, so Nate took out his smartphone to pass time. All last night as he lay in bed he was thinking about Tora and how to get her to meet him again. The photos she'd taken were as great as he'd expected them to be based on her portfolio, but that couldn't be the end of their communication. He called Sunny. "What's up, baby sis?"

"Hey," she said, her voice low.

Nate sensed the sadness and sat up in his chair when he heard her sniffle. "What's going on? You all right, Sunny?"

"Yeah," she said, sniffling again. "I'm all right, what's up?"

"It don't sound like it. Tell me what's going on."

"It's nothing, Nate."

"Sunny…"

"Me and Levi just had a fight."

"*A fight?*" Nate stood up from his desk and walked to the other room when he realized he caught the attention of a couple of his gym mates. "Did he hit you?"

"No, Nate. He didn't hit me. We were just arguing that's all. And I'm emotional. It happens all the time when I'm pregnant."

He never heard anything from Sunny about Levi being violent, but Nate didn't put anything past the guy. "You know you can tell me if he ever gets crazy with you, right?"

"Brother, I'm not the little girl anymore that you have to protect from everything and everybody. I'm an adult, remember? The same age as you. I think I can handle myself when it comes to my fiancé. We're just two people in love having a little spat, okay?"

"Well, you know I don't like you crying. Especially over that fool."

"I know, but as always, we will be fine. My hormones are in overdrive and I'm probably not the easiest to be around right now, so I know I'm causing him just as much stress as he's causing me."

Nate shook his head. She was always making excuses for Levi's behavior.

"But anyway… why did you call me?"

Hearing his sister cry made him quickly forget the reason for his call. And now he wasn't sure he should even ask. "Oh… uhh… I just had a question about the engagement party, but never mind."

"What about the engagement party? I thought you said you weren't coming."

"Well… I just remember you saying you needed a photographer and… I know somebody. I just had her take the pictures for my website. She's really good and I think you should use her. I can call her for you."

"I don't care. I really don't have the energy for all of this," Sunny said. "That's why I'm so grateful for Mama and Kaneesa."

"Why are you doing it then, Sunny?"

"I mean… I'm excited about getting married, but it's all the planning I don't have the energy for."

"Maybe you should wait until after the baby comes. It'll give you some more time to think this thing through anyway."

"Nate," she sighed, "you need to hurry up and get married so you can have your own wife and business to worry about."

He chuckled and left the room, returning to his desk. "I just want my sister to be happy."

"I am happy. I'm getting married to the love of my life, the father of my children."

"I don't know, baby sis. He got you over there crying. I still say you need somebody better."

"Goodbye, Nate," she said.

Vaughn looked just as annoyed and disinterested as he did the other day, but Nate still smiled brightly at him and offered his hand to the kid. Vaughn took it for a brief, limp shake and shoved his hand back into his hoodie. "You ready to get started, man? We're gonna have a real workout today. I let you take it easy last time, but we gotta hit it today."

Vaughn said nothing.

Leticia told Nate, "I'm taking the spin class that's about to start in a few minutes, but please come in and get me if he's not cooperating. We had this discussion at home."

"Don't worry about it, Ms. Leticia. I'm sure I won't have to do that. He'll be fine." Nate had his doubts, but his plan was to make Vaughn comfortable training with him, so the worst thing he could do was go running to the boy's mama to snitch on him.

"Okay," she smiled and touched her son's arm. "I'll see you later, baby." She hurried towards the spin room.

Nate led Vaughn to the cardio section. "We're gonna start with the treadmill again today, but only for fifteen minutes, alright?"

Vaughn pulled out his ear buds, but Nate quickly told him he couldn't listen to any music today, either. "You gotta be able to hear me," he said, then watched as they were shoved back inside the pocket with a frown. "Come on, man... don't tell me you're giving me the cold shoulder again today. What's up?" Nate pressed the button for a pre-made workout setting on Vaughn's treadmill before hopping on the one next to it. "Don't do that to me," he smiled, trying to lighten the atmosphere and lift the kid's mood.

Vaughn simply stared at the television overhead. A college game was on.

"Depending on how much time we have left, we can go to the court and play a game if you want to. And if your mom is still in her class. You want to?"

Vaughn shook his head and Nate decided not to press him further and to just make it through another silent workout with him. When the time was up Nate introduced him to some basic muscle strengthening exercises using his body weight. Vaughn was sweating profusely by then, but never got rid of the thick jacket, and said he was tired.

"Just one more set, man. Come on. It's almost over."

Vaughn stood with his hands at his hips, breathing deeply.

"I'll do it with you," Nate said and got into position to start a lunge combo.

Vaughn walked away and took a seat on a weight bench nearby.

Sighing, Nate got up and walked over to him. "You can't give me just one more set? I know you got it in you, man. Don't let me down."

"My legs hurt."

"Well… you'll feel better if you walk around a bit instead of sitting down. It'll cool you down the right way. Let's go to the basketball court."

"I don't wanna go to the court. I said my legs hurt."

Nate didn't know how much more of this he would be able to take. Leticia had paid him in advance, but if the past two sessions with Vaughn were an indication of how the remaining meetings would be he wasn't sure he could maintain his patience. "Can you make it to my desk? Let's have a chat."

"I'm staying right here until my mama gets done." He pulled the hood over his head and plugged his ears.

Nate left him sitting on the bench and headed back to his desk.

TEN

"The cat room again? Or would you prefer to work another area today?"

"The cat room," Tora said.

"Okay, go right ahead. There are only two others in there at the moment."

Tora signed her name on the volunteer check-in sheet and received a badge from the girl standing behind the front desk. The pungent scent of playful animals was in the air and she could hear the puppies and dogs yelping down the hall as she made her way to the cat quarters. It was during one of many weekends she sat in the apartment lacking the mood for her current hobbies and saddened as she thought about how she hadn't been on a date or had sex in two years, and with no place interesting in mind she could think of to go to, she decided to research new ways to spend her free time. She saw a posting online from the local animal shelter about volunteer opportunities, looked up the address, and drove here the same day to sign up for orientation and training. Three times a month for four hours a day she offered love and comfort to all the fur babies waiting to be adopted into a permanent home.

As she helped the other cat room assistants clean the cages and replenish food and water bowls she thought about what she was going to wear to the meetup with Dexter that evening. She was already in good spirits about seeing him because he'd updated his profile photo, which let her know she wasn't meeting someone with decade-old photos of themselves.

"Will you be coming back tomorrow for the mobile adoption?" the girl behind the counter asked when Tora returned her badge.

"No, unfortunately. I work tomorrow during that time, so… I won't be able to make it."

"Ah well, hopefully you can join us at the next one."

"I hope so, too. I heard it's a lot of fun."

* * *

He wanted to meet at a sports bar in The Heights. Tora walked in and sat at the bar since most of the tables were reserved seating or occupied. She was early.

"What can I get for you, gorgeous?" the bar tender asked.

"Just water for now. With lemon. Thank you."

"Water?" he shook his head. "I'm afraid you'll have to go out to the patio with that type of order. These here are money-making seats."

Tora raised a brow. "Are you serious?" He grinned and she relaxed. He filled a glass with water from the tap and slapped a lime on the rim. She grabbed a straw from the caddy and turned on the stool.

Damn!

He walked in looking like a real-life version of the man of her dreams: tall, fine, handsome. In that order. Someone called his name and he walked over to hug the guy and shake his hand. They were wearing the same biker vest. Dexter shook his head no, looked around the bar when the guy motioned to where he had been sitting. Tora knew Dexter must've been telling the gentleman he was there to meet someone.

She set her glass on the bar and stood up.

He saw her, smiled and walked over and she hoped by the end of the night she could cancel her membership with Soul Meet because he was the one.

Tora returned the smile. "Dexter, right?"

"Dex," he said, and instead of taking her proffered hand he pulled her in for a hug. A tight hug, a lingering hug.

Umm… okay. Wasn't expecting this, she thought.

"How you doing?" he asked as his hand traveled down her back, guiding her back onto the stool. "What you drinking?" He called out for the bar tender. "Carter!"

Whatever cologne he wore was doing a number on her senses already. "You know him?"

"Oh, this is my spot. Me and the bike club come here all the time."

He fist-bumped Carter before telling him, "Give her whatever she want. Heineken for me."

Tora ordered the same.

"I thought I was going to beat you here," he said.

"Why? So you could watch me walk in and determine whether or not you wanted to stay or leave unnoticed?"

He laughed, looked at her, and then laughed again.

"So you've done that before?"

"Only once. She wasn't my type." Carter gave them their beers. "Let's go outside. It's too noisy in here."

He brushed the seat of the patio chair with his hand before she sat down. "What's your type?" she asked him.

"You," he said. "I love a woman that takes care of herself, takes pride in her appearance. I even like that lipstick."

Tora's mobile phone rang and she reached in her purse to silence it. A quick look at the screen showed it was Nate calling.

"Is that your homegirl calling to check on you?"

"No. It's not. Just a client I did some work for."

"Oh, I thought maybe you had it set up so she call you if you didn't like what you see."

Tora smiled and took a sip of beer. "Nope. But I like what I see."

"Then that makes two of us," he said.

A waitress came over and he ordered a bucket of more Heineken and a platter for two of hot wings and fries.

Tora didn't expect to enjoy his company so much, but two hours later she was still listening intently, laughing at the crazy things he said. The conversation was easy and laid-back, as if she was having dinner with someone she'd known for a long time.

He walked her to her car. "What're you about to do now? You wanna come back to my place? We can hang out some more."

"Absolutely not," she said.

He laughed. "I was just testing you."

"Uhn-huh. Sure. What would you have done had I said yes?"

Grinning, he said, "Take my number. We definitely have to get together again, but I want you to call me when you get home, let me know you made it."

Tora waited until after she'd taken a shower and got in bed to call him. He didn't answer, so she sent a text message thanking him for the good time. Then she called her mother.

"It was just a very mellow date," she explained to Sharon. "He said we have to go out again."

"So my guess is he meets all your standards?"

Tora laughed. "Yes! He does! Tall and fine. Nice personality. Good job."

"Well, I'm glad you had a good time. Hopefully it works out."

"I hope so, too, because it's been way too long, Mom… if you know what I mean."

"Oh dear. Good night, sweetheart."

Tora laughed again and ended the call. Turning off the bedside lamp, she turned over on her side and pulled Silk closer to her. She wondered how soon it would be before Dexter asked her out again. She looked forward to telling Candace how great the date was and how, in her eyes, this one has potential. But when she woke up the next morning there were three messages from Dexter. The first two were pictures of his swollen penis, one showing the complete ejaculation running down the length of it.

The final message read: *If you had said yes...*

ELEVEN

"He wasn't this stubborn until after his brother left. That was three years ago, but he still blames me." Leticia walked beside Nate. It was the walk to cool down after their Saturday morning training session. She'd asked him to meet her at the track field at her neighborhood's high school.

"May I ask what happened with his brother?"

She sighed. "He wouldn't go to school, so I told him if he was living in my house he would have to go to work. But he couldn't keep a job more than a month or two. Then I found out he was selling pills for one of his friends. Vaughn really looked up to Deon. He was his only friend pretty much, but I couldn't have that going on in my house. He calls and talks to Vaughn, but not me. I made a lot of mistakes with Deon. I was young, didn't know any better, but I didn't have much help either. And I just want things to be better for Vaughn."

Nate nodded as he listened.

"He's always been quiet," Leticia continued, "and socially awkward. There was some teasing at school because of his size. So being with Deon was his escape from all of that. But I need him to be stronger and to stop worrying about what his peers say. He'll be a freshman in high school this year and I don't want him to have such a hard time there, too."

Nate looked at her when he heard the crack in her voice.

"And this is cheaper than therapy," she said. "I think he just needs someone to talk to." She threw her arms in the air and laughed weakly. "But I don't know why I'm even telling you all of this, Nate."

"No, it's fine. At least I know now why he's the way he is—doesn't like to talk much."

"I really want to put him in some sort of extracurricular activity just so he can socialize and make friends. Something not affiliated with his school because, otherwise, he won't participate."

"Hmm… I wish I could help you out with that, but all I know is sports and martial arts, and it seems he's not interested in that."

Leticia shook her head. "I believe once he loses some weight he'll feel better about himself and, hopefully, open up and try new things."

"I believe he will," Nate agreed.

Nate called Jordyn after he left the track with Leticia. She didn't answer, so he left her a voicemail message: "Hey Jordyn, just calling to check on you as promised. I know you're probably having a good time with your family. Are you making smart food choices today? Get some exercise? Call me and let me—"

There was an incoming call from Tora. He quickly pressed the button to switch from the voicemail to answer.

"I'm sorry I'm just now getting back to you, Mr. Walker," Tora said. "Yesterday was a busy one for me."

"It's no problem but, please, just call me Nate."

"You said you needed me for a wedding, Nate?"

"Yeah, my sister is getting married and I told her how good of a job you did for me and that she should hire you for her engagement party and wedding pictures."

"Wow. I'm glad you love my work. Thank you."

"I really hope you're available."

"I have nothing else lined up right now. When is the engagement party?"

Nate was stumped. He didn't even know because he hadn't planned on attending. "I'm sorry. I'll have to get back to you on that. It's sometime within the next few weeks, that's for sure, but I will call her to find out and call you right back in about two minutes."

He felt like a fool after dialing Sunny because she didn't answer, and he'd tried twice. *What is it with people not answering the phone today?* Any other day she answered his call right away. He was the same way about her.

Now he had to wait for the opportunity to talk to Tora again. One step forward, two steps back.

TWELVE

"So… tell me again why you declined his lunch offer?" Candace browsed the photos of Nate at the park on Tora's laptop as she sat at the dining table. She came over to get her hair braided—a simple cornrow updo. It was another of Tora's hobbies, which doubled as a way to earn extra income. "Because you weren't lying," Candace went on. "He is definitely fine as hell." She popped her gum.

Tora guessed Candace had to have the strongest jaw in the world because she was always chewing gum. Ever since she'd known her Tora couldn't remember a time not seeing her chomping on a piece. "Right? I mean… just beautiful." Tora sighed. "But, as always… too short."

"*How short*, Tora?"

Tora raised her hand to her earlobe. "Maybe about here."

Candace twisted her lips. "That's not that short."

"I was wearing sneakers," Tora said.

"So what? Stop wearing heels," Candace laughed.

"I'm not gonna be able to do it," Tora shook her head and took a seat at the table.

"That's sad. And yet the fool you said was perfect and you had a good time with was sending you pictures of his private by the end of the night."

"I know, I know," Tora pouted. "I was so disappointed. I thought for sure we would be going on a second date. Was actually looking forward to it."

"Mmm-hmm," Candace smirked. "So that just reiterates the old adage: never judge a book by its cover."

Rolling her eyes, Tora said, "The cover is what attracts a person and makes them want to find out what's inside."

"And I'm sure you know sometimes the cover can be bad, or not what you expected, and lo and behold, the interior—the story—turns out to be the best you've ever read."

"But how would I know that if the cover didn't pique my interest enough for me to even look inside?"

Candace pointed at the laptop screen. "You've already said he's gorgeous. So what if he's a couple inches shorter than you, Tora? Is it really that big of a deal?"

"Yes!" Tora said with a bit more emotion than she intended to. "I don't want a man shorter than me. It doesn't look right. I wouldn't feel confident walking next to him."

"Unbelievable," Candace said, shaking her head. "Ruki could be five inches shorter than me, but you can best believe I wouldn't've turned him down."

Tora sucked her teeth. "That's a lie and you know it."

"I'm serious. Height is not an issue for me. Now, if he had bad teeth or a bad walk I couldn't do it."

"A bad walk?" Tora asked, confused.

"Yeah, a bad walk can make or break everything for me. I wouldn't be able to deal with a knock-kneed man or one that walks pigeon-toed. It ruins the whole aesthetic for me." Candace shuddered with disgust and Tora burst out laughing.

"Now *that's* crazy. I have no problem admitting I can be a little shallow in the looks and height department," Tora said. "I have my reasons, but I don't think I've ever turned down a man because of his walk." Then she put a finger to her chin, thinking. "But you know what? I don't think I've ever come across one with a bad walk, so I can't say whether or not I would've turned him down."

"Exactly," Candace laughed, "but I have. Poor guy. His pants were always bunched up between his thighs because he was so knock-kneed."

Tora laughed out loud again. "You really need to stop." She got up from the table to start on Candace's hair.

"So, how many other dates do you have lined up this week?"

"None," Tora answered flatly. "I haven't even logged onto the site. Between Jason and Dexter I think I've had enough bad contenders to last me for the next month."

"Which is why you need to call Nate and tell him you're free for lunch," Candace said with two loud pops of the gum.

"No. But he's asked me to do the photography for his sister's wedding."

"What? Are you serious?"

"Yep. He called me yesterday."

"Well… maybe there will be some tall and single groomsmen at this wedding," Candace said.

"You've got a point there, girl."

They laughed.

* * *

Tora heard her mobile phone ringing as soon as she turned off the shower and left the bathroom in a hurry to answer it. It was Nate.

"I was just about to leave you a voicemail," he said. "I thought maybe it was too late and you were already in bed for the night."

"I was preoccupied and didn't hear it ring." She pressed the button to place the call on speaker before setting the phone on the bed in order to dry off her body. Mink hopped on the bed, poking her nose around the phone when she heard a voice coming from it.

"My sister finally got back with me, so I have the date and time details now. The engagement party is the Saturday after next at The Ballroom downtown."

"Oh, that's a beautiful venue. Perfect for a wedding, too."

"The party starts at seven."

"Okay, sounds good." She made a mental note to put in a vacation day request as soon as she made it to work tomorrow morning. "If you don't mind, please give me your sister's telephone number. I need to call her to get a bit more detailed information about what she wants and what to expect as far as cost."

"It doesn't matter. I've already sent her the link to check out your work on your website. She saw my photos, too. She loved them. And she trusts my judgment. I'm her twin brother."

"Oh?"

"Yeah, we're really close. She's pregnant right now and told me she's too tired to be dealing with trying to find people to work the wedding. So me, my mama, and her best friend are helping out."

Tora nodded. "Oh okay. So everything I need to know I get the information from you?"

"Yeah, I'm responsible for everything to do with the photography for that night."

"I will email you a questionnaire. Get it back to me as soon as possible and I will follow with the deposit invoice—"

"Email?" Nate said. "Don't you think it would be easier if we meet up to discuss the details? I'm still trying to get that lunch date with you."

"Nice try, Nate. An email will suffice." She ended the call and, despite what she'd told Candace, she logged onto Soul Meet and set up another meeting with a potential candidate. Aunt Kit's motto came to mind: *Keep trying until you get Mr. Right.*

THIRTEEN

"It's about time you brought your ass out of the house! We haven't seen you since last year."

"Yeah, man… where the hell you been?"

Nate laughed and shook hands with two of his closest friends before taking a seat at the table. "Kev, what are you talking about? It wasn't last year the last time we hung out."

"That's what it seems like," Kevin said. "Every time we try to hook up you got some excuse for why you can't come."

"Exactly," Jamal agreed. "I never thought I'd see the day where you become a hermit. What's up with you?"

Nate shrugged. "Been busy as usual," he told them. "Between training and podcasting my weeks are tied up."

"Yeah, yeah, yeah." Jamal waved him off.

Kevin said, "Well, I'm glad you found the time to get out tonight though."

It was a rare occasion where Nate wanted to go out for a drink on a weeknight, but the Astros were playing the Cubs and he knew the guys would be watching the game at one of their frequented bars. He waved over a waitress to order his drink and the only healthy appetizer listed on the menu. "Where is Chauncey?" he asked the guys when the waitress walked away.

Kevin grunted. "You already know."

"Where else would he be?" Jamal laughed.

"Don't tell me he's still messing around with that married woman," Nate said, shaking his head.

"Every time her husband leaves town for business he run his ass over there."

"That fool is going to end up hurt and in the hospital one day," Nate said.

"Or worse… dead," Jamal added. "I told him he's gonna cross the wrong man one day messing around with somebody's wife."

Just then the bar exploded with a clatter of shouts and whistles, forcing Nate and Jamal to turn their attention back to the giant TV screens above them. The Cubs struck out and the Astros were up to bat.

Kevin said, "Nate, what's been going on? How is the family? It's been too long since you invited me back over for Sunday dinner. I still have dreams about Mrs. Walker's pot roast." He rubbed his stomach.

"Everybody's doing good, man. Sunny's getting married, so they're all excited about that."

"For real?" Jamal said. "That's cool."

Kevin pursed his lips and shook his head. "She could've been Mrs. Kev had she given me a chance."

"You're still harping on that? Man, that was five years ago."

"Heck yeah! Sunny is bad. Even after the kids," he laughed. "And you know I've always had a weakness for a woman in a business suit."

"Well, I don't wanna think about you and my sister like that," Nate said, "but, honestly, I'd rather she marry you than this dude she's marrying." As she did about most things going on in her life Sunny had told him about the few times Kevin asked her out on a date just months before she met Levi.

Kevin waved a hand. "She said I was a good guy, but she couldn't go out with me. What kinda sense does that make? I thought all women wanted a good guy. I mean… what is there not to like?" He began to posture: stroking his beard, popping his collar. "I make good money, got a nice condo, nice car. I can be romantic."

Jamal shrugged. "Could just be their way of saying you're not their type."

"That's the thing. Women say they want one thing, but when it's presented to them they dismiss it."

The waitress finally brought over Nate's food.

"Well, obviously they wouldn't dismiss you if you were what they wanted," Jamal said. "I don't care how much we sit around and gripe sometimes about how we're the good guys and we're what women need, there's a reason why we're all still single."

"Meanwhile jokers like Chauncey get all the girls," Kevin said with a touch of bitterness in his voice.

Nate and Jamal laughed.

"They like the challenge," Jamal continued. "I believe they really think they can change these men into the type of man they want him to be."

"Or they could just be into sorry dudes like my sister," Nate said, chomping on a raw carrot from his appetizer platter.

"And that's what I don't unders—" Kevin and the rest of the bar patrons jumped to their feet in applause when the Astros made a home run.

"Did you see that?" Jamal said. "The ball barely missed his face!"

Nate looked to the screen for the replay since he had been focused on his plate and missed it.

Once settled in his seat again, Kevin said, "Sunny is a prime example. Why would a woman of her caliber settle for the man she's with? How was he even able to get a chance with her? I thought a man is supposed to complement you, have something to offer?"

Jamal said, "Fellas, I'm out of the loop. What's the deal with Sunny's boyfriend? What's so bad about him?" He looked at Nate.

"He's a user," Nate shook his head with disgust. "And my sister's too blinded by her obsession with him to see it."

"But they've been together for some years now though, right?" Jamal said.

"Yeah, and all he's given her in five years is three babies."

"Wow." Kevin shook his head too.

"Well I'm sure Sunny don't necessarily need him for money, so there's gotta be something else he's bringing to the table. Let's be honest."

Both Nate and Kevin glared at Jamal, doubt on their faces.

Jamal laughed. "It took a long time for me to understand this but, for a lot of women, they just want somebody there. Maybe he's good for her in other ways. Good with the kids… I don't know."

Nate sucked his teeth. "Y'all don't know the half of it," he said. But he wasn't about to go running his mouth and telling his friends his sister's business. Moving the topic away from Sunny, he said, "I met this lady—"

"Ohhh," Kevin nodded, "so that's where your ass been."

Chuckling, Nate said, "I just met her a few weeks ago. I've been trying to get her to meet me for lunch, but she keeps brushing me off, saying she's not good for me." He reached into his pocket for his wallet. Pulling out her business card and handing it to Kevin, he said, "That's her."

"Oh shit. She looks fine, but what's up with that thing in her nose? And what does she mean she's not good for you?" He gave the card to Jamal to take a look.

"I don't know. She won't be straight-up with me when I ask."

"Where did you meet her?" Jamal slid the card back over to Nate.

"This little deli over in River Oaks. I was there to meet Sunny and my mama for lunch. She walked in and I swear my heart was about to jump out of my chest."

Kevin burst out in laughter. "What?"

"Seriously. She walked in looking like a top model. All tall and brown and super sexy. Everybody in that place stopped what they were doing and stared." Tora was walking through the door in Nate's mind all over again. "It was like a scene in a movie."

"Damn," Jamal said.

"I went over to talk to her, ask her for her number, but she said she didn't wanna waste my time. So when I saw the cashier throw her business card in the garbage I asked her if I could have it, get it out of the trash can. I couldn't let her get away."

"Wait, what?" Kevin said. "You got what out of the trash can?"

Nate told them the story of how he watched Tora in conversation with a young girl behind the counter and that she'd handed over her business card. When she left the deli, the girl promptly threw the card in the trash and Nate went up to ask about Tora, telling the cashier Tora looked like someone he knew. The girl explained that Tora heard her chatting with her coworker about needing a photographer for some graduation photos and was just promoting her services.

"I convinced her to let me have the card and contacted Tora to do the new photos for my website," Nate said. "We met at the park for the photo shoot."

"So she wouldn't give you her phone number, but she came to meet you at the park?" Jamal asked.

"Of course she did," Kevin said to Jamal. "She wasn't gonna pass up that business opportunity."

Nate said, "Well, she didn't know who I was until she arrived at the park. I didn't tell her I was the man she turned down at the deli."

Jamal shook his head. "Dude, that sounds kinda stalker-ish, don't you think?"

"I'm telling you that's how beautiful she was. I couldn't give up just like that. She had me hooked at first sight."

"But she told you she wasn't right for you. That should be a red flag right there."

Nate chuckled. "Naw, there's something else… but she just won't tell me."

"And you wanna waste your time trying to find out?" Jamal gave him a sideways look.

"She was reacting to me at the park that day. I saw the way she was looking at me. At one point she was fumbling with the camera."

"Maybe she's married," Kevin said.

"She said she's single. I think she said no that day in the deli just to say no, but she didn't expect me to come looking for her."

Jamal grunted. "Believe me, if she was interested she would've had no problem giving you her phone number. Women know what they want."

"Well, I'll see about that Saturday night," Nate said. "She'll be at Sunny's engagement party."

"What? So she knows Sunny?" Kevin asked.

"No. I convinced my sister to hire her to do the photography for the party."

"Man, you are crazy," Kevin shook his head. "A woman only has to tell me one time she's not interested. I'm not jumping through hoops just to get somebody."

Jamal agreed with a nod.

"For me, she's worth the effort," Nate told them.

FOURTEEN

Tora pulled out her compact mirror to check her face and hair as she waited. Her makeup was still in tact; she smoothed down a few wayward strands of hair near the part on the side of her head. She was waiting for Eric. He was ten minutes late for their meeting and she decided if he did not show up in another three she was grabbing her purse and leaving. She took out her phone and logged onto Soul Meet to see if he'd left a message notifying her of an emergency or something else delaying his arrival.

"Tora? I'm so sorry we're late."

She looked up to see Eric standing next to the table, but she didn't get the chance to fully take in his face because her eyes immediately went to the young lady standing beside him.

"I wanted to call you, but… I don't have your number of course," he said. He pulled a chair out from the table and the girl sat down.

Okay… what is going on here? she thought.

"I told Whitney she was taking too long getting ready and that you might be gone by the time we get here, so… I'm glad you didn't leave." Then he bent down to kiss Tora's cheek, leaving her at a loss for words. He took a seat across from her at the table.

Tora could only smile at the girl as she waited for Eric to explain.

"Remember what I told you on the way over here, Whitney?

We're on a tight budget this month until your credit card bill is paid down, so remember your limit."

Tora cleared her throat. "Eric, are you going to introduce me to your…?" She didn't want to assume anything, but the young woman could be a sister, niece, daughter, or cousin. Regardless, she hadn't expected this would be a three-party meeting.

"Oh! This is my daughter, Whitney. I've told her so much about you, but I forgot you two don't know each other."

How can you tell her about me when you and I don't even know each other? Tora shook the girl's hand. "Nice to meet you, Whitney," she smiled.

"You as well," the girl said.

"Eric, you could've told me you were hanging out with your daughter today. We can re-schedule for another time. I don't want to impose on your time together."

"No, no. It's fine. Whitney always comes with me on my first dates. To get to me you have to go through her."

Tora looked at the two of them as they grinned back at her. "Ohh… kay," she said finally, and picked up the menu.

"It's just that I'm a package deal, and I figure if we are going to be together it's best you get to know my daughter as well, that way we have the opportunity to see if we'll make a good team."

Tora couldn't argue that point, but she wished she was given a choice on whether or not she was ready to meet a man's family before she got to know him herself.

They ordered when the waiter came over.

"Now's the time for the fun part," Whitney said, smiling at her dad.

"Uh-oh," he winked at Tora. "This is our favorite part of the first date."

Tora raised a brow and watched with curiosity as Whitney went into her purse and pulled out a folded sheet of paper. There was handwriting on the front and back, which looked like a list of questions.

"I have some things I want to ask you," Whitney said.

"Oh? I didn't know I would be interviewed." She looked at Eric across the table and reached for her glass of water to take a sip.

Eric said, "This is just her way of getting to know you. She gets a kick out of doing this with all of my dates."

"I see. But I thought you told her about me already."

"Yeah, well, all the information I could find on the Internet."

Tora couldn't believe her ears. "I'm sorry. What?" She knew the only personal details she'd given him about herself were her first name."

"Well, there aren't too many Toras out there who love both photography and the Pittsburgh Steelers. I was able to narrow that down and find out who you really are. You just can't trust people sometimes on these dating sites, and I just wanted to have a heads-up on who we were meeting tonight."

"Okay," Tora said. "I guess it is a smart thing to do considering you take your daughter along with you."

"This is why I was so surprised when you suggested we meet without having a couple of conversations over the phone at least," he said.

Tora shrugged. "I'm not much of a phone person. I prefer we cut all of that out and meet in person to get a feel for each other."

Whitney cleared her throat. "Can I start with the questions now, Daddy?"

Eric rubbed his hands together. "Go ahead, baby. Let's see what Ms. Tora is all about."

She didn't know what to expect, but something told her just the fact that she was on a first date for the first time in her life with a guy that included his child was going to be a peculiar one and she knew Candace would want to hear about it, too.

"Tora, what's your occupation and where do you see yourself professionally in five years?"

Fair enough, she thought. "I work in retail, and I also have a few things I do on the side—such as photography. I sew, too. In five years I hope to have my own photography studio or my own little boutique selling women's and children's clothing."

"Do you have any kids and, if not, do you want some?"

"That looks like a long list you got there," she said to Whitney. "Are all of them two-part questions?"

"Only a few of them," the girl said.

"No. And yes, I want kids." Whitney wrote something down on the paper. *Am I being scored?*

"Okay… when was your last relationship and why did you guys break up?"

Tora looked at Eric. "Seriously? Who created this list?"

Eric smiled. "She came up with some of the questions, and I came up with some. She's done enough of these to know what to ask though."

Tora wasn't sure how deep these questions were going to go, but she had no plans of sharing too much of her personal life with Eric just yet. And especially not with his child. "A couple years ago," Tora answered. "We realized our life goals didn't align."

"Did you grow up with your father in the home?" Whitney asked.

"Until I was five."

The girl made another notation on the page.

"What kind of relationship did your parents have?"

Tora said, "They divorced when I was five, but they are still friends to this day."

"Sharon and Myles, right?" Eric said.

Her heart skipped a beat and she glared across the table at him.

"I saw the article about your dad and the place where he works."

That was over a decade ago. She'd almost forgotten about it herself. It was the plant's move and grand opening in a new, high-tech facility. She and Sharon were there to support her father and posed as a family together when the reporter interviewed Myles as the plant's new shop manager.

Tora was beginning to feel a little uncomfortable, wondering just how much information Eric had on her. She made a mental note to do some research of her own name when she made it home.

"Don't worry," Eric said. "I wasn't trying to find your social security number or anything."

Tora let out a nervous chuckle and reached for her glass. "Could've fooled me."

He laughed out loud. "Next question, Whitney. I'm enjoying this."

"How important do you think it is to form a relationship with my daughter?"

Tora said, "My guess is this is one of the questions you came up with, Eric?"

"Yep."

"Well, hypothetically-speaking of course, *if* I were in a relationship with someone who has a child, I would think it would be very important to have a relationship with the child, too. I understand the whole package-deal thing. And I can only hope it would be a situation where I would want to love him or her as much as I love my own."

Whitney smiled. "I like her already, Daddy."

"Me too," Eric said.

Tora wasn't won over just yet. She asked, "Is this going to be a one-sided interview?"

"Oh no. You'll have a chance to get to know me as well. This is just stage one."

"Stage one?"

"Stage two will be our second date."

"Second date?" Tora questioned.

"Yeah, Whitney and I decide if a second date is necessary, and then she comes up with a day of activity for us."

Tora's forehead crinkled. "So, you take her on all of your dates?" Whitney laughed.

Eric said, "No. Only the first one. I just let her plan out the subsequent dates. She loves being involved in the whole process, I'm telling you."

Tora nodded, thinking how weird it all seemed.

"All of his dates have given me compliments for my ideas," Whitney said.

"Oh really?" Tora nodded again. "It sounds to me like your dad goes on a lot of dates."

Glancing over at Eric, Whitney said, "Well… we just haven't found the right one yet."

"I see. So, not too many make it past stage one?"

"Oh yeah," Eric said. "Almost all make it past stage one. It's at stage two where a lot of them freak out."

Freak out? "Stage two is the point where they get to know you, correct?" She felt ridiculous using his terminology, as if this was a game show and she was a contestant competing for a chance to advance to the next level.

"They get scared," Eric shrugged.

"Scared? Of what?" Tora asked, frowning. The waiter brought their food, interrupting Eric's response. Tora thought once the waiter walked away Eric would continue, but for the next three minutes he and Whitney gushed over each other's platters, taste-testing the other's selection.

Tora's phone rang and she reached into her purse to get it. "I'm sorry," she said to Eric, "I need to take this phone call." She stepped away from the table and walked towards the restrooms to answer. "Hey, Nate," she said.

"Tora, hey. I'm just calling to touch base with you about tomorrow."

"Alright. I'm supposed to meet you at The Ballroom at six o'clock, right?"

"Well, there's been a little change of plans. I talked to my sister today and she said we're gonna meet at my mom's house first. Sort of like a little get-together before the big party, you know?"

Tora nodded. "Okay, so…?"

"So… can you be at my parents' house at three-thirty?"

"Will I be taking photos there, too? Because this will increase the price. I have to be honest with you."

"I understand," he said. "We got you covered."

"Text me the address and I will see you tomorrow at three-thirty."

"Will do," Nate said.

"You okay?" Eric asked when she returned to the table.

"Oh yeah. That was just a client. I'm working an engagement party tomorrow."

Whitney squealed and clapped her hands. "I *love* engagement parties," she said.

"She wants to be a wedding and event planner," Eric said at the surprised expression on Tora's face. "That's all she watches on television."

"Well, it's a profitable business to get into. There's always an event or wedding to plan somewhere."

"What do you think about my dad?" Whitney asked.

The question caught Tora off guard. "Well," she said, "I don't know much about him. I was the only one being interviewed, remember?"

"When you walked away he said you are incredibly sexy," Whitney blushed. "He likes skinny women."

"Oh," Tora said, although she didn't consider herself skinny. She was slim, but not skinny. Looking at Eric across the table, she said, "I like his eyes." She decided to leave it at that because she didn't feel it necessary to go on about the man's assets in front of his daughter.

"Do you like live music?"

"Yeah, I do."

Whitney clapped her hands again. "Good! Because I planned for you guys to have dinner and then go to Music On The Plaza next Friday night."

I guess checking to see if I had any prior plans don't matter. "So this means I've passed the test to make it to round two? Without answering all the other questions?"

They both laughed.

Whitney said, "We really like you. And I'm a pretty good judge of character."

Tora thought the girl seemed wise beyond her years. She hadn't asked the question, but she placed her around fifteen or sixteen years old.

"Will you go out with my dad again?"

How could Tora say no to the girl? Plus, Eric seemed decent enough, worthy of a second date.

After dinner they exchanged phone numbers and Eric promised to be in touch before Friday.

Once home, Tora read over Nate's answers to her photography questionnaire again. She laid out her outfit and got all of her camera equipment together for the engagement party. Saturday was going to be a long day.

FIFTEEN

"Jordyn, it's Nate again. You've missed several workouts in a row now, and I'm worried about you. I hope everything's okay and that you haven't given up. Remember it's a process. And a couple bad days in a month won't ruin the hard work you put in. The key is to get back on the wagon as soon as possible. Give me a call and let me know what's going on, please." Nate ended the voicemail. He hadn't seen Jordyn since the last time they worked out together before the weekend of her family reunion. And she wasn't returning his phone calls.

He took a seat on the bleachers. It was a few minutes before 8:00 a.m. and he was waiting for Leticia and Vaughn. In the meantime he thought about all he had to do before tonight's party: pick up his shirts from the cleaners since he had been too lazy to do it the day before, stop by the barbershop for a beard trim and line-up, the mall for a new tie and to have his shoes shined because, after all, he was seeing Tora tonight and he wanted to look good. He would have his truck washed, too.

Leticia and Vaughn finally arrived. Nate suggested they warm up by completing some basic calisthenics exercises. Once done he instructed Leticia to do a walk/jog combination around the track—to jog the straight portion and walk around the curve—while he and

Vaughn did something similar using the bleachers instead.

"Just follow me and do what I do," Nate said to Vaughn. He knew the boy would be more inclined to go along with his commands since his mother was just a few feet away.

Nate started on the stairs and ascended them slowly. Once they reached the top he walked the length of the bleachers, increasing the pace slightly, until they reached the stairs on the opposite end and descended them. When they walked to the halfway point at the bottom of the bleachers, Nate stopped and they performed ten squats.

"What grade will you be in when school starts," Nate asked as they ascended the stairs again. He remembered Leticia telling him Vaughn was headed to high school, so it was just Nate's way of trying to get him to talk.

"Ninth," Vaughn answered.

"High school will be some of the most fun you'll have in your life. At least it was for me. The games, the pep rallies, the after school get-togethers with friends. You looking forward to it?"

Vaughn shrugged dismissively.

"There's gotta be something you wanna get into. Getting involved in some extracurricular activities will help you meet people and make the time at school a lot more fun. What do you like to do? Act? Sing? Play music?"

"I draw sometimes."

"Oh yeah? That's cool." Nate smiled, glad to get more than one word out of him. "You gotta bring some of your drawings with you next Tuesday and let me check 'em out. I would love to see what you do." He stopped mid-squat to walk over to Vaughn and remind him to keep his back straight and to not let his knees go past his feet as he lowered himself to the ground. "You should check the school's website to see if they have an art club or something. I bet you'll like that if they have one."

For the next forty-five minutes Vaughn didn't have much more to say but, for the most part, he continued through the workout at Nate's set pace. His bright red hoodie was soaked through, but he still refused to part with it, and Nate realized it was a sort of security blanket for him.

They left the bleachers for the track.

"Looks like you jumped in somebody's pool," Leticia joked with her son when they caught up to her.

"He did much better today," Nate said. "Not one complaint. I'm impressed."

"Well, good. That's what I want to hear."

"I had my eye on you out here, too," Nate told Leticia. "Remember when you couldn't even jog to the first curve?"

"Oh yeah, that was embarrassing. And I feel pretty good now. I feel like I can do another two or three laps, but I probably shouldn't push it."

Nodding, Nate said, "Yeah, don't wanna push yourself. Save some of that energy for our next session."

They sat on the track to do some stretching.

"We'll see you next Tuesday," Leticia said when they reached the parking lot.

"Alright, have a good weekend. Vaughn, don't forget to bring your drawings for the next session."

"Bring his drawings? For what?" Leticia looked at Nate.

"He told me he likes to draw and I asked to see them the next time we meet."

Leticia smiled and replied softly, "Thank you, Nate."

SIXTEEN

A Mediterranean oasis. This was Tora's thought when her navigation system announced she'd arrived at the address. She placed her jeep in Park to check the text message from Nate again just to be certain it was the correct house. In the few years she lived in Houston she'd heard about the River Oaks area, but never had a reason to explore this side of the city. It was definitely the place where some of the wealthiest citizens resided, she'd said to herself as she drove down Kirby Road, captivated by the exquisite homes tucked behind evergreen trees in yards spacious enough to hold an additional single family size home in front.

Looking at Nate's parents' grand house with its curved archways, private terraces, and Italian Cypress trees, she knew it would serve as a beautiful backdrop for some of the party photos.

Tora pulled into the driveway and immediately thought how her candy apple red Wrangler seemed out of place amongst the four shiny black luxury vehicles. She wondered which one belonged to Nate as she grabbed her purse and got out.

It was her second ring of the bell before she heard footsteps on the other side of the dark mahogany wood double doors. A woman answered resembling what Tora imagined Old World royalty looked like, and she hoped when she reached middle age she would look half as good as this woman with gorgeous, untouched skin, a head full of silky gray hair, and majestic style. But, while Tora stood admiring the stunning beauty, the woman looked back at her with critical eyes.

Maybe the lipstick is too much, Tora thought. But the matte teal color was her top favorite and every time she wore it out she received compliments. "Hi," she said, "are you Mrs. Walker? I'm here to meet with Nate."

The woman studied her from head to toe as if to say Tora couldn't possibly know anyone associated with this address.

"I am. Who are you and how do you know my son?"

"My name's Tora Jamison of Take Two Photography. The photographer for the engagement party tonight?"

Mrs. Walker's eyes settled on Tora's nose. "You are?" she asked, her voice full of skepticism.

Tora shifted her weight from one leg to the other. *Maybe I should've taken the ring out, too.* "Yes. He told me to meet him here at three-thirty."

It seemed like a full minute of intense study from Mrs. Walker before she finally stepped back and opened the door for Tora to enter. "Come in," she said.

Tora's mouth dropped when she stepped into the foyer behind Mrs. Walker. The grand, winding staircase to their left, the chandelier hanging above it, the pristine white columns, the furnishings, the art. Her eyes quickly took it all in.

"Have a seat in here," Mrs. Walker said, motioning towards the room to the right of the entryway.

Tora did as she was told and Mrs. Walker disappeared to the other side of the wall without another word to her.

She sat alternating between looking out of the big, floor-to-ceiling windows behind her and at her smartphone as time passed. Twenty minutes had gone by and neither Mrs. Walker nor Nate had shown up and she needed to get her camera equipment out of the car. She heard kids playing somewhere on the second floor above her head. *Maybe he's upstairs getting ready,* she thought.

The front door opened suddenly and Tora looked up. A woman came in carrying three boxes. She was a short woman, so the boxes stacked atop each other hid her face. Tora wondered if it was Nate's sister and was about to ask if she needed help, but the woman zoomed through the foyer before she could get the words out of her mouth.

"I'm back with the cupcakes, Vicki," Tora heard her say. "Whose army-looking truck is that outside?"

"It belongs to that young lady in the sitting room."

"What young lady?"

"You passed her on your way in."

"I didn't see anybody when I walked in."

"She said she's the photographer."

"The photographer?"

"Sent here by Nate."

"*Sent here by Nate?* But we already have a photographer, and Nate is not even—"

Quick footsteps came down the hall. The woman stepped into the room and Tora stood up. The woman's reaction didn't surprise Tora. She looked up at her, shock evident on her face as Tora towered over her. Tora was five-eleven in her bare feet, but today she was sporting her classic pointy-toe black pumps with a five-inch heel.

Tora held out her hand. "I'm Tora of Take Two Photography."

The woman looked at her the same way Mrs. Walker had done half-an-hour ago: up and down as if she had mud on the bottom of her shoes and had tracked filth all over her polished floors. Then she looked at Tora's outstretched hand a second before she finally took it.

"Kaneesa," was the woman's bland reply. And before Tora could say anything else, Kaneesa turned on her heels and left the room.

Okay, the women in this house aren't very friendly, Tora said to herself.

Their voices were lowered this time, but Tora still heard what they said:

"*Who* is that?"

"I told you she claims she's the photographer for tonight."

"Victoria, we already have a photographer. He should be here shortly. How is she the photographer?"

"I have no idea what's going on, and of course Nate didn't answer when I called him."

"Nate said he wasn't coming to the engagement party."

This bit of information stoked Tora's attention.

"We don't need two photographers tonight," Kaneesa continued. "And Nate hired her?"

"Apparently so."

"Does Sunny know about this?"

"I have no idea. I doubt it, or else she would've told me."

"Yeah, she would've told us," Kaneesa said. "Well, I'm going to tell this woman she can go. And do you see how she's dressed? With that god-awful blue lipstick? I mean… c'mon. This is a formal event. And she calls herself a photographer? Must not be a professional one."

"My sentiments exactly."

"We already have a photographer, Victoria."

"I'm with you, Kaneesa. Nate has lost his mind."

Tora couldn't believe her ears. *So they already have a hired photographer? Was this just Nate's way of trying to get a chance to have a date with me?*

Mrs. Walker and Kaneesa appeared. Mrs. Walker said, "Apparently there's been a miscommunication somewhere, but we already have a photographer for tonight's event, so my son couldn't have hired you for the occasion."

Tora said, "Nate called me seeking my services as the photographer for his sister's engagement party and wedding. He's already paid the deposit for tonight." She looked at Kaneesa. "Are you his sister?"

"No, I'm not," Kaneesa said, "but I am his sister's best friend and I know what she likes. There's someone already working the party tonight. A vetted professional. Someone whose work is of high quality."

Tora was pissed. She needed to get to her jeep so she could call Nate and have a few words with him. She grabbed her purse, stood, and walked out the door without a word because if she opened her mouth she would've said something she knew she would later regret. And Sharon had raised her to always be the gracious one when in the face of conflict.

She rushed out the door and crashed chest first into a hard body. The purse slipped off her shoulder and fell to the ground. "I'm sorr—" she began until she realized it was Nate.

"Hey, Tora," he said, and bent down to retrieve her bag at the same time she did, their heads colliding.

"Ouch! Shit." Tora put a hand to her forehead.

"Oh, man. Are you all right? Sorry about that. I'm in a rush to get here to see you. I'm glad you're here."

Tora snatched her bag from his hand. "I bet you are," she said, and stepped around him, heading to her vehicle.

"Huh?" he said to her retreating back. "Tora? What's going on?"

Her heels clicked angrily against the concrete. "Is this your SUV parked behind me?" she said. "I need to get out."

"What's wrong? What happened?"

Tora whirled around to face him. "Nate, I take what I do very seriously. I don't appreciate you wasting my time. I took this day off work to be here for you." She yanked open the driver's door and got in.

He came to her window. "What's going on?"

"Let me out, Nate. I don't have time for this."

"Tora, what are you saying? I honestly don't know what you're talking about."

She glared at him. "Was this your scheme to get me here? Your sister doesn't need me. She already has a photographer for the party."

"No she doesn't. That's why you're here."

Tora reached behind her shoulder for the seatbelt. "This was a childish thing to do, Nate. Embarrassing. And I don't appreciate it." She cranked the engine.

"Who told you she has a photographer?"

"Your mom told me. And Kaneesa."

"What? They did?"

Pressing the clutch and brake pedals, she put the jeep in Reverse. "Move your truck so I can go."

"I'm going inside to see what's going on."

Tora shook her head. "Just let me out, Nate."

"Please wait right here, Tora. I'll be right back."

"Nate—" she started to protest, but he turned and walked towards the house. "Shit," she muttered again. She turned the knob for the air conditioner and the blast of air hit her in the face. She was upset and needed to cool down. And she didn't want her makeup ruined by the summer heat. More than that, she needed to calm her body. Even in her state of anger she couldn't get over how beautiful Nate looked in his crisp white shirt and black bow tie. His locks were the most glorious set she had ever seen on a man, adding to his allure.

Several minutes passed before she heard a commotion. She looked up to see Nate headed over to her vehicle, Mrs. Walker and Kaneesa following behind him. She lowered her window.

"Come on," he told her, "turn off the car and get out. You're the photographer for tonight. You're staying here with me."

She grabbed her purse and got out.

"We already have somebody working tonight," Kaneesa was saying.

Nate said, "I already told you you need to call and cancel him. Tora is the one we hired for the party."

"I told Sunny *I* would be the one in charge of getting the photographer, Nate, and he's on his way. I just talked to him," Kaneesa said. She waved her mobile phone in the air. "You're not even supposed to be here!"

"Kaneesa, I was just upstairs talking to my sister. Call her if you need to, but Tora is staying."

Victoria said, "Nate, why would you do this? Just look at the confusion you've caused."

"Mama, I don't know what she's talking about, but when I called to talk to Sunny about the photographer a couple weeks ago, she didn't mention Kaneesa."

"I'm calling her now," Kaneesa said.

"Put it on speaker so we can all hear it," Nate told her.

Tora stood not knowing if she should retreat back inside her jeep or remain in this awkward position, caught in the middle of his family's quarrel.

"Sunny," Kaneesa said into the phone, "are you really going to let Nate make decisions for your party? He doesn't know what you need. No one even knew he was coming."

"Well, I'm just happy he decided to attend," Sunny said. "So can you let him help out, too? I'm really not in the mood for the madness right now."

"But Sunny, he's not even supposed to be here!" Kaneesa yelled.

"I'm sorry, Kaneesa," Sunny said. "It's my fault because I totally forgot you told me you hired somebody."

Nate said, "Where is he? He's not here yet. Whoever he is, he's late."

Kaneesa gave Nate a look as if she wanted to set him on fire. "He's caught in traffic, but he's not even ten minutes away now. I talked to him not too long ago."

"Call him back and tell him his services are no longer needed. He's canceled," Nate told her.

"I'm not canceling anything! Sunny, have you seen this woman he's hired? This is a classy event and she's dressed like she's going to a gothic ball with this black lace dress and turquoise lipstick. She has a septum nose ring, Sunny! A nose ring?!"

Tora shifted on her heels as the three of them looked at her. The dress was a long-sleeve black lace number that stopped just above her knees, which she believed was sensible attire for the event. In the questionnaire she sent to Nate was the inquiry about event dress code and whether the family preferred she wear a certain outfit or specific colors to be in uniform with the rest of the party. Nate had answered she could wear anything she wanted, that it was only the engagement party. So she chose this simple cocktail dress and black pumps, adding her signature lip stain for a pop of color.

He nodded in approval as his eyes traveled over her now. "And she looks just as beautiful as she did the first day we saw her," Nate said.

Kaneesa frowned in confusion. "Sunny, you know this woman?"

Tora wanted to remind Kaneesa of her name, but chose to bite her tongue.

Sunny said, "I don't think so. Who is she, Nate?"

"You'll remember when you see her," he said. "She's the woman I said was going to be my wife."

Tora's head swooned from Nate's admission. She had no idea what was going on and she needed to sit down.

Kaneesa said to Nate, "So that's why you decided to come to the party? Just so you can show off your little girlfriend?"

"She's not my girl—"

"Brother, you didn't tell me you were bringing a date with you," Sunny cut in. "I didn't even know you had a girlfriend. This is something I definitely need to see. I can't wait to meet her."

Tora couldn't believe the exchange occurring in front of her eyes. She wanted to say something, but at the same time didn't want to bring anymore attention to herself or add to the stressful situation.

"I'll be downstairs in a few minutes," Sunny said.

Kaneesa groaned loud enough for the neighbors three houses down to hear, and stormed off.

Victoria gave Tora another once-over. "Young lady, I suggest you at least get rid of the lipstick if you intend to work my daughter's event tonight." And with that, she turned and slowly walked back into her home.

SEVENTEEN

Nate was glad that situation was settled, and now he could give his attention to Tora. "I'm so sorry you had to see all of that," he said. "Do you have something you need me to help you take in the house? To set up?"

Tora finally looked at him. "To be honest, Nate, I don't even feel comfortable working the event anymore." She took a wet wipe out of her purse and rubbed her mouth, wiping away the lipstick.

Nate wished she didn't. The color was beautiful against her brown skin.

"This was a very cruel thing to do," she said. "Normally, deposits are non-refundable, but in this case I would be happy to return it to you just so I can be over this day and not have to deal with you or your family."

Nate was crushed. He sighed. "Tora, you have to believe me. I had no idea about the other guy. You heard it from my sister just a minute ago. She didn't tell me."

"I don't doubt one bit that this wasn't a ploy to force me to be here with you."

"Well, that's not the total truth," he said. "I was trying to help my sister out, and since I love what you did to enhance my website, I knew you would be perfect for her big day. Being able to see you at the same time is just a bonus."

She glared at him a second before turning to open the trunk.

He didn't want her to be upset, but the annoyed look on her face turned him on. "Let me carry the bag for you."

"I got it," she said and closed the trunk. "Just show me where the bathroom is when we get inside."

Nate stood looking out of the patio door into the backyard. Tora had her camera and was taking pictures of his nieces—Bryanna and Melody—in the garden. She didn't have much to say to him ever since they came into the house, so he was keeping his distance and giving her space.

But he couldn't take his eyes off her. The sexy black dress, those ultra long legs held him captive.

"Baby brother, are you going to tell me who she is? I've been watching you watch her for the past hour."

Nate smiled as Geo came to stand beside him. "Her name's Tora."

"I know that much," Geo said. "You forgot already that you told us her name when me and Evelyn came in?"

"Oh. Just the woman that's been running through my mind since I saw her a few weeks ago."

"I overheard the women talking when I went to lay Evan down in the guest room. I'm a little disappointed that I'm just now hearing about your new girlfriend."

Nate looked at him. "Well… she's not my girlfriend, but when I have visions of what Mrs. Nate Alan Walker looks like, she definitely fits the description."

Geo said, "I knew once Sunny got married you would start getting serious about settling down. You're the last one."

Chuckling, "Naw, it's not that serious," he answered. "I just think she's a beautiful woman. And I'm hoping by the end of the night I can convince her to give me a chance."

"Why did Mama want us all here anyway if the party doesn't start until seven? I could've been home reviewing student paperwork and met up with y'all at the venue downtown."

"I'm sure this was just her way of making sure we were all together so we can be there at the same time. Especially me."

Geo laughed. "Probably so. But it looks like Levi is the only one missing this time."

Nate's thoughts had been so consumed with Tora that he didn't realize his sister's fiancé wasn't around. "There's no telling where he is," Nate said. He suddenly realized Sunny hadn't come downstairs yet, either.

"I'm going to get a plate of these hors d'oeuvres and go to the rec room. Come and get me when it's time to leave," Geo said.

Nate's attention returned to the backyard when his brother walked away. The girls were holding Tora's hands, leading her back into the house.

"Uncle Nate, we're gonna show her the playroom," Bryanna said when they entered.

"It's pretty hot outside. I was wondering how much longer y'all would last out there." He looked at Tora. "They're not driving you crazy, are they?"

With a tight shake of her head, she said, "I don't mind. It's better than sitting around twiddling my thumbs."

Nate could only smile as she passed without a second glance at him. He knew the sassy remark was in response to his mother's directive for Tora to wait for instruction before she set up her camera equipment and made her wait in the library for quite some time shortly after they'd come into the house. But his nieces had been so fascinated with the leggy stranger and her camera that they begged their grandmother if they could have their picture taken.

Bryanna, especially, couldn't wait to show off and pose in her new fancy dress.

He heard the cries as he walked up the steps to the top floor. It took a minute before he heard Sunny tell him to come in.

"What's going on, baby sis?" he asked, closing the door behind him. "Everything okay in here? I was waiting for you downstairs."

"She's been like this all day," Sunny said. "Tantrum after tantrum. I don't know what's wrong with her."

His four-year-old niece was beside herself. Squirming and kicking and crying as Sunny tried combing her hair. Her face was red-hot with tears.

Nate walked over and knelt in front of her chair. "What's wrong, Anaya?" He reached for her, but she screamed louder and turned away from him. Nate stood. "She need a nap?"

"She woke up not too long ago. Just one of those days I guess."

Nate heard the tiredness in his sister's voice. "Where is Levi?"

"He had to go and pick up his sister from work. He'll be here in a little while."

Pulling his smartphone out of his pocket, Nate checked the time. Anaya quieted down and walked over to him. He knew she wanted his phone. It was something she'd learned from her cousin Bryanna. Uncle Nate's phone could be used to play games or watch videos anytime if you let Bryanna tell it.

Sunny just shook her head. "Really? Is that all it takes?"

Nate laughed and lifted his niece into his lap as he sat on the edge of the bed. "Just a minute ago you wanted nothing to do with me, but as soon as you see my phone…." Anaya looked up at him with those big brown sad eyes and he couldn't help planting a kiss on her tear-stained cheek. He opened the video app on his phone and Anaya rested her head on his shoulder.

"It's crazy," Sunny said, eyeing her daughter with impatience.

"She just doesn't feel like getting her hair combed," Nate said. He patted Anaya's head gently. "What's wrong with letting her wear it like this? Wild and free? I like it."

Sunny shot him a pointed look. "Are you going to be at my house tomorrow morning to help me de-tangle it?"

"How hard could it be?" Nate looked at his niece's mass of curls again, grabbed one between his fingers and gave it a gentle stretch before letting it spring back into place. "Just spray it with water and she'll be good to go."

Sunny shook her head again. "You are such a sucker for your nieces and nephews. But wait until you have your own. We'll see how much you let them get away with." She took a seat in the chair Anaya had abandoned. "Anaya can take a break for now, but she knows she's not leaving this room without getting her hair combed."

"Other than this, everything okay with you? I know I don't have to ask if you're ready for your party tonight."

With a small smile, she said, "I want you to tell me what made you decide to come? Especially since you were so adamant and had no plans to attend just a few weeks ago."

Nate chuckled. "Well—"

"And who is this woman Kaneesa is so up-in-arms about?"

Nate was happy to skip over her first question. "She's the one from the sandwich shop where I met you and Mama for lunch that day."

Sunny thought back. "So much has gone on since then. Refresh my memory."

"She was tall. Sexy tattoo. The one you said was trashy?"

"Brother, you have got to be kidding," she said, narrowing her eyes. "The half-naked chick?"

"She was fully-clothed," Nate replied. "And beautifully so."

"Typical male response." She rolled her eyes. "You're in your thirties. You should want a woman, not a teenager."

"Oh, she is definitely all woman," he grinned. Legs and lace flashed in his mind.

"I recall seeing a shirt small enough to fit Anaya. And this is the woman you want to bring home to Mama and Daddy?"

"She has the body for it. What's wrong with showing it off?"

Sunny rolled her eyes again. "You have weird taste."

Nate wasn't going to entertain that statement considering how she was just a few months away from committing herself for life to a man with a little boy's mentality. "I should go back downstairs. She's probably looking for me," he said. He stood and Anaya began to cry again as he handed her off to Sunny and tried taking his phone back.

"Cut it out, Anaya," Sunny warned.

"Just let her keep it for now. I'll get it later." He kissed his niece on the cheek again and left the room in search of the lady in lace.

EIGHTEEN

Tora stood in the library, her camera hanging from her neck, as she studied the books on the shelf. Encyclopedias, law and medical science books, collectors' editions of literary classics. She was bored out of her mind. She was under the impression the whole purpose for being here was to take photos of the pre-engagement party, but no one has said anything to her about what she needs to do. She had no idea where Nate had disappeared off to, and she didn't feel comfortable roaming the massive estate, especially after that lackluster welcome she received from Mrs. Walker.

She pulled out her phone to check the time. It was six o'clock. Eric had sent her a dozen text messages throughout the afternoon, most of them telling her what he was doing at that particular moment in time:

1:57 PM: Just dropped Whitney off at the mall to hang out with her friends. I have about three or four hours to myself now.

2:32 PM: I was home and suddenly got the taste for some Burns BBQ. Drove all the way to Acres Homes to get some. Have you ever been there?

3:49 PM: Catching up on my recorded TV shows. Whitney is always getting on me about taking up too much of the recording space.

4:51 PM: Just woke up from a power nap. I don't know if I can wait until Friday night before I see you again.
5:30 PM: I have a house full of bubbly teenage girls… Yikes!
5:48 PM: How is the engagement party?

Initially she wasn't going to respond because she thought it unprofessional to be on her phone while working, but quickly dismissed that logic since for the past two-and-a-half hours all she's done was a bunch of standing around.

She punched in a reply. **The party doesn't start for another hour, but I'm here at the family's home. Bored.**

"There you are," a voice came over her shoulder just as she pressed the Send button.

Tora turned around to see Nate leaning on the door frame looking like a distinguished gentleman—a hand in his pocket, one ankle crossed over the other. His lovely features highlighted by the stark white shirt. She was tempted to raise her camera and capture the shot, but was still rather annoyed with him and how this whole situation came about.

"Nate, I really don't understand why you needed me here. What exactly am I supposed to be doing?" she asked, her voice full of frustration.

"Well… come to find out… my sister's fiancé is not here, so that's why everybody's kinda just hanging around. I'm sorry. But I think we will be leaving soon. Do you need anything? Did you help yourself to the snacks and hors d' oeuvres in the dining room?"

She wanted to ask what would make him think she would help herself to anything in this house without first being offered. "No. I'm fine," she said. The toast and orange juice she'd had for breakfast were long gone, but she decided to ignore her stomach's growl and wait until later to eat. "Just anxious to start what I was supposedly called here to do. That's all."

He nodded. "Yeah, I can understand that. And, believe me, you will be compensated for your time. No doubt."

"Oh, that goes without saying," Tora quipped, but quickly regretted her tone. No matter how agitated she was at the moment he was still a client and she didn't need to be rude towards him.

His smile in response made her feel worse. *God, he is so handsome,* she thought. As a matter of fact, his entire family was handsome. She'd noticed by the poster-size photo of them hanging on the library's wall, and by the gentleman she'd encountered as she left Bryanna and Melody in the playroom.

Someone called out for Nate and he stepped into the hallway. They told him everyone was ready to go.

Nate came back into the room. "See? Just that fast and we're ready." Then he walked right over to Tora, leaving just an inch between them as he stood in front of her. Not even her body's natural reflex had time to react as he invaded her personal space.

Quietly, he said, looking up at her, "I just want you to know my heart is racing right now at the sight of you in this dress."

Outside, Tora was still trying to process what Nate had said. The heavenly scent of his cologne was still in her nose. He'd left her speechless in the library. Mainly because she was worried about who might be in earshot to hear her comeback at his remark. Even still, she didn't really have a comeback because her heart was racing too.

She sat in her jeep waiting for Nate and his family to get settled in their respective vehicles. His SUV had her blocked in the driveway and she watched as he went back into the house three times for something. Finally he walked out carrying a boy toddler on one arm, a diaper bag on the other. Tora guessed the woman walking behind him clutching the hand of a little girl was his sister. She recalled him telling her she was expecting.

How cute, Tora thought, *he has a twin sister.*

Nate assisted with putting the kids in their car seats. Then he walked over to her vehicle.

"Come ride with me," he said when she lowered the window.

"What? Why would I do that?"

"Because I want to talk to you."

"Then how will I make it home after the party?"

"I'll bring you back here of course. To pick up your car."

"Nate, that doesn't make sense."

"Okay. So, how about I ride with you instead?"

Tora frowned at him in confusion. "Isn't that the same thing?"

He chuckled and tapped her door before turning and walking away.

She shook her head as she watched him through the driver's side mirror.

One by one the cars filed out of the driveway. Tora backed out once she had clearance and Nate pulled his truck into her spot before hopping out and joining his sister in the car.

What could he possibly want to talk to me about? she wondered as she started down the street. She couldn't imagine being in such close proximity with him. Her mind was still swirling from the proclamation he'd made a few hours ago about wanting to marry her.

While at a stoplight, she finally read the text message from Eric she'd had to ignore when Nate found her in the library.

Give me the address to where you are and I will come and keep you company. Be your assistant.

She replied back. **That won't be necessary. We're headed to the venue, so I'm good now.**

I would love to see you. I bet you look stunning in whatever you're wearing. How about a late dinner once you're done?

Of course she didn't know how long the party would last and she was prepared to remain there until Nate—or his sister—dismissed her for the evening. **I don't think so. It may be around 11 or later.**

I will still be awake. It's only Saturday night you know. Perfect night.

That's too late to meet for a first date.

She set the phone in her lap and checked her mirrors. She didn't see Nate's sister's car and didn't know whether or not they'd passed her on the street.

Another text message came in from Eric minutes later. **I'm going to have Whitney re-schedule our date. Friday night is too far away. What time should I pick you up tomorrow morning? Is 9:00 too early?**

She should have been focused on the road ahead instead of trying to reply her disapproval at his request. The sound of screeching tires snatched her attention back to the windshield just as the car ahead of her did a hard swerve to the left. Tora didn't have a second to register what the driver was dodging or to hit the brakes before the passenger side of her jeep plunged into the pavement with a hard bang followed by a grisly pop that rattled her from her feet all the way up to her shoulders.

What the…? The jeep wobbled as she steered slowly to the far edge of the street.

"What the…?" she said aloud as she placed it in Park and got out, walking around to the other side.

Her tire was blown.

She looked back to the street to see what she'd hit. A pot hole that was more of a crater than a hole. "Oh my god."

Passing drivers noticed the damaged pavement and were able to dodge or straddle it at the last minute, saving them the same fate.

"Shit," she muttered and went back into the vehicle. *Of all days, this would happen when I'm on my way to a photography commitment,* she thought. How was she going to explain this to Nate's sister? She grabbed her phone to call her, but quickly remembered she didn't have her phone number, so she called Nate. He didn't answer.

She hung up and called her insurance company for roadside assistance. She'd never had to change a tire in her life. Myles made sure that she knew how to, but he always came to the rescue when she and her mother had car trouble when she was back home in Pittsburgh. And she had been fortunate in the years since to not be caught stranded. So the money she paid monthly for emergency assistance via her auto insurance policy would finally be put to use.

After speaking with roadside assistance, she called Nate again. She called him a third time and decided to leave a message when he didn't answer. "Nate, I had a blowout. Please tell your sister I am so sorry, but it looks like I will be a few minutes late. I will be there as soon as I can. I'm waiting for roadside assistance."

She exhaled in frustration, pressed the button to turn on the hazard lights, and waited.

NINETEEN

"Nate, my man! How've you been, man?"

A hand landed roughly on his shoulder from behind. Nate turned around to see one of his and Sunny's high school classmates. "What's up, Travis? What's going on?" Nate shook his hand, noticing his red face and glassy eyes and wondered how in the world Travis was drunk already when the party hadn't even fully started.

But he shouldn't have been surprised. Travis Ferguson was the kid in high school who hosted the best house parties because his dad was some big time corporate executive and never home, so Travis often invited friends over and they helped themselves to the food in Senior Ferguson's pantry, his whiskey, and sometimes his Cuban cigars. By their final year in school, Travis couldn't make it through two class periods before he was sneaking outside to his car for a sip from his thermos. To this day Nate is still surprised that Travis was able to make it through college and law school and go on to become a successful attorney.

"Hey, man..." Travis replied, "just enjoying life. Doing the things that make it all worthwhile: drinking and fucking! Hopefully there's a hot single chick here I can take home with me tonight and get lucky."

Nate glanced around to see if anyone heard the crass remark.

Victoria definitely would've had Travis escorted out if she'd gotten wind of it. He chuckled uneasily. "Sunny has quite a few single friends, but I doubt you will be able to get any of them with that type of thinking."

"Bullshit," Travis sputtered. "I've tried the whole romantic nice guy thing. Chicks don't want that. They want a man who doesn't give a fuck about them—just take them home and screw their brains out. That's what they want."

A waiter passed carrying a tray of champagne to distribute to the guests and Travis grabbed one. Nate was watching the entry doors because they'd been there nearly twenty minutes and he hadn't seen Tora. He returned his attention to Travis. "How much have you had to drink today, man? Because you're talking kinda crazy." He laughed a little so the question would appear more light-hearted than judgmental.

Travis gulped the champagne down like water. "Only a couple beers with my colleague before I came."

Nate knew with certainty he was operating on something more than just a couple of beers. It was seeping through his pores.

"But you know it's true," Travis went on. "I was prepared to buy her a ring and everything. We went out shopping for houses together, too. Everything was great. Or so I thought. But, out of the blue, she told me things were moving too fast, that she wasn't quite ready for the next step. But I found out just a few weeks ago she's moved in with some guy who treats her like shit!"

Nate had no idea who or what Travis was talking about, and he doubted Travis realized it, but he decided not to say anything. His eyes were still scanning the room for Tora.

"So that's my attitude about it right now," Nate heard Travis say. "I will be the asshole they want."

Nate shook his head. "Man, that's a sad way of viewing things, but hey… if it works for you…. I would just hate to see you get a glass of champagne thrown in your face tonight. My sister's friends don't play any games." He reached into his coat pocket for his cell phone.

"Alright," Travis said with a devilish grin. "I'll be nice."

Nate patted Travis's shoulder. "I need to go and check on something. I'll see you around," he said, and walked off.

Sunny was in conversation with someone when he found her, and he didn't want to interrupt just to ask for his phone. He'd realized it wasn't in the pocket of his suit jacket. He spotted Geo and walked over to him. "G, have you seen Tora?"

"No, I haven't seen her," Geo shook his head.

"She should've been here by now, but I haven't come across her yet," Nate said.

"Maybe she's in the ladies' room. Have you checked there?"

"No. But I don't think she would've been in there this long if she was."

"You never know. She may be like Evelyn. Whenever we go out for our date nights she has to go straight to the restroom when we get to where we're going and check her makeup. Does makeup come off or something in a car ride from the house to the venue?" Geo laughed softly.

"She left the house at the same time we did, so why isn't she here?"

"If I see her I'll let her know you're looking for her," Geo told him.

He scanned the room again before walking back over to Sunny. "Hey, sis, let me get my phone from you."

"What? I don't have your phone," she looked at him.

"Yes you do. I gave it to Anaya, remember? So you could finish her hair?"

"Check Deuce's diaper bag. It may be in there. I don't know."

Victoria had requested a separate space in The Ballroom be designated for small children so parents attending the party wouldn't have to worry about finding a sitter. That's how thorough she was about everything. She wanted to ensure there would be no excuses for invitees to give for not being able to attend her daughter's affair.

Nate headed for the room on the opposite end of the hall where he and Sunny had dropped off Anaya and Baby Levi when they arrived. A thought occurred to him as he made his way down the corridor. Did Tora renege on him? She was pretty upset earlier about the photographer mix-up. Was this her way of getting back at him? He quickly dismissed the thought. She didn't strike him as a vindictive woman. But, then again, he knew nothing about her.

His phone was not in the baby's bag, so he returned to Sunny. "It's not in there, sis. What did you do with it?"

"Nate, I don't know what happened to it," she answered breathlessly, clearly frustrated.

"Did you leave it at Mama's house?"

"This is exactly why I don't allow the kids to play with my phone," she said. "If it's not in the car, then I'm sure it's still at Mama's house."

"Then let me use yours. I need to make a call."

Kaneesa approached the table as Sunny searched inside her handbag. With her arms crossed and an eyebrow raised, she said, "Nate, so I hear from Geo that you can't seem to find your little girlfriend. Is she lost? Or is she the unprofessional I knew she would be?"

He could have easily told her to mind her business, but decided against it. He grabbed the phone from Sunny and stepped out into the corridor. Although he'd called Tora only a few times, her telephone number was ingrained in his memory.

She answered right away.

"Tora, what's going on? You having trouble finding the address?"

"I had an accident, Nate. Didn't you get my message?"

"What? No. My sister misplaced my phone. An accident? Are you all right?"

"Yeah, a blowout. I hit a pot hole in the street. Please tell your sister I am *so* sorry."

Nate was already headed back inside before he said, "Tell me where you are and I'm on my way." When she told him where she was, he ended the call and said to Sunny, "Give me your keys, sis. Tora had a flat. I need to go and help her out."

"What?"

Kaneesa sucked her teeth and rolled her eyes. "How fitting. A damsel in distress."

Shaking his head bitterly, Nate said, "Kaneesa, please worry about yourself tonight. Don't you have something you could be doing instead of bothering me?"

"*You* are the problem," she sneered. "We're supposed to be taking pictures with the guests right now, but because you decided to hire somebody from God-knows-where with an unreliable car we—"

"I'll keep your phone with me, Sunny, so I can be in touch with Tora," Nate said, completely ignoring Kaneesa.

"You can't take my phone," Sunny replied. "I need it in case Levi calls me."

He didn't argue and handed over her phone before hastily making an exit for the elevator.

Tora was parked on the side of the road, her emergency lights flashing. Nate pulled up behind her and got out. He inspected all four of the tires before approaching the driver's side window.

"I am so sorry, Nate," she apologized again. "Did you tell your sister?"

"It's fine," he waved her off. "Accidents happen."

"I called roadside assistance again and they told me wait times are longer than usual today."

"That is a pretty big hole," he said, glancing back towards the street. "I hope the city comes and fixes it soon before it ruins a lot more cars. A pot hole like that can do some serious damage to your front end. I'm surprised you didn't see it."

She looked away from him and towards the windshield as if she was embarrassed.

"Do you have a jack? I can change the tire for you."

"Nope. I don't." She shrugged. "But hopefully they will be here soon."

Nate couldn't help staring at her lovely face. The earring dangling from her ear brought his attention to her long and slender neck. "You know all of this could've been avoided had you just got in the truck with me?"

She looked at him. "With the way this day is going my luck probably would've been much worse. I think this is a sign."

He chuckled despite the blow to his feelings. "Are you trying to say I'm bad luck? That hurt." He thought he saw an inkling of a smile curve her lips, but she said nothing. "I'll check in my sister's car to see if she has a jack kit in there," he said.

Sunny's trunk was full of junk. Most of it belonged to Levi: a gym bag, several pairs of scuffed and smelly tennis shoes, dirty clothes, loose paper documents, restaurant take-out bags, empty soda cans, a half-full liter of orange juice.

Nate shook his head in disgust and closed the trunk. "She doesn't have one, either," he said to Tora.

"It's fine. Thanks for wanting to help. All I can do is wait." She sighed. "I'm sure your sister is pissed with me right now."

"I doubt it. She's more concerned about her fiancé. He hadn't even shown up yet by the time I left the party." Nate walked around to the passenger side and got in. "I hope you don't mind, but I don't wanna get hit," he said, closing the door.

She picked up her cell phone and began to thumb through it.

After several minutes of sitting in silence, Nate cleared his throat. "So… Tora… how long have you been in photography?"

She continued typing a text message before finally looking up at him. "About five years professionally, but I've always loved taking pictures since my parents bought my first camera when I was in high school."

"Oh okay. So it was your parents who turned you on to it? That's cool. I'm always interested in how people end up in their occupational fields."

"I think my parents had run out of ideas on what to buy me for my birthday and decided I might like a camera. It wasn't something I asked for. But I ended up falling in love and took it with me everywhere I went."

"Well… you're very good at it from what I can tell. I get so many compliments on my website."

There was no mistaking the pride that glowed on her face now.

"Thank you," she smiled. "I hope your sister will feel the same way about my work. If only I can hurry up and get there." She checked the rearview mirror, looking out for roadside assistance.

Nate said, "Believe me. It's cool. We have the rest of the night to take pictures." He reached up and touched the lanyard hanging from the mirror. "You like the Steelers?"

"That's my team!" she answered proudly.

"*What?* How can you be a Texan and not represent the Cowboys?" he asked, giving her a sideways look.

With an index finger in the air, she said, "First of all, I'm not a Texan, and second of all, the Cowboys ain't all that. What have they done in the past decade?"

"What do you mean 'what have they done'? They're not called America's team for nothing."

She looked at him smugly. "But who has the most championship rings?"

Nate chuckled. "Only by one."

"It doesn't matter. It's still one greater than your little Cowboys."

He wished to lean over and squeeze her tight before planting a kiss on her sassy mouth. "You said you're not a Texan, so… where are you from?"

"Pittsburgh."

"Really? I had no idea."

"Yep," she nodded. "Born and raised."

"You could've fooled me. I wouldn't't've guessed you were from there. So what brought you to Texas? You have family here?"

"Nope. No family. I just wanted to be somewhere with warmer weather."

"Gotcha."

Her cell phone pinged, stealing her attention away from him. He stared out of the window as she carried on a conversation via text message. He wondered who she was chatting with. Was it the boyfriend she won't admit she has? The man behind the reason she won't go out with him?

She set her phone down after a while and sighed heavily. "I did not expect it to take this long. What could be the hold-up?"

"It's Saturday night. I can imagine it would be busy. Or it could be your insurance company. Are you sure you have a good one?"

"Excuse you?" she cut her eyes at him.

Nate laughed. "I'm just joking."

"My insurance is great, thank you very much."

"So… when can I take you out for lunch, Tora?" He intentionally threw the question out there to catch her off guard.

She tossed her head back and rolled her eyes. "Oh, god. Not again."

"You have no choice now that I'm right here in front of you. If the answer is no, I need to know why. Specific answers only. None of this 'because I said so' craziness, either."

"You are very demanding," she said.

"I don't think I am. Just want to take a cute lady out and hopefully get to know more about her." Nate caught the blush on her face before she turned to look out of the window. "Was that your man you were talking to?" he asked.

"Okay, now you're just being nosy."

"I'm not sure why it's so hard for you to just come out and tell the truth. Is it one of those situations where you two are still together, but not really together?"

She stared at him a moment before she said, "It's nobody."

"Okay. Well… now that that's understood, the least you can do is have lunch with me. I won't be inconsiderate and ask for a discount off tonight's services. A simple lunch will suffice. To use your term."

Her eyes widened in disbelief. "Nate, are you seriously resorting to coercion now?"

He chuckled.

"If anything, your sister is the one I'm indebted to, not you."

Nate shook his head and raked a hand over his locks. "I swear I've never had to work this hard."

"My guess is you're used to getting every woman you want. Which doesn't surprise me."

"No. That's not what I'm saying." He wondered if he was wasting his time. If maybe he should just accept that she held no interest in him and he should move on.

But he couldn't do it.

Never in his life had he met a woman with such sex appeal. And he wasn't ashamed to admit his infatuation was purely physical since there was nothing else he could base it on. The women of his past were the strait-laced types. Women like his mother and sister who projected modesty in their style and dress. There was absolutely nothing wrong with modesty he believed, but he also admired a woman who was comfortable in her body and had no reservations about showing a little skin. The tattoo and nose ring Tora wore let him know she was a wholly different type of woman—something he'd never experienced. It didn't even bother him that she had a few inches over him in height, either. To him, looking up to her was to look up into the face of a goddess.

"Finally," she huffed.

Nate looked over his shoulder to see roadside assistance had arrived. "You're not off the hook," he said, touching her forearm. "I want my answer by the end of the night."

She laughed and exited the jeep.

TWENTY

He was doing it on purpose. Every time she turned around he was staring right at her from across the room. And he was easy to spot because, while all the other men in attendance sported their dark suit jackets, Nate had shed his and walked about in only the suit bottoms and crisp shirt. The clothing fit him as if they were tailor-made exclusively to showcase a lean and fit body such as his without being too tight.

Tora wandered over to a corner, keeping an eye out for another perfect photo opportunity. She'd apologized profusely to Nate's sister when they arrived and got right to work in attempt to make up for the lost time. The guests were eating now and listening to the jazzy tunes put forth by the live band. She had to pretend Nate didn't have an affect on her, so she focused her attention elsewhere: at the tables where light conversation and laughter were punctuated by the clinking of silverware against glass plates, at the servers working diligently to refill champagne flutes and water goblets, the redhead that had winked and smiled at her on more than one occasion, down at her shoes as he appeared to be headed her way now.

He came to stand beside her against the wall. "You're probably thinking what I'm thinking," he said.

"What's that?" Tora asked without looking at him.

"That this is the most boring engagement party in the world. What kinda bullshit is this?"

Tora laughed out loud but quickly covered her mouth.

"This isn't a party at all. More like a banquet. Where's the music? Where's the dancing? Everybody's just sitting around."

"Well… everyone's eating right now," she said. "Maybe they'll have energy to dance afterwards."

"With that crap they're playing?" He gestured towards the front of the room where the band was perched on a low platform. "We need some *real* music. The kind that gets people moving. Ass-shaking music."

Tora pursed her lips.

He held up his hand. "I'm Travis by the way."

"Tora," she said, taking his hand. He was a handsome one despite the scruffy hair and beard, with a pair of eyes so light she couldn't determine if they were blue or gray.

"T-N-T," he chuckled.

"Huh?"

"Our initials. T and T. So you know if we come together it'll be dynamite."

She rolled her eyes. "Really?"

"I've been watching you all night."

She only smiled before glancing back across the room. Nate was looking right at her. "How do you know Nate's sister?" she asked him.

"Oh… Sunny and Nate? I've known those two since high school. We grew up down the street from each other. Great friends."

She nodded. "Ah, okay. So you're from the River Oaks area, too?"

"Yep," he answered with an emphasis on the 'p'. He turned to look at her. "But I came over not only to introduce myself, but also ask if you would be willing to hook up with me sometime?"

"Not this one. You can forget that."

Both Tora and Travis looked up to find Nate who seemed to appear out of thin air.

Travis grinned and slapped his arm around Nate's shoulder. "Dude… I'm enjoying the party. It's real laid-back."

Tora looked at Travis quizzically.

Nate said, "I'm glad you are, but why don't you go and mingle with the other ladies? She's here on business, and she's not the woman you wanna mess with. Trust me." Then he held a hand in front of his mouth to speak something into Travis's ear.

Travis removed his arm from Nate's shoulder and looked at Tora before shaking his head and walking off.

"Umm… *what* did you tell him?" she asked Nate.

He chuckled. "You don't have to worry about him for the rest of the night that's for sure."

"Why? What did you say?"

He chuckled some more.

"Are you cock-blocking?"

Shrugging his shoulders, he said, "Call it what you want, but I'm not having it."

"Having what?"

"You going out with him. Not in this lifetime."

She chuckled. "If my memory serves me correctly I am a grown woman with my own mind and right to choose whatever the hell I want to do."

"He's not it. I mean… he's a cool dude, got a bit of a drinking problem, but… no."

"How do I know you're not just saying things to put him down? He said y'all were good friends."

"That's not what you need."

Tora was amused by his not-so-subtle efforts to claim her. She'd lost count the number of times he'd voiced something of the sort throughout the day.

Suddenly, the music ceased and everyone's attention went to the center of the room where Victoria stood with a mic in her hand. She cleared her throat before raising it to her mouth. "I just want to take a few minutes of your time and say a few things before you all start trickling out of here. I know it's late and you want to get your babies home and put them to bed. And a few of you are ready to get in bed yourselves. I'm at the age where my mind and body begins to shut down around eight o'clock, so I understand."

Handclaps and laughter flowed through the room.

"It's a wonder I'm still standing here at this hour," she continued. "But I just want to say thank you for coming out to celebrate this occasion with my daughter. It's been a long time coming, but we all are excited—her father and I especially—to finally see her start on the marriage journey. It's unfortunate my son-in-law couldn't be here so you all could meet him—the ones that don't know him, but a family emergency held him up...."

"That's some shit," Nate said under his breath, surprising Tora.

"But I am wishing Sunny and Levi a long and happy life together," Victoria said. "Her father and I have been married for thirty-five years and are still very much in love as we were on the day we married—"

More applause and sharp whistles echoed around the ballroom.

Tora watched Victoria turn towards the table where her daughter sat.

"Sunny, marriage takes compassion and patience and understanding and sacrifices and the devotion to do what it takes to keep the love going strong. I pray you have the type of relationship you witnessed between your father and me and that the two of you are happy for the rest of your days together. I love you and I'm so very proud of the hardworking, upstanding lady you've become."

Victoria had to wait for the ovation to subside before she spoke again. "Sunny, would you like to come up here and say something to the guests?"

Sunny dabbed at the tears falling from her eyes and shook her head no.

Victoria chuckled and turned back to the audience. "Well… she's a little choked up right now, so I won't pressure her to speak. She also thanks you for coming and wish you all will be attending the wedding in the next couple months. Invitations will be going out soon." Taking a deep breath, she said, "Well, I hope you all are enjoying the party. Mr. Walker and I don't intend to leave until the last person is gone, so please don't feel obligated to rush out of here if you'd like to stay awhile and listen to the band and have a few more glasses of champagne. There's plenty of food left, too, so please… help yourselves. Oh! While I'm at it, I also want to thank the people who came to my aid and allowed me to put this together on such short notice. The Ballroom…"

"Are you ready to go?" Nate asked Tora.

She looked at him. "What? I can't leave until your sister leaves. You heard your mom say they'll be here for a while."

"You don't have to stay until the very end. You've done your part."

"Nate, I can't do that. Especially since I showed up late in the first place."

"Well, I'm ready to go, and I need a ride home. Be right back," he said, and walked off.

Tora jutted her lip and blew some air. She was ready to go as well. Her stomach was practically turning in on itself she was so hungry. And the heels she wore had stopped being comfortable about an hour ago. But she was committed to her client and wouldn't leave.

She watched Nate walk over to his sister's table and whisper something in her ear, then he approached their father.

"Let's go," he said when he returned.

"Nate, are you sure your sister is okay with this?"

"We wouldn't be leaving if she wasn't." He grabbed her bag and led her out a side exit door at the rear of the ballroom.

They were headed towards the elevator banks in the corridor when Kaneesa called out from behind. "*Excuse me!* Nate, *I know* you're not leaving before the party is over."

They turned around. Kaneesa was looking directly at Tora although she'd addressed Nate.

"How dare y'all try to leave now!"

Nate said, "Sunny is okay with it, so there's nothing for you to worry about, Kaneesa."

"Y'know… it's really blowing my mind how selfish you're acting right now. This is your sister's engagement party!"

"You need to lower your voice, Kaneesa," he said. "Sunny no longer cares about this party since the main person that's supposed to be here with her is not here. And yet I'm the selfish one?"

"That's beside the point, Nate."

"No, that is the point. You think I want to stand in there and see my mama having to lie to these people to cover Levi's punk-ass? Or see my sister crying? Don't tell me you actually believed Sunny's tears were tears of joy?"

"Nate, you have no idea what you're talking about. He is helping his sister. Y'know… like you had to help *her*," she motioned towards Tora.

Tora felt as though she was right there in the Walkers' driveway again, being a witness to the family's drama.

Nate said, "Kaneesa, days or weeks or months from now when my sister looks at the pictures from this night, I doubt she will remember how I left an hour early, but *she will* remember how her fiancé—the father of her children, the one who's supposed to be her biggest supporter for life—didn't love her enough to go through hell or high water to ensure he would be at this party tonight." Nate grabbed Tora's hand and left for the elevator.

Tora realized whatever was going on with his sister bothered him a great deal, so she made no complaints about his fingers entwined with hers. And he was still holding her hand as they exited the elevator and stepped into the parking garage.

It wasn't until he'd assisted her in the jeep and took his place on the passenger side that he apologized. "That's the second time today you had to see something like that. I'm sorry. We're not this way all the time."

"It's fine. I completely understand." She started the jeep and pulled out of the garage, headed towards Nate's parents' house.

They rode in silence for awhile before she said, "I feel bad for your sister." At the party, Tora thought it was strange then that the fiancé wasn't present for any of the photos, but she had no idea the reason behind it. She only focused on doing her best to capture beautiful memories for her client. But now she knew he hadn't even shown up.

"I do too, but that guy—" he shook his head. "Well… I don't even wanna talk about him right now. I wanna talk about something else."

Tora glanced at him out the corner of her eye. She wanted to keep her attention on the road this time for fear of another disaster involving a pot hole. But she knew what Nate was going to say before she asked the question, "What do you want to talk about?"

He looked over at her. "Us."

Her stomach answered before she could. And because they were sitting at a stoplight near the turn onto the Walkers' street, it was loud and clear. A growl. Long and slow and mournful like a lost dog.

Her eyes widened as she looked at him. Then the two of them burst with laughter.

Nate said, "Are you hungry or did you eat something bad?"

"Hungry," she said. "All I had this whole day was some toast."

"Then we definitely need to get you something to eat," he chuckled.

"I will as soon as I get back to my apartment." She pulled in front of the Walker estate. "By the way… your parents' house is gorgeous. A dream house," she said, placing the jeep in Park and releasing the door locks. "I love those private terraces."

"Come inside. I'll give you a tour."

"It's late. I should go," she said, shaking her head. "I will start on your sister's photos tomorrow morning."

Nate reached over and turned the key in the ignition, shutting the vehicle off. "I don't want you passing out from hunger on your way home. We still got leftovers from earlier. It won't take long."

She sighed in resignation and got out of the jeep. As soon as she stood on the pavement her feet throbbed in protest. The pumps she wore were one of several pairs that didn't cause discomfort after all-day wear, which was the reason why she'd chosen them, so she wondered what was different about today. But perhaps her body was just irritable and in need of sustenance to revitalize blood flow.

Her phone began to vibrate in her handbag as she stood waiting for Nate to unlock the door. She knew it was either her mother or her father calling since she normally would have called them by now.

"Is that Nobody calling to find out where you are?"

"Ha. Ha." she jeered playfully, stepping into the foyer with him. Her father was just one of the missed calls she noticed. All five of the others—including a couple text messages—were from Eric.

She followed Nate to the kitchen and he told her to have a seat at the island while he went to the sink to wash his hands.

"Can I have a cupcake?" she asked. A box of the tempting treats sat on the counter in front of her. She remembered seeing Kaneesa haul them in earlier.

Nate turned from the sink to face her. "I thought you wanted some real food."

"I do. But I want a cupcake, too." She was so hungry she couldn't wait another second. "I'll eat this while you warm the leftovers."

He shook his head and smiled. "Knock yourself out."

And she did in four bites.

A half-hour later she was enjoying her second helping of the shrimp kebabs and jasmine rice he'd warmed in the microwave. She'd slid out of her shoes and had her toes curled around the rungs of the bar stool. It was the relief she needed.

"I'm ready for my answer now," he said, looking at her as he stood on the other side of the island. His bow tie had been loosened and his shirt unbuttoned, revealing the white tank underneath. He'd helped himself to only a couple of the kebabs and stood as he ate them.

She looked at him just as she was biting into a pineapple chunk. "I'm here, aren't I? And we're eating."

He frowned. "Oh, so this is considered our lunch date?"

"I don't see why not. You said it was just lunch. Nothing major, remember?"

He chuckled and Tora looked down into her plate to keep from looking at him and his hardened nipples. At the ripped abs beneath the thin undershirt. She thought of how it was just eight hours ago when she was upset with him, believing he'd deceived her into coming here. But with the way her body was reacting while in his presence, how could she remain angry?

He gave a slight shrug. "Well... I guess I have to accept that. You ready for me to show you around?"

"Yep," she said, and pushed her empty plate and glass towards him. "I appreciate that. It was very good." She slipped on her heels, but just as quickly got out of them. Her feet needed a little more time. She waited as he scraped the crumbs into the trash can and placed their dishes in the sink. He led her through a narrow archway on the opposite side of the kitchen and down the hall.

He said, "So… back here is the rec room. This is just where we kick back and watch TV when we're all here."

Tora stepped into the dim room and looked around. The L-shaped sofa itself was big enough to hold a dozen people. A barrel pub table sat in one corner. A dry bar occupied another. She imagined how great it would be to watch one of her favorite movies or a Steelers game on a massive projector screen like this one covering the majority of the wall. They exited and continued down the hall.

"These windows are amazing but kinda spooky at the same time. I can't believe you guys leave the curtains open." The house where she grew up in Pittsburgh had only three windows. All were on the front of the house facing the street. Leaving the interior exposed for outsiders to see in was unthinkable. "I take it you all don't worry about a Peeping Tom or a—"

"They can peep if they want to," he answered haughtily, cutting her off midsentence, "but if they try to come in…"

Tora laughed, the sound of it surprising her as it reverberated off the walls and tiled floor. She followed him into the room where she had imaginary tea with Bryanna and Melody earlier.

"This actually used to be a wine room," Nate said. "But my mama had it re-done for the kids to play in."

She nodded and they continued on. He showed her the guest room and then they retraced their steps back to the front of the house. He pointed in the direction of the master suite before leading her up the winding staircase. "How many bedrooms is it?" she asked.

"Just five. Two down here. Three upstairs."

Just five? Most of the people she knew back home had only two. Three if they were lucky enough to have a well-paying job. "Is this the house you grew up in as a kid?"

"No," he shook his head. "We didn't move into this one until me and Sunny started high school. We used to live in a house not too far from here though."

"Travis told me y'all grew up together."

"Yeah, his dad still lives down the street." Without opening the doors, Nate pointed out Bryan and Sunny's old rooms.

"By the way," she said, "what did you tell him about me?"

Nate chuckled. "Oh, I just told him he was wasting his time because you recently joined a convent."

She sucked her teeth. "*Men… I swear…*"

He turned the door handle for the room at the end of the hall. "This was mine," he said.

Tora was surprised by how sparsely furnished and decorated it was. She was expecting to see the cluttered room of a teenage Nate— all the memorabilia he'd left behind once he moved away from home. The only furnishings were a king-size bed, two nightstands, and a lone dresser on the opposite wall facing the bed. A couple paintings adorned the walls. It was as if the room had been staged for a retail showing.

Soft light shone through the door leading out to the terrace. "I love this," she said as she stepped outside. "I would sit out here every morning with my cup of tea. And probably every night before bed." Nate came to stand beside her as she looked over the railing onto the yard below. "It's so peaceful and quiet."

"I used to come out here all the time," he said.

"How many girls did you sneak up here when you were in high school?"

Nate laughed out loud. "Just one."

"Are you serious?" she looked at him.

"Heck naw! My mama would've kicked my butt if I tried something like that."

Tora laughed too.

"No girlfriends were allowed upstairs when we were younger. We had to stay downstairs in the living room. Or on the patio in the backyard where she could see us."

"I'm surprised you were allowed to date in high school. Mrs. Walker seems like the short-leash type of mom."

Nodding his head, he said, "She was. She didn't even want us talking to girls until high school. My sister used to cry all the time about that. All of her friends could go to the movies and the mall with their boyfriends, but Sunny couldn't even talk to hers on the phone." He chuckled at the memory.

"Well, by the looks of it, it seems like you guys had a lot to keep you occupied at home anyway."

Nate walked over and took a seat on an arm of one of the chairs. "Well… we lived good if that's what you're hinting at. But she was strict about what we could and couldn't do, and who we hung out with. Every once in a while she would let us do something out of the ordinary, but it was rare."

"What do your parents do?" she asked, turning to face him.

"My dad is a corporate attorney and my mama is a medical scientist."

"Oh wow. They are some hard-working people." She didn't know what their occupations entailed exactly, but they sounded fancy enough. And anything with scientist attached to it automatically screamed smart according to her definition.

Nate nodded in agreement. "Sunny's an attorney, too. She just made partner, and so is Bryan. My brother Geo is a professor at Rice U."

"Wow," she said again. "So you're from a family of excellence." *And all I do is dress mannequins and store displays for a living,* she thought.

"I was an attorney myself," he continued. "Criminal lawyer. I did that for a few years."

"Are you serious? So what happened with that?"

"I didn't like it."

She looked at him in surprise.

"I've always liked health and nutrition, so… I knew I wanted to work in fitness."

"I see." *From attorney to fitness trainer.* She rolled it over in her head. Silence fell between them and she turned back to look out over the yard again. And to keep from looking at him and all of his sexiness under this moonlight. "I just have to say it again… I love the peacefulness of this neighborhood."

He said nothing. She knew he was watching her from behind.

After a while she felt the sleepiness coming on suddenly, and said, "I need to go. Gotta make this drive all the way back towards Katy."

"You live in Katy?" he asked, standing.

"Well, I'm not in Katy proper, but my apartment's not too far from it. Off Highway Six."

"You serious? I live off Highway Six! On Park Row."

Now why did I open my mouth? She'd forgotten how close he lived to her.

"Where off Highway Six?" he asked eagerly.

A vehicle door slammed shut below and Tora leaned slightly over the railing. "I think somebody just pulled up," she said.

"Most-likely my parents."

"My purse and my shoes are still in the kitchen."

Nate led her back inside. He held her hand and she didn't know if it was because he believed she needed assistance walking down the stairs or if it was to protect her from Mrs. Walker's wrath. Mr. and Mrs. Walker were entering the foyer as she and Nate descended the steps. Unhappiness showed all over his mother's face, but Nate acted as if he didn't notice.

"So y'all finally making it back, huh?" he said.

"Nate, why on earth would you leave the party early?"

"I was tired, Mama. And what was the point of being there? I didn't like seeing Sunny sad like that."

"What do you mean you were tired? We all were tired, Nate, but Levi showed up just minutes after you left."

"Oh he did?" Nate said, shocked.

"*Yes*, he did," Victoria answered sharply. "There was no way I would've allowed you two to leave had I known about it." She glared at Tora.

Tora shifted her eyes, glancing at Nate's father as he stood nearby listening.

"So what was his excuse for showing up so late?" Nate asked.

"I don't know. But Sunny was glad he could make it, and so was I. And you should've been there…"

Nate sucked his teeth.

"You claim to be tired," Victoria continued, "but here you are—the two of you—gallivanting around my house this time of night when *you* were supposed to be with family. And doing your job." She looked at Tora again, her eyes traveling all the way down to her bare feet.

Tora squeezed Nate's hand. "I was just telling him how much I love your house, Mrs. Walker. And he decided to show me around."

Victoria grunted. "Yeah, well, my husband and I work very hard to be able to afford these things. It's something we tried to instill in our children."

"Yes," Tora smiled. "Nate was telling me about that, too."

She raised an eyebrow and looked over at her son.

Nate walked down the remaining steps, pulling Tora behind him. "We just need to get her purse and then we're leaving."

Tora quickly slipped on her shoes and grabbed her handbag once they were in the kitchen.

"You can take a cupcake home with you if you want."

She gave him an '*Are you crazy?*' look, and he chuckled.

Victoria had disappeared, but Nate's father stood at the door, waiting to lock up behind them. "You'll be here tomorrow for Sunday dinner right, son?"

"Of course," Nate nodded.

"It was nice meeting you, Mr. Walker," Tora said, and took his hand when he offered it.

"You, too. Thanks for your help today."

"It was my pleasure."

"I told you leaving early was a bad idea," Tora said to Nate once they were outside. "Give me your sister's telephone number. I will call her first thing tomorrow morning and tell her not to worry about the final payment. And I will gladly meet her somewhere for another photo shoot to include her fiancé. It will be on me."

Nate shook his head. "Tora, that's not necessary."

"How can you say that?" she asked, her voice rising slightly in the night air. "She was depending on me to do a job!"

"And you did it," Nate stated calmly. "It's not your fault he wasn't at the party. You were hired to be here starting at three-thirty and he wasn't here then. That has nothing to do with you. Sunny is not mad about it, trust me."

"How do you know?" Tora folded her arms.

"Because I know my sister. Taking pictures was the last thing on her mind for worrying about where *he* was."

"I knew I shouldn't've listened to you. This whole day was a mess. And totally not how I like to conduct business." She pulled out her phone. "What is your sister's number?" she asked again.

"Tora, it's *fine*."

"Nate, why is it such a problem for you to give me her number? This is crazy!"

He called out the number and she punched it into her phone, saving Sunny to her contacts list.

"When do I get to see you again?" he asked as she got into the driver's seat and started the jeep.

She had to laugh to stop herself from screaming at him. She wanted to scream because despite being so frustrated the majority of the day—and him being the root cause of it—she was having a hard time controlling her body's response to him. Perhaps it was the after-midnight hour and the fact that it had been two years since the last time she'd had sex, but looking at him standing there with an air of nonchalance about the entire day, with his top shirt still unbuttoned, his hands resting in his pockets, looking like the adonis he was, was driving her crazy. His brothers were just as handsome, but taller, and they were married—which didn't surprise Tora—and she wondered why Nate had to be the one lacking in the height department.

It just wasn't fair.

She said, "Now that I have your sister's number, there's no need for us to meet up again, right? And after what happened today I highly doubt she'll still want me to work the wedding. Kaneesa will convince her to go with the photographer she'd chosen, I'm sure."

"Stop," Nate said. "Everything is cool. Don't even worry about that." He leaned down, resting his forearms on the driver's door. "This has nothing to do with the wedding. I'm asking *you*... when can *I* see *you* again?"

She chuckled and threw her head back, looking up at the ceiling.

"Nate… *what* is it? *What* do you want?"

"To get to know you."

She looked at him. *What did I do to deserve this?* she wondered. The finest man she'd ever met wanted her and, because she knew there couldn't be anything serious between them since he didn't meet one of the main requirements she sought in a mate, she had to turn him down. But there was no way she could come right out and tell him he was wasting his time pursuing her because he didn't measure up, so she said the only thing she could say to spare his feelings: "We can be friends."

She thought he would be grateful and happy to hear she was giving him permission to remain in contact with her, but the half-smile, half-smirk on his face told a different story. "Be safe going home, alright?" was all he said before getting in his SUV and driving off.

TWENTY-ONE

Nate studied the images as he flipped slowly through the notebook, each charcoal sketch more impressive than the one on the page before it. He was amazed by the kid's level of talent. If a stranger had shown any of the drawings to Nate he never would have guessed they were created by a fourteen-year-old. They were sketches of random objects and scenes: sports cars, reptiles, a messy classroom, video game consoles, a group of girls sharing French fries, superhero characters, kids playing basketball.

"These are really, really cool, man," he said to Vaughn again as he sat across from him at the table. It was the attention to detail that fascinated him. But while most of the images were cute and innocent, a couple of them raised his curiosity. "Tell me about this one though," Nate said. A kid was gagged with wadded paper in his mouth; a pencil gouged one of his eyes.

Vaughn shrugged. "Just what I felt like drawing."

Nodding his head, Nate asked, "What about this one?" Another kid was lying on the pavement bleeding, his limbs violently contorted, with a crumpled bicycle nearby.

"I just wanted to draw that one, too."

"How does your mom feel about your art? I know she must like it because, man, you are talented that's for sure."

"She don't see all of it," Vaughn said.

Nate closed the notebook and slid it back over to him. "What about your friends? You ever share it with them?"

Vaughn shook his head.

"Well, I'm going to tell you right now this is too good to keep to yourself. You gotta let people see this! I can't even draw a decent circle, but here you are creating top-notch art like this. Man, if I were you I would be showing everybody I know. Because you never know who you'll meet. Somebody might know somebody that can introduce you to other artists."

Vaughn's mouth twitched.

"And since you're headed to high school it's the time to start thinking about what you wanna do after you graduate. It's not too early. That way you can take the proper courses or join clubs and really zone in on what you like to do. Man, I'm telling you, if I was as good as you, had this type of talent, I would be bragging, showing it off to all my friends." Nate knew he was pushing it, but he felt he was on a roll since the kid was responding to him. "So what else do you like to do? What do you and your friends get into?"

Vaughn sucked his teeth in response. "I don't talk to nobody."

"Why not?" Nate asked.

"Because they don't talk to me."

Now we're getting somewhere, Nate thought. "Why is that?

He frowned and shrugged his shoulders.

"Have you ever tried talking to them?"

"No."

"Well, how do you expect to make friends if you won't talk to people?"

"They always saying stupid shi—" Vaughn looked at Nate.

"It's cool," Nate nodded.

"They always saying stupid stuff about me," Vaughn continued.

"Like what?"

"Calling me Big Bird or Chewbacca. And calling me retarded and that I can't talk."

Nate shook his head in disappointment. "Unfortunately, that's just how a lot of kids are, man. They're ruthless. And can say some of the craziest things. But I think it's because they don't understand you. You probably intimidate them a little, too."

Shrugging his shoulders, Vaughn said, "I don't care."

"I used to be teased when I was in school," Nate confessed. "I wasn't always this fit. I was a skinny kid growing up, and there were these dudes that used to talk crap about me, and had something to say because I mostly hung out with my sister and her friends. I won't lie and say it didn't get under my skin, but I just had to realize no matter where you go people will say something—be it good or bad. And it turned out those same dudes talking smack had nothing to say to me when I was winning on the court or football field. I may have been skinny, but I was strong and fast. And they weren't."

Vaughn chewed on his thumb nail, saying nothing.

"Your mom worries about you, man. She wanna see you happy and socializing, hanging out with your peers. I think you should try. Let your classmates know you're not crazy like they think you are. Somebody is probably waiting for you to start the conversation. You don't want to go through another four years of school without friends."

Leticia pulled into the parking lot and he and Vaughn got up from the table.

"I really appreciate you letting me see your artwork," Nate told him. "I can't believe you're hiding all that talent!" He walked Vaughn to the car to meet his mom. After giving Leticia a brief rundown of their workout, he waited until she drove off before he returned to the track. He did a few leg stretches and high jumps and then took off down the lane. He ran two eight-minute miles before getting in his SUV and driving home to his apartment.

* * *

"She put me in the friend zone."

Kevin spluttered in laughter while Jamal shook his head.

"So if that doesn't tell you that you're wasting your time chasing this woman, I don't know what will," Jamal said.

"I think she got a man," Kevin said. "You sure it ain't Chauncey's chick? It's a small world... you never know."

Nate shook his head and waved his hand. They were sitting at a table in BJ's watching the game. Nearly three days had passed since Sunny's engagement party and Tora was all he could think about. She hadn't even given him a chance to take her out on a proper date and he was already in the friend zone. "Why do women do that?" he asked his boys. "If I approach a woman, I'm not trying to be her friend."

"Control," Kevin said. "She don't want you, but she don't wanna give you up completely either. Just in case she doesn't get the man she really wants, then you're the backup plan."

Jamal said, "Man, forget that. She basically told you from the start that you were wasting your time. So... what? You didn't believe her?"

Nate waved his hand again, dismissing him even though what he said was the bitter truth. Tora had let him know that day in the park her stance regarding his pursuit of her. So either he was going to settle for a platonic relationship with the woman who stirred a deep lust within him, or he was going to swallow that bitter truth and forget he ever met her.

"We're always hating on Chauncey," Kevin said, "but women practically throw themselves at him. Married or not. He's out here having fun and we're sitting on the sidelines missing all the action."

Jamal said, "Yeah, but you know Chauncey has never really been about quality. He gets with those types of women because he doesn't have to work hard to be with them. They meet up a couple times a month and do their sneaking around and then go their separate ways until the next month. But he doesn't have to deal with the every day responsibilities of maintaining a relationship. There's nothing appealing about that if you ask me. I want the whole nine. I wanna watch my woman while we get dressed together in the morning for work, send her flowers during the day, cook dinner and take a bath with her at night. Extended vacations. Sit down with her while we plan our fiscal moves in life. Kids. All that."

"And how long have you been waiting for her?" Kevin asked.

"Well… I'm being patient. I know how hard it is to find a good woman out here, but that doesn't make me think about settling for just any old thing in the meantime though."

Kevin nodded his head. "Man, you're right. And maybe I'm just a little bitter about things, but it shouldn't be this hard. I'm a good dude!"

Nate and Jamal laughed at him again.

"And you're starting to sound kinda whiny about it, too," Nate said.

"It just pisses me off sometimes when I think about it. Women are out here ruining themselves with these losers, and then when they're left heartbroken and burdened with kids they wanna wisen up and get a good guy."

Jamal patted him on the shoulder. "Dude, what's in your drink 'cause you're being extra sentimental right now? Everything's gonna be okay. Your queen will be here sooner than you think. I promise."

Kevin laughed and pushed his hand away. "I'm just tired of meeting women that don't know what they want."

"The one that wants you as much as you want her is definitely out there," Jamal told him. "Keep the faith, brotha."

Kevin looked back at him. "Man, you always try to have the perfect thing to say," he laughed.

"So…" Jamal asked Nate, "what do you plan on doing about your situation? You settling for the friend zone and taking your position as her shopping and movie buddy?"

Nate shook his head, taking a sip of his drink. "Naw, I'm definitely not settling for the friend zone."

<h1 style="text-align:center">TWENTY-TWO</h1>

"I don't like it."

"Why not? It looks fine to me."

Tora stood with Candace outside the store looking at the window display she'd just completed—a beach replication to showcase their newest swimwear collection. "Maybe if I swap that floral suit for the solid blue on her, and then switch his swim trunks to the floral. I think that would be better, don't you?"

Candace shrugged. "I give up. You've changed this thing three times already."

Laughing, Tora said, "I know, but it has to be the right color combination. And I'm feeling the blue suit versus the red. It makes the white cat-eye glasses stand out more."

Candace turned her head quickly as a sneeze overtook her.

"Okay… are you sure you're cured because I have a date tomorrow night and don't need you getting me sick."

Waving her hand, Candace said, "I told you it's not a cold, it's my allergies." She sneezed two more times.

"Uhn-huh. Well, I don't need you giving me allergies, either." She walked back into the store to change the mannequins' attire again.

"I still can't believe you turned Nate down," Candace said. She had been home sick all week, so Tora filled her in on the fiasco that was Nate's sister's engagement party when she finally made it to work for the day.

"Girl, believe me, it was hard because he's so damn fine!" Tora stomped her foot and shook her head in frustration. "His whole family's gorgeous! And paid!"

"I'm still tripping on the things you said about his mama though. Sounds like Ruki's mama and how she is with me."

"Yeah, it was crazy. She basically looked me up and down like I was a ten-dollar hooker. '*Who are you and how do you know my son?*,'" she said, mocking Victoria.

"So where is this big date you speak of? Where is Eric taking you?"

"He wouldn't tell me. He said it's a surprise. And that I need to wear my best dress."

"Sounds exciting. I remember me and Ruki's first date."

"He's been trying to get me to go out with him all week, but I was busy working on the party photos for Nate's sister." Tora pulled out her phone. "He doesn't hold a candle to Nate looks-wise, but he's not bad. And seems sweet so far. Look at the texts I've been receiving from him every morning."

Candace nodded as she peered at the messages on Tora's phone and said, "I love a thoughtful man. My Ruki is like that. A call just to ask me how I'm feeling or to wish me a beautiful day. I'm counting down the days until it's official and we move in together. I'm so looking forward to waking up to my baby every morning."

"How is the wedding plans coming along?" Tora asked. "Have you finally decided on the number of bridesmaids you're having?"

"It's a struggle because you know Ruki has five sisters and I feel obligated to include them as bridesmaids, but if I do that there will be no room left for me to include my own sisters and friends."

"Who says you have to include them in your wedding party?"

"Well, I thought it would be rude if I didn't include them, especially since my brother is one of the groomsmen."

"Just select the one you like the most and it's a done deal."

Candace laughed. "And have the others looking at me sideways because I didn't choose them? I can just hear Ruki's mom now."

Tora shook her head and wrapped a sarong around the standing mannequin, readjusting the arms to rest its hands on its hips. "This is *your* wedding. The bride chooses *her* bridesmaids while the groom chooses *his* groomsmen. His mother should have no say-so in any of this."

"Girl…. I just don't want any problems going forward. It's bad enough she doesn't like me simply because I'm from the wrong side of the globe."

"Well if I were you I would choose none of them and go on about my merry plans."

Candace suddenly put on a broad smile. "Maybe after your date tomorrow night you'll be planning your own wedding this time next year. And I can be your matron of honor."

"Whoa," Tora looked at her. "Now, while I do anticipate my big day, I'm not getting ahead of myself. This is only our second date."

"You know me," Candace giggled. "I love love. And I just want to see everybody else in love."

"Yes, *I know*," Tora rolled her eyes playfully.

* * *

She sat on her couch Friday evening, absentmindedly watching a *Real Housewives* show, waiting for the call from Eric. They'd spoken on the phone earlier and he reminded her to be prepared to have the time of her life because Whitney had done a great job planning a special night on the town for them.

She picked up her mobile phone to call Myles, but quickly hung up, realizing he would still be asleep before his night shift. She called Sharon instead. "Hey, Mommy. What are you doing?"

"On my way out the door for a quick break with a coworker. How are you?"

"Good. Just wanted to call you now because it will be late when I get home tonight."

"Oh. Tonight is the night that you meet with…?

"Eric," Tora reminded her. Sharon had laughed, calling the situation strange and funny at the same time the day Tora told her about her first date with Eric and Whitney.

"I hope you have a good time."

"I do, too. What are your plans for the weekend?"

Sharon chuckled. "Sweetheart, you talk as if you'll be showing up here this weekend to hang out with me."

"I'm just asking, Mom." Every now and then Sharon still made it known how sad she was about her daughter being so far away from her, however subtle in the message.

"I don't have any plans at the moment. Your Aunt Kit may call me up to go someplace with her. She's been doing that a lot lately."

Tora's phone beeped, signaling an incoming call. "This is Eric on the other line, Mom. I have to go."

"Be safe and enjoy yourself."

"I will. Talk to you tomorrow. I love you," she said, and they hung up.

Oh my god, Tora thought as a pearl white S-class Mercedes-Benz slowed in front of the curb where she stood. The wide-body vehicle gleamed and sparkled as if it was fresh off the showroom floor.

She'd told Eric not to bother trying to enter through the gates of the apartment complex, that she would meet him at the entrance. Giving him her apartment number so soon was out of the question.

It was bad enough she'd let him convince her to come this far versus meeting him at the place where they were going, but he insisted, saying he wanted to treat her to a proper date, acting as her chauffer.

"Wow!" he said as he got out of the car and came around to open the passenger door. "Look at you! I swear you are the sexiest, most gorgeous woman out of all the ones I've been with."

"Thanks," she said, surprised when he kissed her cheek. "You're looking good this evening, too." He wore a navy sports jacket, white knit shirt underneath, with blue jeans.

"Jesus Christ," he muttered as she slid onto the leather seat. "Your hair. Your dress. Everything."

She was awake until one o'clock in the morning working on her hair, deciding to add some extensions for length and volume to create a ponytail updo. It turned out perfectly for the red off-the-shoulder skater dress she'd chosen as her outfit, complete with gold caged sandals and accessories.

Eric reached into the backseat once he settled on the driver's side. "I got these for you," he said, producing a bundle of assorted roses.

"Aww… they're so cute!" Tora smiled. "Thank you." She laid them across her lap. "Were these part of Whitney's plan?"

Eric laughed. "No. Those were my idea. However, I did let her pick them out." He pulled away from the curb and turned down Highway 6 towards the I-10 freeway.

It was the strangest thing to happen, but Nate popped into Tora's mind out of nowhere after they had been driving several minutes and approaching Park Row.

"We're going to Brennan's," Eric said. "Have you ever been there?"

"Nope. Never heard of it. What type of place is it?"

"Well, you're in for a treat. It's a Creole restaurant downtown. Some of the best food you'll ever have. Whitney and I have been several times, and it's always a memorable experience."

"Sounds good," Tora agreed.

Traffic stalled as they approached the 610 loop, so Tora thought it was the perfect time to ask the question he never answered on their first date.

"You haven't finished telling me why the women you've gone out with freak out after the second date. Is there something I should be worried about?"

"I just think they have a problem with how straight-forward I am. I lay everything out on the table so they understand from the beginning."

Tora looked at him. "What do you mean?"

"Whitney will be sixteen this year. I'm over this whole dating thing. I'm looking for a *wife*. Some stability for my daughter. At our age, a woman has to know what she wants. So I let them know, hey, if you're not looking to be married within the next year or two, then we're wasting each other's time."

"Just like that, huh?" Tora said.

"Just like that," he nodded.

Brennan's was everything he said it would be. Tora tried dishes she never would have given second thought to trying if it wasn't for Eric's coaxing: oysters, turtle soup. However, she drew the line at frog legs, no matter how much he wanted her to believe they 'taste like chicken.' After a dessert of bread pudding and white wine they left Brennan's for the plaza where *Salsa Night* was taking place. Tora watched as beautifully dressed couples danced, their bodies moving in tandem with the high-powered rhythm thumping from the speakers. Eric wasted no time and grabbed her hand, pulling her through the throng to a spot on the platform.

He proved to be a much better dancer than she was, grooving along like salsa came natural to him. She did the best she could and found herself laughing out loud as he whirled her around on numerous occasions. She felt ridiculous because her movements weren't nearly as smooth and fluid as the lovely, silky dark-haired beauties that danced around them. Latin music was out of her element, but she made the most of it, taking every opportunity to twirl in her cherry red skater dress.

"I think I've finally met my match," Eric told her.

"What?" she said, leaning towards him trying to hear over the music.

"You're good at this!"

She knew he was gassing her up, but she just smiled and nodded and continued to twist her hips and shake her ass to the beat.

A couple hours later Eric led her four blocks over to a booth on a corner, just outside a hotel entrance. A horse and carriage were waiting at the curb. She looked at him.

"Yes, this is for us," he smiled.

She returned the smile and said, "Cool, but I need to find a restroom before I embarrass myself tonight."

Eric laughed loud and long—startling the horse even—as if she'd just told the best joke he'd ever heard in his life.

She used the ladies' room in the hotel's lobby, freshening up as best she could, and touched up her makeup with the little she had in her clutch bag.

Both Eric and the coachman assisted her into the carriage when she returned, and they started down the street.

"This is my first carriage ride," she said after a while.

"Well, I'm glad to hear that. I will be sure to let Whitney know it was an excellent choice. Did you enjoy the salsa as well?"

"Yep. That was cool, too. Where did you learn to dance like that?

Did you take lessons? You were looking like a professional out there."

He chuckled. "I learned just by studying others. My friends and I used to go to all types of clubs. It wasn't hard to pick up."

They rode in silence, enjoying the atmosphere and watching the downtown patrons shuffle along the sidewalks and cross the streets for the bars and restaurants. Eric threw his arm across the back of the seat and touched her shoulder, trying to pull her closer.

She looked at him. "I'm fine."

"You're just so beautiful. I can't believe it. If I'm not careful, I may fall in love with you tonight."

She let out a half-hearted laugh. "Surely you're just joking,"

"No, I'm not. I told you I'm very serious about what I want. There's no beating around the bush with me."

Tora smiled, but said nothing, and looked back towards the street.

"Tell me," he said, and removed his arm from the seat to adjust his wristwatch, "what is it that *you* want?"

"I want a relationship," she said without hesitation. "A serious, monogamous relationship."

"I'm your man then," he said. "Don't you look any further."

It reminded her of what Jason the fool had said. "Well, I don't think it's wise to make a decision so soon. There's still a lot we need to know about each other."

"What else is there you need to know? I'm sure you did some research on me?" He laughed quietly. "At least I hope you did."

And she had. Her Internet search revealed he was an award-winning salesman of a local food distributor. He was an active member in his church's men's ministry where they volunteered often, mentoring youth and visiting local prisons. A search of the state's marriage records showed he was twice married. Nothing came up when she searched for criminal records.

She said, "I'm enjoying this so far. Let's just continue this nice evening, take it one date at a time."

* * *

Eric stopped the car in front of her apartment building. "I had a really nice time," he said, looking over at her. "Hands down, this is the best date I have ever had. And I'm not lying."

"I had a good time, too," Tora said. "Thank you. Tell Whitney she did a good job planning this for us."

"Definitely. I've never connected with a woman like I did with you. Not once did you complain about anything. You just went with the flow and enjoyed yourself."

She shrugged. "What was there to complain about?"

He shook his head. "You won't believe some of the stuff I've gone through trying to show women a good time. One woman would complain about the type of restaurant we went to, or one would've had something to say about dancing in an outdoor plaza, getting sweaty and ruining her makeup. Another would've complained about having to walk to the carriage ride." He grabbed her hand. "And I've already told you you're the sexiest I've ever seen."

She laughed. "You really need to cut that out. I'm more than just my body."

"Oh, I know. It's just that I can already tell you're the one for me."

"Eric…" she rolled her eyes playfully and looked out of the window.

"Seriously, Tora. You are exactly what I have been searching for."

"Why do y—" She gasped when she turned back around to find his face just centimeters from hers. "What?" she tried to say, but his hand was already on her neck pulling her face to his.

Tora recoiled, rearing so far away from him that her head bumped against the window.

"I can't have a kiss?" he asked, frowning.

"Umm… no, you can't."

He grinned and leaned closer, his hand crawling up her thigh. "Come on. It's the perfect ending to our perfect night."

She grabbed his wrist, her other hand on his shoulder, pushing him away. "Eric, are you crazy? No!"

"Didn't you have a good time? Don't tell me you're the type to pretend you won't kiss on the first date after it's been established you want the guy."

"What the hell are you talking about?" she pushed him again, but she may as well been pushing a brick wall because his body didn't budge.

His free hand squeezed her hip as he puckered his lips.

"Eric!" she said, and raised her arm, ready to elbow him in the face.

He chuckled and withdrew. "I'm sorry." Shaking his head, he said again, "I'm sorry," and got out of the car.

Tora grabbed her purse and exited the vehicle without waiting for him to come around and open the door. She didn't appreciate him forcing himself on her. Yes, it was a beautiful date, but that didn't mean she was ready to lock lips with him. "Good night, Eric," she said and started up the sidewalk.

"Well, damn. I guess I've ticked you off now, huh? You won't even wait for me to do my gentlemanly duty and see you to your door."

"I'm fine," she called over her shoulder. "Good night."

She entered her apartment and went straight to the bedroom to undress and take a shower. It was only after she'd settled in bed that she checked her phone for the first time that evening. Nate had sent a text message just minutes after Eric picked her up.

Hey friend. Wanna go see a movie tonight?

TWENTY-THREE

Nate eased down on the sofa. He knew he should have stopped after the first slice, but he couldn't resist a second one, and now he was stuffed and miserable. His mother's meatloaf was just one of her famous dishes that held power over him, dominating his resolve, causing him to go against everything he preached to his clients about discipline and willpower.

"Look at you, son… about to burst, aren't you?"

Nate laughed as his father came into the room and joined him on the sofa. "Yeah, I definitely can't move right now."

Gerald chuckled. "That's why I have to push myself away from the table sometimes, or else I would be in the same predicament."

Nate sighed and laid his head back on the sofa.

"You doing all right, son? Everything still good with the training business?"

It was the question his father asked every couple of months it seemed. He never came right out and questioned him like his mother did, but Nate knew his father also wondered if his choice for a profession in fitness was just a phase and if he would be returning to his 'real' career in law soon.

"Everything's cool," he assured him. "It never feels like work. And I'm having fun."

"Well, that's good. As long as you're able to take care of yourself without struggling… that's all that matters."

"Exactly," Nate nodded.

Just then Bryan and Geo entered.

Bryan said, "Man, I ate way too much," and exhaled a burp loud enough to wake the dead.

"You have to exercise self-control or you'll hurt yourself," their father said, laughing along with Nate and Geo. "Has she sliced the pie yet? I made sure to leave some room for dessert."

Geo said, "Not yet. They're in there about to start working on the wedding invitations now."

"I tell you… your mother just likes to spend money," Gerald said. "Now why couldn't she use the same invitation she sent out for the engagement party since she's inviting the same people? It could've been a one-for-two invitation."

"You know how Mom is. She's going all out for Sunny, glad she and Levi are making it official. She can't have her daughter walking around with three children and unmarried."

Nate sucked his teeth. "Which is dumb. What's the point if the guy is a deadbeat? He couldn't even make it to their engagement party on time. And he knew how much work Mama did to put this together for them. But I bet you she didn't say anything to him about it."

The three of them looked over at him.

Gerald shook his head. "You're right about that, son, but that's your mother. And she wants things a certain way."

"And where is he today? This is the second Sunday in a row he's missed. Had it been either of us skipping dinner she would've had a fit."

His father chuckled. "You're right about that, too. She says she doesn't labor in the kitchen all morning for y'all not to show up."

The Sunday after the engagement party neither Sunny nor Levi had come over for dinner. Nate called Sunny that night to apologize for convincing Tora to skip out early on the party. She told him not to worry about it, that she was happy Levi was able to make it.

It was exactly what Victoria had said.

They didn't care that Levi was late; they were appreciative that he decided to show up.

Nate woke up, not recalling when he'd fallen asleep. His father was sleeping silently on the sofa next to him. Bryan and Geo were gone, and he didn't hear any other commotion in the house from his nieces and nephews, so he knew they'd all left for home. He pulled out his phone to check the time. It was a few minutes before nine o'clock. Tora had finally returned his text message from two nights ago. *Damn, was I that tired?*, he thought, and left the room in search of his mother to kiss her good night.

She was snuggled under a blanket in the corner of the living room sofa, looking studious and youthful with her tortoise-shell glasses on, her hair in a ball on the top of her head.

"Me and Pop were knocked out back there," he said.

"I know," she replied, not looking up from her book. "I came in to check on you two."

"What're you reading?" he asked, surprised to see it wasn't one of the medical tomes she usually had her nose in.

She held up the cover.

"Walter Mosley," Nate read aloud.

"Black Betty," she added. "It's part of a crime series. It's pretty good."

Nate nodded his head and covered his mouth as a yawn came on. "I'm gonna head on out now, Mama. Dinner was delicious." He leaned down to kiss her cheek. "Thanks, as always."

"Have you been making preparations to start re-paying me and your father like we discussed? Your first payment is due soon."

His shoulders sagged. He'd been trying not to think about it. Three hundred dollars extra per month was just something he could not give up without feeling financial strain. But he knew his mother was dead serious about her money, and she wouldn't tolerate any excuses.

"Yeah," was all he said.

"Good. And you still have the paper I gave you, correct? With the account information so you can have the payments routed directly to us?"

"Uhn-huh."

"Perfect. Be careful going home, son."

* * *

He was in a sunken mood when he left his parents' house, and it was too late to call Tora once he'd made it to his apartment, so he called her as soon as he opened his eyes early Monday. "Good morning, my friend," he said cheerfully.

"Good morning to you, Nate."

"I was hoping you were an early riser."

"Actually, I'm not," she said, "unless I have to work the opening shift at my job."

"Oh man… I'm sorry to disturb you. I'll just call back in a few hours then."

"Well I'm awake now. What's up?"

"How is my friend on this lovely morning?"

She laughed softly. "I see you keep stressing the 'friend' part."

He chuckled. "Forgive me for not getting back to you last night. I was at my parents' house for dinner and fell asleep afterwards."

"It's cool. I was only letting you know I didn't see your text until later that night. And this was my weekend to work, so… and I was busy."

"Okay, but when are you free? Since we're friends now, I want to know when can we hang out?"

She laughed again. "I see I've set myself up for this one, huh? Why are you up so early?"

He shook his head and lifted his feet to rest them on the coffee table. She was dodging the question. "I'm gonna go for a run before I head over to the gym. I'm working late tonight, too. One to ten."

"You actually work out before going to train with your clients?"

Chuckling, he said, "Well, yeah. When I train with them it's at their pace, so I'm really not working my body very much."

"I see. I always wondered how that worked."

"You wanna go for a run with me?"

"Please," she snorted. "I can count on one hand the number of times I've exercised in my adult life. The only time you'll catch me running is if somebody's chasing me."

Nate laughed out loud. "You were definitely blessed with some good genes, but you still want to treat your body right and get some exercise. For your heart. And how do you expect to get away from your chaser? You'll burnout within the first fifteen seconds."

"Whatever," she said. "A light and easy walk is the most I'll ever do."

"Okay, well… I'm leaving in about twenty minutes. You wanna meet me at Bear Creek Park?"

"What? I'm sleeping in."

"Come on, Tora. You will feel so good after getting a few minutes of exercise this morning you'll want to do it again tomorrow."

"I doubt that," she said.

"If you don't then I owe you lunch."

"I see what you're trying to do."

Nate smiled.

"I don't even own something suitable to work out in," she said.

"Of course you do. All you need is a T-shirt and some shorts. Nice try."

She laughed and agreed to meet him in a half-hour.

* * *

A jolt of heat rushed to the center of him as soon as she stepped out of the jeep. That sexy brown mid-section of hers was on full display again. She wore a white T-shirt tied in a knot underneath her breasts, and a pair of knee-length light blue sweatpants with the word 'Pink' in bold white letters down the front of her left thigh. White Chuck Taylors covered her feet. She definitely didn't intend to do any running in those types of shoes, Nate thought.

He wished he could put his arms around her, but he had to remind himself he was just a friend. Much like Kevin and Jamal and Chauncey were his friends, and he didn't greet them with a hug whenever he saw them.

"I can't believe I let you talk me into this," she said. "I'm supposed to be turning over in bed right about now."

"It's the perfect time to start an exercise routine," he smiled at her. "And I'll train you for free."

"I am here to walk. And that's it."

"Okay. Walking is a good way to ease into it. It's not too strenuous and will get your heart rate up."

They crossed the street for the track and started down the asphalt path.

It wasn't until they reached the half-mile marker when he said, "Should we pick up the pace a little bit?"

"You can go right ahead if you need to. I'm already getting winded."

"You gotta be kidding me," he said laughing. "We haven't been walking a good ten minutes yet."

"I'm sure it's because my body's not well-rested, considering someone felt the need to call and wake me up at eight o'clock this morning."

Her directness wasn't surprising, but she gave him a look and a smile that let him know she didn't mind that early-morning phone call. "Were you hanging out late last night with your girlfriends?"

"There you go being nosy again," she said.

"Well… we're friends now, so we should be able to share everything with each other, right?"

"Umm… our *friendship* is just… what? A week old?"

He chuckled. "So we have a lot of catching up to do."

They continued to walk along the path as joggers and other brisk-paced walkers whizzed past them. He looked over at her to see beads of sweat dotted her nose, and her mouth was slightly parted as she breathed. He was reminded of his first training session with Jordyn and how she thought she could just hop on the treadmill and walk at 5.5 mph for thirty minutes straight because 'walking was easy.' She quickly realized how difficult it was when the heart's not conditioned for prolonged activity.

"How you feeling?" he asked.

"Good," she said, and wiped her forehead with the back of her hand. "How much further do we have to go?"

"Not too far, but we can take a break if you want to."

"Yeah, because I need one." She exited the trail and cut across the grass to a bench.

Nate chuckled as she plopped down on the seat. "I definitely need to whip you into shape," he told her.

She raised her eyebrows but said nothing, as if she was too tired to offer a comeback. He continued to stand while she sat for several minutes until her body calmed.

She completely threw him for a loop when out of the blue she asked, "Why are you single?"

"Well… it's been a while since I've come across someone I'm interested in."

"What happened with the last one?" she asked.

He shrugged his shoulders and kicked lightly at a rock near his shoe. "Just grew apart I guess."

She looked skeptical.

"Different viewpoints about things. Really… she didn't like that I gave up being a lawyer to become a fitness trainer. She was an attorney herself."

"Wow. So you're just surrounded by lawyers everywhere in your life, huh?"

"We were in the same circle."

"I see," she nodded.

He wanted to ask her a relevant question—why she was being so vague with him—but it would be redundant at this point.

She finally stood and brushed at her backside with her hands. "I'm ready."

They walked the remainder of the track to reach the lot where they parked their vehicles. Nate tried his luck and asked if she wanted to join him for breakfast.

He didn't expect her to agree so readily.

Or to do so with a smile that warmed him all over.

TWENTY-FOUR

Tora pushed her food around the plate with her fork. She didn't know why she ordered such a big platter because she rarely ate breakfast, and the times she did it was usually something light.

And she didn't know why she agreed to have breakfast with Nate, either. It was like the more she saw of him the more she was reminded of her unfortunate luck.

"I still can't believe you're from Pittsburgh," he said, interrupting her thoughts.

"Why is that so surprising?"

"I guess I just assumed you would be from here. You fit right in with us Texans."

"Oh no... I'm far from it," she laughed. "But it's been cool. I can honestly say I see myself staying for a while. The money stretches a little bit further down here that's for sure."

"What was it like in Pittsburgh? I haven't visited too many states up north."

"Well... I grew up in a place called The Hill District." She shrugged. "It was like being in any other inner city hood, I guess. Far, far different than your River Oaks neighborhood."

He chuckled.

"Your bedroom at your mom's house is bigger than our old living and dining rooms combined."

"Wow."

"We didn't move from there until my last year in middle school… when my mom remarried."

"So… what made you settle in Texas of all places? Especially with no family here?"

"I first moved to Florida. I had this dream of living an idyllic life there in Miami… near the beach and shopping and having a cute little photography studio somewhere. But I couldn't deal with the hurricanes. I had to go. Then I moved to Atlanta because, as they say, it's a good place for us. From there I went to Tennessee. And finally… here I am in Texas."

"Wow. You moved around quite a bit."

"I wanted to be somewhere with mild weather, but California is too expensive. Besides, it was interesting to be someplace different every few years."

"So Houston is it, huh?"

"Well… the flooding creeps me out," she laughed. "It's why I moved to a third-floor apartment. I get nervous every time it rains."

Nate waved his hand. "It's nothing to worry about. You'll be fine."

"Nothing to worry about?! I saw the freeways flooded!"

He laughed. "It's survival of the fittest."

"It's crazy! Something definitely needs to be done about these drainage systems. The people at my job already know to not expect me if it rains too much. I can't handle it."

"Are you an only child? You have no brothers and sisters?"

"Yep," she nodded, "an only child."

"So you just up and left your parents?"

Tora swirled the straw around in her orange juice. "Of course I miss them. I call every single night before bed. And I go home around the holidays… if I can get the time off approved. They've been here a few times to visit, too."

"I can't imagine not being near my family," Nate said.

"And I've always wondered what it would've been like if I had a sister or brother. What about you? What's it like having a twin? Is it true what they say? That you feel each other's energy and whatnot? And can complete each other's sentences?"

"Well… I don't know about all that," he grinned, "but me and Sunny are really close. Closer than I am with my brothers. We used to do everything together."

"I think that's so sweet. I saw how helpful you were the day of the engagement party."

"Well… that comes natural. She's my sister."

Tora smiled and took another bite of food.

Silence settled between them as they returned to their meals and listened to the low chatter amongst the other diners. She kept her eyes on her plate for the most part, or glanced out of the window watching other patrons enter the restaurant, but as soon as Nate looked away, she couldn't help staring at his chest and arms in the long sleeve trainer shirt. His body was so tight, but so damn huggable.

And she imagined what it would be like to do just that. To lay her head on his chest while she wrapped her arms around his waist.

If only….

* * *

"I was out having breakfast with a friend. Yes, I got 'em. Yes, I got those too."

Tora was scurrying through the apartment trying to dress for work. She and Nate had gotten so relaxed in their conversation at IHOP they didn't realize how much time had passed. Calls and text messages from Eric buzzed her phone throughout their meal, but she was determined to not let his persistent rings dampen her mood. He'd sent her a text message Friday night after she'd gone to bed, apologizing for attempting to kiss her. She hadn't responded by the next morning so he called, leaving a voicemail the second time to find out if she'd received his text message the night before. A note on her door from the Leasing Office as she left for work that morning notified her of a package she'd received. He'd sent two dozen roses with a note attached: *'Because you liked them so much'.*

This morning it was a teddy bear and a chocolate-covered fruit arrangement.

"You don't seem to be too happy about them," Eric said.

"It's a nice gesture, but you don't have to call or text me every ten minutes."

"Well, if you would answer me I wouldn't have to."

Tora rolled her eyes and pulled on a pair of slacks from the dryer. "Honestly, Eric, what you did just rub me the wrong way. I didn't appreciate that at all."

"I said I was sorry."

"Your hand was on my neck and my leg, forcing me to kiss you!"

"I thought you had a good time."

"I *did* have a good time, but that doesn't mean I'm ready to go that far yet."

He chuckled. "C'mon, dear. We're both adults. This is not junior high school. Don't you find me attractive?'

"You're old enough to know there's more to relationships than physical attraction," she said, grabbing a shirt and her vest from the closet.

"And you're old enough to know that there's absolutely nothing wrong with two adults sharing a kiss after a special night out."

"Exactly. But it has to be what both parties want."

His laughter annoyed her.

"I'm running late for work, Eric. I have to go."

"What time do you get off? Let's go out for dinner."

"No thanks," she said.

"Tora, seriously? Are you seriously making a big deal over a stupid little kiss? Like… seriously? I didn't even kiss you!"

"Talk to you later, Eric," she said, and ended the call.

* * *

Driskell & Co. at The Woodlands Mall was their biggest store location with greater inventory selections. Tora kept to herself, working diligently in a corner setting up a table display for their Summer Tee Clearance Sale. She was still pissed about the conversation with Eric. No one had ever treated her that way before. He may have considered what he had done no big deal, but for her it was a total turn-off.

And no amount of flowers or candy was going to change that.

Instead of going to the food court during her lunch break, she went to Macy's and bought two new lipsticks from the MAC Cosmetics counter: Ruby Woo and Flat Out Fabulous.

She smiled as she thought about Nate over breakfast. He'd told her he was looking forward to seeing her blue lipstick again, that he had never seen anything like it on a woman, and she wore it well. Tora was completely bare-faced for their workout and he also commented that she looked much younger without makeup.

—With these under-eye circles?

—Well… they don't look too bad. They don't make you look old, I mean.

—I think you're just saying that.

—I'm serious. Why would I lie?

—Trying to make me feel good.

—You don't feel good already?

She left Macy's and stopped by a cart vendor to buy a new cell phone case, and then Great American Cookie for a brownie.

For the remainder of her work shift she tried dismissing Eric from her thoughts, but she worried about what she might find once she made it back to her apartment.

TWENTY-FIVE

Nate ended the call after leaving a voicemail on Jordyn's phone. He'd already called her sister she listed as an emergency contact just to make sure Jordyn was alive and well. She'd missed an entire month of workouts now and he needed to know nothing tragic had occurred, preventing her from showing up to their scheduled meetings. Although hopeful, he had a feeling she had given up. He'd seen it happen so many times before with other clients. They set super high expectations for themselves only to be disappointed when they didn't achieve the results they wanted in the timeframe they wanted. In Jordyn's case she couldn't see beyond the numbers on the scale even though she'd lost a considerable amount of inches off her body overall.

He sat at his desk jotting down ideas for his next podcast episode while he waited for Leticia and Vaughn. Not even five minutes into his brainstorming and he was already itching to talk to Tora. His finger was pressing the button to dial her before he could stop himself.

"Ready for today's workout?" he said by way of greeting.

"What? I don't remember agreeing to another workout with you."

"Sure you did. I told you I would train you for free, remember? You didn't decline the offer."

"Nate, I am in my bed."

"Still? It's eleven o'clock. We gotta get our workout in, and eat a good breakfast so we can tackle the rest of the day energized."

"My day will start once my alarm goes off in another thirty minutes and not a minute before."

Nate chuckled. "I'm just playing around with you. I'm at the gym right now waiting for my next training session. How are you feeling after yesterday? You wanna go for a walk again, don't you?"

"No," she laughed quietly. "My ankles hurt."

"I don't doubt it, but that's just your body's response to the shock since you don't exercise regularly. So now you need to do it again and develop a routine and make it a habit."

She exhaled sharply. "Don't count on it."

Nate smiled and shook his head. "I was hoping we could meet again today, but I see you're working late."

"Yep, I am closing again tonight, but I'm off tomorrow. Wednesdays are my weekday off."

"You serious? I'm usually off on Wednesdays, too."

"Yeah right," she laughed.

"I'm serious," he said. "So I think… since we're friends we should make it our day to hang out. You know… like I'm sure you and your friends do… get together for your knitting club—"

"Knitting club?" she laughed.

"—or Happy Hour. But instead, we'll work out and then have breakfast or lunch."

"You're really trying it."

"It worried me how winded you were from the walk. You're too young for that—"

"Excuse you?"

"I want to help you. We'll start off slow. Just once a week for a full month. Then we'll take it from there." Nate knew he was pushing it, but it didn't hurt to put the offer on the table.

"Nate, I'll be just fine," she said.

"C'mon… tell me you didn't feel good afterwards."

"Okay, I'll admit I had a slight boost of energy. Only slightly."

"See. So imagine if you exercised more often."

"Ask me again tomorrow. Today I'm not making any promises."

He chuckled. "I most definitely will."

Nate ended their call when he saw Leticia walk through the door. "Where is Vaughn today?" he asked as he approached her. She was always so generous with hugs whenever she saw him, something he was still trying to get used to. He didn't mind them—loved them, actually—but just wondered what prompted them.

"At home. He claimed he wasn't feeling well, so… I left him behind."

"Oh man," Nate said, "today was his weigh-in. I was looking forward to seeing the results with him."

"That's probably why he didn't want to show up," Leticia chuckled. "Now that I think about it."

"Has he fallen off the plan?"

"I do my best to make sure the kitchen is stocked with healthy snacks, and I've started cooking lighter meals for dinner, but there are times when he's there by himself, so I'm not able to monitor him twenty-four-seven, y'know?"

Nate nodded his head. It was during the first week of working out with Vaughn that he covered the basics of nutrition with him as he did with all of his clients. He also told Leticia it would make her journey to getting healthier a lot easier and less stressful if she and Vaughn were on the same meal plan. He was surprised to find out she had been cooking two different meals every day—healthy fair for herself and hearty meals for her son.

"So how are you doing today?" he asked her.

"Doing good. Ready to get this session over with to tell you the truth."

Nate smiled. "What about your numbers? Blood pressure down?" It was the reason why Leticia had come to him in the first place. Her doctor recommended she take her health seriously and finally do something about her pressure, or she would be placed on medication. Leticia wasn't a large woman, but she confided in Nate that she had trouble controlling stress: stress at work, stress from family, worrying about Deon. And now Vaughn.

"I don't see the doctor for another couple weeks, but I've been following his orders as closely as I can." She shrugged. "We'll see."

Nate looked at her. "Well, you look good that's for sure. And I would brag and tell him how you're able to run a quarter-mile now without stopping."

She squeezed his arm as she laughed. "Isn't that the truth? Even if my numbers don't turn out great, that alone should be rewarded."

He led her to a private room. "I figured we could switch things up a little bit today. We're gonna do a circuit drill workout."

Leticia stood with her hands on her hips as she gazed around the room, looking at all the equipment laid out on the floor: miniature cones, a rope ladder, fitness ball, dumbbells, a set of three steps, and a thick twisted black rope that looked like something fit for a game of tug-of-war for pro wrestlers. "Nate, I'm much older than I look," she shook her head pitiably.

Laughing, he said, "Don't worry, we'll take it easy and modify some things if we need to. This is just something different so your body doesn't get used to the same ol' routine."

TWENTY-SIX

"I agree with Eric. I think you're overreacting."

"What? How so?" Tora pulled out the straight-pin she held pressed between her lips, using it to fasten a knit blouse behind a mannequin torso to achieve a fitted look for the otherwise square-shaped top. "Are you telling me you would've kissed him after the first date?"

Candace blew a gum bubble before sucking it back in with a piercing snap. "First of all, it wasn't y'all's first date. Second of all, *hell yes* I would've kissed him. I kissed Ruki after our first date. I wanted to kiss him *before* the date actually got started to tell you the truth," she laughed.

"He brought his daughter on our first date, so that no longer counts as a date."

"Didn't you like him? You said it was a really nice time, so what was the problem?"

"I don't *know him*, Candace. We're supposed to be spending the first couple months just feeling each other out."

"He was attracted to you, Tora. Wanting a kiss is not a bad thing."

"His hand was practically underneath my dress!"

Candace sighed. "Okay... so he's apologized and now he knows it's not something you feel comfortable doing. I say you should give him another chance."

"And he's turned out to be a pest you see?"

Every day for the past three days Eric had called her no fewer than ten times. And each time it just so happened she was in the middle of doing something or on her way to do something—or dining with Nate—so she dismissed the call and planned to return it when she had the spare minutes. But then he'd follow up with a text message, demanding that she give him a call as soon as possible.

"Now just a few days ago, Tora, you were saying you appreciated how thoughtful he was."

"That's before he showed his jerk tendencies. I'm sure if he found out some young boy was pushing his hand up his daughter's skirt and trying to kiss her without permission he would've been ready to beat his ass."

Nodding her head, Candace said, "You got a point there. Still, I really don't think he meant any harm."

The pocket of Tora's vest began to vibrate. "Speak of the devil," she said as she looked at the caller ID.

Candace smirked. "You may as well tell him now how you really feel so he can stop calling."

Tora walked towards the rear of the store as she answered. "Hey, Eric."

"Wow. I'm surprised you picked up."

She rolled her eyes at the sarcastic tone of his voice. "I'm here working. What's up?"

"Well I'm grateful for you blessing me and taking a few minutes out of your busy schedule to grace me with your attention…"

"Eric—"

"How are you doing, Tora?"

"I'm fine. How about you?" She sat on the edge of the desk in the office.

"We're doing well over here. I came home to have lunch with my daughter today. But Whitney has something she wants to ask you."

Tora didn't have a second to process what he said before Whitney was on the line.

"Hi, Tora. I apologize for calling you at the last minute, but I *really, really, really* need a *huge* favor. Like… *huge*. My dad has given me permission to go to my friend's party—it's her Sweet Sixteen— and it's a big deal. Like… *really* big deal. And we found the perfect dress, and it was the only one they had in the store like it, and I *had to* have it, and I told Daddy there was no way we were going to find anything prettier at another store, so there was no way I was going to leave and go home without it…"

Tora's mind whirled as Whitney rambled on, wondering what was her point and what it had to do with her.

"…And I already have the perfect shoes and the perfect bag… but there's just this one tiny thing," Whitney said.

"Okay," Tora said hesitantly, the word coming out of her mouth as a question.

"It's just a little bit too long. And so I told Daddy we would have to find a tailor that could cut a few inches off the bottom, but he said that I should call you. That you would do it for me. And I had totally forgotten that you like to sew. Will you hem my dress for me? Please, Tora?"

Tora bit her bottom lip. Eric had done it again, using his daughter to put her in an awkward position to help fulfill his request. "Let me talk to your dad again, Whitney." Once Eric was on the line, she said, "There are many tailors who can fix her dress on the same day. It'll just cost you a little extra."

"I know that, Tora," he said briskly, "but I don't have time to try and find one. It's the reason why I suggested she call you. I thought maybe you can help us out with this."

"How soon does she need the dress?" she asked him impatiently.

"Thursday night. They're having a sleepover and all of the girls are gonna be at the Parkers' house, so that's where I'm dropping her off Thursday night."

Tora thought for a moment about her schedule and what she had to do the next couple of days. "Alright. I'll do it."

"Oh my god! Thank you so much!" Whitney screamed. "Yes! Yes! Yes!"

Tora hadn't realized she was on speaker.

Eric said, "So what time will you be available tomorrow evening? I can leave work an hour earlier if you need me to. Should we go to your apartment or do you want to come to our house?"

"Did you let him down easy?" Candace asked when Tora returned.

"I didn't get the chance to. He called because his daughter needs someone to hem a dress for her tomorrow. She's going to a Sweet Sixteen this weekend."

"Awww…. See? He likes you, Tora."

Tora sucked her teeth. "He did this intentionally, using his daughter to get to me. I'm only doing this because she practically begged me to. What would it have sounded like for me to say no?"

"I still say you shouldn't let that little kiss be the reason you write him off so soon. He seems like a decent guy. He just got excited about seeing you in that dress that night. And after all the fun y'all had, he couldn't help himself."

Tora rolled her eyes. "Whatever you say, girl."

* * *

The next morning Tora pulled into the parking lot of LA Fitness. Nate did exactly as he said he would do and called her again at eight o' clock sharp to ask if she was working out with him. She'd yelled at him, called him crazy for disturbing her sleep, told him she was tired since it wasn't until after three a.m. when she'd finally gone to bed. She had spent the night binge watching *Power*.

But she left the comfort of her plush mattress and dressed anyway, fussing at him the entire time as she held the phone, deciding to just do the workout and be done with it for the day.

She walked into the gym and immediately spotted him chatting with someone off to the side of the member services desk. *God help me*, she thought as she looked at him. Even in the basic uniform of gray shirt and black track pants Nate was a sight to behold. His locks hung loosely at his shoulders and shook slightly with each nod of his head as he spoke with the gentleman standing before him. But the gentleman's eyes had fixated on her, which prompted Nate to turn around.

His face lit up as if he was surprised she'd shown up afterall.

She couldn't help returning his smile. He turned back to the gentleman and shook his hand before leaving him.

"Tora, look at you, distracting folks as soon as you walk in the door. How you feeling?"

She laughed. "Tired, Nate. Just tired."

"Well let's get right to it," he said. "I don't want you to change your mind and run out of here."

She had to present her ID and sign a waiver before the clerk behind the desk gave her a 3-day guest pass. She'd told Nate she had no plans of joining his gym, that it would be a complete waste of money if she did, so he convinced her to try it out for free for three days.

After a tour of the facility he led her to the cardio machines. "Which one you wanna do?" he asked. "Stair climber, treadmill, bike, or elliptical?"

"Bike," she said, and took a seat on one. "This looks like the easiest of them all."

He chuckled and showed her how to work the settings and took a seat on the bike next to hers.

Tora glanced around at the other members. At the joggers and walkers on the treadmills watching news and sports highlights on overhead TV monitors, the elliptical trainers who appeared to be skiing in place, at the one stair climber who was doing more posing than stair climbing as she held her cell phone in the air taking selfies. On the opposite side of the room was the weight training area. Tora noticed the dichotomy. On that side were the muscle men and women whose bodies were fit for glossy magazine covers. The outfits were sleeker, more revealing to show off all the hard work they'd put in. They strutted back and forth between the machines and weight benches, admiring their own reflections in the mirrored walls as they passed.

"So this is the gym life, huh?" Tora said to Nate after a while.

"You've never been to the gym?" he asked.

"Nope. Never had a reason to."

"That's crazy. We definitely have to change that, Tora."

"Like I told you before… don't get your hopes up."

He laughed. "I'm determined to get you to fall in love with exercise. You'll see. You've already taken the first step by showing up today even though you didn't want to. So… that's a good sign right there."

She rolled her eyes playfully. "You're lucky I like you."

The words were out of her mouth before she realized it. She didn't mean it the way it sounded. She definitely didn't *like* him. At least, she believed she didn't. What she liked was *looking at* him.

But the smile on his face told her he'd taken her words literally.

"What're you doing after this?" he asked.

"Going home to take a shower and get back in my bed."

He chuckled. "Okay… what are you doing after that? I know

you're not spending your whole day off in bed. This is our day to hang out, remember?"

"Later this afternoon I have something to do—around four—but I am free after that," she said. "I have to go to Spring and shorten a dress for someone for a party they're attending Friday night."

"Oh yeah? One of my partners lives in Spring. My partner Chauncey."

Tora nodded. "So I have to drive out there. That's one of the things I'm still not used to about Houston. You have to drive so far to get to places."

"You're right about that," he agreed. "So what time should I call? How long do you think it will take you?"

"It shouldn't be too long. Around five I guess."

"Cool," he said.

An hour later Tora left the gym without having broken much of a sweat. She and Nate did more talking than working out. The entire time she was near him she could only think about how handsome and fine he was and why she had agreed to meet with him later. She was only setting herself up to be tortured all over again in his presence.

* * *

Tora parked her jeep next to the shiny white Benz. Eric's house was the two-story red brick one in the center of a quiet cul-de-sac. With her sewing machine kit in tow she rang the doorbell.

Eric answered with a wide grin on his face. "Hey sweetheart. Thanks for coming."

He leaned in to kiss her cheek as she stepped into the foyer, but she held up a hand. "Please, Eric," she said, "I'm here to do this for Whitney."

"Well alright," he chuckled. "I see how you're acting." He shook his head and licked his lips as she moved past him. "With your sexy self."

Tora rolled her eyes.

"Hi, Tora!" Whitney bounded down the stairs followed by a pretty teen with the most glorious haircut style Tora hadn't seen in decades. It was a high-top fade with a streak of gold in the front. Intricate design parts were cut on the sides. Tora could definitely see herself rocking something like it if her hair was thick enough to pull it off.

"Hey, Whitney. How are you?" Tora asked, smiling. Whitney walked up to her and wrapped her arms around her, surprising Tora.

"Doing good. Thank you sooo much for coming," she said.

"Oh, you're welcome. Glad I could help out."

"This is my friend, Faye." With a wave of her hands she introduced her friend as if she were presenting a game show prize.

"Hi, Faye. I absolutely *love* your cut."

"Thanks."

"Her brother did it," Whitney provided. "He's in barber college and she's his guinea pig. It's awesome, right? I told Daddy I want to get mine cut like that, but he said no. Not until I'm eighteen when I have free reign to do whatever I want to do." She gave a look at her dad.

"Well... where should I set up?" Tora asked. "And how about you go ahead and change into the dress, Whitney, so I can get started." She didn't want to be there any longer than she had to.

They led her to the dining room. Eric covered the cherry wood table with a bed sheet before she set up and plugged in the sewing machine.

"We'll be right back," Whitney said, and she and Faye disappeared.

Tora made it a point to not make eye contact with Eric as she removed her tools from her bag.

"We really appreciate you doing this for us," he said.

"Like I told Whitney… it's no problem."

"So… how was your day?" he asked.

"Fine," she answered dryly. She stood next to the table, looking over her threads and needles, waiting for Whitney to come downstairs.

"Y'know… I really think we should sit down and talk." He took a step closer to her and raised his hands as if he wanted to grab her shoulders.

She took a step back. "Eric, I've already told you why I'm here. Let's just leave it at that. This is not the time."

"Well, when will you have time, Tora? I'm sick of playing phone tag with you!"

Tora looked at him. *Did he really just raise his voice at me?* She unplugged the sewing machine. "Eric, I'm sorry, but you're gonna have to tell your daughter you will find somebody else to help her with the dress. You are crazy if you think you're gonna talk to me like this." She picked up her bag and slung it on the table.

He grabbed her arm but quickly released it as she glared down at his hand.

Raising his hands in surrender, he said, "Look, Tora… I'm just a little perplexed by this whole situation. I really don't understand why you're making such a big deal out of nothing."

"And that's your problem… you keep saying 'it was nothing.' You have a daughter, Eric. What if someone did to her what you were doing to me?"

Just then Whitney appeared in a beautiful gown with a beaded bodice and pink chiffon skirt. She held it gathered in her hands to lift it off the floor.

"Oooh… this is beautiful on you," Tora said, forcing a smile to hide her anger with Eric.

Whitney dropped the dress and turned around slowly. "It's the best, right?"

"You are gorgeous, honey," Eric said.

The girl was truly beautiful, Tora thought. It was just too bad her father was a jerk.

"Do you have a stool?" Tora looked at Eric. "Something she can stand on while I take the measurements?"

"Hmm… I'll see what I can find," he said.

Yes, you do that, she thought as he left the dining room. She went into her tray of threads to find the closest match for the pale pink dress. "I think you're gonna have on the prettiest dress at this party," Tora said to Whitney.

"Oh no. You should see my friend Monique's dress. Hers looks like a princess gown. She said nobody can outdo her at her own party."

Tora laughed. "What about you, Faye? Are you going to this party, too?"

Faye grinned and nodded, running a hand over the sides of her head. "Yes, ma'am. I'm going."

Whitney said, "She doesn't wear dresses though. Faye said she's showing up in a tuxedo."

Both of the girls laughed again.

"A tuxedo can be cute," Tora said. "There are some really nice ones out there for girls." Tora's phone pinged in her purse. It was a text message from Nate.

There's a bar and restaurant out there where you are called Bombshells. Me and my partners are going to watch the baseball game tonight. You wanna meet me there? It's only if you want to. Or do you prefer it's just us?

She smiled and replied back.

"Is this okay?" Eric returned with a dairy crate.

Whitney laughed. "Daddy that looks like it's going to hurt my feet."

He left the room again and came back with a thin blanket and folded it in half to lay on top of the crate.

Eric and Faye watched in silence as Tora measured and marked and pinned the dress to Whitney's liking. Then the girls went back upstairs so Whitney could change.

"I like to have me a cocktail sometimes after work. Can I get you one?" Eric asked.

Tora shook her head. "I'm fine."

He went into the kitchen. "Taking time out of your day for her just further proves the type of woman you are. I love that about you. And that's how I know you're good for me."

Tora pretended she didn't hear him.

Whitney returned and Tora hemmed the dress in no time. Whitney beamed proudly while Eric took photos and Faye looked on admiringly.

"Daddy, you act like this is my prom night." Whitney rolled her eyes as her dad snapped pictures with his phone.

"Well, you know I like to document every little thing."

"I *know*," Whitney groaned.

"I'm going to send this to your mother, too, so she sees what she's missing out on."

"Oh god, Dad, just let it go already."

Tora returned her supplies to her bag and packed up the sewing machine.

"How much do I owe you?" Eric asked.

"Nothing. Don't worry about it."

"Are you sure?"

"Yes. I didn't mind doing this for her."

"Awww… thank you so much, Tora," Whitney said and came over and wrapped her arms around Tora again. "I love it."

Eric said, "Why don't you stay and have dinner with us then? We're going to order in."

"Yes!" Whitney exclaimed. "That would be cool. And me and Faye can show you the dance routine we choreographed."

Eric nodded. "Oh yeah, Tora, you definitely have to see this. These girls have been working hard on this routine. They are amazing."

All three of them stared back at her expectantly, both Whitney and Faye with proud grins on their faces, waiting for her to tell them she would love to stay and see their remarkable dance routine.

She smiled. "I'm sorry girls, but I can't stay. I have somewhere else to go in a few minutes."

"It'll only take five minutes," Eric told her. "You have to stay and see this."

"Yeah, just five minutes," Whitney agreed with a cheeky smile. "Just let me go and take off my dress!"

Whitney was smooth, but Faye definitely had better timing and energy. Tora sat on the couch wide-eyed, watching as they pop-locked and snaked and rolled.

"She gets her dancing skills from her father," Eric said.

Tora clapped her hands when the song ended and the girls stood there in their defiant poses. "Check y'all out! That was really good!"

Breathless, Whitney said, "Thanks. We love dancing."

"Maybe you should invite Tora to see your dance competition next month," Eric said to Whitney.

Tora shook her head. "Eric, stop doing that. I have so much going on, and between working most weekends and volunteer obligations, I don't know what my schedule is gonna be like." She didn't need him trying to include her in anymore of his plans.

"Are you sure you can't stay and have dinner with us?" he asked as she grabbed her things to go.

"Yes. I'm on my way to meet a friend."

Whitney hugged and thanked her once more.

"It was good seeing you again, Whitney," she told her. "Nice meeting you, Faye. I hope you guys have fun at the party."

She ignored the bitter look on Eric's face as she walked out the door.

* * *

Seeing him was like a breath of fresh air. She'd texted him when she arrived at the restaurant and he walked outside to meet her.

"It's packed in there," he said.

"I can tell. I was worried I wouldn't find a parking space."

"It's always like this when the 'Stros play. You know how that goes. Wait… you're from Pittsburgh, I forgot. So…"

She rolled her eyes with a sly grin. "Don't you even try to start some mess today."

He chuckled and held the restaurant door for her. "My partners are already at a table. They were giving me a hard time when I told them you were coming."

"Oh really? Should I leave?"

"Naw… they were just talking smack."

Nate's friends' expressions were not anything she hadn't experienced before. She was used to the curious stares wherever she went. If it wasn't the way she occupied so much vertical space in a room, it was her wild makeup and sexy attire. She wasn't expecting Nate to ask her to meet him before she made it back to their side of the city, so she had to make do with the baggy jeans and T-shirt she'd thrown on to go to Eric's place. On her way to Bombshells she'd stopped at a Wendy's for a restroom stall to apply some makeup, cuff her jeans, and knot the blue T-shirt behind her back—a habit she'd started ever since she got her torso tattooed. In the trunk of her jeep were the orange pumps she had been intending to take to the shoe doctor to get the tips repaired. She figured they could survive one more day of wear.

Kevin was the first one Nate introduced her to—a beautiful bald brother with a killer smile. A spectacled and plump Jamal held her hand between the both of his as he bowed his head and introduced himself. And then there was Chauncey—a rival of Nate's in the looks department—whose gaze lingered on her a little bit too long, forcing her to look away.

Nate stole a stool from a nearby table and placed it next to hers. "You hungry?" he asked. "I can get you something."

She looked at the loaded plate in front of Jamal. "I want whatever that is."

"It's pulled pork nachos," Jamal said. "They're really good, too." He pushed his plate towards her. "Try one."

She did. It felt strange how they were all watching her as if she were a judge and they the contestants of a cooking show waiting with bated breath to see if their dish would receive her approval. "Yep," she said, licking sour cream off her thumb, "that's what I want."

Nate and Jamal laughed and Nate beckoned a waiter.

Twenty minutes later she was drinking a cold beer and eating the best nachos she'd ever had, enjoying the lively atmosphere around her as the sports fans shouted with glee or groaned in frustration at the television monitors. On more than one occasion Nate got excited at a play and his thigh bumped against hers underneath the table, or he relaxed on his stool and rested his arm across the back of her stool.

She knew he was just caught up in the game and didn't realize what he was doing.

"Everything cool?" he asked after a while.

Tora nodded her head and smiled. "I'm cool."

She couldn't believe she'd eaten the entire platter of nachos and was looking down at the plate, scraping the remaining ingredients on her last chip when she heard someone approach the table with, "Hey fellas. How y'all doing?"

She looked up to see Eric extending his hand to Chauncey but looking right at her as he went around the table shaking the guys' hands.

"I noticed this beautiful lady, Tora, here sitting with a group of guys and had to come over and introduce myself. Which one is the friend you said you were coming here to meet?" he asked her.

Tora's blood boiled. How dare he come to their table questioning her? What the hell was he doing there anyway she wondered. Had he followed her to the restaurant?

Nate's friends were looking at her with curious expressions while Nate studied Eric. She was too heated to say anything.

Eric looked at Nate again and appeared to take notice of how closely he sat next to her, his arm across her chair. "She and I have been spending the last few weeks trying to get to know each other," he said to Nate. "Just thought I'd stop by and meet her friend, that's all."

Nodding his head, Nate said, "I gotcha."

Tora glared at Eric.

Eric glanced at one of the overhead TV screens. "What's the score?" he asked to no one in particular.

And no one answered. Kevin and Jamal and Chauncey were still trying to figure out what—if anything—was transpiring in front of them.

The last thing Tora wanted was to cause a scene, but she needed Eric to go about his business and leave her alone.

He finally turned back to her. "The girls are in the car waiting for me. I'm gonna tell Whitney I saw you in here."

It was only after he turned and walked away from the table she noticed the to-go bag he carried in his hand.

* * *

"So your man caught you on site."

"Please… he is *not* my man," Tora said. She pulled out her keys as she and Nate approached the space where she'd parked.

"I don't know about that. He seemed pretty upset to see you sitting next to me."

"He's just a guy I went out with a couple times, which I now realize was a huge mistake."

Nate nodded. "Oh. I see." He glanced around the parking lot.

Tora noticed Eric had left her a voicemail message. She settled in the driver's seat and cranked the engine. "Thanks for inviting me," she looked up at Nate. "I don't even like baseball, but the drinks and food were good."

"*What?* Why didn't you tell me?"

She laughed. "It's cool. Like I said… the food was very good. And you seemed to really enjoy the game."

He smiled. "Be safe going home," he told her and stood waiting until she pulled away.

Tora pressed the button to listen to the voicemail from Eric once she was on Highway 45 headed south:

"I really can't believe you would lie to me and my daughter like you did. But I shouldn't be surprised. So was that guy really your *friend* or is that just the crap you told us? Better yet, what type of woman would be hanging out the way you were with a bunch of men drinking beer and watching sports? Are you really a lesbian or are you screwing all four of them?…"

Tora overheated. She took the next exit off the freeway and pulled into the entrance of a car dealership lot. She pressed the button to call back Eric, her eyes blurry from anger. "You have completely lost your fucking mind!" she yelled as soon as he answered. "What the hell is wrong with you calling my phone leaving a stupid message like that? Just who the fuck do you think you are?!"

"Whitney was really disappointed when she found out you lied to—"

"Cut the shit, Eric," she said hotly. "Leave your daughter out of this!"

"Here I am trying to get to know you, but you won't give me a chance all because of one simple mistake. It's a damn shame. I see you had no problem getting chummy with those guys."

"Are you really that stupid and sexist?"

"I just found what I witnessed today very interesting. Call me old-fashioned, but a woman hanging out with a group of men and no other woman in sight is just not a good look."

"I don't give a damn about looks or what you think, Eric."

He chuckled. "You are completely out of line."

"Lose my number," she said, and hung up.

She was still fuming when she made it back to her apartment. After taking a shower she called her mother and told her everything. They talked for two hours. When she finally hung up with Sharon she listened to the voicemail from Nate that she'd ignored as she was on the line with her mother. He wanted to know if she'd made it home safely.

She texted her reply: **I did. Thanks.**

TWENTY-SEVEN

Nate sat at his computer setting up weekly automatic payment drafts to be transferred to his mother's bank account every Monday. Money would definitely be tight now that he had to shell out three hundred extra dollars per month. On top of his monthly living expenses he also paid a fee to the gym for use of the facility to train his private clients.

Maybe he would need to cancel his cable TV service and stop going to bars with the guys he thought. But he couldn't imagine a life without ESPN. And, as far as saving money on entertainment and dining out, he could always host a game night at his apartment and invite Kevin and Jamal and Chauncey. His fitness podcast was only a couple years old and not yet bringing in substantial income, but he wasn't about to give it up. His number of subscribers was steadily growing and he loved engaging his listeners.

He clicked the button to shut down the computer after he was done and folded the paper with his mother's account information, placing it back in his wallet for safekeeping. Tora's business card was tucked in the bills slot. He pulled it out and stared at her picture. He hadn't spoken to her since Wednesday night. After she'd left the restaurant that night and he returned to the table with the guys, Kevin and Jamal warned him to stay away from her:

—I knew she had a man. There's no way a woman that fine is single.

—You definitely got to leave this chick alone, Nate. That ain't nothing but trouble.

—She told me he's just somebody she went out with a few times.

—Naw, that dude came over here mean-mugging us like we were chillin' with his wife. She's lying to you.

—I believe her. Why would she have to lie about something like this?

—Fool, are you crazy? Women lie about shit like that all the time! Now you know why she was giving you a hard time, talking about she wasn't a good fit for you. It's because she already had a man.

—Exactly!

—Or if he's not her man then he's her sugar daddy.

* * *

Nate could tell by the look on Vaughn's face it was going to be a difficult training session. Leticia looked just as perturbed as her son. She eyed Vaughn as he exited the vehicle before turning to Nate where he stood on the curb.

"Let me know if he gives you any trouble today because he definitely tried my patience this morning. I'll be back in an hour."

Nate held out his hand to Vaughn for a shake after Leticia drove off. "What's up, man? How you feeling?"

Vaughn shrugged and walked ahead of him.

He decided to dismiss the kid's attitude and just let him have his moment. "We're gonna do a HIIT workout today," Nate told him. "You ever heard of it? High-intensity Interval Training. And what that means is we're gonna do an exercise, go hard at it for thirty seconds, and then rest for fifteen seconds, then go right into another rep. I'll be doing it with you, so you're not working out by yourself today."

It was eight-thirty in the morning and already eighty degrees outside, yet Vaughn sported his usual hoodie. He was making Nate feel hot just looking at him.

"Let's start with a warm-up. We'll jog in place and do some high-knees to get our heart rate up. Ready?" Nate was set to start the timer on his stopwatch, but Vaughn shook his head and stood with his hands loosely at his hips. "What's up? You giving me a hard time today? How about you call your mama right now and tell her to come back and pick you up since you don't wanna work out. How about that?"

Vaughn shook his head again and looked away from him. Nate noticed the sadness in his eyes. He wasn't just being defiant this morning, Nate thought. Something deeper was going on with him.

"You got something you need to talk about?" Nate asked cautiously.

Vaughn rested his arms on the top of his head, looked up at the sky.

"Let's go over here and sit down a minute." Nate led him over to the bleachers and they sat. "Everything okay? Tell me what's going on."

Vaughn sucked his teeth and continued to shake his head. "I'm just tired of the shit," he finally said.

"What happened?"

"Them stupid dudes down the street, man."

"Down what street? By your house?"

"Yeah," Vaughn answered. "They always talking shit to me. And I'm tired of it. It's stupid."

Nate waited for Vaughn to expound further, but he fell quiet for a couple minutes until Nate asked, "What did they do?"

"I was jogging down the street yesterday, doing my exercise, when Rashad and Zack drove by. I had my ear buds in, so I didn't hear them at first, but then Rashad blew his horn. They said something stupid like, 'It's about time you got some exercise, you fat fuck.' And then Zack ol' stupid-ass tell me I need a bra because I have big titties like a girl."

Nate shook his head in disgust. "You didn't respond to them, did you?"

"No," Vaughn said. "I just stopped running, but I didn't say nothing to them. Rashad drove off and I thought they were gone. I started jogging again, but they came back. And Zack started throwing shit at me out the window. I looked down and it was tomatoes and apples and shit."

"That's crazy, man. Did you get hurt?"

"Hell no. Zack can't throw for shit. And when I started running towards the car Rashad burned off."

Nate shook his head again. "People like that… you just have to ignore them. They got nothing better to do with their time."

"Easy for you to say," Vaughn grunted. "I'm tired of them. Next time I see Zack I'm gonna punch his ass in the mouth. Rashad, too!"

"Naw, naw. You don't wanna do anything like that. It's not worth having a fight on your record. Just let it go. As long as they don't put their hands on you, then all they can do is talk. Just be the bigger person and walk away."

"Man, do you know how long I've been walking away?! I told you they're always saying crap to me! Ever since seventh grade!"

Nate looked over at Vaughn. This was the most verbal he had ever been in the entire month and a half he'd been working out with him. Frustration and desperation reddened the kid's face and Nate watched as his jaw twitched with anger.

"Were these guys in your class at school?"

"Zack was. Me and him had the same English class. Rashad is in a higher grade, but we all catch the same school bus. That's where that shit started. On the school bus when Rashad started calling me Big Bird. Zack is his sidekick and always following him around."

"I can understand it makes you mad, man. Remember I told you I dealt with the same type of crap when I was in school? Eventually they stopped messing with me once they realized I wasn't fazed by what they were doing. And, look at it this way… what Rashad and Zack did only proves the punks they really are by their reaction when you ran up to the car. It was two of them against you, but you see how they ran off? That lets you know right there they ain't nothing but a bunch of talk." Vaughn nodded his head, but Nate wasn't sure if he was taking what he said to heart. He held his hand out to him, "All seriousness aside, I'm glad you were out getting your jog on. You're down twelve pounds, so that tells me you're doing something right. So how about we go ahead and get this workout over with before your mom comes back to pick you up?"

* * *

He couldn't help himself. He needed to see her again. It was a few minutes past twelve o' clock in the afternoon as he sat on his couch feeling energized after the morning session with Vaughn. It was the first time he'd ever worked out hard while training a client at the same time. He encouraged Vaughn to channel all his frustration into the workout and to forget about Rashad and Zack's stupidity.

He dialed Tora. "What're you up to, Ms. Lady?" he asked when she answered.

"I am working," she said. "What's up?"

He hoped he wasn't just imagining the smile in her voice. "Just chillin' at the crib, thought about you, wondering when I'll have the chance to hang out with my *friend* again."

"Cut it out," she laughed.

"Are you closing tonight?"

"No. I get off at six. Why? And don't say because you want me to meet you somewhere at a sports bar because the answer is no."

"Why not? Are you afraid you're gonna run into that dude again?"

"Please," she sucked her teeth, "I'm not worrying about him."

"Then… what are you doing tonight?"

"I'm relaxing at home. I have no plans. It'll be a lazy Friday."

Nate proceeded with caution. "How about you come to my place?"

"Hold on," she said.

She was in conversation for several minutes with someone in the background and he thought about hanging up to allow her to get back to work, but hanging up would not give him the answer he was waiting to hear.

"Nate, are you crazy?" she said once back on the line, but she was smiling again. He was sure of it.

"What? Don't tell me you and your girlfriends don't get together and hang out at the house sometimes. I would find that hard to believe."

"You are a mess."

"Seriously… I have Netflix. We can watch a movie. Just relax, hang out."

She heaved a sigh before finally responding. "I'll call you later for the address."

TWENTY-EIGHT

Tora couldn't believe she agreed to hang out with Nate at his apartment. But she figured, why not? It beat sitting home alone on a Friday night.

He was standing in the middle of a parking space when she pulled around to the visitors parking area.

"Are you literally standing here so no one else gets this spot?"

"You thought I was playing?" he said.

She shook her head and laughed. He'd told her to call him when she was on her way and that he would meet her outside to ensure she found someplace near his building to park versus having to walk from the other side of the massive complex.

"I told you parking spots are hard to come by around here. Especially on the weekends. I think all of my neighbors are homebodies. I've already had to turn two people away."

"Are you serious?" she said, exiting the jeep.

"Yeah. One threatened to call security, saying I couldn't hold a space for somebody, but I told him I'll be here waiting for him *and* security when he comes back."

"Oh my god, Nate. Are you really going to go to jail over a parking space?"

"They better not come back around here tripping with me

tonight. It's not that serious."

"You think?" she said, laughing again.

He looked her up and down, smiling. "How are you this evening?" he finally said. "You had me waiting forever. I was worried you changed your mind."

"Umm… I told you I didn't get off work until six, it takes about thirty minutes to make it home, and I had to take a shower."

"Oh okay," he nodded. "So you had to go home first to put on something more comfortable. I guess I was too excited, thinking you would come straight here after work."

He was too stinking cute, she thought. "I see you're looking pretty comfortable, too," she said, noting the Texans football T-shirt and the soft lounge pants he wore. Adidas slides on his feet. She raised her hand and flicked the tail of the silk wrap covering his locks. "What's up with this though?"

He chuckled. "I just put it on since I'm chillin' tonight. I wear it to bed."

"Oh. I see." She followed behind him as he led her down a long sidewalk to his first floor unit. She couldn't tear her eyes away from his ass as they went.

She was surprised how neat and tidy his apartment was. She was half-expecting the usual bachelor pad: mix-matched furniture, minimal décor, things stored in places where they shouldn't be. But everything was orderly, the living room so cozy and inviting.

A woman definitely had a hand in this, Tora thought as she scanned the room admiring the charcoal gray furnishings with black and white accents. *Probably his mother. Or maybe his ex.*

He took a seat on the sofa and she sat down next to him. "What you wanna watch?" he asked, grabbing the remote from the coffee table.

"How about Power? Do you like that series?"

"I've heard of it, but never watched it," he said.

"Are you serious? I can watch that show every day!"

"I know it's pretty popular, and I've heard my partners talking about it a few times, but I never really paid much attention to it."

"Oh my god, Nate. I can't believe you don't watch Power. Who doesn't watch Power?" She playfully rolled her eyes at him.

"Well… tonight's a good time to start I guess. What is it about?"

She grabbed the remote from him and found the episodes listing. "The main character, Ghost, is this big-time drug lord who also owns a night club. He wants to get out of the drug business and just work the club so he can focus on family and making money the legit way…." She sat up in the couch, "Wait… what kinda snacks you got? I like to munch while I'm watching the show."

He chuckled and got up from the sofa for the kitchen pantry. "Umm… I got some mixed nuts in here, and protein bars." He opened the refrigerator. "Granny Smith apples."

"What?" Tora stood and joined him in the kitchen. "No chips? No cookies? No popcorn?"

"I'm sorry. I don't keep junk food in the apartment because I don't want to be tempted."

Tora shook her head pitifully. "We have to go to the grocery store, Nate. I can't watch my show without snacks."

He laughed. "Let me grab my keys."

* * *

Back in Nate's apartment, Tora sat on the sofa with everything she'd bought at the store laid out on the coffee table in front of them. She didn't want to have to get up for a refill of anything once she started the *Power* episode.

Five minutes into the show and Ghost already had her swooning. "Omari Hardwick is so damn fine."

"Who?" Nate looked over at her.

"Him… Ghost," she gestured at the television with the *Little Debbie* snack cake in hand. "That's his name in real life."

"Oh okay," Nate nodded his head. "He kinda looks like the dude in Coming to America."

Tora whipped her head around. "What?"

"The actor in Coming to America. The Soul Glo dude. What's his name?"

"He does *not* look like no Eriq La Salle!"

"To me he does," Nate chuckled.

"Eriq *wished* he was as fine as Omari."

"Well, I don't know about his level of fineness, I'm just talking about how he looks."

Tora rolled her eyes.

"So you think he's fine?" Nate asked.

"Most definitely," she said. "He is gorgeous."

"Okay… so if you were to see him walking around in the grocery store, would you still say the same thing?"

"Yes I would. And what are you trying to say, Nate?"

Shrugging his shoulders, he said, "I'm just asking. I find it interesting how women will see a man on TV and go crazy, but see the same type of man in public and won't give him a second look."

"That's not true. There are no Omari Hardwicks walking around every day." Perhaps she needed to retract that statement, she thought, because Nate was definitely an Omari Hardwick-type. And so were his brothers. As a matter of fact, they were levels above Omari if she were honest. "But men do the same thing," she said. "Y'all expect us to look like the women on these reality shows when even those women are average-looking at best once you strip away the makeup and hair extensions and fancy clothes."

"Well… not all of us think that way. Confidence more than

anything is what gets my attention."

She rolled her eyes again. "Sure… of course you'll say that."

"I'm serious. That's what hooked me when I saw you that first time. You walked in there like you owned the place. Nose in the air and everything."

Tora laughed out loud. "I did not!"

"Okay… you didn't really have your nose in the air, but you definitely had a presence. Everybody stared."

"Let's… let's just watch the show," she said, and picked up the remote.

It was a poor choice Tora quickly realized halfway into the episode. As was typical once Ghost and his love interest, Angela, were behind closed doors, they were all over each other. And the scene was certainly hot as Ghost made love to Angela while they stood knotted together against the penthouse window overlooking a city skyline. Nate was silent next to her and it was a long, awkward sixty seconds. *It's been two years*, Tora thought. *I definitely don't need to be watching this with him sitting right next to me.*

Nate cleared his throat once the scene was over and got up from the sofa. "You want anything while I'm up?"

"I'm cool," she answered even though she was anything but.

He came back a minute later with a new glass of water. "It seems like a promising show," he said when the episode ended. "I'm down to watch another one if you are."

"Really? So you liked it?"

"Yeah, that was pretty good."

She wondered if he genuinely enjoyed the show or if he was just looking forward to another steamy sex scene. Tora smiled and scrolled through the episodes list, quickly scanning the show descriptions to choose one she believed would be less taxing on both of their senses. "I need to take a bathroom break before I start the show," she said.

"Okay, it's just right there... down the hall."

Tora found the bathroom and noticed it was just as tidy as the rest of the apartment. Even the toilet seat was down. She peeked behind the shower curtain as she always did when visiting someone's home and using their facility for the first time. Maybe it was a childhood fear that rolled over into adulthood, or maybe she was just being certain no one was hiding in the tub.

She didn't realize how much liquid she had to get rid of until she sat down. Nate's phone rang. Tora guessed it was one of his friends when she heard him say, "Y'all can go on without me. I'm chillin' at the crib tonight, hanging with Tora." It made her smile, and she didn't know why.

He was still on the phone when she left the bathroom so she took the opportunity to have a glance in his bedroom as she passed. *Either he cleaned up right before I came over or he's really a neat freak,* she thought. The only thing out of place was a pair of tennis shoes he'd obviously kicked off near the foot of the bed.

"After all the sweets I had, now I need something salty," she told him when she returned to the sofa. He just shook his head as he watched her open the bag of tortilla chips and jar of chunky salsa.

"I don't wanna hear one complaint from you at our next workout," he said.

"Who said there's gonna be another workout?"

"*I'm* saying it." He looked at her with a playful seriousness.

"Do you mind getting me some more juice?" she held up her glass. He had no idea what looking at his beautiful face and tight body did to her.

"Not at all."

With the exception of a few droplets of commentary to help him understand what was going on, they watched the next episode in silence. Tora didn't feel uneasy being in his apartment with him.

He'd put his feet up on the coffee table and she did the same after he offered her a blanket. *Why am I sitting here on his sofa eating snacks and watching TV as if we've been best buddies for years?*

"I might have to start from the beginning and watch the whole series," Nate said once the show ended.

"I think you'll love it. It's one of the few television shows I can watch again and again and never get tired of it."

"Well, maybe you can come back tomorrow and we watch it together."

His eyes met hers as he waited for an answer. *I have no idea why I agreed to be friends with him. This was definitely not a good idea.* "We'll see," she said, and dropped her feet from the coffee table. "I work the opening shift tomorrow, so I need to get going." She stood and folded the blanket, handing it over to him.

"Time went by too fast. I was enjoying your company." He got up and stretched.

Tora averted her eyes to stop herself from staring at the center of him. "It was a nice evening." She began to gather the snacks and clean her mess.

"I'm tempted to have you leave everything here so you have an excuse to come back tomorrow."

Laughing, Tora said, "Absolutely not. These snacks are going home with me tonight in case I get a craving later."

"Are you telling me you wake up in the middle of the night to snack?"

"Sometimes," she admitted, smiling.

Nate chuckled. "Yeah, we definitely need to work on your eating habits."

"Mind your business," she said. "I told you before I'll be fine."

"Alright," he raised a palm, "just trying to offer some advice to a friend."

"Well… your advice is unwanted." She enjoyed giving him a hard time.

He smiled and shook his head, leaving the room to return the blanket to the linen closet in the hall.

Tora walked over to the computer desk in the corner, noticing the fancy audio equipment set up. "What is all this?" she asked when he returned.

"I have a podcast show—"

"Do you really? I didn't know that."

"Yep. This is where I record. For now. Hopefully, in the near future, I will have a separate recording studio. When I get a bigger place I mean."

"What is your podcast about?" she asked.

"It's a fitness podcast, so I offer tips and motivation about that. Nutrition, too, and how to develop healthy eating habits. A healthy lifestyle overall."

"I should've known," she rolled her eyes playfully.

"Do you wanna record an episode with me? I can bring you on as a guest, talking about your experience as a person who's never exercised in her life, but is making moves to change that."

"You're really trying it," she laughed, "but no thanks. Maybe I'll listen to an episode or two to support you. How about that?"

He shook his head and grabbed her bags.

Tora didn't realize it was after midnight until she got in her jeep and started the engine and the clock on the dashboard glowed blue.

"Text me when you make it home, okay?" Nate said, closing her door.

"I will," she smiled at him and backed out of the parking space.

All the way home she wondered why this beautiful man was sent into her life. It was torture.

* * *

The next morning she could barely make it out of bed. Early mornings were never her favorite time of day. She reluctantly threw back the covers and went to the kitchen to warm water for tea. Her cell phone rang, sending her back to the bedroom to answer it. She sucked her teeth when she checked the caller ID.

"Eric, I thought I told you to lose my number?"

"Well… it's been two days. I figured I would give you some time to cool off so you can talk to me like an adult."

"Excuse me?"

"Tora, I really wish you would give me a chance to make things right. Please."

She sighed and rolled her eyes. "Eric, I—"

"Let me come and pick you up. Let's talk about it over breakfast."

"I'm leaving for work in a few minutes, Eric."

"Well… what time do you get off? I wanna take you out for a nice dinner."

She sighed again and sat down on the bed. She realized she just needed to be straight forward with him. "Eric, you're really wasting your time at this point. We just aren't compatible, so it makes no sense for you to continue contacting me."

"What?" he said in a tone that he was utterly dumbfounded that she would turn him down.

"I'm being honest."

"You know what… I'm so *sick* of women like you who don't appreciate real men like me! You seem to be the type who prefers thugs anyway. Maybe I should put some fucking weave in my head and wear some nappy-ass dreadlocks, too! Would you like that?"

Tora couldn't believe her ears. The guy definitely had more than a few screws loose. "You are so far gone this is unreal. How would you like it if someone talked to your daughter like you're talking to me, Eric?"

"You leave Whitney out of this! And as a matter of fact, I'm raising her to understand to appreciate the good guys like her father. I know she won't turn out to be a woman such as yourself who doesn't realize when a man wants to give her the world."

Tora had to bite her lip to stop herself from laughing out loud at the irony of his statements. It wasn't even worth responding to, she thought.

"Whitney loves you," he continued, "and she had a fabulous time at the Sweet Sixteen party. She suggested we buy you an appreciation gift. It's one of the things I was calling to tell you."

She wasn't falling for it this time. There was no doubt in her mind the gift thing was all Eric's doing. "Thanks, but no thanks," she said. "A gift is not necessary."

"Tora, are you serious?! Are you really gonna turn down a gift from my daughter? What an ungrateful, cold-hearted bitch you are!"

Tora closed her eyes as she saw red. "Eric," she said as calmly as she could muster, no longer hearing what he was saying as he continued to shout expletives at her. "I'm glad you showed your true colors. I'm blocking your number."

At work, and two hours into her shift, she was still fuming, pissed that she'd answered Eric's phone call in the first place. Just who did he think he was? Badgering her as if he was God's gift to women and she the dunce for not recognizing the blessing sent her way?

She wasn't in the mood to socialize with anyone, so she worked in the storage room unpacking the shipment that had come in Thursday afternoon—the shipment which the sales clerks claimed they never got around to unboxing because the store had been so busy. But Tora knew the real reason was because Candace—the most stern of the store managers—had the past couple days off work and not around to enforce the clerks to do anything.

It was the reason why Candace frowned, looked at her questioningly when she finally made it in for her shift and found Tora hanging and tagging trousers. "Okay… why are *you* doing that and not Brittney and Lupe?"

"I don't mind," Tora waved her off. "It's best I work back here with the way I'm feeling right now."

"Girl, what's wrong?" Candace asked after she'd stepped into the office to lock her purse in the desk drawer.

"I canceled my Soul Meet account. For real this time. I am *done* with the online dating crap."

"Really? Why? What happened now?"

Tora gave her the rundown of Eric's shenanigans over the past few days.

Candace's mouth hung open as she listened. "Oh my god," she spoke finally, "how fucked up is that?"

"Exactly," Tora agreed.

"He is definitely crazy. Good thing you blocked his number." She grabbed a security tag from the bucket sitting between them and pinned it to a trouser leg. "I'm sorry you had this experience."

"There is nothing to be sorry about. It's not your fault."

"Yeah, well, this guy seems like a psycho for real. I was hopeful you would meet someone as beautiful and loving as my Ruki. Maybe you can try again in six months. Take a break from it."

"Girl, are you crazy? Didn't you just hear me say I am done with online dating?"

Candace shook her head sympathetically. "Well… Ruki has a couple single friends, but I'm afraid they won't measure up to your standards."

Tora detected sarcasm in her voice. "What are you trying to say?"

"That they are not six-foot-five even, with perfectly-proportioned faces and model features."

She rolled her eyes at Candace.

"Seriously… they are some very nice men though. Both of them. And they have good jobs. One's a nurse and the other is in banking."

"Okay… what's the catch?"

"Well, one is about five-nine, the other one five-six, *maybe* five-seven on a good day."

"Forget it!" Tora laughed out loud.

"See what I mean?" Candace sighed. "You're so quick to write people off over something they have no control over."

"Please. Don't be fooled. I've been discriminated against by men too, y'know? For being too tall, or not having enough ass and small breasts. Why is it that they can have their preferences, but we're labeled as shallow and too picky when we do it?"

Candace exhaled sharply. "I don't know why there's a double-standard when it comes to that, Tora, but I just hate the thought of you passing up a decent guy over something as trivial as his height."

Tora tossed their trash and grabbed another box to unpack. "Well… it's not something I like to think about, but… I dated a short guy once."

Candace sucked her teeth. "Yeah, right."

"I'm serious. He was the last guy I was truly in love with. If it wasn't because of him I would probably still be in Tennessee."

"What do you mean?"

"I had to get away from him. We were crazy in love."

"Isn't that the whole point? To be crazy in love with each other?"

"No. We were crazy in love, but not in a good way."

"Huh?" Candace frowned, looking at her.

"He was so jealous and insecure I couldn't do anything without being accused of wanting to be with someone else. We were together for three years and it was the best time of my life. I had never felt so sure about anyone else. There was nothing he wouldn't do for me, and I felt the same about him. Then… for some reason, things changed… and I couldn't understand where his attitude was coming from. But I loved him and stuck with him thinking it was a phase he was going through. He became too controlling, calling to find out my every move, wanting to know what time I got off work so he could calculate the exact time I should be home. We could be out having a nice date—or out anywhere—and if I just happened to notice a tall guy walking past us he would ask me if I wanted to be with that guy instead since he was taller."

"Oh my god. Are you serious?"

"It was crazy and sad. So then I started going out of my way trying to appease him, to make him understand that I was genuinely in love with him."

"But I don't get it," Candace said. "What made him all of a sudden doubt your love for him?"

Tora sighed. "I think his friends were putting things in his ear. He told me they were skeptical of me from the beginning—a lowly department store clerk as they put it—and thought I was only with him because of who he was. You ever heard of Mike Stack?"

"Of The Mike Stack Morning Show?"

"That's him."

"Are you serious? I love that show! I listen to it every morning. His show is one of the most top-rated in the country, right? How on earth did y'all cross paths?"

"At an industry party in Memphis. I was invited by a friend who knew someone working there. He came over and introduced himself, and we just started talking. It was the weirdest thing because I had never heard of him, so he was shocked about that. He asked if he could call me later, and the only thing that crossed my mind was the audacity of this itty-bitty man to ask me for my phone number."

"I've only seen head shots of him," Candace said. "He's a good-looking guy from what I can tell, but I never imagined he was short. How short?"

"Five-five."

"Nooo. Are you for real?"

"Yes."

"And you—Ms. I-refuse-to-date-a-man-that-is-not-taller-than-me-with-my-heels-on—actually went out with him? Unbelievable."

"He was really cool the more I talked to and got to know him. I decided to give him a shot. It was a true whirlwind romance. I traveled all over with him, met some famous people in the music business. We had a lot of fun together. In the beginning, I sometimes wondered why he chose someone like me when he had connections with gorgeous women all over the country."

"Well… maybe it was the fact that you didn't know about him. You are gorgeous, too, y'know, and men like gorgeous women."

"It got to the point where I was doing things out of character. I quit my job and moved in with him, becoming the trophy girlfriend who just sat around all day dolled-up waiting for him to come home, or went shopping with his credit card. For a whole year I was not myself. My mom would've killed me had she found out how I was living."

"You mean she didn't know? How did you keep that a secret?"

"She knew I was dating a radio show host, but I didn't tell her who he was. I wanted it to be a surprise when I took him home to meet her and my dad. We never got around to it. I was done once he accused me of fucking his groundskeeper—a tall Dominican guy."

"What the hell? You have got to be kidding!"

"Absolutely not. What's even more crazy about that is he had security cameras everywhere. Why would I cheat on him if I knew there were cameras on me?"

"Exactly."

"I asked him the same question and he said it was because I knew where the cameras were and how to avoid them."

Candace shook her head. "I'm sorry, girl, but it sounds like something else was going on with this guy for him to be so paranoid."

"After that experience I said I would never ever again get involved with a man shorter than me. I cannot deal with them and their insecurities."

"Well that's no reason to dismiss them all. He just had his own issues. But I'm truly shocked you dated him in the first place. A five-foot-five man at that. He must've felt like a midget walking next to you with your heels on."

"That's another thing. I didn't wear them as often when we went out so our differences in height wouldn't be so jarring. It was bad enough the stares we got whenever we held hands in public."

Laughing, Candace said, "I feel like I needed to see it with my own eyes to believe it. The way you talk about them I was under the impression you were absolutely repulsed by men shorter than you."

"He was the first and definitely my last that's for sure."

* * *

Tora laid the throw blanket across her legs and Silk jumped into her lap. It was only six o' clock in the evening and she was already dressed for bed, stretched out on the living room sofa with the television geared up to play one of her old favorite shows: *The King of Queens*. She needed comedic relief after that phone call from Eric nearly twelve hours earlier. His malicious words still bounced around in her head and she was having trouble dismissing them. She'd blocked his number, but a part of her wanted to call and cuss him out for good measure.

Her cell phone rang and she checked the caller ID before pressing the button to answer. She wouldn't be surprised if Eric tried to reach her from an unidentified number.

"Hi, Nate," she said.

"You know I'm calling to find out if you want to hang out tonight. What are you up to?"

"Relaxing at home again. It's been a stressful day."

"You wanna tell me all about it over dinner somewhere?"

"Honestly, I don't feel like doing anything. I'm in my pajamas sitting on my couch, but you are welcomed to come over here."

"Cool. Should I stop by the store to pick up snacks?"

She laughed. "No. You never have to worry about that at my place. My pantry stays loaded with all the goodies. Just bring food instead. Your choice."

TWENTY-NINE

He smelled Tora's cat as soon as he stepped into the apartment. And there it was perched on the back of the sofa, its tail hanging and curled like the handle of an umbrella. Nate shuddered at the sight of it. He was allergic to cats.

"That better not be a bag full of rabbit food you got there," Tora said.

"Naw. It's fajitas. Steak and chicken."

"With all the toppings? Sour cream and cheese and guacamole, right?"

"With all the toppings," he confirmed and set the bag on the counter.

"Thank you! It's a perfect night for fajitas." She grabbed plates from the cabinet while he unpacked the bag.

"I forgot to pick up drinks, so... please tell me you have something here."

"Yep. I do." She opened the refrigerator to a rainbow of juices and soft drinks. "I told you you never have to worry about anything."

He could only shake his head and smile. "Just give me a water."

The cat watched them intently as they loaded their plates. Tora walked over and took a seat on the sofa. Nate waited to see if she would shoo the cat away because he didn't want to be anywhere near it. The only other seating in the living room was a chaise lounge, which looked uncomfortable and not fitting to relax and enjoy his meal. More than that he wanted to sit next to Tora.

He reluctantly took a seat on the chaise when the cat hopped down from its spot and settled against Tora's thigh. "Are you watching Power again?" he asked.

"Not this time, believe it or not. I'm watching The King of Queens."

"I've never heard of that one."

"It's old, but I still record and watch all the episodes. It's great whenever I need a good laugh."

"Oh, okay." It was definitely not his type of show he quickly realized. The humor was too corny for his tastes.

At the third commercial break Tora got up to refill her drink.

Nate said, "Tell me what made your day stressful."

"Oh," she sucked her teeth, "just that stupid guy again. He called me, talking crazy and cussed me out because I want nothing to do with him."

"He cussed you? What's up with him?" The thought of the guy disrespecting Tora—or any woman—ticked him off. He had a low tolerance for men like that.

"He has a problem accepting no for an answer apparently. I blocked his phone number so he can't call me again."

"That's good. Hopefully he gets the hint."

She'd said she'd only gone out with the guy a couple times, but for Nate it was a couple times too many. He wondered why he couldn't get a real date with her. The times they spent together so far were enjoyable, but he wanted a true date—the kind that ended with a passion-filled kiss followed by a night of heated lovemaking.

She returned to her show and Nate was glad to hear her laughing, that she wasn't letting the chump sour her evening. He settled back on the chaise and that's when it began: along came the first sneeze.

He knew the symptoms would show up eventually. He'd been there almost an hour and was surprised he'd gotten by that long.

"Why are you sitting way over there?" Tora asked him.

"Well… I see you and your kitten are pretty comfortable. I didn't wanna take up space."

"This is my baby," she drawled while running her fingers along the cat's side. It stretched its limbs in satisfaction. "This is the spoiled one. He won't let me out of his sight whenever I'm home. Right, Silk?"

"Silk?"

"That's his name," she laughed. "Mink is around here somewhere."

"Wait… you have *two* cats?" Nate said.

"Minky Pooh, where are you?" Tora cooed.

And sure enough another white feline came trotting from somewhere around the corner and leapt into Tora's lap. It was identical to the other one except for the string of blue pearls around its neck.

Tora bounced and hugged and sweet-talked the cat as if she were handling a toddler. When she nuzzled its nose and the cat licked Tora's lips, Nate wanted to cry.

He sneezed again.

"Preseason starts next week. Will you be watching any of the games?"

"Of course I am," she said. "The Steelers play the Cowboys."

Nate chuckled. "Are you really a fan of the game or just your team?"

"I watch others every now and then. I like the Giants, too. But when my team is playing I'm front and center without question."

"And how did you become such a fan of the game? I mean… I'm not surprised because I can't imagine there's anything else to do in

Pittsburgh. Still… I find it interesting."

She tossed him a sassy look before answering. "I had no choice but to be a fan considering my dad was a super fan. He lived for football. It was always on in our house and it's all he talked about. We used to go to pro games. He coached Little League for a short while, too. When I first moved to Florida he would call me to see if I was watching the game, and we would be on speaker phone screaming and shouting together."

"For real?" Nate laughed.

"Yep. We still do that sometimes to this day. He's silly, but that's my daddy."

"That's cool. I see the merch you got around here," Nate said. There was Steelers memorabilia throughout the apartment. "All I got is a few Texans and Astros T-shirts. Oh… and an Astros cap. Your collection puts mine to shame."

"Well… considering your teams' records, I wouldn't be inspired to spend my money on merchandise either."

Ouch! Nate was about to serve her a comeback, but two consecutive sneezes thwarted the plan.

"What do you want for dessert?" She got up from the sofa and went to the kitchen, opening the pantry.

His eyes began to water. "Do I get to have anything I want?"

"Of course. It's the least I can do since you bought the fajitas." She stood looking at the shelves. "Something salty or sweet? I got all kinds of stuff in here. Name something and I bet you I got it."

"Tora." He sneezed again.

"Huh?"

"That's what I want."

"What?" She turned around to face him.

Another sneeze. *Fuck!*

"Are you coming down with a cold or what?"

He coughed lightly to clear his throat. "Something must be in the air. I'm all right."

"I know what we should do," she smiled.

I know what we should do, too, he wanted to say.

"Make root beer floats."

"I can't remember the last time I had a root beer float. Or ice cream to tell you the truth."

"And that's a shame. I'm going to make you one. I even got some whipped cream."

"Naw. I probably should skip dessert this time." *Unless it's you topped with whipped cream,* he thought.

"Oh c'mon, Nate! I know you're into eating light and healthy all the time, but it's okay to live a little too, y'know? Have something good every now and then."

He chuckled. "I do. My mama cooks every Sunday and she usually makes a dessert. Sundays are my cheat day."

"Well… today is Saturday, and I'm making you a float."

"If you insist," he winked at her.

It puzzled him to see her put the container of ice cream into the microwave, but then he realized she only heated it a few seconds to soften it, which made scooping easier. She filled two tall plastic tumblers with vanilla ice cream, poured the root beer, and topped them with *Reddi Wip.*

"I think I still have a jar of cherries, too," she said, and opened the refrigerator. "It's been in here a while though." She studied the jar. "Aww, man! They expired a month ago."

"Trash 'em."

"They should still be good."

"Naw. I wouldn't trust it."

She twisted off the cap and sniffed. "They still smell good. And they look good. They've been in the refrigerator the whole time, so…

I think they're okay."

"I'll pass," Nate chuckled.

She rolled her eyes and ate a cherry before dropping two more in one of the tumblers, and then tossed the jar in the trash can. "There's nothing wrong with them. It's not like it was a jar of mayo or something."

"Alright… we'll see how you're feeling later on," Nate teased, and accepted the cup from her. "Thanks."

"You really don't have to sit over there, y'know. We shared a couch just last night, remember?"

It was the second time she'd said it. He didn't want to think too much into the suggestion, but he was moved by the fact that she wanted him next to her. If only the damn cat would get lost.

"I won't be attacked, will I?" he asked jokingly, and left the chaise for the couch.

"My cats are real sweethearts. They won't bother you."

There was another sneeze as he eased down on the opposite end of the sofa, as close to the corner as he could get. Silk appeared unbothered by his presence.

Tora looked at him. "Are you sure you haven't caught a cold?"

"I'm okay," he sniffed. "Whatever it is will clear up soon." He wasn't sure how much longer he would last, but he didn't want the night to end either.

They talked through another show. Nate wanted to hear more about her life in Pittsburgh and all the other places she'd lived. He asked about her dreams, if she had any fears.

He loved listening to her recount special moments, and was surprised when she shared some of her embarrassing moments. He wasn't expecting her to be so open with him considering she'd told him before when he wanted to know something about her that he was being too nosy. He learned that, despite her affinity for bold makeup, tattoos and piercings, she was a woman who wanted a simple life where she was free to express herself creatively and make a living with her art. Like him, she couldn't fathom being tied down with an ordinary nine to five desk job.

"What about a life partner?" Nate asked. "I know you wanna create memories with someone special, right?"

She sighed and looked over at him. "Of course I want someone to go through life with. Who doesn't? My parents divorced when I was young, but I'm still amazed by their friendship. They genuinely care a lot for each other after all these years. I look forward to that type of lasting love for someone."

"But you're not just talking about friendship only, right? You want more than a platonic relationship eventually?"

She laughed and he worried that he was coming across too desperate in his questioning.

"Well… with the losers I've met in the last couple months… things aren't looking too good."

She got up from the sofa before he could say anything else and told him she was going to the bathroom. He took the opportunity and escaped to her balcony for fresh air, leaving the door slightly ajar. As soon as he was outside he took a deep breath and worked to scratch his itchy throat. Of all things, he mused, why did she have to be a cat lover? There was no way he could ever hang out in her apartment again.

"Did he leave?" Nate heard her say minutes later.

"I'm out here," he answered.

"What made you come outside?" She stepped out onto the balcony. In the short time she was gone she had changed out of the clouds-printed pajama pants and into a purple satin short set. He caught a whiff of perfume, too.

"I have a confession to make. I'm allergic to cats."

"What?" she said, her eyes wide. "Are you serious? I had no idea! Is that why you're sneezing all over the place?" Then she laughed. "Why didn't you tell me?"

Nate wasn't expecting her to touch his chin, raising his head to look at her. Even in his state of misery that simple touch caused a stir inside him.

"Your eyes are kinda red, too. You poor thing. I can't believe you didn't tell me!"

"I should be okay after a few more minutes out here," he said.

"I'll lock the cats in my bedroom," she chuckled, and went back inside.

Nate tried his best to hang, but he was miserable. She'd switched the television to an episode of *Power*, but between constantly trying to clear his throat, sneezing, and wiping his watery eyes he couldn't relax and enjoy her company.

"Tora, I hate to say this," he said finally, "but I have to go. I'm having a hard time right now."

"Aww… you poor thing." She stood and walked him to the door. "How sad to be allergic to cats because they are the best creatures in the world. I can't imagine life without my babies."

Nate chuckled. "I see. Next time we'll just have to meet at my place again."

"Apparently," she said, smiling.

He wanted to pull her body into his for a warm hug.

"Thanks again for the fajitas," she said.

"No problem. I really wish I could stay longer, but…"

"And you should have told me you were allergic!"

"I know," he smiled, "but I really wanted to spend some time with you."

"Just crazy," she shook her head and laughed.

Nate opened the door and both of them were startled by the man standing there.

"Eric, what the hell are you doing outside my door?" Tora yelled. "What the hell are you doing at my apartment?"

He glanced at Nate. "I came over to talk to you, Tora."

"You need to leave right now or I'm calling the police. How *dare you* show up to my front door!"

"Oh, come on. You're being overly dramatic. I just want to talk to you."

"I've told you before we have nothing to talk about, Eric. Especially after all the shit you said to me."

"Look… I was upset, okay? And just talking out of my ass."

"Eric, leave," Tora said tightly.

Nate stood between them watching and waiting. Waiting to see if he would need to intervene on Tora's behalf should the guy try something crazy.

Eric looked at him. "Will you give us a few minutes, buddy?"

Tora tried to step around him, but Nate raised his arm to keep her back. "Hey, man," he said to Eric, "I'm not sure who you are, but she's a friend of mine. And she asked you to leave. So why not respect her wishes and go?"

Eric stared Tora down. Shaking his head, he finally turned to Nate. "Yeah, well, it looks like you got farther with her than I did. Congratulations," he said, and walked off.

"You son-of-a-bitch!" Tora screamed as Nate closed the door.

"What's up with that guy, man?" Nate said.

"He's an arrogant bastard," Tora said.

"You need to call the police and report him." He followed her back over to the sofa and sat down next to her.

"I know he must've followed someone in the security gates."

"Right," Nate nodded his head. "I've always thought those gates were a joke myself. Has he ever done this before?"

"No. I haven't even known him that long. We went out only two times."

"Well, this guy is definitely crazy if he's showing up to your place uninvited, so you should go ahead and call the police just so it's on record." He stepped out onto the balcony as she made the phone call. He scanned the sidewalks just to be certain the punk wasn't still hanging around.

When the police arrived, Tora gave a report of all she knew about Eric, how they met, and details of their conversations. Nate tried not to be jealous as he listened to her recall their nights out together.

One officer pulled him aside and questioned him, surprising Nate when he said:

—Listen…we come across women like her all the time. Are you sure she didn't set this whole thing up? It wouldn't surprise me one bit if she did just to have you two fighting over her. We've seen it plenty of times before.

There was no way he was going to leave her alone tonight, Nate thought, so when the unenthused officers left, he said, "You might as well pack an overnight bag and stay with me tonight. In case that fool comes back and tries something."

"Nate, I'm not gonna let him run me out of my apartment! I'll be fine."

"Are you sure?"

"Yes. I'm not going to give him control over me. I have a Taser. And will have no problem zapping his ass if he shows up again acting crazy."

"Alright, well… call me if you need me." This time he did wrap his arms around her and told her to stay safe before he walked out the door.

But it wasn't until he pulled into his own apartment complex that he was compelled to return to hers. He picked up his smartphone and called her. "Tora," he said, "I can't do it. I won't be able to sleep tonight. I'm spending the night with you."

"What?" she said. "You don't have to do that, Nate. I am fine."

"I don't trust him."

"What about your allergy?"

"I'll tough it out."

THIRTY

"If that doesn't make you wanna drop your hang-ups and give that man a chance, then you are the dumbest woman in the world for real. Just saying."

Tora rolled her eyes, but smiled at Candace. "It was so sweet of him to do that. Poor guy sneezed and coughed all night. And when we woke up the next morning his eyes were so red and swollen. I felt so bad for him!"

"Allergies are no joke. Some people die from theirs, Tora. He could've died trying to protect you from a jackass!"

"I know." Tora shook her head sympathetically. "I asked if he wanted me to take him to the emergency room, but he told me he felt okay and just needed some fresh air. He refused the Benadryl I offered."

Candace popped her gum and a devilish grin curved her lips. "So… where did he sleep?"

"Oh god, Candace. He slept on the couch!"

Candace tsked. "What a shame. The man puts his health—and life—at risk to take care of you and you made him sleep on a hard couch. I would've had that fine, sexy man in my bed so fast!"

Tora laughed out loud. She wouldn't tell Candace the thought had crossed her mind. That night, in the early predawn hour, she'd gotten out of bed for a drink of juice as she oftentimes did in the middle of the night. She thought Nate was sound asleep on the sofa, and she tiptoed through the kitchen, but just as she opened the cabinet to grab a glass his voice echoed in the darkness.

—You okay? he said.

Tora turned around and almost dropped the glass at the sight of him standing there wearing only his boxer briefs. Even in the dark room his silhouette left nothing to the imagination and Tora found herself clutching the counter for balance as her heart and stomach cartwheeled at the outline of every curve of every muscle on his body.

—Just getting a drink, she said. Are you okay?

—Yeah. Just went to the bathroom to grab some tissue.

—I'm so sorry.

—It's nothing. I just wanna make sure you're good. That you're not losing sleep over this crazy dude Eric.

—I'm sleeping fine. Just got thirsty.

—Well… come and get me if you need me for anything.

She'd climbed back into bed with a knuckle between her teeth to stifle a whimper because the man was so damn fine and she definitely needed him. Needed him in her bed, between her legs….

"He insisted we be friends after I told him there couldn't be anything between us," Tora said to Candace. "So… that's what we are. I told you I was burned before. I'm not going through that again."

Candace rolled her eyes heavenward. "Fine," she said, "but I don't wanna hear nothing out of your mouth when some other woman snatches him up."

* * *

"Ohhh… you are such a cutie, I wish I could take you home with me." Tora returned the cat to its cage—a beautiful fat and fluffy Maine Coon who was the newest addition to the shelter. After leaving

Driskell & Co. for the day Tora decided to put in a couple volunteer hours. Nate was all she could think about as she tended to the fur babies. When he walked her to her jeep the morning after he stayed the night, he warned her to be on the lookout for Eric and to also report him to the Leasing Office so they have a description of his car. She'd told him she appreciated his concern, but she was a big girl and knew how to handle Eric if necessary. But he'd given her a no-nonsense look and told her to do as he suggested, and she had to admit it turned her on as he stood there, swollen eyes and all. He then told her he would call later that night to make sure she'd made it home safely, which he did.

And he'd called every morning and night since then.

She wondered what he was doing now as she cleaned her hands in the restroom before heading to the front desk to return the volunteer badge. She was still feeling bad for how he suffered through the night at her apartment.

She wanted to see him. A thought came to mind just as she was exiting the doors of the shelter.

"Oh, Tora?" the receptionist called after her.

"Yes?" she turned around.

"We were viewing your profile and noticed that you're also a photographer. We're getting ready to update the adoption photos in preparation for fall. Is this something you would be willing to help us with?"

Tora smiled. "Of course. I'd love to."

"Okay. We will be starting that sometime in the next couple weeks, so we will give you a call and work out a schedule soon, okay?"

"No problem. Thanks."

"No, thank *you*. We really appreciate your commitment to the shelter."

* * *

She still had Nate's gate access code saved in her phone, but instead of entering the gate she idled at the curb and called him. It was a risky thing to do and she hoped he was in the mood for company; otherwise she would have to return to her apartment and eat the pizza and hot wings she picked up all by herself.

When he answered she said, "Kickoff is in thirty minutes. Are you ready to witness this Steel City beatdown?"

He laughed out loud—a glorious laugh—and she couldn't help laughing along with him.

"Man, you are crazy for real. I like that. What's up?"

"I'm outside your apartment."

"You are?"

She noted the surprise in his voice. "Yes. With pizza and hot wings. Do you mind if I join you to watch the game?"

"Tora… if you could see the grin on my face right now," he said. "I'm on my way outside to meet you."

"You are such a bad influence. Do you know how hard I had to work to reverse that root beer float last weekend?" He reached over to grab a slice of pizza and she slapped his hand away.

"I got the veggie pizza for you for that very reason." She laughed at the shocked expression on his face.

"You serious? So you're not sharing?"

"Nope," she said, crossing her legs and taking a bite of the slice she held in her hand. An Italian sausage meatball fell in her lap and she picked it right up and popped it into her mouth. "I figured you would have something to say about my choice, so I got you your own pizza… thin crust veggie." He pouted sadly and Tora thought it was the cutest thing.

They were sitting on his sofa eating pizza and hot wings straight from the boxes as they watched the pregame commentary. It was the first preseason game and the Steelers were playing the Cowboys.

He asked, "Still no word from that fool, huh?"

"Nope. Not one phone call either. I checked my blocked calls list."

"Good," Nate nodded. "If he knows what's best for him he won't come around again."

"I hope so. Because I seriously don't want to be the reason he ends up in jail and away from his daughter."

"I doubt he'd like it if somebody was stalking his little girl."

"Exactly! That's *exactly* what I told him!" She slapped her palm with his. "I'm glad you were there though. I think seeing you made him take me seriously this time."

"And I will gladly do it again if necessary." He looked at her.

"Thank you," she smiled and turned towards the television as the game's start was announced. Clapping her hands excitedly, she said, "You should go ahead and get a box of tissue now because your team is getting stomped tonight."

"Oh, so you talk a lot of noise, don't you?" he laughed. "If you're like this for a preseason game, I can imagine how cocky you are during the playoffs or Super Bowl."

"Hey… I'm just letting you know how serious I am about my team."

They settled back on the sofa and for the next two-and-a-half hours they rooted for their respective team, trash-talking each other at every significant play. It was a low-scoring game with the Steelers ahead by only a field goal, but that didn't stop Tora from getting in Nate's face, rubbing it in so to speak.

"There's still plenty of time for us to score," Nate said, "So I wouldn't get too excited if I were you."

"Save it! The Cowboys will lose this one… *again*. As they always do." She got up to go to the kitchen, but Nate snatched her as she passed him, pulling her down onto his lap. She squealed, "Nate! What are you doing?"

"I've had enough of your sassy mouth." He captured both her hands and pinned them above her head. "Now what? Huh?"

Laughing, Tora said, "Don't get mad at me because your team's weak. They've got the rest of the season to practice and improve, but we both know that's highly unlikely."

Nate shook his head. "You're so…. So…"

"So what?" She squirmed trying to break free of his hold. "The truth hurts, I know."

He held her wrists with one hand and squeezed her side with the other, causing her to flop like a fish.

"Please don't! I'm ticklish," she laughed.

"Oh yeah?" He squeezed again and Tora nearly fell out of his lap trying to escape, but he held her firmly against him. "You're just so damn sexy. And beautiful."

"I think you're sexy and beautiful, too," she admitted.

Nate lowered his head to hers, but quickly pulled back. "Wait… did you kiss the cats today?"

"What?" she giggled.

"I gotta know."

"No. No, I did not."

"Good," he said, and lowered his head again.

When his lips touched hers, her body's response was immediate. With her arms still clasped above her head, she arched into him as he kissed with a plaintive tenderness. Not once, but three times.

With each kiss Tora wondered how she ended up here. Lying on her back across this man's lap while he kissed her as if she belonged to him.

But she enjoyed it. At the same time, she regretted how much she enjoyed the feel of his mouth on hers.

He released her hands and she sat up. "What was that?" she asked.

"I don't know. I mean… I couldn't resist. I hope you're not—"

"We're supposed to be watching the game. That's why I came over here." She said it as though she was trying to convince herself more than she was trying to convince him. The truth was, she was attracted to him, but she'd made a vow to herself two years ago that the next time she slept with a guy would be in a committed relationship. There were many casual, friends-with-benefits types of hookups in her past, and the Tora of two years ago wouldn't have had a problem going all the way with Nate, but she wanted more than just romps between the sheets whenever she needed a release.

Her cell phone rang in her purse and she got up to answer it. A smile crossed her face when she checked the caller ID. "I'm gonna take this," she said to Nate and walked down the short hallway towards his bathroom. Pressing the button to answer the call, she said, "Well, well, well… hello, stranger. You've finally come down off Cloud Nine long enough to give your best friend a call?"

Cynthia laughed. "It has not been that long since the last time we talked. Don't even try it."

"Ever since you got yourself a new man I don't see or talk to you as much anymore."

"That's not true. You're exaggerating."

"Well, that's what it seems like," Tora said. She entered Nate's bedroom and took a seat on the floor at the foot of his bed.

Candace was her work associate, but Cynthia Williams was her best friend. They met shortly after Tora moved to Houston, when she was looking to connect and make friends in her new city. Last summer, following a breakup with her boyfriend, Cynthia went back to her hometown to recover and spend some time visiting with her grandmother, but ended up meeting a dream man. Since then, their girlfriend get-togethers were few and far between according to Tora because Cynthia's weekends were tied-up with her significant other.

"What's up with you?" How are you doing?" Cynthia asked her.

"That's what I should be asking you. I'm surprised you're still awake and not knocked out after a hot sex session with your beau."

"Oh lord, Tora. Holiday doesn't drive down until tomorrow afternoon."

"Mmm-hmm… I can't believe you still call him Holiday."

"I know, but it's what I'm used to. Besides… it suits him. Each time I'm with him it feels like a holiday, so…"

"Quick… somebody pass me a bucket! I'm gonna be sick!"

"Whatever," Cynthia said, laughing.

"I'm here at Nate's apartment. We're watching the game."

"Nate? Is that the guy you told me about that was—"

"Fine as hell, but short," Tora finished for her.

"Girl, if you don't stop being so picky you'll never meet your soul mate."

"And I'm so tired of hearing that!" Tora rolled her eyes. "I know what I want, okay? Don't fault me for it." Then she smiled. In a low voice she said, "But he kissed me…"

"Wait… what? How did that happen? I thought you weren't interested in him like that?"

"That's the problem. I like him, but I don't want to."

"What kind of sense does that make, Tora?"

"This whole abstinence lifestyle sucks. I'm horny and he's available, but I don't want to do it because I'm not looking for a fuck buddy."

"Did he tell you that's what he wanted?"

"No. He's a real gentleman."

"And just because he doesn't meet *one* of your requirements you—"

"Can't do it," Tora said, and sighed in frustration.

"I can't believe you're the same woman who told me I was out of my mind when I was questioning whether or not I wanted to give Holiday a chance."

"Your situation was different. And you see he's turned out to be the best thing that's ever happened to you."

"You should take your own advice and quit being so shallow."

"It's deeper than being shallow. You know that."

"Okay, so, the little man you were madly in love with broke your heart and you swore you would never go there again? But are you telling me that if a handsome man broke your heart just the same, you would start dating ugly men exclusively?"

Tora laughed out loud.

"See… you laugh because you realize how silly all of this is."

"That's not true! Between you, my mom, and Candace, y'all just don't understand because you've never been the tallest woman in the room. You've never had to deal with the stares, being asked constantly, 'How tall are you?', hearing snide remarks from men, like, 'That's one tall tree I would like to climb.' Or being single for most of your life because there just aren't enough tall men to go around. Dating a man shorter than me is just a constant reminder of all that."

"T, you're missing it!" Nate yelled from the living room. "Where you at?"

"Girl, you got me missing the game," Tora said to Cynthia. "I'll have to call you back later."

"Don't bother. I'll be asleep by then. But you better open your eyes and see what's right there in front of you."

"Bye, girl," Tora said, ending the call.

"I told you to never underestimate those Cowboys," Nate said. "You were talking all that noise earlier, but look what happened?"

"I step away for ten minutes and the Cowboys were able to score a touchdown?"

"Yep, yep," Nate smiled and winked at her.

"But they missed the field goal?"

"That doesn't matter. They scored. They won. End of story."

She re-joined him on the sofa. "It's just a preseason game, so it's no big deal."

"Oh now it's not a big deal?" Nate chuckled.

Neither one of them mentioned the kiss again that night. They sat, talking and watching more television as they had done in Tora's apartment. Just two friends laughing and enjoying each other's company until several hours ticked by and, by then, Tora was too tired to drive home, so Nate suggested she stay the night. On the couch they both remained until their eyelids closed. They slept upright underneath his University of Texas blanket, their feet resting on the coffee table amid the boxes of half-eaten pizzas, discarded chicken bones, and grease-stained paper napkins.

THIRTY-ONE

Nate stood when Sunny entered the restaurant so she would see where the waiter had seated him. She was a lot fuller with this pregnancy than she was when she carried Anaya and Baby Levi. Her face and neck were plumper, and her ankles reminded him of the elderly ladies he'd seen over the years suffering with edema in their lower limbs. Sunny lacked the same energy, too, but Nate figured maybe this baby just required more of her.

"What's up, baby sis?" He held the chair out for her to sit.

"I can't believe you are actually waiting for me this time."

"You need to stop with all that for real," Nate chuckled.

"Did Mama call you? She's not coming. She couldn't leave the office."

"She didn't, but okay."

"So we can go ahead and order now."

Nate flipped through his menu again and the waiter came over and placed a basket of bread on the table before taking their beverage order.

"So this means you got the tab this time, right?" Nate said when the waiter left.

"Nope. I'm gonna need to see you show up on time for something more than once before I buy your lunch."

"You're wrong for that, man," he shook his head, smiling.

Sunny asked, "So, what have you been up to?"

"Nothing really. Just trying to figure out how I can bring in some extra income. Did Mama tell you what she's doing to me?"

"No. What?" Sunny dunked some bread in olive oil and took a bite.

"I have to pay her back for college."

"Are you serious?"

Nate nodded his head. "Three hundred dollars a month."

"Oh my god. I know she had been saying that for a couple years now, but I didn't think she would actually do it. Wow. So what are you going to do?"

"I'm not sure right now. It's not like I can work extra hours at the gym. I just... I don't know."

"You know she won't be happy until you're practicing law again."

"That's not gonna happen that's for sure. I wasn't in love with the profession like you, Dad, and Bryan are."

"The first few years are always tough as you're trying to establish yourself and build a clientele," Sunny said, "but I can't imagine doing anything else."

"I know, *partner*. You were taking me to court every other weekend, remember?" Nate smiled, recalling the many times his sister begged him to play Courthouse with her during their adolescent years. Of course Nate always had to play the criminal, and she the prosecutor. She was the judge too, and he could never seem to escape the maximum sentence for his crimes. It was during their final year in junior high school that Sunny decided she wanted to study family law after her best friend's mom lost the custody battle to her estranged husband simply because he made more money. Nate witnessed his sister fall into a deep depression that lasted three months when her best friend had to leave Texas for Oregon to live with her father.

"Don't try to pretend you didn't like playing along. We were just practicing for what we were meant to do."

"What *you* were meant to do," Nate corrected her.

"How long do you have to pay Mom the three hundred dollars?"

"Until the debt is paid off. She told me I'm responsible for half of what she and Dad paid in tuition."

"Wow," Sunny said. "So you're basically paying back a student loan."

Nate shrugged. "Basically."

"It's funny, and it's not funny at the same time."

"She gave me the list she had typed up. It shows everything—right down to the pack of gel pens I loved to use."

"Oh my god," Sunny said again, laughing. "Are you really surprised though? Remember that time I accidentally broke her antique music box? She didn't give me an allowance for four whole months. I had to pay the cost of the repair."

"Well, you kinda brought that on yourself to be honest, baby sis, because you know she always told us to stay away from it."

"I know, but still... sometimes I felt like she went a little overboard when trying to teach us a lesson."

The waiter finally returned to take their order and Sunny requested more bread with her entrée. She'd eaten the entire basket by herself since Nate didn't touch any of it.

Her phone rang. "That better not be the office. I told them I was taking an extended lunch today." She retrieved the phone from her purse and looked at the screen. "It's Kaneesa," she said, and set the phone down on the table. "I'll have to call her back. I'm sure she just wants to tell me about another cool idea she came up with for *my* wedding. Or maybe to talk about you."

"Talk about me?" Nate said.

"She's still upset about the whole photographer thing. She didn't appreciate how I chose your friend over the guy she hired. She said I was showing favoritism because you're my brother. But you know she's still in love with you, right?"

"Sunny—"

She laughed because she knew he didn't want to talk about Kaneesa.

"We really haven't had the chance to talk about your new friend. What's her name again? Tory?"

An immediate smile came to his face. "Tora." It was nearly a week ago the last time he saw her—the night he kissed her precious lips. They hadn't seen each other since then, but he still performed his nightly and morning phone calls to ensure she was safe in her apartment. Their conversations were usually brief, and a few times not, but she didn't say anything about the kiss—and he was afraid to—which made him wonder if he'd overstepped his boundaries that night. At the time, she seemed to enjoy it, in his mind she welcomed it even, based on the way she kissed him back, but perhaps she's had time to reconsider her feelings about it.

"Are y'all dating?" Sunny asked him.

"Just friends," he said. "I've been spending some time with her. She came over to watch the game with me Thursday night. We chilled, relaxed. It was cool. I like her."

"Oh yeah? What's so special about her?"

"Other than her being the sexiest woman I've ever seen?"

Sunny rolled her eyes. "I swear that's all you men care about. What does she do for a living?"

"She works in retail. A department store in the mall."

"Impressive," Sunny said. It sounded like something their mother would say when she was being sarcastic.

"She loves it," Nate said. "And she does photography on the side."

"I'll admit… I absolutely love how our photos came out. She did an excellent job."

"See? Now aren't you glad you didn't listen to Kaneesa?"

"You did her so wrong," Sunny shook her head. "I thought I'd never hear the end of it after you left the engagement party. Why don't you like her, Nate?"

"Sunny, we've discussed this before, and don't act like she hasn't told you what I told her. I'm just not attracted to her in that way. We're better off as friends. Besides… I love you sis, you know that, but you and Kaneesa are too close. I don't need my sister knowing the specifics of what I do in the bedroom."

Sunny almost spit Dr. Pepper all over the table as she laughed out loud. She had told him Kaneesa told her about their night of sex upstairs in his bedroom while everyone else was on the first floor drinking and being merry at their parents' Christmas party.

"I still can't believe she did that," Sunny said. "Mama probably would've torn through the house like a tornado clearing everybody out if she knew what was going on."

"I'm trying to forget," Nate shook his head at the thought.

"You owe her. You were wrong for treating her the way you did."

"I was drunk. She was the one who initiated it. I wish I were strong enough that night to say no, but I wasn't. I've apologized and told her where we stand. She'll be okay."

"Heartless." Sunny pursed her lips.

"I was honest."

They were in the middle of their meals when Sunny's phone rang again. Nate knew it was Levi when she answered, "Yeah, babe?"

He pulled out his own phone to see if he had any calls or text messages, to see if there was a word from Tora. In the guys' text message group Jamal had sent a link to some video about women and the top qualities they sought in a partner. He was always sending links to videos and articles. If they weren't about the plight of society—black society in particular—they were about relationships between men and women.

Kevin was the only one to respond. **Fool, didn't i tell yo ass before ain't nobody got time to watch a video? we at work fool!**

Nate put his phone away when Sunny's voice raised a notch.

"I have no idea what you're gonna do, okay? *You* created this mess. I can't believe you would do something like this, Le, considering all of what we have going on right now… the wedding, the baby." Her fork hovered above her plate as she listened, her eyebrows knitted in frustration. "No. No. No, I'm not. *You* call around and ask. This is your problem!" She threw the phone down on the table.

It was the first time Nate had ever heard her talk like this to Levi. "What's going on, sis?" he asked.

She put a palm to her forehead and closed her eyes. He watched as she shook her head, her chest expanding and contracting as she took slow, deep breaths. Her eyes finally opened. "Nothing," she said, and reached for the salt shaker. "It's nothing."

He knew it made no sense to try and probe further because the stubborn set of her mouth let him know she didn't intend to say anything about whatever was going on in her household.

He returned to his salad and for the remainder of their lunch date all she would discuss was her newfound position as third partner of Thomas, Baker & Walker—a women-only practice specializing in family law—and the baby girl she couldn't wait to meet.

* * *

"Look." Vaughn grinned proudly as he stood on the scale.

"Another three pounds already? Look at you, man!" Nate gave him a high-five. "So this just proves you're making good choices all around. This makes my day."

"My shorts are baggy on me now, too." He lifted his hoodie to show Nate the extra room in the waistband of his gym shorts.

"It feels good, don't it?" Nate said, matching his smile.

"Yeah. I feel like I got more energy, too. I started riding my bike again."

"See? I told you that was gonna happen. Now you just have to keep it up. That's what counts. The point is to get your body moving as much as you can every day." Nate led Vaughn back over to his desk to sit since Leticia was still in the sauna. "Now that you're down fifteen pounds, it's a good time to think about the overall goal. We have to figure out the healthy weight range for you so you know what you're striving for." Nate was glad to see a genuine smile on the kid's face, and it seemed with each session Vaughn was getting more comfortable talking to him.

While they sat waiting for his mother, Nate discussed with Vaughn his plans for their remaining training sessions. "School starts for you in the next couple weeks, right?" Nate asked once they were done.

Vaughn nodded.

"Have you figured out what you're gonna do to get more involved?"

"No. My mama said they got a art club though. She looked it up online."

"I think you'll love it, man. It's the perfect way to meet other artists. Have you made anything new?"

"I draw every day," Vaughn told him.

"I hope I get to see more of it. When's the last time you saw your brother?"

He shrugged slightly. "I don't know. It's been a while."

"How is he doing? Have you talked to him lately?"

"Good I guess. He stay out in Crosby now. With his friends."

"That's cool," Nate nodded. "He'll probably be shocked the next time he sees you since you're slimming down."

Vaughn chuckled. "Yeah."

When Leticia emerged from the women's locker room Nate gave her a recap as usual of what he and Vaughn did that morning. Leticia wanted to make sure her son was still cooperating and not giving Nate any problems.

He watched them as they exited the gym, and Nate hoped it wasn't his imagination, but Vaughn seemed to walk with a little pep in his step.

THIRTY-TWO

She hadn't completely made it in her apartment door when Nate called to tell her to come over. Her knee ached, she smelled like dog, and all she planned to do was shower and relax on the sofa. It was adoption photo day at the shelter and she'd spent the last three hours photographing every kitty and pooch in the building. She'd asked the director's permission to jazz up the photo shoots with simple props and accessories from her personal collection—a plaid throw blanket for the cats to lie on, a beret to add to a dog's head, a ball to wrestle with—just to make the fur babies that much more endearing to potential adopters. The day turned out to be more exhausting than she imagined. One particular pup—a 70-pound chocolate Labrador—was all too eager to play with Tora, his tongue lolling and his tail wagging as he jumped all over her. Even the young girl assisting Tora was having trouble containing the friendly animal. Neither of them noticed the leash that somehow wound itself around Tora's ankle, so when Tora tried to get away she was tripped up and fell knee-first on the cement floor.

She packed an overnight bag because she had no intentions of returning home and subjecting her knee to another three-story climb.

Nate opened the door and a frown creased his forehead. "Tora, why didn't you call me? I would've come out to meet you."

"I did call. You didn't answer." *God, he looks so good,* she thought. There was something fresher about his face, but she couldn't place her finger on it.

"I'm sorry," he said. "Maybe I didn't hear the phone ring." He stepped aside for her to enter. "Were you able to find a close parking space?"

"Yeah, thank God. Because my knee is throbbing like crazy."

"Why? What happened to your knee?" He grabbed the bags from her shoulder as she limped over to the couch.

"It happened at the animal shelter today. I got tangled in a dog's leash."

"And hurt your knee? Why didn't you let me know? I wouldn't've made you leave your apartment if I knew you were in pain, Tora."

He said it in a tone like he was really upset she didn't tell him.

"Which one is it?" he asked. She pointed to her right knee and he sat down beside her. He gently lifted her leg and placed it across his lap.

That's what's different, she thought to herself as she watched him examine her knee. His sideburns were gone and his beard and goatee had been trimmed way down.

"It's a little swollen right here," he said, poking the area lightly with his finger. "I'm gonna get an ice pack for you."

"Do I smell some cooking going on?" she said when he left the couch.

"Yeah," he chuckled. "It's just a little somethin'-somethin' I put together. Stuffed chicken breasts, pasta, garden salad. Y'know… something light."

"It smells really good."

"Thanks. I figured we didn't need another junk food night."

She laughed. "What are you trying to say?"

He returned to the living room with a Ziploc bag filled with ice cubes. "That you make it hard for me to stay focused, but I'm determined tonight."

The look on his face made her believe he wasn't just talking about his diet.

He suggested she turn sideways on the couch to stretch her legs across his lap. He placed the baggie on top of her knee. "The chicken should be ready in about another ten minutes," he said. "You hungry?"

"Mmm-hmm." The bag was cold. "I don't know how you expect me to keep this on my knee. I'll end up with freezer burn."

"No you won't," he said. "I know how to do it. Just relax."

She propped a throw pillow behind her head and did just that.

"What were you doing at the shelter?" he asked.

"We're getting ready for the fall adoption campaign, so I was helping out with the photos to update the web roster."

"Is this like a second job or—"

"Just volunteer work. I try to go there at least three times a month; no less than two. I help out wherever I'm needed. We clean the cages, clean the animals, assist with playground time."

"You really love animals, don't you?"

"I really do," she smiled. "They're like children to me. Sweet and innocent and just so loveable. We always had pets when I was growing up. My daddy is a dog lover, but I prefer cats most of the time." Then she laughed. "And what's so funny about my dad is that he always named our dogs after his favorite classic cars. We had a German Shepherd named Fleetwood, a Boxer named Regal. DeVille was his favorite of them all, I think. She was a Pit Boxer mix."

"Now I know where his daughter gets it from with the unusual pet names."

"You're probably right," she laughed again.

When the food was done he told her to stay put and that he would make her plate.

"What should we watch this time?" he asked when he returned to her side. "Power again?"

"Sounds good to me."

His sheets were soft and smelled like lavender. He said he'd changed them while she was taking a shower. That was an hour ago and she lay in his bed wondering how she was going to fall asleep without a TV. He didn't have one in his bedroom and she was used to watching television until she dozed off at night.

She turned over on her side, but the light from an outdoor lamp shining through the blinds forced her to turn back. There was no curtain covering the window, which she thought was strange considering how carefully decorated the rest of his apartment was.

She hadn't thought to pack her night mask, either. She would rather have the couch, but he insisted she sleep in the bed because of her knee even though it was feeling much better than when she first arrived. After dinner Nate had spent a few minutes massaging her leg and neither one of them would admit they were turned on by the small gesture. She smiled as she recalled how he'd teased her calf and she'd turned into a giggling, squirming mess all over again.

"Oh, you're still up?"

Tora turned towards the door where he was standing. No shirt. Black boxer briefs. *He knows exactly what he's doing to me,* she thought.

"I just came to get another pillow," he said.

Her eyes followed him as he went to the opposite side of the bed. *Have mercy. Them GQ models ain't got nothing on this man.*

"You comfortable?" he asked.

"Oh yeah. The bed is wonderful. Just having trouble going to sleep without a TV to put me to sleep."

"I'm sorry. I don't like televisions in the bedroom."

She couldn't even look him in the eye for staring at his chest. "Why not?" she asked.

"For me, the bedroom is a place for only two things."

In her mind her tongue was tracing the creases in his abs. She finally looked at him. "And what's that?"

"Sleep and sex," he said.

She cleared her throat. "I see."

"You're welcomed to join me on the couch," he said.

"So does this mean no sex occurs on your couch?"

His laugh was loud and unexpected in the quiet room. "Well… these couches are only a couple years old and… no, they haven't seen any action."

She left the bed, pulling his blanket behind her.

They were watching TV for only a half-hour before she started yawning. "I guess I can return to bed now," she said, and stood.

"Aww, man. I was enjoying you sitting next to me. Now the couch is all cold." He gave that puppy dog pout again, and she fell for it.

"You don't have to sleep out here if you don't want to."

His eyes searched hers and she knew he was wondering what exactly she was proposing.

"We survived sleeping together a few days ago," she shrugged.

"And you have no idea how much pain I was in, either."

"Pain? Why were you in pain, Nate?"

"Because I had the beautiful, sexy woman I've been fiending for since I first laid eyes on her alone in my apartment, sleeping next to me on my couch and I couldn't touch her."

Her pulse quickened at the intense way he gazed at her as he confessed.

"Telling me to lay down next to you in a bed *just to sleep…*" he shook his head. "I'm not even gonna put myself through that."

It was a bad idea because there was no way she would be able to lie next to him either without feeling a tug in her loins.

But maybe that's exactly what she wanted. It had been two years too long.

"I don't want you to have to give up another comfortable night of sleep on account of me, Nate."

The way he lay there on the couch looking up at her, one arm resting behind his head, she was tempted to go and get her camera.

"Tora," he finally said, "please don't play games with me."

"I'm not—"

"If I come in there, I'm making love to you."

A quiet breath pushed past her lips when the heat that began at her knees rushed to her head. She didn't expect he would be so blunt.

"It took forever just to get you to hang out with me, you tell me we can't be anything more than friends, and now I'm supposed to share a bed with you like it's nothing?"

"I mean…" she shrugged again, at a loss for words. He was right. She had said there couldn't be anything between them, and she was trying her hardest to not give in on her promise to abstain from casual sex. He didn't deserve that if he was seeking something more than a platonic relationship.

"How do you like your eggs?"

The question came out of left field. "What?" she said.

"I make breakfast every morning. How do you like your eggs?"

"Oh," she chuckled. "Scrambled is fine."

He turned over on his side and pulled the blanket up to his shoulder. "Good night, beautiful. I'll see you in the morning."

Who am I kidding?

She was no longer sleepy. Instead, she lay wide awake in the dark,

Nate's declaration replaying in her head: '*If I come in there, I'm making love to you.*'

Why was she doing this to herself? She wanted this man as much as he wanted her. There was no denying that. She knew there were no guarantees in life and she needn't be too proud to put aside her list of standards, especially when there was a man in the next room who sent her mind and body into a tizzy whenever she was around him.

Yes, she wanted to make love to him, too, but there were a few things she needed to know.

She sat up in bed. "Nate?"

THIRTY-THREE

He hoped he wasn't imagining things. His heart leapt to his throat when he heard his name called from the bedroom.

He left the sofa and walked down the carpeted hallway to the room. Easing the door open, he was relieved to find her sitting up in bed. It was real.

"Come here," she said. She sat Indian-style on the edge of the bed and smoothed the sheet over the space next to her.

He took a seat and looked at her.

She exhaled and said plainly, "Nate, I want to make love to you, too."

He was grateful the only light in the room was from the courtyard outside because she couldn't see how his body went hard.

"But we need to talk."

Huh?

She reached over and turned on the bedside lamp. The plunging neckline in the cream satin pajama short set she wore gave a little peek of her breast as she leaned forward and Nate wondered what they had to talk about when he would rather get straight to the loving.

"Nate, it's best we go ahead and get this out of the way now. To put everything on the table."

She was making him anxious because he didn't know where she was headed.

"I'm at the point in my life where I want something meaningful."

Nate waited.

"What I'm saying is… I've made the decision that the next person I'm intimate with will be someone who's looking for the same thing I am. Back in the day, I didn't have a problem with casual flings and hopping in bed with people just to get off."

His heart dropped to his lap. *How many men has she hopped in bed with?* He ran his hands down his thighs.

She turned her body to look squarely at him. "Nate, what do you want? Are you looking for a relationship with me?"

He cleared his throat. "Well… I've been telling you since the beginning I wanted to know who you are. I don't mean that in a casual way."

She nodded. "But I just want to be sure we're on the same page."

He reached for her hand. "Tora, when you walked through the doors of that sandwich shop, I knew I had to have you." He leaned forward and kissed her neck. "I told my sister and my mama that you were mine."

"Really?" she giggled.

He kissed her soft lips. "Yes."

"Before you even knew my name?"

"Maybe I knew it then. That's why I've been so obsessed with you." She closed her eyes as he kissed her neck again. "I've been waiting for this for a long time. Can I make love to you now?" He guided her hand down to his lap. "See how you got me?"

She massaged the outline of his penis and returned his kisses. "Yes," she said.

He lifted the satin top over her head. Her breasts were only big enough to fit in the palms of his hands, but they were beautiful and he took his time to savor each one.

He moved her over to the center of the bed before pulling down her shorts and underwear, and when she spread her legs he couldn't help smiling down at her.

He loved hairy pussy, and he couldn't remember the last time he'd saw one.

Nate first explored her body using only his hands. He caressed and teased and rubbed it down before retracing the entire length of her with his tongue. Her skin went from warm to hot, and when the scent of her arousal was in the air, he knew she was ready.

He stood to remove his own shorts and to grab protection from the drawer in the nightstand. Once they were protected, he united his body with hers, and inside her smoldering center is where he remained for the rest of the night.

THIRTY-FOUR

"Okay, I've never seen you so anxious to leave work in a long time. What's up?"

Tora laughed as she placed the sign posts back in their boxes.

"You're walking around cheesin' all day and everything. Did you hit the lottery and ain't told nobody or what? What's really going on?"

"First of all, if I won the lottery I wouldn't be standing here working that's for sure," Tora said.

"Well… something's definitely going on and you're not telling me. So, spill the beans, girl."

"Why does something have to be going on? I can't just be in a good mood and excited about going home after a long day of work on my feet?"

"Nope, because whatever it is got you glowing like a light bulb. You weren't walking around glowing like that last week."

Tora shrugged and smiled. "I'm just excited to be going home to my man, that's all." She grabbed the boxes and headed to the back of the store for the storage room.

"Girl, what?"

She laughed as Candace came following behind her.

"Hold up. What did you say? *Your man?*"

"Yes. *My man.*" Tora set the boxes on the metal shelf and turned to face Candace. Candace's eyes bounced left to right as if she were watching a fast-swinging pendulum, and Tora couldn't help laughing again.

"What exactly do you mean, Tora?"

"Nate," Tora said. "We're officially dating."

Candace turned away, beckoning Tora with a wave of her hand. "Come… come in here, girl. I need to sit down for this one."

Tora giggled and followed Candace to the office.

"This is a complete surprise," Candace said once they sat down. "How did you go from, *'we're just friends'* to *'he's my man'* in a matter of days?"

"We had a conversation," Tora said. "I told him what I wanted, and he agreed it was what he wanted, too."

"Which is?"

"Something serious. I'm not looking for a casual partner."

Candace grinned and reached across the desk to give her a high-five. "Congratulations for coming to your senses."

"I'll admit I could no longer stand it. He's too fine and sweet and beautiful for me to ignore. And oh… after what he did to me the other night and the next morning, I regret I was wasting my time looking for guys on Soul Meet."

"Wait… are you telling me you were out gettin' your groove on and I didn't know anything about it?"

"Well, sis, did you really expect me to stop the man in the middle of his downstroke so I can give you a call?"

Candace rolled her eyes. "You know what I mean. I seriously believe you knew you were going to go there with him all along, and you were playing hard-to-get just because."

"That's not true," Tora said. Then she sighed. "It was just getting harder for me to ignore the way I felt when I was with him."

"Mmm-hmm… I told you so. Now imagine if you didn't snatch him up and he moved on to another chick? You would've been the *friend* watching that beautiful man from the sidelines loving someone else."

Tora shook her head. "I don't even want to think about it."

* * *

She let herself into the apartment with the key he'd hidden underneath a bush near his front door. He sent a text message earlier to say he wanted her there when he came in from work, butt naked and waiting in his bed.

"Good girl," he smiled when he found her lounging nude in his queen-sized bed. "I was counting down the hours at work because I couldn't wait to be here with you."

"You and me both," she smiled back.

He took off his T-shirt and pants and crawled in beside her. "I've been thinking about this all day," he said, and covered her mouth with his in a slow, passion-filled kiss.

She loved how he kissed in slow motion, his mouth lingering on hers as if he intended to leave a light visible imprint. His tongue teased her lips around the edges, soft and feather-like, and slid in and out of her mouth. He cupped a breast in his hand, gently twisted the nipple between his fingers. Tora leaned into him when he released her breast and his hand traveled down her torso to her legs and parted her thighs. Chill bumps rose on her skin as he gripped the hair, tugging lightly at the most sensitive area, and Tora felt all of her nerves rush towards his touch.

Nate's tongue was still in her mouth when he began his four-one rhythm down below. Slowly and tenderly his finger caressed her clit in a circular motion before dipping in the warm center. One-two-three-four-one. One-two-three-four-one.

Tora spread her legs wider as the minutes passed and Nate wasn't stopping. She wound her hips in the motion of his hand and thrust forward as a finger pushed inside her. One-two-three-four-one. One-two-three-four-one.

She buried her face in his neck, panting softly as the heat intensified. The more he rubbed, the wetter she became, and it wasn't long before he slipped all four fingers inside. His palm brushed her clit as he went faster and deeper. Tora squeezed her eyes shut, the tempo vibrating her whole body. Electric-like currents zipped up her spine, curling her toes from the sensation. She had never experienced anything like it, and she lay there spread-eagled—her nipples taut, her skin hot and cold at the same time—as Nate proved what his hands were capable of.

When the heat rose from the bottom and the wave rushed to her center, she turned her face into Nate's shoulder and screamed.

"Mmm," he breathed, and kissed the side of her face.

Her heartbeat thudded in her ears as she lay there, breathless.

Tora eased her legs closed, but Nate guided them back open.

He wasn't done.

She looked up at him and he dipped his head to kiss her lips. Then she felt those magical fingers on her again. He was in her hair, caressing and pulling as gingerly as he did before. How soothing, those hands, the way they stroked her back to calm. He rolled over on top of her and kissed her again. Her lips, her cheek, her neck.

He started to move.

Still in his boxer briefs, Tora felt the solidness of his penis as he glided back and forth. She was a slippery slope down there, her clitoris swollen and tender, but that didn't stop her from wrapping her legs around his waist, encouraging him to keep going.

It hurt so good.

Nate filled her mouth with his tongue again, cradled her head between his hands, and rocked her until she reached another soul-shaking, heart-pounding climax.

THIRTY-FIVE

He sat at the end of the conference table in the back of the room. His supervisor, Luis Morales, was giving a presentation, but Nate wasn't paying attention. It was their mandatory quarterly meeting that all of the trainers had to attend, whether or not they were scheduled to work that day. The objective was the same: how to bring on new clients, how to retain the ones they have, and to always remember to mention their supplements. Nate never suggested supplements to his clients. He didn't believe in their use and preferred to do things the natural way. As usual, Luis was standing at the front of the room reading straight from his PowerPoint slides as if they couldn't read the bullet points for themselves. Nate always thought it strange how Luis was such a lively personality in one-on-one conversations, but a total bore when it came to these meetings. He wished Luis would just send the entire presentation to them via email so they could review it on their own time.

Nate wasn't concerned about the meeting notes because he was busy texting Tora with his phone hidden beneath the table.

Will you be there again tonight? I need more of you.

She replied back, **Probably not. I don't wanna spoil you. I must ration it out.**

Nate crooked his elbow and coughed into it to hide his laugh. He texted back, **Too late. I'm already spoiled. I'm sitting here in a meeting but all I can think about is you. I wish I didn't wash my hands.**

You're so nasty.

You haven't seen nasty yet.

I'm still thinking about last night too. No one has ever made me cum while still wearing his clothes.

Nate looked up and towards the front of the room. He nodded his head in agreement as if he was listening to Luis. He replied back to Tora, **Next time there won't be anything between us. And I'm gonna show you what my tongue can do.**

He put his phone away because he was getting hot, his body stiffening at the thought of tasting Tora, hearing her sweet whimper as he took her to ecstasy.

Leticia was warming up by doing some brisk walking on the treadmill when he emerged from the conference room.

"I hope you wasn't waiting too long," he said. "I thought the meeting would never end."

She shook her head no. "It wasn't too long. I've only been here twenty minutes or so."

Nate noticed Leticia was sporting a new hairdo—one of those old-school French rolls in the back, and a cascade of Shirley Temple curls framing her face in the front. "I like your hair," he said. "Looks like Ms. Leticia's going on a date tonight," he teased.

She grinned coyly, patting the back of her head. "As a matter of fact I am."

"Really?" Nate laughed. "That's all right, Ms. Leticia. Do your thing."

"You won't believe where I met him," she said. "At the doctor's office when I went to get my check-up."

"What?" Nate said in surprise.

"Yeah, he was there for a check-up, too. We started talking about our issues to each other, and before we knew it, we were laughing so much the other people in the waiting room were looking at us crazy. He asked for my phone number and I told him I didn't have time for anything like that because I'm focused on raising my son. But do you know that fool was waiting in the lobby for me after my appointment?"

"For real?" Nate said. "He was determined."

"A whole hour later," Leticia said. "He told me he had no intentions of taking me away from my son, that he would love to meet him, but he hoped I would join him for a cup of coffee and a couple hours of conversation."

"And you couldn't refuse?" Nate smiled, thinking of how even the middle-aged man had to work hard for a date.

"So that's what I wanted to tell you. We have to take it easy today because I don't want to ruin my curls."

Nate laughed again. "I gotcha, Ms. Leticia. I promise I won't work you too hard. We will do some core and lower body training. How about that?"

"Alright. Sounds good."

He led her to a private corner in the weights area. "You haven't told me what the doctor said though. Is everything cool?"

"Oh yeah," she said. "He was impressed with my results. I see him again in six weeks for a follow-up."

"That's great. I love to hear it."

"I'm proud of Vaughn, too. Since he's lost a few pounds, he's feeling himself now. You should see him… when we're at home and I'm making my plate or something, he'll tell me to watch my portions, or if I'm going for seconds on a bowl of ice cream, he'll say 'Do you *really* need more ice cream or are you just losing your willpower?'"

Nate chuckled. "He wants to make sure you're staying on track too, huh?"

"I guess he figures we're in this together now even though it was just a few months ago when he was looking down on my healthy cooking. Working with you has helped a lot, and I see that you've inspired him to do better, and I thank you for it."

"Hey, it's what I'm here for, Ms. Leticia. I'm just glad I could help. I admit I was a little worried about him in the beginning, but… he came around."

"And you're a cool dude," Leticia smiled. "That's what Vaughn told me."

* * *

He'd just finished a podcast recording when he heard the key placed in the lock. He turned around in his seat at the computer desk to see Tora enter the apartment. It warmed his heart that she decided to come over afterall, but her attire raised his eyebrows. "It's nighttime and damn-near eighty degrees outside, Tora, why are you wearing shades and a trench coat?" He appreciated the shiny black pumps however.

Without a word she walked over to him, dropping her bag on the floor along the way. Her face was expressionless behind the sunglasses as she stood looking down at him.

"What's up, baby? Everything okay?"

She shook her head somberly, and he was concerned, until she untied the coat sash and undid the buttons. Then a wry smile curved her lips. She was naked underneath.

At the sight of her smooth brown skin Nate felt his temperature rise. He reached up, grabbing her waist, but she pushed his hand away. She shrugged off the coat and stood before him unmoving, quiet still. He reached for her hips this time, and she just as quickly batted his hands away. He sat back in his seat and waited. As the seconds passed, his eyes roved all over her body. From the delicate curves of her shoulders to her teacup-sized breasts, flat stomach, and straight hips; the soft thighs and ultra long legs he fell in love with at first sight.

She propped a foot on his thigh, and Nate didn't care that the heel of her shoe pierced his leg because the thing he craved most was just inches away from his face now. The bushy triangle, the hypnotizing scent of it—a sweet musk—drove him wild, and he licked his lips unconsciously.

With both hands she gripped the sides of his head and pulled his face forward. He couldn't help squeezing her ass. She tsked and shook a finger at him, then in silent command forced his hands on his knees. Nate understood now, and when she tilted hr pelvis towards his mouth, he stuck out his tongue.

He licked and sucked and savored.

Nate felt his penis straining against his shorts, and he wanted so badly to free it, to sink inside Tora's hot body. He was already having trouble keeping his hands under control. They trembled with the urge to hold onto something, anything as he thrust his tongue inside her.

Tora's fingers curled around his locks, holding his head in place as she began to rock her hips, rubbing his face in her sex. From his mouth up to his nose, and then down to his chin she smothered him.

Nate's face glistened with her sweet nectar, and it turned him on to hear her moans grow louder, to feel her body tightening as she rode it freely, uninhibited, until her body shuddered from the powerful orgasm.

"You should come with me tomorrow to my parents' house. For Sunday dinner," Nate said later as they lay in bed.

"Why would I do that?" Tora said.

"What do you mean 'why'? For dinner like I said. And because I want to introduce you to them."

"You forgot I already met them at your sister's engagement party?"

"That don't count. You were just the photographer then."

She turned over to face him. "And what am I now?" she smiled.

"You tell me," he said.

She leaned forward and kissed him. "What do you want me to be?"

He rested his hand on her hip. "Right now? My freak."

Tora grabbed the pillow and pushed it into his face.

"Seriously," he laughed. "You may as well get to know my family." He rubbed his thumb across her cheek. "And they need to know my lady."

THIRTY-SIX

It was her first time inside Nate's SUV—a blacked-out GMC Yukon with limousine tint and black rims. She wondered how he was able to see at night because, although it was only five-thirty, the tint made it appear much later outside. She sat in his passenger seat, bobbing her head along with him as they listened to 97.9 The Box's Sunday mix. The drive to Nate's parents' house for dinner made her think about her own parents and how much she missed going out with Sharon to their favorite soul food restaurant when Sharon wasn't in the mood to cook, which was most of the time because she had never been very good at it; or going to her dad's house after he'd call to tell her he wanted to have a cookout and she needed to come over, and yes his new girlfriend and her kids would be there, but he also wanted the company of his own daughter.

She wished she could convince her parents to move south so they could be close again, but they were adamant Pittsburgh was home, and they had no intentions of leaving.

Tora was as equally amazed as she had been the first time she entered the Walker estate. She couldn't get over the vastness of it. Not before or since her short time with renowned disc jockey Mike Stack had she witnessed anyone living a life of such opulence.

Bryanna and Melody ran up to their uncle, nearly knocking him off balance because he wasn't expecting them to jump into his arms. "Yo!" he laughed as he held one in each arm and they blew raspberries on his cheeks.

Tora laughed, too. It was cuteness overload.

He set them on their feet and Bryanna promptly told him, "Uncle Nate, we had a sleepover here last night with Nana and Grandpa. We played games and watched movies and ate popcorn."

"We ate… and we ate popcorn!" Melody echoed excitedly.

"So you had a fun night with Grandma and Grandpa, huh? That's cool," Nate said. "Hey, do y'all remember Ms. Tora?"

The girls looked up at her and she smiled back. "Hi Melody. Hi Bryanna."

"Hi," Bryanna said, and she turned and skipped off, Melody right behind her as they left the foyer. The two of them almost crashed into Kaneesa as they went.

Kaneesa sucked her teeth, a look of disdain on her face as she glared at Tora and Nate. "Oh. It's just you. I thought it was Sunny and the kids."

"Well, hello to you too, Kaneesa. How you doing?" Nate said.

She rolled her eyes and turned back around. Nate made a gesture as if he wanted to back-hand slap her across the back of her head.

Tora swatted his hand down. "Nate, don't do that."

"I'm sorry, baby, but she likes to try me sometimes." Then he kissed her shoulder. "Don't worry. I'm not gonna embarrass you or nothing like that."

"You better not," she said, and he grabbed her hand and led her across the threshold towards the lively dining room.

It looked like a holiday feast was going on. The room buzzed with the chatter of Nate's family as they sat around the long table. A number of colorful dishes were scattered across the tabletop.

The buzz ceased when Nate spoke and announced she would be joining them for Sunday dinner.

"Welcome," Nate's father said, followed by Nate's brothers. The women, whom Tora remembered were his sisters-in-law Sharday and Evelyn, smiled and said hello.

"Nate, why didn't you call to tell me you were bringing a guest?" his mother asked. And she looked Tora up and down as if she were checking to see if she looked decent enough to invite to her table.

Tora had asked Nate before they left his apartment if he thought she should remove her nose ring before visiting his parents, and he had shook his head, told her to be herself.

"I wanted it to be a surprise," Nate told his mother as he bent down to kiss her cheek.

"You know I like to be aware of these things to ensure we have enough for everyone."

"Ah, c'mon, Ma," Nate groaned. "You know we always have enough. I tell you what… I'll let Tora eat my portion first, and if there's anything left after everybody else gets theirs, then I'll eat. Is that alright with you?"

Everyone laughed expect Kaneesa and his mother.

"Don't start with me, son," his mother said.

Nate held out a chair at the corner end of the table and Tora sat down. "Thanks," she said quietly. He took the chair at the end right next to her.

"Nate, you know Sunny and them are coming, and that's where they sit. Why would you put her there?"

Oh God, Tora thought. She looked at Nate for confirmation if she needed to move.

"Kaneesa, please," he said. "It's enough seats here for Sunny and the kids. Levi can find somewhere else to sit. They're the ones late this time."

"Oh my god. Really?" Kaneesa looked at his mother. "Vickie, how is he able to do this? He knows his sister will be here for dinner. She shouldn't have to find a seat elsewhere."

"Kaneesa, why are you even talking to me? Last time I checked your last name ain't Walker, so maybe you should give up your seat if you're really concerned about Levi having one."

"You know what? Screw you, Nate!"

"Alright. Alright," Nate's father said calmly, trying to bring order, but Kaneesa was fired up.

"Don't come in here trying to show out in front of your little girlfriend, okay?"

Victoria said, "She's right, Nate. This is exactly why you should've let me know ahead of time."

Tora wanted to leave. She hated feeling like she was the cause of another argument between his family.

Nate said, "Mama, is it really that big of a deal? It's not like we don't have extra chairs in this house. Do you want me to bring in one from the library for Levi?"

"You are not removing my chairs from the library, son—"

"Then he can sit at the bar in the kitchen. Or will that be a problem? Better yet, me and Tora will take our plates to the kitchen. We'll eat in there. Come on, baby," he said, and Tora was glad to go.

"Sit down," Victoria yelled. "Both of you."

Tora eased back into her seat, her eyes on the table as if she had just been reprimanded by her own mother.

"I swear, Nate, you're really being dramatic right now."

"*I'm* being dramatic?"

Tora wanted to shake him and tell him to just let it go. She glanced at his father, who gave her a look as if to say he was just as embarrassed as she was.

"Sit down, son," Victoria said again. "All of us eat together. As a family. You know this."

His brothers and sisters-in-law never said a word.

Nate finally plopped down in his seat. He pointed a finger and said, "Mind your business, Kaneesa."

Kaneesa pushed back from the table and rushed out of the room.

* * *

Tora lay in bed waiting for Nate. He was in the kitchen cooking breakfast for her. It was a little after two in the morning and she woke up hungry. The atmosphere at the Walkers' Sunday dinner was tense the entire time—for her especially—and she'd lost her appetite and couldn't eat. It all started when Nate's sister and her fiancé finally arrived. Kaneesa found her way back to the dinner table and took the opportunity to badger Nate again. And it seemed she couldn't wait to rehash Tora's lack of professionalism at Sunny's engagement party, which prompted Victoria to question her work ethics as well. Nate came to her defense and reminded them it was his idea to leave the party early, and that if they didn't see a problem with Levi's absence for the majority of the engagement, they should have nothing to say about his and Tora's leave. Levi didn't like this, however, and it led to a heated exchange between him and Nate.

Tora sat there dumbfounded, disbelieving that all the chaos began over a seat at the dinner table.

Mr. Walker was finally able to calm everybody down and Tora took a bite of food just to do something with her hands.

Mrs. Walker's cornbread dressing was full of onion and celery. Tora tolerated celery, but she flat-out detested onion. The raw smell of them, the taste of them always nauseated her. Perhaps Mrs. Walker sensed her disgust because she glanced at Tora at the precise moment she'd gagged and spit the dressing into Mrs. Walker's platinum-colored paisley cloth napkin.

—Is there a problem with the food?

Tora felt like a cat caught with the family's pet bird in her mouth. All of them were looking at her.

She couldn't admit she disliked the dressing due to the onion, because to say that would have been the equivalent of saying she didn't like Mrs. Walker's cooking. So she said the first thing that came to mind.

—I thought there was a hair.

Mrs. Walker stared at her a moment before turning to her husband:

—Gerald, in the thirty-five years I have been cooking for you, have you ever had a hair in your food?

Mr. Walker shook his head no. Then Mrs. Walker went around the table asking each one if they'd ever encountered a strand in all the years they dined at her table.

Tora felt herself sinking with embarrassment, wanting to disappear into the wall.

"Of all the things I could've said, why would I say something like that?" She sat up in the bed when Nate entered the room. "Why couldn't I just tell the truth and say I don't like no freakin' onions?" She shook her head and rolled her eyes.

"You're really making a big deal out of nothing, babe. I told you it's nothing to worry about." He handed her the plate and set a glass of water on the nightstand.

"I didn't mean to insult her," Tora sighed.

"Will you stop? You did not insult her. You thought there was a hair in your food, so—"

"But it wasn't!"

"Okay, but it can happen. No big deal," he shrugged and climbed in bed beside her.

She appreciated that he was trying to make her feel better about the situation, but it also frustrated her at the same time because he didn't understand how much of an embarrassment it was.

He kissed the side of her arm and said, "I can get used to this."

"To what?" she asked.

"Breakfast in bed with you. Can I have a bite?"

She rolled her eyes playfully. "Why didn't you make enough to have a plate of your own?" She fed him a forkful of the blueberry pancakes.

"I don't eat this late." He laid back on his pillows and watched her as she ate. "There's something I gotta tell you," he said after a while.

She scraped the last bit of crumbs into her mouth and set the plate on the nightstand. She took a drink of water. "Okay?" she said.

"Me and Kaneesa hooked up."

She turned to him, an eyebrow raised.

"I just wanted you to hear it straight from me first."

"What do you mean you *hooked up*? When did this happen?"

"Last Christmas. At our Christmas party."

"Oh. So y'all used to date?"

"No. We were just good friends for a very long time."

"I see," she nodded. "Friends with benefits?"

"Not even that. We hooked up just that one time. I was drunk."

Tora rolled her eyes. "Now it all makes sense. Now I know why it seems she has a problem with me. What did you do to her?"

"I didn't do anything. I mean… I told her where we stand, that we can't have anything going on. Sunny and my mama think we're perfect for each other though. Not me. She's like my sister."

Tora twisted her lips.

"Seriously. And I regret we did it because now she hates my guts."

"The awkwardness of it all," she groaned, and settled underneath the covers. "I guess I won't make it in Mrs. Walker's good graces, either."

He pulled her close to lay on his chest.

"I don't want any drama, Nate," she nudged his side.

"What?"

"From Kaneesa. Or you. Or anybody else."

"There won't be any drama. What are you talking about, woman?"

"I'm just letting you know."

"C'mon," he chuckled, and kissed her forehead. "We need to get some sleep for our workout in a few hours. I let you off the hook these past couple of weeks, but we gotta get back at it. My alarm is set for seven."

"Please," she said. "You can work out all you want to, but when that alarm goes off you better not disturb my sleep if you know what's best for you. I'll be here when you get back." She ignored the stunned look on his face and closed her eyes as she snuggled closer to him.

THIRTY-SEVEN

It was a rare thing for Geo to send a text message; even rarer for him to make a phone call, so when Nate glanced at his smartphone to check the time while Vaughn performed leg curls he was surprised to see both a text and missed call from his brother. He knew it had to be something major.

Have you talked to Sunny? read the text message.

Nate texted him back. **No. why what's up?**

Geo's response came ten minutes later. **The wedding is off. Levi did something stupid. I'll call you after my workshop.**

It was the wrong thing to tell Nate because now his mind was racing, wondering what exactly Geo was talking about. What did Levi do?

He couldn't stop thinking about it as he coached Vaughn through some weighted squats, and he considered leaving Vaughn alone while he snuck away to make a call to Sunny, but he wouldn't walk away from his client unless there was an absolute emergency. Geo would have mentioned it if Sunny was hurt.

At least, Nate hoped he would.

"I'm taking him shopping for school clothes this weekend," Leticia said when they all sat down at Nate's desk. "He's excited about that because his old clothes are so loose on him now."

Nate nodded at Vaughn, who sat trying to be cool and not blush. "I'm excited for you, man. You worked hard these past few weeks. I'm really proud that you've been keeping up a routine on the days we don't see each other. It's gonna be tough now that you're going back to school, with your new schedule and everything, so I want you to come up with a plan to still get some exercise in. After school, maybe."

Leticia said, "You'll see us around. He asked me to add him to my membership. I was surprised he wanted to join me on a walk around the neighborhood yesterday."

"That's the way to do it. It makes exercise fun sometimes when you have a partner." Nate was truly proud to see Vaughn making changes, and the way Leticia beamed at her son he knew she was, too. His phone vibrated in his pocket. "Unless you need anything else from me we can call it a wrap."

They stood and Nate walked them to the door. "See you tomorrow," Leticia said, giving him a brief hug.

He made a mental note to ask her at their next session how her date went.

Back at his desk, he returned Geo's call. "What's up, G? What's going on with Sunny and Levi?"

"Actually, Bryan is the one who told me about it. He said he called Pop about something and Pop told him. Supposedly Levi is caught up in some kinda gambling scheme and owe some people some money. Pop said like ten grand—"

"Ten grand?!" Nate said. "Who the fuck would loan Levi ten thousand dollars?"

"That's what we all wanna know, but Bryan said Pop told him Sunny called Ma all upset because Levi is supposedly receiving threatening phone calls, and he let Sunny listen to one of the messages, and so now she's all upset and worried. She told Ma she had about thirty-five hundred in savings, and asked if she and Pop could loan them the rest."

Nate shook his head in disgust. He knew early in his sister's relationship she was dealing with a trifling man, but he never imagined Levi would have her involved in something like this.

Geo said, "So Sunny told Ma they need to just cancel the wedding altogether, and of course this pissed Ma off because of all the money they spent on everything and she already sent out the invitations—"

"This is so fucked up, man," Nate shook his head again, "but I'm glad she canceled that shit to be honest. What the hell is Levi doing gambling if he don't even have a job? Was he taking money out of Sunny's account or some shit?"

"I have no idea about that, but this is crazy. Ten grand?" Geo whistled. "How can you owe someone ten grand? Wouldn't you stop lending them money after they didn't pay back the first grand? The first one hundred?"

"Something's not right," Nate said. "And what's really fucked up is how Sunny has to cover for him."

* * *

"What are you sitting there looking mad about?"

He didn't realize his feelings showed on his face. He smiled despite how pissed he was. Seeing Tora lifted his mood a little. "I was pouting because I came home and you weren't here."

She dropped her purse and tote bag on the floor and rushed over to the couch, hopping onto his lap.

"Girl?!" She laughed and kissed him softly and he decided it didn't matter that she'd just body-dived on top of his penis.

"I had to go home and check on my babies," she said. "It's bad enough I leave them alone and I'm spending so much time here with you. Silk followed me around, whining the whole time I was packing my overnight bag. I think he knew I wasn't coming back home for the night."

"You're gonna have to get rid of your cats."

She looked at him as if he'd told her to hose them down with water before electrocuting them. "Are you outta your mind? I'm not getting rid of my cats!"

"Chill, babe," he chuckled, "I'm only joking."

"Don't play with me about my babies, okay?"

"So how are we gonna do this? You know I can't stay at your place. And I like the idea of coming home to you every day."

She tilted her head to consider it, then said, "I don't know what we're gonna do, Nate, but my cats ain't going nowhere that's for sure."

"Well I guess you'll be driving home every day after work to check on them before coming here."

"You are crazy!"

He leaned forward and kissed her neck. His lower half throbbed in response to her straddling his lap.

"Seriously though... why were you looking so mean when I walked in?" Tora asked.

His mood quickly deflated. "I was just thinking about my sister and her stupid-ass boyfriend. That's all. Oh... and the wedding's off."

"Oh my god. Why? What happened?" She slid out of his lap and sat beside him.

"The guy is in some kind of financial trouble, owing somebody thousands of dollars, and he got my sister involved trying to bail his ass out of the situation."

"That's terrible. Who does he owe money to?"

"I have no idea. I tried calling my sister after I left the gym to find out what's going on, but she didn't answer my call."

Tora shook her head.

"It's fucked up. She don't need to be dealing with this type of shit while she's pregnant."

"Exactly," Tora said.

"Anyway…." He wrapped his arm around her shoulder and kissed the side of her face. "I don't want to talk about it anymore because it just pisses me off. What do you want for dinner? Should we order in or do you wanna go out?"

"Oooh… I could use a margarita right now. Let's go out."

Nate got up from the sofa to grab his keys from the bar counter. "A spontaneous dinner out with my lady on a weeknight? This is what I live for now," he smiled, and followed her outside.

THIRTY-EIGHT

Maybe it was her body's need to make up for lost time, or maybe it was just that he turned her on, but the pulsing between her legs made her roll over on top of him for the third time.

"Again?" he said, smiling up at her.

Tora leaned forward and kissed him in response, her hand moving down between them for his penis. She guided him inside. She straightened her back and began to roll her hips. It took only a second before his flesh swelled to its full length, sending ripples of ecstasy up her spine at the feel of it sliding in and out of her. No matter how many times they made love she was always anticipating the next time.

Her pace quickened and soon her body was slick with perspiration. Sweat trickled down behind her ears and down her neck onto her chest.

Nate palmed her breasts, firmly squeezing them as if they were his anchor for the wild ride she was giving him. His breath came out in sharp gasps as Tora rode him faster and faster, the bed screeching in rhythm with her movements.

She closed her eyes and threw her head back. No other man's body melded so perfectly with hers. No one else had felt this good.

Tora reached back and gripped his knees with her hands as she bucked her hips with unbridled fervor.

"Get up."

Her body sizzled. Every nerve was on fire.

"Get up," she heard him say again. But she couldn't get up. Not when she was in a state of heated passion, just on the verge of euphoria. Tora leaned forward, planted her hands on his chest, and began to bounce her hips. Nate sucked in deep breaths, and Tora felt his legs tighten beneath her.

Sweat rolled down her forehead, stinging her eyes, but not even the irritation could slow her down. She squeezed her eyes closed, giving in to the forceful climax overtaking her body.

Nate's outcry, the liquid warmth of his satisfaction, mingled with her own.

* * *

The apartment reeked of hot garbage when she entered it two days later. She honestly couldn't remember the last time she'd taken the trash out, but that was the least of her worries because her kittens came trotting out from her bedroom when they heard the jingle of her keys, mewing loudly as if they hadn't seen her in ages.

"Hi," Tora cooed. "I missed you, too." She picked them up and carried them over to the sofa and sat down. Whoever said they preferred dogs above cats because cats are not affectionate just didn't know her cats. She giggled as Mink and Silk appeared to be in competition with each other to see who could give her the most licks and headbutts. And she welcomed all of that love because she had no plans to see Nate later that evening.

"You wanna go outside? We can go outside," she told them. It was a gorgeous day and she figured they could use some sun. After gathering the trash to take to the dumpster, she put Mink on a leash and carried Silk in the sling tote.

Once outdoors, she took her time walking to the trash receptacles since Mink was her usual curious self and wanted to sniff every bush and caress every flower along the way. They turned a corner and had to step around two young men carrying a sofa. She was a few feet past them when she heard one of the guys say:

—Dude, you see that shit? She's carrying that cat like it's a baby. A fuckin' baby! And what's up with the one on the leash? That bitch is confused!

Tora rolled her eyes and kept walking. It was too beautiful a day to let a manchild spoil her mood.

She tossed the trash at the dumpster site and then led Mink towards the courtyard. A woman and young girl around the age of four were sitting at one of the tables enjoying ice cream cones. Suddenly Tora wanted an ice cream cone. A chocolate fudge-dipped one from Dairy Queen.

"Mom, look! Kitties!" the girl said, leaving her cone on the table and hopping down from the bench before her mother had a chance to stop her. She ran right up to Mink and dropped to her knees.

"Harley, no!" her mother shouted.

"It's okay," Tora laughed as the girl roughed Mink's head.

"I'm so sorry," the woman said. "She does this every time she sees animals. Cats especially. I try to warn her that not all animals are friendly and she needs to be careful."

"It's not a problem. I was the same way when I was a little girl," Tora said. It was a good thing Mink was her most personable cat because had it been Silk the kid ran up to she may have been lying on the ground crying from a scratch to her face for frightening him.

"Mom, see the kitty? He likes me," Harley said, and took possession of the leash.

Tora and the woman sat down at the nearby table while Harley walked with Mink around the courtyard.

"My brother has a cat Harley just loves and—" she paused, "I'm Lauren by the way—"

Tora nodded and smiled. "I'm Tora."

"Oh, that's a lovely name."

"Thanks."

"Whenever we visit him, my brother, she's all over the cat. The poor thing doesn't stand a chance." Lauren licked the sides of Harley's cone to keep it from running all over her hand. "She wants to take him home with us every time."

Tora chuckled.

"I thought about getting one for her, but her father disapproves. He doesn't like indoor pets."

"Oh," Tora nodded.

"Honey, your ice cream is melting. If you don't want it I'm gonna toss it, okay?" Lauren called out to her daughter.

Harley was too busy laughing at Mink waltzing across one of the tabletops.

"See what I mean?" Lauren shook her head. "She begged for this ice cream and now she's not even thinking about it." She got up and threw both of their cones in the trash can when Harley didn't respond to her second call. "But I may do it anyway. He's rarely home, so it's not like he'll have to deal with it."

"Her dad?"

"Yeah. He travels a lot for work, so he's gone for weeks at a time. It'll be a nice surprise for her." She smiled.

"How sweet," Tora said.

Lauren reached over and patted Silk's head. "Who's this little guy? He's sitting here like he's the king."

"He's the spoiled one. He doesn't like to be outside too much."

"He's beautiful. I can tell he's well-taken care of."

"He is. Both of them are."

For the next hour they sat and chatted and kept an eye on Harley. Lauren complained to Tora about her upstairs neighbors whose child sprinted from one end of the apartment to the next all day long, and about her next door neighbor who woke up every morning coughing up phlegm. She said she'd tried to become a member of the social committee board but was told she had to have been a resident of the complex for at least six months. She and her husband just moved to the area from Tomball four months ago.

Tora told her that she'd chosen the third floor apartment because she was afraid of being flooded out during Houston's infamous rain storms, and because she didn't like anyone living above her. She told her about the animal shelter where she loved to volunteer and how it would be a great place to look if Lauren decided to get a cat for Harley. She told her about the guy who called her a confused bitch right before she came over to the courtyard.

Harley threw a fit as soon as Lauren said it was time for them to leave.

"In a minute! I just want to play with him," she cried.

"We have to go now, Harley. It's lunch time and I need to start the laundry."

Harley didn't want to hear any of it and plopped down in the grass, still holding on to Mink's leash.

"It's okay. You'll see us around again soon," Tora tried to calm her.

Eventually they both had to leave their seat at the table and go to Harley when she wouldn't come over as her mother demanded.

Tora grabbed Mink's leash. It broke her heart to see the girl's feelings crushed. "Thank you for playing with her today, Harley. She really likes you, too."

Lauren had to pull her daughter off the ground. Fat tears rolled down the girl's face as Lauren waved goodbye to Tora and carried Harley away kicking and screaming.

THIRTY-NINE

When Sunny didn't respond to his text messages or return the phone call after he'd left a voicemail, he decided to dial her office. He had a special rapport with the receptionist and knew he wouldn't have any trouble getting through to Sunny right away.

"Good afternoon. Thank you for calling Thomas, Baker, and Walker. How may I direct your call?"

Nate smiled. It was several years ago when he first heard that voice—a soft and breathy tone that was more fitting for nighttime radio than a stiff law office. He was so taken aback by the beauty of it he'd asked Sunny to tell him all about the lady with the sultry voice and if he could schedule an appointment to come in and see what she looked like.

Then he learned she was married.

But Veronica had no problem letting him know that if she ever decided to betray her husband he would be the one she'd risk it all for if he indeed was the handsome brother in the photo on Sunny's credenza. Nate knew she was being facetious, but every once in a while he would call the office just to have his ego stroked.

"Mrs. Tramell, how you doin'? It's Nate Walker."

"Well hello my lover-in-waiting… it's been a long time."

Her voice really could make a man give up everything. It was just that sexy.

"How has life been treating you?" she asked.

"Life's great. I can't complain about anything."

"Still wasting time with that bougie chick?"

Nate chuckled. She was referring to his ex-girlfriend—the one who dumped him, the one he was still mourning when the incident with Kaneesa occurred. "Naw. She's been out of the picture for a while now. I've moved on to someone better."

"Ohhh… I see. So *now* you're cheating on *me?*"

"Mrs. Tramell, you left me no choice. Did you expect me to wait forever?"

"Is she good to you?"

"Oh yeah. She's perfect."

"Well… when she acts up, I'm here if you ever need to get your mind off things."

Nate chuckled again. "We really need to stop talking like this before someone thinks we're serious."

"You're right," she laughed. "What can I do for you?"

"Is Sunny available?"

"Hold on, let me try—"

"No, don't tell her it's me."

"Why not?"

"She might not answer."

"She's definitely not going to answer if I don't announce who you are. She has me screening her calls today."

"Alright. Tell her it's me, and it's an emergency."

"Is everything all right, Nate?"

"Oh yeah. I don't mean like a tragic emergency… just… I need to talk to my sister. That's all."

"Hold on."

Nearly seven minutes passed before Sunny picked up the line.

"Sunny?"

"Yes, brother?" she answered, her voice edged with annoyance.

"What's going on with you, baby sis? Why you not answering?"

"Is that why you're calling my office?"

"Yeah. I've been worried about you."

"There's nothing to worry about, Nate."

"That's not what I heard."

She sucked her teeth.

"And I'm kinda disappointed I had to hear it from Geo."

"So is that what y'all are doing? The whole family knows? This was supposed to be between me, Mama, and Daddy."

"Well… they said the wedding was canceled, which surprised me because me and you just had lunch not too long ago, and you didn't mention that anything was wrong."

"Nate, don't try to act like you care about the wedding now."

She had a point there, but it still bothered him that Levi was causing her grief. "Sis, I'm just trying to make sure you're okay. Once I heard about the threatening phone calls and how Levi got you involved, my main concern is you, Anaya, and Deuce—"

Sunny remained quiet.

"So what's going on with Levi? What kinda mess is he in?"

She sighed heavily. "He has a little gambling addiction, Nate."

"Little? Sunny, I heard he owes somebody ten grand, and now they're calling for him to pay up. Sis, there's nothing 'little' about that."

"Everybody has an addiction to something, Nate, whether we acknowledge it or not. For some it's cigarettes, or food, or shopping, or playing video games. Levi likes to bet on things and he went way overboard this time."

Nate shook his head. "Sunny, are you covering for him? Ten thousand dollars is a lot to owe somebody over a few bets."

"So now you think I'm lying? I really don't have to explain

anything to you or anybody else for that matter, Nate. I'm going to figure it out."

He didn't want to upset her any futher, so he decided to quit with the questioning while he was ahead. "Do you need my help with anything? I mean… do you need me to take the kids off your hands for a few days?"

"Yeah, right," she said. "You wouldn't last two hours with them. And how would you pull that off with your work schedule? Are you on vacation or something?"

"No. Just trying to help you out if I can."

"I'm sure Levi would like a break from them for a few days, but… that's his job. He's the stay-at-home dad."

Nate held back his thoughts on that one. "Talk to you later, sis. Call me if you need anything."

"Alright, brother. Bye."

FORTY

The bristles of his beard tickled her skin.

"Wake up, sleepy head. Aren't you gonna be late?"

Nate was kissing all over her face. The crisp cool scent of his bath soap filled her nose. His face was damp like he hadn't completely dried off his body. Tora groaned. "What time is it? I just need fifteen more minutes."

"Seven-thirty. Don't you leave at eight when you work the early shift?"

She raised her head to check the time for herself then plopped back against the pillow. "I really don't feel like going," she groaned again.

Nate chuckled. "Why not?"

"Because a certain somebody wouldn't let me get any sleep last night."

He smiled and kissed her forehead. "That's strange because we both got the same amount of sleep, but I woke up energized this morning."

"I'm sure you did," she smirked as he left the bed. Last night Nate was insatiable. Her body was still tender from the number of times he'd taken her.

She watched as he stood pulling clothing out of the dresser

drawers, and she thought how natural it felt to wake up next to him and see him go through his morning routine.

"I'm about to make breakfast," he said. "Should I pack yours to go?"

"I think I'm gonna call off."

"Really, babe? Are you being lazy today?" He slipped on a pair of those jogger pants she loved on him—the ones that showcased his firm ass.

She pulled the bed sheet up to her chin. "You should, too."

Nate looked at her. "What's wrong?"

"Nothing's wrong. I just don't wanna go to work today. And I want you to stay here with me."

He came over and sat on the edge of the bed. "Let me get this straight.... You want me to call off work just so we can do nothing?"

"Yes. I just wanna relax."

"I don't think I've ever called off work," he said.

"Today would be the perfect day to do it. Let's just chill."

He chuckled and shook his head. "You're really a bad influence, you know that?"

"Will you bring my phone from the living room so I can call my boss? It's in my purse on the floor by the coffee table."

* * *

"It'll be just our luck somebody sees us."

"Will you stop saying that? Nobody's gonna see us," Tora said.

Nate accepted the tickets and property map from the cashier and they entered the gates to The Houston Zoo.

"It's called Murphy's Law. Something is bound to go wrong."

Tora rolled her eyes. "I never would've guessed you of all people would be a scaredy-cat."

"I'm just saying..." he chuckled. "How will I explain to my

supervisor if someone mentions they saw me out today?"

She'd convinced him to call off work after all. Following breakfast in bed they took a two-hour nap, and when they woke up Tora decided she no longer wanted to spend the day indoors and suggested the two of them go out for a day of fun.

"It's not gonna happen, Nate. Relax." She took the map from him. "What do you wanna see first?" she asked.

"Doesn't matter," he said. "Wherever you go, I'll follow."

"I'm surprised you didn't grow up to become a zoo keeper or a veterinarian," he told her after they had been walking for a while.

"It seems the most logical career for me considering my love for animals, right? But I loved fashion and photography just as much, and I believed I could do more professionally in those fields."

Several of the animals she had been excited to see weren't even outside of their caves, but she and Nate got a kick out of watching the baboons and chimps' mischievous behavior.

"I know you can't be around cats, but do you ever think about having like a dog or something?"

"Eh," he shrugged. "I mean… I never thought about it. I guess having one could be cool, but I don't know if I'm ready for that type of responsibility. You gotta walk them and bathe them and take 'em to the vet. It's almost like having a kid, y'know?"

"Exactly, and that's why I've always favored cats. They're pretty self-sufficient. Just leave some food and water out and they're good alone for a few days. I used to have a rabbit, too, when I was a little girl, but she got out of her cage some kinda way and I never saw her again. My daddy swore up and down our neighbors found it and was holding the rabbit hostage in their house," she laughed. "We had a parrot. He was so pretty! We named him Mr. Bentley. My mom didn't care for him though. She said he made too much noise and the cat we had at the time was always messing with him, which made him squawk even more."

"So you had your own zoo when you were a kid?"

"Pretty much," she said.

They chose to stop and have lunch at the deli. Nate found an empty, moderately clean table for them to eat outdoors. As soon as Tora set their tray of sandwiches down a crow fluttered onto the table, and Nate nearly knocked over their drinks fanning it away. The bird landed on the next table, two more swooped down beside it, and all three stood watching, waiting for Tora or Nate to drop some food.

Nate said, "Maybe we should eat inside."

"No. Let's stay out here. They're not gonna bother us. The weather's too perfect to not have lunch on the patio."

"If you say so," he laughed. "I'm just trying to save us from a bird attack."

She took a chunk of bread from her sandwich and tossed it to the crows. The swiftest of the bunch snatched it and flew away.

"Babe, why would you do that?!"

Tora giggled.

"I see now you're a big kid sometimes," he shook his head smiling.

She blew him a kiss and started on her turkey sandwich.

"I admit this turned out to be a very relaxing day," Nate said.

"It is. I wish we could stay out here forever," Tora sighed.

They were coasting around the lake in a pedal boat at Hermann Park. Tora had suggested they go to the park when they left the zoo because she had never been there. They spent the first hour touring the park on rental bikes when they came upon the lake.

"I may end up falling asleep out here," Nate said. "It's comfortable." He yawned.

"You and me both," she said, and yawned too. "I told you we didn't get enough sleep last night."

"You're probably right," he said, giving her a sexy grin.

His phone rang in his pocket.

"What could my dad be calling me about this time of day?" he said, looking at the screen.

Tora glanced around the lake. "Maybe he sees you," she laughed.

"Oh, you got jokes, huh?" Nate reached over and squeezed her thigh as he answered the call.

Tora was busy looking at the turtles in the water when her attention returned to Nate when she heard him exclaim.

"I thought the baby wasn't due for another month? So she went into labor early?!"

"What's wrong?" Tora asked when his call ended.

"My sister just had the baby. Like an hour ago, my dad said."

"Well… that's good news, right?"

"She wasn't due until the end of next month."

"Oh," Tora said.

"My dad said she was in a lot of pain yesterday, so she told Levi to take her to the hospital late last night."

"But she and the baby are okay?"

"I guess so. Dad didn't say. He said he and my mom are going up there to see her when they get off work."

"Well… congratulations on your new niece or neph—"

"I know it's all Levi's fault. He has her stressed out over his bullshit."

Tora looked at him. "You really think that's why she had the baby early?"

"I know so. But Sunny will never admit to it."

"I noticed you don't seem to like him all that much. Why is that?"

Nate shook his head. "He's just *the worst* dude for my sister. He don't do shit for her, barely do anything for the kids, don't contribute nothing to the household, ain't trying to be nothing. He's just there.

Living off her and spending her money."

"She obviously loves him, so—"

"I just feel like I'm watching her slowly waste her life away with this dude."

"Yeah, but, Nate I'm sure you know there is nothing you can do about that."

"Sunny is too smart to settle for a low-life."

Tora shrugged. "Maybe there's something she sees in him that she lacks herself. It can happen. Smart women fall for their polar opposite all the time."

He sighed heavily and shook his head again. "The baby is a month premature because of his punk ass."

"Are you going to the hospital to see them?"

"I want to, but with the way I'm feeling right now I might end up cussing Levi's ass out."

Tora sucked her teeth. "Nate—"

"I'm serious," he said.

"Your sister's relationship with that man has nothing to do with you, so you need to stop all this crazy talk."

He reached over and grabbed her hand. "I'm just worried about her. That's all."

"I understand," Tora said, "but saying something to him is not gonna make Sunny love him any less. If anything it'll probably make her love him more. And hate you."

Nate chuckled. "I hear you, babe. Now let's go home and take a quick shower so we can go and see my new niece."

Tora smiled and they pedaled the boat around, returning to the dock.

She liked the sound of that: *Let's go home.*

FORTY-ONE

Sunny was alone and just waking up when he entered her room. A slight frown creased her forehead when she saw him. Then she smiled.

"Brother, what're you doing here?"

"I came to see you. Duh."

She rolled her eyes.

"How're you feeling?"

"I feel okay. Just tired."

He took a seat on the bench next to the window. A bucket of white flowers sat on the table next to him, along with a teddy bear and bouquet of pink, and black and white polka dot balloons.

"What about the baby?"

"She's fine. They have her in NICU right now."

Nate knew it was the place where they kept the preemie babies. The ones who needed prolonged extra care. The ones who had the potential for developmental issues. "She got all ten fingers and toes?"

Sunny rolled her eyes again. "Yes, brother, she has all ten fingers and toes."

"Alright," he laughed. "Just making sure." He picked up the teddy bear. "I'm sorry I didn't think to get you a gift."

"Those are from Kaneesa and the ladies at the office."

"Where is Levi?"

She straightened a leg, wincing as she readjusted the blanket at her waist. "I told him to go home so he can get some sleep. He was very tired this morning."

"Are the kids with him, too?"

"No. He took them to their grandma's—his mama's house—last night. Anaya was crying when I talked to her this morning because she wants to see the baby. I told her her daddy is gonna bring her up here later so she can see her little sister."

"You know she's gonna be all over her like she was with Duece."

"Oh god, yes," Sunny smiled and shook her head. "I still think about that day I walked into the nursery and she was trying to pull Duece out of his bed. He was about as big as she was at the time! And she really thought she could carry him. At two years old!"

Nate chuckled and returned the teddy bear. "What did you name her?"

"Skylar."

"Walker? That's pretty dope."

Sunny twisted her lips. "She's a Fontenot, you know that. Just like Anaya and Baby Levi."

He sat back against the bench. "Will I be able to see her today?"

"Yeah, I just have to tell the nurse and she'll escort you down there. They'll probably ask you a few questions to make sure you're not sick or anything."

"Tora is with me," he said. "She wants to see the baby, too. She's in the waiting room."

Nate's first thought was that she looked just like her daddy. She already had Levi's unibrow, and lips that appeared to be in a perpetual pout. The only thing Nate could see the baby inherited from Sunny was her long lashes.

"Awww," Tora said, standing beside him as they peered through the Plexi-glass. "How cute."

"Another little munchkin added to the bunch." Nate hoped his niece grew up to look more like her mother than her father. He leaned in closer to the glass. She was so tiny and all he could think about was how she should still be inside the womb.

"This makes number six, right?" Tora asked.

"Yep. Number six," he nodded his head. "Another little one for Uncle Nate to spoil, according to Sunny."

"She's right, because it seems Bryanna and Melody have you wrapped around their fingers."

Nate could only smile proudly. It was true. Bryanna, Melody, Evan, Anaya, Baby Levi, and now Skylar could have anything they wanted from him.

His mother and father had made it to the hospital by the time he and Tora returned to Sunny's room.

"How did you make it here before us?" Victoria asked after he'd given her his standard kiss on the cheek and then a hug to his father. "I thought you would've been working late."

"I took a sick day."

Sunny and Victoria gasped at the same time.

"Brother, you told me you weren't sick!"

"Why would you go visit the baby if you're sick, son?"

"You're not supposed to be around the baby if you're sick!"

His mistake didn't dawn on him until he saw the concern on both of their faces. "Relax. I'm not sick."

"You just said you were sick, Nate," Victoria said.

"I said I took a sick day."

"Isn't that what a sick day is? When you take a day off work because you're sick?"

"Yeah, but we just took the day off to relax and hang out."

Victoria looked from Nate to Tora and then back at Nate again. "Son, are you telling me you lied about being sick just so the two of you can *hang out*? You're abusing your employer's benefits?"

"Ma—" Nate groaned, closing his eyes. He wished he'd kept his mouth shut.

"What if you get sick for real, Nate?" she said. "If you start calling off work arbitrarily, when you really need days off you won't have any to take, or your employer won't believe you—"

"Oh, god." Nate raked a hand through his locks.

"This is why a lot of companies are doing away with sick time and going PTO. Because of situations like this where people abuse the system. That's what weekends are for, Nate, if you wanted to *hang out*." She looked over at Tora as if she just knew Tora was the reason he decided to call in sick from work.

"Ma, can we please not—"

"You know I didn't raise you to be unethical, Nate."

He looked at his dad who stood chuckling and shaking his head.

"Pop, haven't you called in sick before when you just didn't feel like going to work that day?"

"Uhhh… maybe when I was younger, son. Sure, I've done that a few times."

"See, Ma?" he said, smiling.

Victoria sighed and adjusted her purse on her shoulder. "Honey, let's go so we can see our grandbaby," she said to Gerald, and they left the room.

* * *

"Are you the black sheep in your family or something? No offense, but it seems like your mom doesn't like you at all."

Nate busted out in laughter. He and Tora were lying in his bed on their backs, staring up at the ceiling.

"What makes you think that?" he asked.

"She seems annoyed by you. But I noticed she doesn't act like that towards your sister and brothers."

"Well… I wouldn't say that she doesn't like me. She's just a strict parent, and she wants things to go her way all the time."

"That's not strict, that's controlling, Nate. And she talks to you like you're still a child. I'm sorry, but I wanted to say something so bad today when she was going on and on about us taking a day off."

"Why didn't you?" he said.

"My mom taught me to respect my elders at all times."

Nate chuckled. "You stood there and let me take the heat all by myself. That wasn't cool."

"I just didn't wanna cause any more stress for anybody."

"I'm used to it. I've been dealing with Victoria Helena Walker's attitude all my life."

"How does your dad deal with her? He's so cool and relaxed. I wonder if he feels like he has to walk around on pins and needles when they're at home together."

"Not really. She caters to him, actually. He does the same for her, too."

Tora huffed. "I find that hard to believe on her part."

"Are you talking about my mama?"

"I'm just saying… she's not very nice when it comes to you. Or me for that matter. And I don't like it. I'm so close with my mom and dad, and I know for sure if I were to take you home to meet them they would invite you in as if you were their own son. Your mom may as well spit on my shoes with the way she looks at me."

"Stop it," Nate shook his head. "She's not a cruel person at all."

"That's how I feel sometimes. I hate to say it, but it's almost like I'd rather not be around her if she's gonna act like that."

Nate reached over and pulled her close to him. He knew his mother was a tough woman to warm up to. A couple of his past girlfriends had the same complaint, but he hated Tora felt this way. Spending time with his family was an obligation, and now that she was officially his woman, he couldn't imagine not having her by his side at their gatherings.

FORTY-TWO

"Gosh!" Tora yawned for what seemed like the dozenth time within a few mintues. "I am having the hardest time keeping my eyes open."

"That man keeping you up every night, ain't he?" Candace laughed and popped her gum. "Believe me, girl, I understand."

"You are so crazy," Tora said. "Sometimes we do stay up pretty late at night watching Netflix, but—"

"Uhn-huh. Are you sure y'all be watching Netflix or does Netflix be watching y'all? Tell the truth."

"You know what?… I'm not even going there with you, girl," Tora laughed, and commenced to pulling outfits from the racks to start the new window display for the fall season.

"I know how it is when you can't get enough of each other. You don't mind losing a little sleep just to get a fix."

Tora yawned again. Her eyes were watery because she'd yawned so much. "I need a nap. It seems like for the past couple of weeks all I wanna do when I get home is take a nap."

"Really?" Candace said. "Maybe your energy is low. Do you take vitamins?"

"I used to. Years ago. But those things made me hungry."

"Hmm… that's a new one for me. I've never heard before of vitamins making someone hungry."

Tora pulled out her mobile phone to check the time. She had two hours left of her work shift and was tempted to go to the restroom stall and sit on the toilet just so she could close her eyes for a few mintues. She was that tired.

Candace said, "Oh! I know what I meant to ask you. What are you doing after work today? There is something for the wedding I want to go and look at, and I want your opinion."

"Didn't you just hear me say I need a nap? I am going home to get in my bed."

"Aww, c'mon, Tora. I want you to come with me. There're these hats I'm thinking about getting for my bridesmaids. I think they'll go great with the dresses, but my sister said they're ugly. She doesn't have much fashion sense, so I don't trust what she says anyway."

"Why do you want the bridesmaids to wear hats? What kind of hats? Sounds old-fashioned."

"It's not old-fashioned," Candace said. "I think it's classy."

"Everybody doesn't like to wear hats. You might wanna take that into consideration, too."

"But it's *my* wedding."

Tora shrugged. "Just trying to warn you."

"I have a picture of the hat I can show you," Candace said, reaching into her pocket for her phone. "I got the idea from a photo I saw in Vogue magazine."

Tora looked at the photo. The hat wasn't ugly, but it wasn't cute either. "I'll have to see it against the dress," she admitted.

"You don't like it? I think it's beautiful."

"If you like it, that's all that matters. It's *your* wedding as you said."

They ended up someplace on Harwin Drive which, to Tora, was nothing more than a low-budget flea market. Underneath dim overhead lights were rows and rows of tightly-packed racks containing gowns and tuxedos and pant suits, and every formal event accessory imaginable. The clutter and density of it all gave her a headache. She believed they were there to see a particular hat, but nearly an hour later of shadowing Candace, Candace still hadn't shown her this hat she just had to see.

"I'm going to find a place to sit down," Tora said. Her patience was gone.

"What's wrong?"

"I told you I'm tired, girl," she said, stifling a yawn. "You wanted me to see the hat, now where is it?"

"Ohhh… it's not in this store. It's at the one down the street."

Tora's eyes narrowed. "Candace—"

"Alright! Alright! I promise we won't be too much longer."

"Why are we here anyway when you've already chosen the bridesmaids dresses? And please don't tell me you got them from this store because, if that's the case, I could've made the dresses for you myself."

"Oh nooo." She laughed. "I just like to come here to see what they have and to get some ideas."

"Ideas for what?"

"I don't know. I just like to browse, okay? I'm in love with all things wedding right now."

Tora sucked her teeth.

"You'll understand once you start planning yours."

"Well… that's not happening anytime soon," Tora said.

They were in the kids' section now and Candace picked up a dress that could have easily been a poodle on a hanger because that's exactly what it looked like.

"I still haven't decided if I want one or two flower girls," Candace said. "I kinda like this."

Tora shook her head. "Will you put down that ugly dress?"

"Now you sound like my sister." Candace turned the dress around to look at the back. "I consider this fashion-forward."

"There is nothing forward about it. It's not even backward. Whoever designed it needs to be shot. Where would a kid where something like that? It's a mess."

"Geez… you must really be tired because you're talking about shooting people and everything."

"I'm beginning to think your sister is right because if you think that atrocity is cute then, yeah, I question your taste. That's why they have it so dim in here so you can't see how bad this stuff really looks."

Candace laughed out loud and returned the dress to the rack. "Fine."

"Can we leave this place already? It stinks in here, too."

"Oh god, Tora… are you sure you're not pregnant because I've never seen you aggravated before?"

"What?! Girl, no! Definitely no. I'm on the pill to make sure there won't be any accidents."

"Ruki and I decided we're gonna wait a couple years before we start our family. Travel a little bit. I may even take a few classes on visual design. Ruki's dad lives in London, and he hasn't seen him in like six years, so we're hoping to go and visit him. Actually, he has a lot of family in London he told me."

"His dad's not coming to the wedding?" Tora asked as they exited the store. She was glad to be outdoors and away from that musty interior.

"There're some issues with his visa, and I don't know all of the specifics, but Ruki said it's a high chance he won't be able to attend our wedding, which is kinda sad if you ask me. I'd rather he be there than my mother-in-law."

"Oh yeah," Tora nodded in agreement. "I can definitely relate to that sentiment."

* * *

She didn't realize she'd slept so long until she woke up and noticed she'd slept right through her alarm and saw the missed calls and text messages from her parents and Nate.

Mink mewed softly, and Tora was surprised to find her lying right next to her. Mink never slept in her bed, preferring her own cat bed in the den.

After a quick trip to the bathroom Tora called Myles, then Sharon, before calling Nate.

"Woman, I'm glad you called because I was sitting here right now putting my shoes on, about to head over there."

"What are you talking about, Nate?" Tora smiled.

"I was wondering why I haven't heard from you all day."

"I hung out with Candace for a little while after work, and then I came home and fell asleep."

"You know I need you here," he said. "I had to eat dinner and watch Power all by myself. I didn't like it."

Tora went to the kitchen and opened the refrigerator. She was starved. "I can't spend every night at your place, Nate. I have cats to take care of, remember?"

He sucked his teeth and she laughed.

"I may stop by after work tomorrow."

"May? Naw… I'm thinking you need to come over right now."

"It's damn-near midnight, Nate, I'm not leaving my apartment this late."

He chuckled. "I don't expect you to, but… I'm bored. And I'm lonely without my lady."

Tora blushed and rolled her eyes at the same time. She grabbed the box of *Hot Pockets* from the freezer and popped them into the microwave."

"I talked to Sunny today," he said. "She told me they might let her come home Sunday."

"Wow. Already? That's cool. So she and the baby are doing good?"

"Well… the baby's not eating as much as she should, so they're trying to figure out why."

"Oh. Is Sunny breast feeding?"

"I don't know," Nate said. "I mean… I assume she's not. She didn't breast-feed Anaya and Deuce."

Tora took her plate and drink over to the living room sofa and sat down. She browsed the list of her recorded TV shows and settled on *Real Housewives of Atlanta.*

She and Nate chatted a few more minutes, and as soon as the call ended she wished she was at his apartment, curled up next to him on the sofa.

Mink's sharp hiss took her attention away from the television screen to see the cat violently paw at Silk's face. Silk was only trying to claim his territory across Tora's lap when Mink pushed him away. The exchange made Tora laugh.

It was the first time Mink had ever been so protective of her.

FORTY-THREE

Nate pulled into the driveway next to Jamal's car and parked. The garage door was up, but he still walked around to the front door and rang the bell. It had been a while since he hung out with his boys, and he decided to stop by Jamal's place for a visit.

Jamal answered the door wearing gray sweatpants and an old faded Sam Houston State University T-shirt that was no doubt from his college days and when he was about twenty pounds lighter. For years Nate had tried convincing his friend to meet him in the gym, but whereas Nate was gung ho about health and working out his body, Jamal would rather work out his mind. Which was why Nate wasn't surprised to see a book in Jamal's hand, his thumb as a place holder between the pages at the midway point.

"What's up, man?" Jamal said, and they leaned in for the ceremonial brotherly hug.

"What's up with you?" Nate followed him inside.

"Chillin'," Jamal said. "Just chillin'."

Nate sat on the couch behind the ottoman littered with books and journals. The TV was on a sports channel, but the volume was low. Nate said, "It's a beautiful day outside. I thought you, Kev, and Chauncey would've been out and about somewhere."

"Naw, man. I haven't even talked to those fools today." He tossed the book on the ottoman and picked up the television remote. "Chauncey had us meet him at this place Thursday night— someplace on 1960—called Whiskey River."

"Was it live?"

"Kevin liked it, but it wasn't my type of spot at all. The crowd was too young and not black enough."

Nate chuckled. "You know how Chauncey is… as long as there are women in the building he's in heaven."

"As usual, he left us early with a new chick on his arm." Jamal shook his head. "I can't do it, man. I can't be laying up with a new chick every other week."

"Hey… that's a dream for a lot of guys."

"Anyway…" Jamal said. "I'm surprised you're out today and not somewhere training somebody."

"Naw, not today. And Tora had to work…. I didn't wanna stay in the apartment all day."

"Tora? Is that the same girl from—"

"Bombshells? Yeah."

"Oh. So y'all are still hanging out?"

"She's my lady."

Jamal looked at him. "For real?"

"Yep."

"You just couldn't resist, huh?" Jamal laughed.

"Couldn't resist."

"Whatever happened with her man though?"

"He wasn't her man. That was some crazy dude she met who wouldn't leave her alone."

"I admit I'm kind of jealous."

Nate laughed.

"She got any sisters?"

"Naw. She's the only child."

"Damn."

Nate laughed again.

"I'm hopeful I'll meet my queen before the end of the year. I definitely don't wanna be thirty-four and still single. I thought I would have a couple little Jamals running around here by now."

"Yeah, I always felt like you would be the first one to get married out of all of us."

"Wouldn't it be some shit if Chauncey is the one?"

"Wouldn't it? And the chick will probably propose to *his* ass."

"Exactly," Jamal said. "It's crazy."

Nate remained at Jamal's house long enough to watch Denzel Washington whoop everyone's ass in *The Equalizer*. He left when the time neared that Tora would be getting off work in order to be home when she made it there.

FORTY-FOUR

"Geez, babe… what'd you do? Put on the whole bottle?"

"What?" Nate said, settling into the driver's seat and buckling his seat belt.

"Your cologne," Tora said.

"I did only two squirts as I always do. Why?"

"It smells like you did way more than just two."

"I thought you liked my cologne," he said.

"I do. It's just really strong today," she said.

He put the SUV in Reverse and pulled out of the parking space. "This morning you accused me of using strange seasonings while I was cooking breakfast. What's up with your nose right now, babe?"

This made her laugh, and she pressed the button on her door to crack the window even though he had the A/C on. "Maybe this is a sign that I don't need to be going to your mom's house."

"Aww, c'mon," he chuckled, and looked over at her. "I knew you were gonna say that."

"I could've stayed at the apartment while you went to have dinner with your family. I wouldn't've minded it at all."

"T, I already told you. We have dinner at my mama's house every Sunday. *Every* Sunday. Like… without question. It's what we do. My brothers have their wives there with them, and since you're my lady now, I want you there too."

She sighed and looked out of the window. "There's no room for me at Mrs. Walker's table." She meant it in more ways than one, but didn't bother voicing it.

"That's not true," he said. "We'll pull a chair from the rec room like we did last time. Besides, my sister and her kids' father won't be there today, so—"

Tora switched the channel on the radio from 97.9 to 102.1. "Still, I'd rather stay home," she said.

He looked over at her. "You serious, babe?" He rested his hand on her thigh. "Don't let my mom get to you, for real. And trust me when I say you're not going through anything anybody else hasn't gone through. It just takes her a while to warm up to people."

Tora sucked her teeth. "Who wants to deal with that type of snooty attitude though? I sure as hell don't."

He chuckled. "I'm sorry, babe, but Pop told me she cooked pork steaks today. I can't miss that." He smiled at her and she rolled her eyes, but not without offering him a smile in return.

"Good lord, I can smell it all the way out here," Nate said as they approached his parents' front door.

"It does smell good," Tora admitted. Nate unlocked the door with his key and stepped back to allow her to enter ahead of him.

"I know Mama is gonna have something to say because we're a little late," Nate said.

"And you better tell the truth, too. It had nothing to do with me."

He chuckled and patted her backside. "It's ESPN's fault."

His sisters-in-law, Sharday and Evelyn, were seated in the living room watching a movie, while his nephew, Evan, pushed a toy truck around the coffee table. Tora loved how Nate greeted his family with hugs and kisses every time he saw them.

The ladies acknowledged her with a smile and friendly hello as they had done on the few other occasions she visited. Tora appreciated how they made her feel welcomed considering Mrs. Walker was their mother-in-law.

Nate said, "Don't tell me y'all ate dinner already." He glanced at a nearby clock. "I know I'm not that late."

Evelyn laughed. "Actually, we just finished about five minutes before you walked in here. We came over a little early."

Sharday said, "And we all agreed this will be the Sunday we *don't* wait for you to get here before we start eating. Everybody was too hungry."

"Ohh… it's like that, huh?" Nate laughed, and shook his head.

"Even Melody is done, and she's normally the last one at the table."

"Y'all are so wrong. I hope there's something left for us."

"We decided to wait until you get here and eat before we made our to-go plates," Sharday said. "It's the least we could do."

"Well, I'm glad to know my family is considerate," Nate said with an air of sarcasm.

They laughed.

He led Tora to the rec room so they could say their hellos to the rest of the Walker clan.

"Where's Mama?" Nate asked his dad after he greeted him and his brothers.

Tora couldn't get over how handsome all of them were. And to see them together, side-by-side, in a room was overload on a woman's senses.

"She went to the hospital to be with Sunny and Levi," his father told him. "She's getting released today. Vicki's been gone for about an hour or so."

Nate nodded. "Are they coming back here?"

"I'm not sure. I doubt it, son. I would think Sunny might want to go home and get some rest."

"You're probably right," Nate said.

"They're keeping the baby in the hospital though," Gerald said.

"Why? What's wrong?"

"She's still not eating very much, so… they want to keep an eye on her."

Nate reached for Tora's hand. "We're gonna go ahead and eat. Evelyn told me y'all decided not to wait for me today."

All three of them blushed with guilt.

Gerald said, "You know if your mother was here she would've made us wait for you, so we took it upon ourselves to make an executive decision in her absence. The food was getting cold, son."

"I'm telling Mama!" he said, and Tora joined in on the laughter.

She and Nate had the dining room to themselves. In the center of the table was the mouth-watering Sunday meal: smothered pork steaks, garlic mashed potatoes, cabbage, corn on the cob, and a basket of dinner rolls. Tora was surprised to see neither of the apple pies had been sliced.

"I can't believe your mom cooks like this every week. No offense, babe, but she seems like the type that couldn't be bothered with getting her nails dirty."

Nate gave her a sideways look.

She laughed and kissed his cheek.

"I'm not gonna let you continue talking about my mama like that," he said.

"You know it's true," she smiled.

While they ate Tora stared out of the floor-to-ceiling windows, which lent a glorious view of the front yard and all the Italian Cypress trees. A squirrel hopped over to the window, its head jutting left and right, trying to peek inside. Tora giggled when it stood on its hind legs.

"You ever wonder why squirrels are so mechanical in their movements?"

"What?" Nate said. He was busy dipping his dinner roll in his mashed potatoes.

"Why they move like robots?"

"Naw, babe. I can't say I've ever really thought about it. Only *you* would wonder about something like that."

Tora scraped the thick layer of gravy off her meat portion. "I'm glad Mrs. Walker isn't here to see me do this," she said. Her voice lowered a notch. "I don't care for the gravy."

"*What?*" Nate studied her.

"It's too thick."

"That's that forty-weight gravy, girl! What're you talking about? It's the best!"

She scrunched her nose and giggled. "It's not for me."

"You trippin'."

"If you say so."

"I forget you're from up north. Y'all don't know how to eat."

"Please," she rolled her eyes. "We're not about to start this 'the north versus the south' bullshit."

"You better stop cussing at my mama's table."

"Shit… you're right," she laughed.

Nate leaned over to give her a kiss. Tora forced him to linger as she tugged playfully at his mouth, sucking pork steak grease from his bottom lip.

"Damn. Y'all need to get a room."

They pulled away from each other and looked up to see Levi standing on the opposite side of the table.

"Hi," Tora said, and returned to her food, grateful it was just him who'd caught them tongue kissing at the family table instead of Nate's father, or worse, Mrs. Walker herself.

Levi held an empty plate in one hand as he lifted the tops on the serving dishes with the other. "I'm trying to see what Mama got for us today."

Nate watched him, chewing slowly on the piece of bread he'd just placed in his mouth. "I thought you were at the hospital with Sunny. Isn't she coming home today?" he said.

"She is," Levi said. He placed two pork steaks on the plate, followed by a huge heap of potatoes.

Tora was waiting for her chance at a second helping of the mashed potatoes. They were so smooth and buttery and downright good.

"So, why you not at the hospital with her?" Nate said.

"She made cabbage, too? Hell yeah. I love cabbage, and it's been a while since she cooked some." Levi set down his plate and, with a serving spoon, adjusted the meat and potatoes on his plate to make room for cabbage. He piled on a serving big enough for three people. Licking a finger, and returning the top over the bowl of cabbage—of which he left the serving spoon inside—he said, "I came to get me a hot plate."

Tora watched Nate watching him. Levi picked up his plate and moved on to the dish of corn. He shook his head and returned the top, deciding on two dinner rolls instead.

"My sister's coming home from the hospital today after having your baby, and all you're worried about is getting a hot meal? Dude, are you serious right now?"

Nate's got a point, Tora thought, raising the corn cob to her mouth.

Levi paused to look squarely at Nate. His forehead crinkled. "Yeah. What's the problem?"

"The problem is you're supposed to be there to help her. To give her a safe ride home. Y'know… what a man is supposed to do for his woman. Oh, but I forget… you're only concerned about yourself."

"*What?*" Levi said.

"You heard me," Nate said.

Levi spread his arms wide, the plate still in his left hand. "Dude, what's your issue with me?"

"After everything my sister does for you? All the shit you put her through? You can't be there when she needs you most?"

"You don't know what the fuck I do with my wife, okay?"

"I know a lot more than you think, homeboy."

Tora put a hand on Nate's thigh, willing him to let his brother-in-law be.

"Motherfucker, if you got some shit you wanna get off your chest, why don't you just say it?"

Nate put down his fork. "My sister busts her ass every day to take care of you and this is the thanks she gets? Stressing over how she's gonna save your ass after you gambled her money away…"

"Nate—" Tora pleaded, but he pushed back from the table and slowly got up, heading towards the other side.

"What goes on in my household ain't your fucking business, *son.*"

"If it wasn't for my sister, you wouldn't even have a home." Nate raised his arm, reaching for Levi's plate.

Tora was looking right at them, but she still didn't see it coming.

Levi shoved Nate and Nate swung his fist.

Tora screamed.

In a second, Nate was on his back atop the table, the dishes skidding towards Tora.

"Stop! You guys… stop!" She jumped up from her seat and hurried around the table to intervene, but thought better of it as Levi's heavy fists punctured the air in front of her face.

With the agility of a martial artist Nate was back on his feet, charging at Levi, and the two of them slammed into Mrs. Walker's curio cabinet, glass shattering behind Levi's back.

Tora ran out of the dining room to get help just as Sharday and Evelyn were rushing in to investigate the commotion.

"Oh my god! What's going on?" Evelyn said.

It was like the sound of rumbling thunder as the two men tussled around the dining room, pummeling each other. Flesh and gristle and bone.

Sharday tried pulling them apart, but was quickly knocked into the wall with an elbow to her nose.

Tora couldn't believe her eyes as Nate and Levi fought like two strangers, their punches violent with deep-seated hate. She didn't notice Little Evan until it was too late as she rushed from the dining room again in search of Nate's father and brothers. She scooped the screaming kid up from the floor and hugged him tight, apologizing as she held him close to her chest.

The raucous brought Mr. Walker, Bryan, and Geo from the rec room just as she turned the corner off the main hall.

"It's Nate and Levi," she said. "They're back there fighting!" And the three of them headed for the front of the house.

"I'm so sorry. I didn't see you," Tora bounced Evan a little and rubbed his tiny back.

"Let me have him," Evelyn said, coming up the hallway.

Bryanna and Melody came out of the playroom, and Evelyn ushered them back inside and closed the door behind her and her screaming son. Tora hoped the kid was okay and left once more for the dining room.

Mr. Walker and Bryan held Levi in restraint, while Geo held on to Nate. Like two angry rams they bucked, trying to get at each other one more time. Levi yelled and cussed, angry spit flying from his mouth as Nate cussed and yelled right back at him.

Tora was stunned by the whole scene. The food and shattered glass on the floor, the damaged antique China cabinet, the giant hole in the wall. But what bothered her most was seeing Sharday standing in the corner with tears in her eyes as she held her nose, blood dripping down the front of her mint green T-shirt.

FORTY-FIVE

Nate closed his right eye and gritted his teeth against the sting as Tora applied alcohol to sterilize the deepest laceration on his face, the one that had his left eye swollen shut. The cut on the corner of his mouth wasn't as gruesome, but his bottom lip was plump, too.

She blew a gentle breath across his eye to lessen the sting.

"I hope this shit doesn't leave a ugly-ass scar," he said.

"A scar should be the least of your concerns," Tora said. "You need to be worried about your eye."

Nate looked at himself in the bathroom mirror. He knew he had gotten some good licks on Levi, but with the cuts and his bruised eyelid it was a question mark about who was the victor of the brawl. He pushed back his locks to examine his hairline and the four empty squares. "Only a bitch-dude would pull hair in a fight. Look at this shit, man." He shook his head.

Tora sighed and twisted the caps back on the alcohol and ointment.

"You might as well get the scissors and cut all this shit off."

"What?" Tora questioned. "Nate, I know you're not talking about cutting off your locks. For what?"

"You see this?" He turned to her so she could get a good view of his plugged scalp.

"It's gonna grow back, Nate," she said.

"It's fucked up."

"It's not as bad as you think. I might have a product at home you can use to help with the regrowth."

"Naw," he looked back at the mirror. "I'm not walking around like this."

Tora lowered the top on the toilet and sat down, crossing her legs as she stared up at him. "I'm not cutting your hair, Nate, only for you to regret it a couple days from now. Don't go doing crazy shit just because you're pissed off. All of this could've been avoided."

"Yeah, because the motherfucker pushed me."

"Because you started it."

"I was only trying to take my mama's food away from him. He don't deserve to eat at our table when my sister's laying up in the hospital waiting for him."

"He's a grown man, Nate. You had no business trying to take something from him."

He looked at her. "You're taking his side? So, you don't have a problem with the way he treats my sister?"

"Nate, this isn't about your sister. This is about you being the instigator and starting a fight just because you don't like him."

"I don't like him because of the way he treats Sunny."

"Okay, but that has nothing to do with you, Nate! That's *her* boyfriend."

"So, I'm just supposed to sit back and let him fuck over her? Let him stress her out, which can, in turn, affect my nieces' and nephew's well-being? He's gambling away my sister's money—money that's supposed to feed and clothe Anaya and Baby Levi—I hate she gave my nephew the dude's name. I like to call him by his nickname... Deuce—and Skylar?"

Tora sighed heavily and shook her head. "Nate, again... you have no control over what your sister allows in her household. It's not your problem to solve."

"He got people calling, threatening him because he owe them money. Am I just supposed to sit back and let something bad happen to my sister? Who's to say these people—whoever he owes money to—don't show up at her house, shooting the place up looking for him?"

"Nate—"

"I doubt he's even a gambler. His ass is probably smoking crack and owe drug dealers."

"Now you're just talking crazy. There's no way he would owe drug dealers thousands of dollars and still be walking around breathing."

"The point is that there's a possibility when there shouldn't be!"

"Nate, no matter what you say or how angry you get, *there is nothing* you can do to help your sister's situation. It's her decision to make."

Nate shook his head. "You don't understand because you don't have any brothers or sisters. You don't have a close family like I do."

"What? That doesn't even make sense. Because I don't have siblings I can't empathize? You are crazy! I know the difference between right and wrong. And you are *wrong*, Nate! What happened today is your fault. Plain and simple."

"I'm wrong for wanting to protect my sister?"

"You are *wrong* for starting a fight with her boyfriend."

"Whatever," he said. "You just don't get it. I don't expect you to know how it feels to wanna protect your family." He turned back to the mirror for another look at his eye and he was suddenly pissed with Levi all over again.

"You know what… I think it's best I go back to my own apartment for the night so you can calm down and deal with your issue alone."

She got up and brushed past him and he didn't try to stop her.

* * *

The next day Nate called off from work. His rib cage hurt, his scalp burned, and he didn't want to have to answer any questions about the condition of his face. He lay on the couch looking at the television, but he really wasn't watching it. He'd called his mother to apologize for the damage to her dining room, but she'd told him she was too upset to even speak to him right now. His call to Sunny also went unanswered. He called Bryan to check if Sharday was okay, and Bryan told him he'd taken his wife to an urgent care clinic last night to ensure her nose wasn't broken.

The day ticked by and Nate remained on the couch thinking. Thinking about Sunny and his mother and Tora.

FORTY-SIX

She knew something was wrong when the taste of her favorite Earl Grey tea turned her stomach. For the past few years Tora began each day with a warm cup of the citrus-flavored black tea, but this morning's drink was like having a mouthful of laundry detergent.

There were the stubborn odors, too. She'd changed the cats' litter box and taken the bag to the dumpster, but she continued to smell garbage. And raw chicken. She didn't even have chicken in the fridge as it had been awhile since she bought groceries, but the scent followed her everywhere.

"It sounds like you need to make an appointment with your doctor," Candace said when Tora confessed her misery to her friend at work later that afternoon. "One of my sisters experienced the same symptoms before she found out she was pregnant."

"I told you I'm on the pill," Tora said. "I think my hormones are just out of whack." For two years she abstained from sex, and after year one with no prospect for a relationship in sight, she decided to give her body a break and ditched the birth control. Following that first night with Nate was when she resumed the regimen.

"Well, it wouldn't hurt to have a check-up anyway, just in case something else is going on."

* * *

There were too many to choose from. Tora picked one up, and then grabbed another to compare the two. She doubted Candace's claims about her being pregnant, but once she made it home from work she decided to do some research. Her period was late, but she knew it took the body a while to sync with the birth control schedule. She left the apartment again anyway, and headed for the local CVS Pharmacy to purchase a pregnancy test.

"Tora?"

She turned around at the calling of her name.

"Hey, girl!" It was Ja'Nett from their book club.

"Hey, girl," Tora echoed. "How are you?"

Ja'Nett leaned in to give her a hug and Tora got a whiff of peanut butter.

"I guess you and Cynthia gave up on the book club, huh?"

"Huh?" Tora said, then she smiled and shook her head. She didn't attend the last two meetings. "To be honest, I've been so busy lately I haven't had the chance to—"

"Save it," Ja'Nett pursed her lips. "Cynthia says the same thing. Her bad habits are rubbing off on you."

Tora noticed the opened package of peanut butter crackers peeking out the top of Ja'Nett's purse. She couldn't remember the last time she'd had a peanut butter and jelly sandwich, and she decided at that moment to stop by the grocery store to buy the ingredients and have one for dinner.

"Girl, you pregnant?"

Tora blinked out of her thoughts. "What?" Ja'Nett was looking at the home pregnancy tests in her hand. "Oh," she said, "I was just looking to see how they—" she cleared her throat and changed tunes. "They're for my niece."

"Your niece?" Ja'Nett frowned. "I thought you were an only child?"

"She's not *really* my niece, I just call her that. She's actually my coworker's niece, but she didn't feel comfortable asking her auntie to buy the test for her, and she definitely couldn't tell her mom, so…." Tora felt ridiculous for lying, but she didn't want anyone in her business right now.

Ja'Nett said, "Be sure to check your email in a few days. I'm sending out the next quarterly newsletter. We're thinking about doing something a little different to switch things up. I got the idea to host a future meeting at a winery bed and breakfast—"

"Oooh… that sounds nice."

"—but I wanted to have a poll to see how everyone else feels about it. Wouldn't it be great? I was thinking we can do it for our October meeting, that way everyone has a chance to make plans ahead of time."

Tora nodded. "I really like that idea. You know Cynthia's gonna love it because she's the serious wine drinker."

"Yeah, sure. *If* she decides to come. And you too," Ja'Nett said sarcastically.

"I promise I'll be at the next meeting," Tora laughed, and tapped Ja'Nett's shoulder. "Which book are we reading now?"

"*Read* your emails, Tora."

She laughed again. "I will."

"I gotta go," Ja'Nett said, and gave Tora another hug. "I'm surprised my daughter hasn't called to find out what's taking me so long. She's waiting in the car. See you at the next meeting."

"I'll be there for sure," Tora said, and waited until Ja'Nett turned off the aisle before she continued her pregnancy test comparisons.

FORTY-SEVEN

It was Wednesday, his off day. He'd called off work Tuesday, and since today made three days in a row he'd been inside his apartment, his body was itching for movement. The swelling on his face had gone down, but the bruises were still visible. He wrapped a bandana around his locks, grabbed his keys, and headed out.

Tora declined his offer when he called to ask if she wanted to get together for lunch, and stated in response to his follow-up question that there was nothing wrong. She didn't come over to his place yesterday after work either.

Nate was disappointed.

He wondered if she was still upset and holding a grudge against him for what happened at Sunday's dinner.

And still, neither Sunny nor his mother wanted to hear anything he had to say.

Instead of going to Bear Creek Park, which was less than two miles from his apartment, he drove twenty miles out to Memorial.

It didn't surprise him to see the park was packed in the middle of the afternoon on a weekday, but he was lucky and found the last empty spot to park his SUV near the tennis courts.

He'd intended to do a light jog, but found himself walking the entire trail, letting his mind wander.

FORTY-EIGHT

"I'm four weeks."

"Four weeks what?"

"Pregnant."

Tora closed her eyes against the silence on the other end of the line, letting the news sink in. "Are you disappointed?" she finally asked her mother.

"No, not disappointed necessarily," Sharon said. "I'm shocked."

Tora nodded as if her mother could see her reaction.

"Is it Nate's?" Sharon asked.

"Of course it is," Tora answered. "Whose would it be?"

"I didn't mean it in a judgmental way, sweetheart. It's just so soon. It seems like it was only a few weeks ago you were crying about being single and—"

"That's the crazy part about it all," Tora said, cutting her off. "But, who knew birth control pills can expire?"

"Is that what happened?"

Tora nodded her head again. "Yes."

"You didn't use anything?"

"We did… at first. Then… one night we…. We… just got caught in the moment."

"Oh god, Tora," Sharon said quietly.

Tora's eyes blurred with tears as the realization hit her all over again. The home pregnancy test results had come back positive, but she wanted a second test. A professional test. Yesterday she was able to squeeze in an appointment with her OBGYN. This morning she got the phone call with the news.

She sniffled and rubbed the tears that slipped down her cheeks with the heel of her hand.

"Why are you crying, sweetheart?"

She sighed. "I'm still in disbelief. I just always said I would never do this. Never end up in this situation. I wanted to be married."

"You're not the first person to do something you said you would never do, and you definitely won't be the last. So all you can do now is move forward."

Tora could always count on her mother to try and make her feel at-ease, no matter how big her problem.

"Are you ready?" Sharon said.

"I have no choice."

"What does Nate have to say about it?"

Mink hopped on the couch then and butted Tora's hand until Tora rested her palm on top of the cat's head. "I haven't told him yet," she said.

"I would think he'd be the first person you called."

"I've been here on the couch all day, processing everything. I'll go to his apartment tomorrow and tell him."

"You know you have my support, no matter what happens. Mine and your dad's."

"Are you gonna tell Dad for me?"

"Of course not. You can tell him yourself. As a matter of fact, here he comes now."

"What's he doing there?" Tora said.

"I had him take my car for a test drive. It's been making this weird knocking sound, and I needed him to check it out."

Tora heard her father questioning Sharon as he walked in the room, wanting to know when the last time she's had an auto oil change, and if she realized her car veered slightly to the right when driving.

"Your daughter's pregnant," Sharon said.

"Pregnant? With what?"

"A baby, Myles. What else could she be pregnant with?"

"Well hell, I just wanna be sure I heard you right."

Tora shook her head and smiled. Sharon's voice muffled as she spoke to Myles in the background for a minute before returning her attention to Tora.

"I told him he's gonna be a Paw-Paw. You know he's a sap when it comes to you. He's got tears in his eyes now."

"Does he really?" Tora blinked back her own fresh set of tears.

"He says he's too choked up to talk right now, but he's happy for you. And excited."

Tora dabbed at the corners of her eyes with her pinky finger.

"I'm gonna have him go with me to see a mechanic right now. Be sure to call me again later tonight, okay?"

"I will."

"We love you."

Tora dipped her hand in the warm water and waved some of the bubbles towards the back of the tub. She turned off the faucet and just as she stood to drape her towel over the shower rack, there was a knock at the front door.

Who in the hell...?

It was almost nine o' clock. She wrapped the towel around her body again and left the bathroom, both Mink and Silk following right behind her.

She stopped in her tracks just beyond the sofa. It had been weeks since that night Eric showed up at her apartment unannounced, and the thought that it might be him put her on edge. She was prepared to call the police if it was Eric on the other side, but she didn't want him to know she was home. Lightly, she moved towards the door, careful not to make a sound once she stepped onto the tiled floor.

She chuckled and shook her head as she peered through the peephole.

"Nate, *what* are you doing?" she said after opening the door. A surgical mask covered his nose and mouth.

He immediately reached for her. "What's up, baby? Where have you been?"

She rested her arms on his shoulders and kissed his forehead. "Here." The towel started to come undone, and she quickly caught it and re-tucked it underneath her armpit.

"You had me worried you were mad at me. I refuse to go another day without seeing you. That's why I'm here." He stepped into the apartment and she closed the door behind him.

"You think that mask is gonna protect you?"

"I won't stay long," he said.

"I was just about to take a bath." She picked up the cats and took them to the den and closed the door.

"So I'm right on time?" He followed her to the bathroom.

Tora hung the towel on the towel rack and stepped into the tub.

"You mind if I join you?" Nate asked.

Tora shrugged. "I don't care." He undressed and got in, settling between her legs. She leaned back and rested her shoulders on the towel she'd rolled into a long tube and placed on the back of the garden tub.

"I need to start doing this. After a hard workout. This is good for muscle relaxation."

She tugged his shoulder, encouraging him to lie back against her chest.

"T, I'm sorry," he said.

"For what?"

"For what I did Sunday. Upsetting you."

"I'm not the one who needs your apology. Have you talked to your sister?"

"No. She's still not answering my phone calls."

"What about Levi?"

"I don't have shit to say to him."

Tora rolled her eyes. "Don't be too proud, Nate."

"I'll never apologize for taking up for my sister."

"So I guess you're planning to start a fight with him every time he does something to Sunny that you don't agree with?"

"I'm not saying that, but if it's necessary, then… yeah."

"Well, I'm telling you right now you need to change your attitude. Especially if you want this relationship to work. Fighting doesn't solve anything, and it can have you thrown in jail. Our kid doesn't need a dad who can't control his temper. Or who goes around beating people up because he's pissed off."

He chuckled. "You're thinking years ahead already, huh? I hear ya, babe."

"No, Nate. Not years. Months from now. As in *nine months* from now."

There was a pause before Nate quickly sat up, water sloshing around them. He slowly removed the mask from his mouth. "What you say?"

"I found out this morning."

"Pregnant?" he said, searching her face.

"Yep."

His eyes bounced from her face to her chest, down to her

stomach, and then back to her eyes. "Oh," he said, barely above a whisper. He returned to his positon and rested his head on her chest again. He grabbed her hand underneath the water and brought it to his mouth. He kissed her palm.

There wasn't a trace of bubbles in the water by the time they got out of the tub.

FORTY-NINE

Victoria didn't cook the family dinner that Sunday. When Nate arrived, most everyone was in the rec room, eating takeout meals from Cleburne Cafeteria.

He thought he would find his mother in the kitchen, but it was Geo.

"What's up, G?" Nate said.

"Hey, what's up?" Geo stood at the island filling Evan's sippy cup with apple juice. "You all right, bro?" he asked. His gaze fell on the nasty scar on Nate's eyelid. "Your eyes are red."

Nate took a seat on one of the bar stools. "I'm all right. I stayed over at Tora's place last night, and she got two cats…"

"Oh yeah. Your allergies, right?"

"Yeah," Nate shook his head.

Geo studied him. "You sure everything's okay, bro? Looks like something's on your mind."

Nate rested his elbows on the island and made a pyramid of his hands. "I'm gonna be a dad," he said plainly. He'd recited the phrase aloud to himself many times that morning, trying to get used to the sound of it, the idea of it.

"Let me take this cup to Evelyn for the baby. I'll be right back," Geo said after what seemed like a long minute.

Nate got up and poured a glass of juice for himself. Seeing Geo involved in the simple act of preparing a cup of apple juice for his son made him think about how that will be him around the same time next year.

When he returned, Geo said, "You wanna step outside and talk about it or—"

"Yeah, let's go out," Nate said, and they left the kitchen for the patio. He didn't realize how soon he'd forgotten his juice until Geo placed the glass on the table in front of him as they sat down outdoors.

"How far along is she?"

"She's a month."

"I'm surprised because the two of you just got together, right? It hasn't been very long at all?"

"I definitely wasn't expecting this to happen."

"You're not too happy about it or what?"

"Not that I'm not happy, it's just... me and Tora are still getting to know each other. We haven't even had our first holiday together, or our first serious argument. I haven't met her parents, don't even know their names. What am I supposed to say when I meet her daddy? 'Yessir, I am the stranger who knocked up your daughter'?"

Geo laughed out loud.

Nate drank from his glass of apple juice.

"You think she's gonna turn crazy on you?"

"Naw. Nothing like that," Nate shook his head. "She's a beautiful person, man. In and out. I'm just thinking about how our relationship just entered a whole new dimension."

"What have y'all decided to do? I mean... how does she feel about it?"

"I think she's numb right now, just as shocked as I am. Last night I was telling her that we have to start making preparations and move in together. She said we didn't need to make any rash decisions just because she's pregnant."

A brow rose on Geo's face.

"Exactly," Nate shrugged. "But she doesn't want to. I think it's because of her cats. She's not trying to get rid of 'em."

"You gotta be kidding, bro."

"Nope. Those cats are like her kids."

"Yeah, but there's no way she'll choose her animals over you, I'm sure."

"You don't know Tora," he said.

She had made it clear to him on many occasions that her kittens were her life and there to stay.

"That's crazy."

"One of them li'l motherfuckers pissed all over my shoes, too."

"What?" Geo glanced at Nate's feet underneath the table.

"Not these," Nate said. "I had to go home and get another pair when I left her apartment this morning. I walked out barefoot because I threw those shoes right in her trash can—"

"Nooo—"

"She took 'em out and told me she was gonna get them cleaned. I told her I didn't want 'em."

Laughing, Geo said, "Why would the cat pee on your shoes?"

"Tora believed it was the boy cat. Acting out because she's been spending a lot of nights at my place."

"She might be right. Animals can be territorial."

"It was sick, man." Nate shook his head in disgust, thinking about the rough night at Tora's apartment. He itched all night long as he tried to sleep between her sheets. At around four in the morning he woke her up and told her he had to go because he couldn't stand it.

"Tora laughed about it," he said. "She thought it was cute and claimed the cat was only trying to protect her."

"Sounds like the two of you got some things to figure out."

Nate leaned forward, placing his elbows on his knees and clasping his hands underneath his chin. He blew out a breath. "Yep. Definitely got a lot to do, man. I still can't believe it. Me? A daddy? Right now? This wasn't supposed to happen for another few years or so."

Geo said, "There's nothing to fear, bro. I think you'll be a great dad. It'll be an adjustment in the beginning, of course, but you'll soon see it's not so bad after all. Evelyn and I were talking just the other day about having another one in the next couple of years. After Evan turns four."

"Oh yeah?"

"Yeah," Geo nodded thoughtfully. "So, it's the right time for you to have a family of your own." He leaned over and patted Nate on the shoulder. "Welcome to the club, bro."

Nate smiled. "I guess so."

Just then Mr. Walker stuck his head out of the patio door. "The girls say they want some ice cream for dessert, so I'm gonna make a run to the store. Y'all want anything while I'm out?"

"We're good," Nate and Geo answered almost in unison.

"Alright. Just checking." Mr. Walker closed the door, but just as quickly opened it again. "Nate, where's Tora? I see she didn't come with you today."

"She's at home. She said she was too tired to come."

Mr. Walker nodded. "Oh, okay. I was worried, thinking maybe she didn't wanna have dinner with us again after what happened last Sunday."

That was probably part of the reason, too, Nate thought, but when he'd called to remind her about Sunday dinner, she told him she was still in bed resting. "Naw, just tired," Nate told him.

"When are you gonna tell the rest of the family?" Geo asked after their father left.

"I guess I should tell them today, huh?"

"Might as well," Geo said. "We're all here. Well… you'll have to call Sunny and put her on speaker phone when you make the announcement."

"She's still not talking to me," Nate shook his head.

"Have you heard the latest news?" Geo asked.

"No. What?"

Geo lowered his voice even though it was just the two of them outdoors. "Bryan told me they had to cut a check for Sunny for the whole ten thousand. Whoever this guy is that's after Levi wanted his money in full and right away. I don't know if it was him, or if he sent somebody, but they showed up at Sunny's house. Luckily, she was at the hospital visiting Skylar at the time. But… supposedly Ma didn't want Sunny any more stressed about it than she already was, and having to take money out of her savings, so… they went ahead and paid the dude off."

Nate picked up the glass and drained the last of the apple juice. It was his way of trying to douse the anger that fired up inside him. He wanted to drive over to his sister's house and shake some sense into her, but only after he'd kicked her boyfriend's ass and thrown him and all his shit out on the street for endangering her and the kids. He thought about Tora and what she said to him. The battle against Sunny's boyfriend wasn't his to fight. There was something greater, more personal, for him to worry about.

He had a child on the way.

"I'm hot now, G," he said, rising from his seat. "Let's go back inside."

Nate wouldn't accept another day of silent treatment. He went to his mother's home office and knocked on the door, and waited until he heard the faint call, granting him permission to enter.

She sat at her desk. The long white curtains on the window at her back were open, casting her in a triangle of sunlight. Tiny dust motes floated above her head like glitter.

"Hey, Ma," he said, and pushed the door closed quietly behind him.

"Hi, Nate," she returned. Her eyes didn't leave the computer screen.

He walked over to give her a kiss, and she didn't tilt her forehead towards him to welcome the affection like she normally did. "What you working on?" he asked as an icebreaker.

There was a click of the computer mouse, and then the ticking sound of the keyboard as she quickly typed something before granting him a response. "I'm preparing some notes for my assistants since I'll be working from home for the next couple of days. The contractor is coming tomorrow to start on the dining room."

Nate sat down in the chair. "I'm so sorry about that, Ma."

She sighed heavily and shook her head before removing her glasses. She looked at him. "What has gotten into you, Nate Alan? Tell me what possessed you to think it was okay to put your hands on Levi? In my house?"

The use of his middle name let him know that not only was she still angry, but saddened, and deeply disappointed, which hurt him more. Following behavior Victoria deemed their worst—he and his siblings realized when they were kids—Bryan was addressed as Bryan André, Sunny became Sunny Marie-Danielle, and since, like their father, Geo didn't have a middle name, he was Gerald Walker The Fourth.

"I didn't put my hands on him first," Nate said calmly, but he really wanted to ask if that was what the bastard told her he'd done.

"Do you have any idea how long that China has been in this family?"

How could he forget? He'd heard the story on many special occasions when it was brought out for use. The bone China with the birds and gold leaves motif was a gift for his great-great grandmother on her wedding day. It was gifted to her daughter—his grandmother—at her wedding, and then, decades later, passed down to Victoria. So, naturally, the next person in line to receive it was Sunny. On her wedding day.

Nate was sick with guilt.

With a solemn nod of his head he said, "I remember."

"You have no idea how livid I was that day when your father called to tell me what happened," she said. "After I dropped Sunny off at home I drove for an hour all over the city, trying to calm myself down. And when I walked in my dining room and *saw* the damage, *the destruction*—" her eyes closed, her head shook slowly, as if she was reliving the scene in her mind. She opened them. "Nate Alan… you have no idea. No idea."

He glanced down briefly at the floor. There was no doubt she would make him pay for the damage to the dining room wall—and possibly the curio cabinet—but the China itself held sentimental value and was irreplaceable.

"Am I the reason you're in here by yourself instead of out there with everybody else?"

"I have a headache and I need to get this document sent out for tomorrow. There's a lot going on right now." She started typing again.

I know. Geo told me, he wanted to say, but he dared not broach the subject with her. He knew better.

"You want me to bring you something from the kitchen? Did you eat already? Dad went out to get ice cream. You want some?"

"No," she stated flatly. "I'm fine."

She wasn't. And he was partly to blame. He'd apologized many times via text message and voicemail over the past week, but what more could he do? He shifted a bit in the chair. "How long do you think you'll be in here? I got something I wanna tell everybody."

"I don't know, Nate," she said with exasperation.

"It'll only take about two minutes of your time. Can you take a break?"

"Son, I'm working, and I don't have time right now."

"It's good news," he said.

She sucked her teeth. "What is it, Nate? I'm really not in the mood."

"Come to the rec room. I wanna tell everybody at the same time."

She looked at him with a slightly arched brow and he believed he saw a glint of curiosity in her eye.

"You're disrupting my time and getting on my nerves. Seriously."

"You got another grandbaby on the way," he rushed out with a smile since she had no patience for him today. He knew the news of a new baby to the family would soften her around the edges and lift her spirits.

He was wrong.

Her face went slack. "Tell me you are lying, son," she said.

"I'm not."

"And this was your idea?" she asked.

"No. It was a surprise to Tora just as much as—"

"Of course she is. *Of course she is!*" Victoria pushed away from the desk in her leather swivel chair. "How could you let this happen, Nate? Didn't you learn anything from the incident in college? Of course she would get pregnant because she walked in here and saw dollar signs. It was all over her face the day she showed up the first time."

Nate was dumbfounded. "Is that what you think of her?"

"I can spot women like her a mile away."

"She's not like that at all, Ma. That's a mean thing to say. And she knows what I do for a living."

"How can you afford to support a family? Do you have any idea how much diapers cost? Formula? Daycare for an infant? This is what your father and I have been warning you about all of your life."

It wasn't the reaction he expected from her at all, and he was suddenly hurt. But more than that, he was pissed.

"I might not make the type of money Sunny and them make, or be able to have my child walking around in Air Jordans like Sunny's kids, or send them to private schools like Bryan and Geo, but I'm going to do all I can to make sure our baby has everything he or she needs."

"Son, what are your career plans? Because when I think of personal trainer I think of it as something people do as a pastime or second job. Does the company even offer you medical insurance? Because the baby will need it."

It was if she hadn't heard a word he'd said. Or maybe she just didn't care. "I can go back to being an attorney and be miserable. Is that what you want?"

"I want you to take your life and future seriously and put to use the education your father and I paid for."

He shook his head dismissively at the thought. "Ma, when I see this kid who, just a few months ago, walked with his head down suddenly walking with self assurance, or seeing him smile because he can fit into a pair of pants three sizes smaller, or hear how his mama doesn't have to take medication because she was able to get her blood pressure under control—" Nate shook his head again "—*nothing* I did when I was a lawyer gave me the same satisfaction."

Victoria sat back in her chair and folded her arms across her chest. She studied him a moment before saying, "I hope you understand, son, that this does not exempt you from paying us what you owe every month. It will be a valuable lesson to you because there will always be unforseen expenses. And the two of you better not call asking us for one red cent."

It was like a second kick to his chest. "Really, Ma? I come to share the good news with you that I'm about to be a dad and this is what you say to me? That we don't have your support? But you have no problem bailing Sunny and her dude out?" He stood up from his seat, his nostrils flared.

"Nate, don't try to flip this around. This is about *you* being irresponsible!"

"I *am* responsible! You might not like what I do, but it is a real job. It's my career. And I love it. You act as if I'm some type of loser, out here without direction, begging for money. I've never asked you and dad for anything. And, as far as the baby situation, things happen..."

"And that's exactly my point! If you were being responsible there would be no surprise baby. It's called family planning, Nate. The thing I've warned you all about since you were teenagers."

Nate exhaled sharply, running a hand over his locks. "Ma, we will be fine. Me and Tora are gonna figure it out."

"This is what I feared," Victoria said, shaking her head. "Why settle for mediocrity, son? Why struggle?"

"Why can't you accept that I'm living my life how I want to live it? I appreciate everything you've ever done for me, but I'm not cutout to be a lawyer! I mean... c'mon, Ma, you can't keep trying to control every little thing we do. All the while we were growing up you controlled what we did, what kind of people we hung out with, how we dressed, who we dated. We're adults. I should be able to choose how I live my life. I mean... aren't you at least proud that I'm making an honest living? Doesn't that count for something?"

"So, I'm a bad mother because I wanted you all to be self-respecting, hard-working, upstanding people? That I wanted you to have stress-free lives with the financial freedom to afford the best?"

"Everybody doesn't want the same things, Ma."

"Oh, come off it, Nate. You're just making excuses now."

He sat back down in the chair. "I'm being honest. I enjoy helping people."

"Lawyers help people, son. Doctors help people."

"You just don't get it," he said quietly.

Victoria sighed. "I'm not sure where I went wrong with my twins. Between your sister and her ridiculous boyfriend, and your lack of drive to do more in life—"

Nate sucked his teeth. "Well, that's the only good thing that's come out of this conversation. I'm glad to hear you acknowledge that Levi's a joke." He got up to leave just as there was a tap on the door and his father came in.

"What're y'all doing back here?"

Nate moved past him and out the door without a word.

"Your son is about to be a daddy," Victoria said to Gerald.

FIFTY

Now every time she entered the bathroom she couldn't help looking in the mirror, lifting her shirt to see the changes. Her belly was as flat as it'd always been. And, although tender to the touch, her breasts were still the same too.

For now.

Sharon had told her she didn't see any visible changes until her fourth month when she was pregnant, and that it might be the same for her.

But Tora wasn't in a hurry. The shock still hadn't worn off.

Never in a million years would she have guessed the chance encounter with Nate that afternoon at a River Oaks deli would lead to a little person developing inside of her just a few short months later.

She had only been longing for a beautiful relationship, heading towards marriage.

A baby wasn't part of her immediate plan.

* * *

"You've been kinda quiet, Nate. What's wrong?"

He extended his arm, inviting her to have a seat next to him on the couch.

She sat and rested her head on the crook of his shoulder.

"Just been thinking about a few things," he said.

"A few things like what?"

"I wanna ask you something, T, but I want you to be honest about it."

"Okay," she said.

"Would you prefer it if I was a lawyer?"

"I thought you hated being a lawyer?"

"I know, but would you like it better if I was?"

She considered it only a second. "No. Not necessarily. Unless it's what you wanna do. Why do you ask?"

"Because… I've been thinking… with the baby coming that I probably should."

"But why, if it's not something you like to do?"

"I just wanna make sure that you and the baby are okay. That we're okay."

She looked at him.

"It's just that ever since I had the conversation with my mama, she got me wondering."

A couple weeks ago he'd told her his parents knew about her pregnancy, but that was all he'd said. The lack of details of how they'd taken the news made Tora feel perhaps it didn't go over too well. She knew it wouldn't be too presumptuous to believe Victoria, especially, wasn't particularly happy.

"Let me guess… your mom has a problem with it?"

"She's just worried I won't be able to take care of y'all."

Tora highly doubted Mrs. Walker had any concerns for her welfare. She ·wouldn't be surprised if the woman shunned her completely, deciding she—and possibly her baby—was beneath her and her well-to-do family.

"Nate, you have to do what's best for you. It's not my decision to make. And, honestly, it's not your mom's either. If you want to go back to practicing law, do it because *you* want to."

"I don't want the baby to go without anything," he said.

"Do you really believe we won't be able to take care of this baby? Between the two of us?"

"And I wanna be able to give you everything you want."

She sighed and rolled her eyes. "I have everything I want, Nate. And if I don't, I can go out and buy it myself. That's not why I'm with you. If I wanted a man to spoil me I would still be with one of my exes."

His body stiffened. "What the hell is that supposed to mean?"

She sat up, looking at him. A thick vein streaked the center of his forehead and she couldn't help laughing at the sight of it. "Calm down, Nate. I'm just saying…. I don't want you thinking that's what's gonna make me happy. Love and respect is what matters most to me. Without those two, everything else means nothing."

"I hear you," he said, and reached for her to lie back against his shoulder.

FIFTY-ONE

It all became real to him as the months passed and her stomach swelled. He was going to be a father. Responsible for the life and well-being of a whole person. Worry had been replaced with anticipation as he watched Tora's growing excitement. They would go to Target or Walmart just to browse the baby section. In grocery stores she would point at the baby carriages sitting in shopping carts and smile and say, "That's gonna be us."

What surprised him most was her sudden interest in going out for long walks. One day on a whim he recorded her walking around the park trail, her full belly on display because she refused to wear maternity clothes, and posted the video online. Within a couple days it had garnered thousands of views and hundreds of comments from expectant moms praising Tora for her determination to remain fit while pregnant and for having Nate's support.

She'd looked at him and said he would be a fool if he didn't make something out of it.

Every free moment was spent with her, video blogging their experience.

It had been weeks since he had Sunday dinner with his family. He gave an excuse each time his father or one of his brothers called.

Out of the blue Sunny texted him, sending her congrats on the baby. She'd teased him, saying: **You might be the one to have twins!!!**

So each time he accompanied Tora to her checkups he asked the doctor if she was sure there was only one baby in the womb.

FIFTY-TWO

"Ohhh… this is so cute! With little matching booties… aww…"

"Candace, will you stop drooling over my baby's clothes and put them in the box? The guys are gonna be here at any minute."

"I know, girl, but these little outfits are giving me baby fever," she whined, clutching the onesie to her chest.

Tora rolled her eyes playfully. "We promised Nate we would have this all packed and ready to go when they get back for the second load."

It was moving day. With just two months left before the baby was due Nate said he'd had enough of her shenanigans and it was time for them to move in together. It ticked him off that they were spending nights apart, sleeping in separate residences. And she had to admit she had grown tired of hiking up three flights of stairs to her apartment every night.

He recruited Kevin, Jamal, and Chauncey to help.

"What happened to your cats?" Candace asked.

Tora's heart lurched. Just the mention of them made her want to cry all over again. For two weeks as she was making the administrative preparations for the move, she toggled back and forth between deciding whether to put them up for adoption and researching how to make life comfortable for a person living in a household with a pet they were allergic to.

She'd contacted Lauren to ask if she was still seeking a cat for Harley, but Lauren said she'd changed her mind, that her husband disapproved.

"They're at Jamal's house," Tora said.

"Really? How did that happen?"

"I told Nate I couldn't give them up, so he called Jamal and asked if he would take them in. He said Jamal had a cat when he was a kid, and that he was trustworthy."

"That was nice of him."

"Yeah. It's only until I figure out what I'm gonna do."

"Girl, once you have the baby you'll forget all about them cats," Candace said.

Tora shot her a pointed look. "No I won't! They were my first babies. I love them just as much. Are you crazy?"

Candace laughed. "Well, excuse me!"

"Yeah, sis. You're excused."

EPILOGUE

"We did good, babe," Nate said, kissing Tora's lips.

She nodded. "Yep, I think so."

The two of them were smitten, staring down into the little pink face of their daughter.

She arrived at 12:29 p.m. that day, a sunny afternoon.

"I think she looks more like me," Nate said.

Tora chuckled. "No she doesn't. She doesn't look like either one of us right now."

"She has my nose." He bent to kiss it, and the baby shuddered in Tora's arms.

"You have to be careful, Nate, so your beard doesn't scratch her face."

"You're right," he said, and kissed the baby's hand.

"I'm already anxious to take her home. To bathe her, and dress her, and watch her sleep."

"Our lives are changed forever, babe," Nate said.

"Exactly." She nodded.

"How soon do you wanna get married?"

There was a knock at the door.

They looked up to see Victoria walk into the room. It was a surprise to both of them.

She carried a vase of white tulips.

"I hope the two of you didn't think I wouldn't show up to meet my grandbaby," she said. Then she walked over and wrapped her arm around Nate for what seemed like a long time. She kissed his cheek. "Hello my son."

"Hey, Ma," he said.

She looked at Tora. "These are for you, dear." She set the flowers on the bedside table. "Now… give me my grandbaby."

Tora released the baby to her grandmother.

"My, isn't she precious?" Victoria said, cradling her in her arms. "Just as cute as she can be. What's her name?"

"Santana Jamison Walker," Nate said.

"Santana," Victoria repeated. "I love that. What a wonderful name. It suits her perfectly." Smiling, she said to Tora, "Let's start over. How are you?"

Questions for Discussion

1. Tora is leery of online dating and Candace is surprised she's never considered it, especially in these times where it is common to talk to and meet people online. How do you feel about online dating? What are your experiences with online dating if you have already tried it?

2. Tora admits she can be shallow when it comes to selecting a partner. Are there any physical characteristics you cannot compromise on?

3. Nate gave up his job as an attorney to follow his dream of a life in fitness and nutrition. Would you give up a high-paying job for a career in a field you love even if your salary would be significantly less? Why or why not?

4. What are your thoughts about Victoria and the high expectations she set for her family?

5. Discuss Nate's relationship with his sister. Do you believe he is justified in his feelings about Sunny's relationship with her fiancé and his need to protect her?

6. Oftentimes unresolved issues or insecurities from past relationships can hinder new relationships. Discuss Tora's confession to Candace about the problems she had in a previous relationship and why she was reluctant to be with a guy like Nate. Can you relate to Tora's viewpoints in any way?

7. What type of future do you foresee for Tora and Nate?

Dear Reader,

Thank you for your time. I hope you enjoyed getting to know Tora and Nate. Please take a few minutes and leave a review online. You can also share your thoughts with me by sending an email to teneka@tenekawoods.com

Visit my website and sign up for my newsletter to be the first to know about upcoming releases, news, receive giveaways, and more!

I want to hear from you!

With love,
Teneka